I0700623

A Gay Mormon Missionary in Pompeii

What is a gay Mormon missionary doing it Italy?

He's trying to save his own soul as well as the souls of others, terrorized by homophobic doctrine into committing acts of cultural imperialism to prove his worthiness.

In these tales chronicling the two-year mission of Robert Anderson, we see a young man tormented by his inability to be the man the Church says he should be. After enduring a major earthquake, encounters with organized crime, a serious bus accident, and conflicts with horrendous mission leaders, he dreams of nothing more than escaping his suffocating existence any way he can.

But one day, he meets another missionary who loves him, and his world changes forever.

Praise for Johnny Townsend

"Told from a believably conversational first-person perspective, [*A Gay Mormon Missionary in Pompeii*'s] novelistic focus on Anderson's journey to thoughtful self-acceptance allows for greater character development than often seen in short stories, which makes this well-paced work rich and satisfying, and one of Townsend's strongest. An extremely important contribution to the field of Mormon fiction." Named to Kirkus Reviews' Best of 2011.

Kirkus Reviews

In *Zombies for Jesus*, "Townsend isn't writing satire, but deeply emotional and revealing portraits of people who are, with a few exceptions, quite lovable."

Kel Munger, *Sacramento News and Review*

In *Sex among the Saints,* "Townsend writes with a deadpan wit and a supple, realistic prose that's full of psychological empathy….he takes his protagonists' moral struggles seriously and invests them with real emotional resonance."

Kirkus Reviews

Let the Faggots Burn: The UpStairs Lounge Fire is "a gripping account of all the horrors that transpired that night, as well as a respectful remembrance of the victims."

Terry Firma, Patheos

"Johnny Townsend's 'Partying with St. Roch' [in the anthology *Latter-Gay Saints*] tells a beautiful, haunting tale."

Kent Brintnall, Out in Print: Queer Book Reviews

Gayrabian Nights is "an allegorical tour de force…a hard-core emotional punch."

Gay. Guy. Reading and Friends

The Washing of Brains has "A lovely writing style, and each story [is] full of unique, engaging characters….immensely entertaining."

Rainbow Awards

In *Dead Mankind Walking*, "Townsend writes in an energetic prose that balances crankiness and humor….A rambunctious volume of short, well-crafted essays…"

Kirkus Reviews

A Gay Mormon Missionary in Pompeii

Johnny Townsend

Contents

The Abominable Gayman of Mt. Olympus

A man with a huge red growth on his forehead stepped in front of me and mumbled. I couldn't understand him and moved on, dragging my two suitcases. I could hear the hiss of train doors closing somewhere behind me along with a hundred voices combining to make an indistinct roar as loud as the train engine starting up. It seemed as if I'd just stepped out of a time machine into another age. Fifty years back? A hundred? I felt a surge of adrenalin and smiled. It was October of 1980, and I was ready to start my new life.

I stepped out of the station and took my first look at Naples. This was going to be my first assignment in Italy. A teenage girl sped by on a motor scooter. Tiny cars jammed the streets around the station, honking and squeezing into places I would never have dared drive into. I'd seen postcards of scenes very similar to this from the teachers at the Missionary Training Center in Utah and had thought at the time, "How quaint." Somehow, though, when the same scene filled the entire landscape instead of just four by six inches, it didn't look quite so quaint. Still, it wasn't as if this were some third world country. It wasn't as if I was in some tiny village in Peru, like my friend Steven from my hometown of Biloxi. When I'd received my mission call, I'd said to my mother, "Guess where they're sending me? It has food you really like."

Her shoulders had sagged, and she replied glumly, "Mexico."

I shook my head. "Nope. What's another kind of food you like?"

Then she'd smiled, and her eyes lit up. "Italy! You're going to Italy!" And she clapped her hands.

I turned to look down another street. Several buildings had identical posters glued to their walls, advertising a movie, the rerelease apparently of *Via col vento*, with Clark Gable holding Vivien Leigh against the backdrop of a burning Atlanta. One half-torn poster flapped in the breeze, Vivien's head beating against the wall. I watched a newspaper blow along the sidewalk until it lodged against a crushed cardboard box lying in the gutter. It's Europe, I told myself. It'll be a great experience. A rat scampered away from the box. It's a privilege to be here, I said to myself. Paul himself had preached not far from Naples. We were in the mouth of the wolf here in Italy, preaching to Catholics, members of the church the scriptures called the "whore of Babylon."

I pulled out the rough map that the elders had made for me in Rome to show me how to get to my apartment. They expected me to find the right bus line and get to my apartment on my own, but I found a taxi instead. The driver listened to my attempt to pronounce the address on Via del Sedile di Porto, glanced over at the paper in my hands, and then we took off.

By looking up the narrow streets as we drove along, like valleys between crumbling cliffs, I could see that the buildings started down at the sea and climbed up some hills surrounding the heart of the city. Vesuvius was off to the south, and it seemed impossible that I could really be near such a famous place. It was the first time I had ever seen a volcano, but I could barely make it out because of the smog rising upwards from some factories outside the city. They were still digging up bodies over there in Herculaneum. It was so…so cultural.

The buildings here were all about four to six stories high and crammed together, almost as if they grew out of each other. Many of the thick wooden doors looked at least fifteen feet high, some with smaller doors cut out in them. The only vegetation I could see was a little grass growing up between cracks in the sidewalk and a tuft of grass on the roof of an aging Catholic church.

The taxi dodged an old man pulling a cart of worn shoes, and I saw a hunchbacked woman selling brassieres at a small stand. I smiled and nodded at her as we passed, and she smiled back. A few seconds later, the taxi pulled up onto the sidewalk in front of my apartment building. The driver handed me my suitcases and I paid him 10,000 lire, about twelve dollars. It was way too much, I thought, for such a short trip, but I didn't feel like arguing. Besides, he was kind of cute. Then I bit my lip to punish myself for the thought. He left and I looked up at my new home.

I stared at a building with cracks running in odd designs across the front. It must have been at least three hundred years old. But it's culture, I told myself. I raised an eyebrow. Or maybe it was penance. I knew I had to be beaten down while I was out here. Maybe it was just as well to get started right away.

"Waat eez yore naim?" asked a boy about eight, walking over with a couple of his friends.

"Waat taheem eez eet?" asked one of the other boys. I understood that they had trouble pronouncing the English and smiled pleasantly at them. We'd been taught in the Missionary Training Center to be careful in our pronunciation of Italian as well, especially when asking someone how old they were. The phrase to be used was "How many years do you have?" but the catch was that the word for year was "anno" and both n's had to be pronounced. Just one n made the word "ano", which meant "anus," and we had to be sure we weren't asking, "How many anuses do you have?" So I could be understanding about the fact that these boys had a little trouble with their English.

"Eet eez naheen-theerty," I answered, and the boys looked at each other and shrugged. I had just a handful of American change left, so I pulled two dimes and a nickel out of my pocket and handed it to them. They smiled and ran off, and I turned back to the building.

The palazzo rose about six stories. It had probably once been painted bright red, but the paint had worn away in many places, and the plaster covering the outside walls was crumbling, leaving patches of dull red where it still clung onto the building. I looked down the street. Several unwashed cars passed by the unwashed cars parked along the curb. Another little boy ran by, carrying a loaf of bread loosely wrapped in brown paper. A heavyset man chased him.

I looked at the list of names underneath the intercom by the door of my palazzo. The word literally meant "palace." How exciting to be able to live in a building called a palace, even if it really just meant "apartment building" now. From the intercom, I could see that our apartment was on the sixth floor. How urban, I thought, smiling. I was truly living in a big city for the first time. It was wonderful. Nothing anywhere in Mississippi compared.

I dragged my luggage inside the building and into the elevator, grateful to find that such an old building had been refitted with one, but the tiny elevator, which barely had enough room to hold me and my two heavy suitcases, wouldn't move. Then I noticed the silver box with the sign that said I needed to pay ten lire. The smallest coin I had was a hundred lire, which wouldn't fit in the machine, so I shrugged and started up the stairs.

The steps were of solid black stone, and a few of them were chipped badly. Taking a brief rest on the fourth floor, I noticed some graffiti on the dirt-stained walls. It was probably just as well that I didn't know what those words meant. It wouldn't help to know how to fantasize sinfully in two languages.

"Hi, Elder Anderson!" said a guy not much older than me, probably still nineteen, when I finally reached our apartment. "I'm Elder Williams. Welcome to the Gut." He clapped me on the back. "How was your trip?" He picked up one of my suitcases and headed off to a room down the hall.

Thank goodness, he seemed nice. It would be so much more fun to be a missionary with a friend.

"It was okay." Of course, I'd had to sit on my suitcase in the corridor right outside the bathroom the whole way from Rome since the train was so crowded, but I was already making up a way to turn the ride into "the joys of Europe" in a letter I knew would make my mom laugh. "What's the Gut?" I added. Maybe that could go in the letter, too.

"We're just outside the 'historical center' of the city, commonly known as the ghetto." He stepped in front of a door and motioned like a game show hostess. "Well, here's our room. Benvenuto to the Napoli One district, Anziano."

"Thank you," I mumbled, unable to say anything more, trying not to let my mouth hang open. It was like no palace I'd ever envisioned. Torn Book of Mormon posters taped to the walls failed to cover up the cracks and stains everywhere about us. A few tiles on the floor were missing, and a few others were loose. Elder Williams's desk looked fifty years old, and mine wasn't much better, with scratches, chips, and missing drawer handles. I was sure we'd gotten the desks out of someone's trash. But at least my chair looked sturdy enough. The pillow cases on both beds were stained, with sweat, I supposed. Maybe the linen had never even been washed. But the two low, metal cots seemed okay, even if the foot of my bed was supported with some wooden blocks and old magazines instead of legs.

And I knew that I couldn't be a jerk. I'd grown up thinking central air and heat was natural, but apparently no one in Italy had air conditioning, and we'd learned in Culture Capsule that no one had screens on their windows, either.

We'd been told in the MTC that we were facing a thoroughly new way of life, that part of what God wanted was to shake us up enough to appreciate the blessing of having been raised in Zion. Of course, other MTC teachers had said we'd be so full of the Spirit that we wouldn't notice any inconveniences. I might have to face a few unpleasant conditions, I realized, but I had to show God I was willing to do anything. And two years would pass in an instant.

"No vacancies at the Marriott?" I asked Elder Williams, smiling. I put my suitcases on the bed and opened them up.

"There's no time for unpacking, Elder. We've got work to do." Elder Williams clapped me on the back again.

"You got here in ritardo," he went on, "so you didn't get to meet the other elders. You'll meet Lysenko and Griffith at lunch later. In a lot of our apartments, we have six missionaries living together, but here in Napoli One, we just have four. You'll like them. They're good guys."

I closed my suitcase and made a quick stop to the bathroom before leaving. "Don't pull the cord," Elder Williams shouted through the door, "or it'll overflow. Fill the bucket from the bathtub and pour it down the toilet." I washed my hands and splashed a little water on my face, smiling at myself in the mirror for encouragement. Then I followed my companion to the front door, where he asked me to say a prayer in Italian before we left. I did so, mostly repeating a short one I'd memorized at the MTC, and we headed down the stairs.

"Don't we ever use the elevator?" I asked. Ten lire, after all, was only worth about a penny.

"It's hard to find ten lire pieces. Sometimes, we get candy as change at the store. So we save them for when we go tracting."

"You mean all the buildings have pay elevators?"

"A lot of them do, at least the ones without portieri who kick us out."

"What's a portiere?"

"A doorman. That reminds me. We're supposed to speak in Italian so you can learn the language faster." He switched instantly to what seemed like fluent Italian, and I tried to catch a word or two here and there to tell me what was going on. It made me remember a day in the MTC during gym when I was playing volleyball. An elder behind me shouted, "Bird in water!" in Italian. I was so puzzled, I'd turned to look and was hit full in the face with the ball. "I didn't know the word for 'duck,'" he apologized. There were clearly many more words yet to learn.

Elder Williams and I talked to some men in the street. Elders weren't allowed to talk to women, to make sure no one thought we were propositioning them. I found women less intimidating and regretted not being able to talk to them, but I knew I probably didn't miss it as much as the other elders, though I wasn't about to volunteer the information to anyone that I had "homosexual tendencies." Perhaps most of the reason I was here was to cure myself, though refusing to associate with women seemed a strange way to do it. My only desire in curing myself was so I'd be more what God wanted me to be. And maybe getting such a full dose of men for two years was what it would take to cure me. All I knew was that I had to do whatever I was told. If that meant only talking to men, then I'd only talk to men. But when a man would pass by, I was too scared even to say hi, so Anziano Williams did all of the approaches for the first hour. Then he looked at his watch. "That was your first training session. Now you try."

Oh, God, this was it. The moment that preparation ended and interaction began. I took a deep breath and set on a man with a moustache. "Excuse me, sir," I said. "I…" The man walked on without even pausing. "Guess I forgot to use my Scope this morning," I said to Elder Williams, who also seemed not to hear me.

"Hello, my name is…" I tried more loudly with another man who also kept walking. Maybe I was being too abrupt, too rude. Would I want to be stopped cold on the street like this? I tried to think of a softer approach.

"Good afternoon, sir. We're here to…" Yet another man ignored me, walking on. I'd been joking about the mouthwash, but now I wondered, cupping my hand and blowing into it. My breath seemed okay.

I looked at my companion, who was nonchalantly studying a crack in a wall. I didn't try to approach anyone else, and finally Elder Williams looked up and we moved along. After a few minutes, he stopped a man, they chatted for a moment, and then the man left. "Your turn," said Elder Williams.

I approached another man, and then another, and then another, without completing a sentence. Then I waited for my companion, who finally approached one more man. As soon as they'd finished talking, Elder Williams said, "Your turn."

This went on for another hour or two, every approach feeling like someone pulling off a fingernail. "Sir," I said to one man, but he walked on before I could add anything else.

"We're representatives of the Church of Jesus Christ…" The next man paused long enough to curl his lip as he looked at me. I tried to smile in return to show how friendly we were.

"Excuse me, sir, I…" Another man glanced at my name tag and quickened his pace.

"Buon giorno," I said perfectly. "We'd like to…" The next man hurried across the street. I felt as if I didn't have any fingernails left. "Elder, they won't listen to me." I looked at Elder Williams and then down at myself. "My tie *is* on straight, isn't it?"

"It takes a little practice to do street contacting. Don't worry. It'll get better."

I nodded but wondered just how much practice it took simply to say hello. I knew I couldn't expect too much of myself the first day of work, but I did expect more than half a sentence. Yet at the same time, I knew that Elder Williams had been out months longer than I had, and although he did at least get to finish his questions, the responses he received weren't very different from the ones I'd gotten. But maybe it was only going poorly today because people could somehow sense that I wasn't what I was supposed to be.

This was what I'd feared ever since I'd gone to the doctor and begun processing my papers to send to Salt Lake to volunteer as a missionary, that my innate sinfulness would make my service useless. We didn't even believe in original sin, except for gays. Our very nature was sinful. Perhaps the other elders would notice, too, as the Italians apparently did, that I wasn't a "real" missionary, and they'd tell the mission president, who would then send me home before I could become straight. I needed faith to be cured, but I had to be cured before I could have faith. What if I needed both before I could be any good out here?

They'd told us in the MTC that we could baptize a hundred people a month if we had faith and weren't slothful servants, no matter which mission we were sent to. Every minute that ticked by seemed like a condemnation, and those minutes were ticking by slowly. I felt like a blond Jew trying to pass as Aryan in Nazi Germany. I wondered how long it would be before the mission president called me for a private interview to find out what unresolved sin was causing the problem.

Our most effective tool as missionaries wasn't language or knowledge but the Spirit, and I wasn't sure the Holy Ghost could reside in me. I knew that gays were an abomination, and though I'd never actually done anything with another man, God certainly knew that I'd wanted to. The Prophet said I was revolting. My stake president at home said being gay was next to murder. My bishop said only selfish people were gay. But one of the apostles had said a mission was good for people who needed to overcome weakness, so I'd worked extra hard for the six months before my mission, volunteering several hours each week doing shopping or cleaning for the elderly members in our congregation, trying to build the spiritual resources my bishop said I didn't have.

I tried not to think too much more about it, listening to my companion's approaches and trying to memorize and practice them. Proving myself and earning a place in the highest degree of the Celestial Kingdom was the only way I'd have a chance at becoming a god one day. And wasn't learning how to become a god the whole purpose of coming to Earth in the first place? It couldn't be hopeless for gays, or God could just wipe us off the face of the Earth and be done with us. He didn't keep us here merely as trials for other people, did He? Surely, we weren't just another plague like mosquitoes or hurricanes. I wanted to be more than a redbug or a flood.

I was exhausted and hungry when we came home for lunch. It felt as if eight or nine hours had passed since we'd left this morning. But it was only 1:30, our regular lunch hour since we never ate dinner, night being the best time to tract door to door. Two meals a day.

"No midnight snacks?" I asked. "Like a pizza?" I tried to look innocent so the other elders wouldn't know at first I was joking, but they didn't catch on at all. Well, perhaps this schedule would help me learn to control my appetite. I could stand to lose a few pounds. I was 5' 10" and weighed 170, having lost seven pounds in the MTC by giving my desserts to my companion there as a sign to God I was willing to give up at least some pleasures. Learning to live with two meals should help in dealing with my sexual appetite, too. And it would make fasting once a month easier as well, since now we'd only have to skip one meal instead of two to complete our required twenty-four hour fast.

The last two months before I went in the MTC, I'd been fasting once a week. I didn't feel much more spiritual, but I did lose four pounds, and then when my stake president set me apart as a missionary by giving me a priesthood blessing before I went to the airport, he'd said, "Robert's going to be the kind of missionary who comes back from his mission thirty pounds heavier." He'd laughed as if that were funny. I was irritated at the irrelevance of the comment but was also afraid it might be true, so I tried to psych myself up now to eat a little less than I wanted today.

Elder Lysenko, one of the other two missionaries in the apartment, made today's lunch, which was ready at a little after 2:00. I thought his companion, Elder Griffith, was a little cuter than he was, but then I pinched my arm for thinking such a useless thought. Walking into the kitchen, I noticed that there were about thirty pieces of dried spaghetti hanging from the ceiling above the sink. The wall in back of the stove was covered in layers of caked grease. We squeezed around the small table in a kitchen barely large enough to contain us, and I sat down in front of a heaping serving of—something.

I didn't say anything until after the blessing, to which I certainly hoped Heavenly Father was listening. "Uh, what is it?" I asked.

"Mission Mash," said Lysenko. Everyone laughed. "It's Friday. I just used whatever was left over from earlier this week." I must have looked doubtful because he added, "Don't worry. It's my specialty."

The other elders seemed to enjoy the meal, and I wondered if I was being overly picky. One measly day, and my good attitude was gone already? The bread was as hard as my mattress, and the glop on my plate had no flavor.

"We don't have to wear hairshirts, too, do we?" I asked. "Or walk on our knees?"

"Huh?"

"I'm just trying to make sure we're Mormon and not Catholic," I said, smiling.

The other elders looked at each other blankly, and I felt stupid for the failed joke.

I looked around at the other elders eating heartily and then nodded and joined in.

After lunch, I watched two roaches crawl across the bathroom sink while I brushed my teeth.

We left the apartment at 3:30, and the evening hours dragged by slowly. We did some more street contacting and then tried to catch a bus to take us to our tracting zone. People were hanging out the back doors even before the bus pulled up, and as soon as it slowed down, the crowd waiting to board began clawing their way forward. "Get ready," said Elder Williams, nudging me.

My mouth hung open in astonishment as I watched the surging crowd. "Elder," I said, "I can't do this." I'd never ridden anything other than a suburban school bus before.

People were pushing and shoving and being *rude*. My mouth hung open again, but somehow I found myself in the middle of the mass, pushed and shoved along toward the back door. Actually, I was heading more for the rear of the bus beyond the doors, but just as I was being shoved out of the competition, a woman standing on the bottom step grabbed my collar.

"Anziano," she said. She must have been a local member. She pulled me forward and forced me into her place before she jumped off. "I can catch the next bus," she told us, smiling with a resigned shrug. I stared back after her as we lurched forward. She was only five feet tall. How had she done that?

"That was awfully sweet of her," I said, struggling over the word for "sweet."

"She knows she'll get blessings for helping the missionaries," said Elder Williams.

I tried to look back at her in the distance through the rear window. Did getting blessings mean it wasn't sweet, I wondered? I fell against a man's greasy hair as we turned a corner. Maybe giving up her place hadn't been such a sacrifice. But I was still touched.

Getting off the crowded bus at the right stop later was just as difficult as getting on, as we'd been pressed well into the bus by that time and had to fight past several people to reach the exit. I wondered what I would do if Elder Williams was transferred to another district at the end of the month, leaving me to show my new companion around the city. I wanted to remember my way about the streets, but it all seemed like a complex, changing maze. Everything seemed to be happening so fast, and there were so many people everywhere. I wanted to just sit in a corner and rest for a minute.

"Why don't we preach to them on the bus while we've got them cornered?" I asked, smiling after we stepped off of the bus. They'd told us in the MTC that if we forced ourselves to smile even when we didn't feel like it, that soon it would come naturally, and our inner happiness would attract people. I needed to reinvigorate my attitude before it failed completely.

"The gospel is not a joking matter, Elder."

I frowned. He'd been smiling in the apartment. Had I been obnoxious? We walked down the street in silence for a few moments, until a man about twenty leaped out of a doorway and stood in front of us. "Ciao!" he said in a childlike voice. "You teach me?"

"Not tonight," said Elder Williams, trying to walk past him on the sidewalk.

"How come?"

"We're late for an appointment."

Elder Williams edged past him successfully and kept walking, not looking back. The man looked dejected, so I put my hand on his arm, and he turned to me. "Not like me?" he asked.

"I like you," I said. "My name's Roberto. What's yours?"

He grinned. "Reni."

Didn't that mean "kidneys," I wondered. "You live here?" I asked, pointing to the doorway of the building from which he'd come.

He nodded. "I not go to school. I—"

"Elder Anderson!" I looked up the street. Elder Williams was standing with his hands on his hips ten yards up the sidewalk. "Get over here!" he said in English.

"You can speak in Italian," I said, wanting to add in English myself, "There's no need to make him feel we're talking about him," but I didn't say that last in English or Italian.

"We'll be late," he said then in Italian, though of course we had no appointment.

I shook Reni's hand. "I have to go," I said, "but it was nice meeting you." Then I joined my companion up the street.

"You're supposed to follow my lead," said Elder Williams.

"But he just wanted to talk for a couple of minutes."

"Elder, he's already going to the Celestial Kingdom because he's retarded. We don't have to waste time on him. He'd want to keep us there an hour. There are more important things for us to do. What if we miss out on someone we *could* teach because you were back there with him?" He turned away from me, and we walked on in silence.

I was missing something. How could Elder Williams seem so nice this morning and not six hours later seem so stern? It must somehow be my influence. My presence had made the Holy Ghost leave us. I'd tried so hard to stop being gay before I came out here, but I simply hadn't managed to do it. It wasn't fair to keep me from the blessings of a mission when I was trying so hard, but everything seemed to be telling me I shouldn't be here. It wasn't fair of me to bring others down just to try to get some blessings for myself. How long could it be before everyone realized that I was the one who was to blame? My soul was going to be naked at some point, and the Germans were going to see I was circumcised.

But I wasn't ready to give up quite yet. I *wanted* to be righteous. And I wanted to make life better for others. So I had to find a way somehow to tap into the Spirit. It had to be possible. It just had to be.

Tracting door to door in the aging apartment buildings in Napoli One was next on our agenda, and I found myself smiling in anticipation, without even trying. The teachers at the MTC had made it sound like the funnest, most successful work in the world, so I felt like we were finally going to be doing something I could like. "You can reach people where they feel most comfortable and least threatened," my teachers said, but we hadn't knocked on three doors before one man answered our knock with a Doberman straining at the leash. Another man answered with a gun pointed at us. Elder Williams looked scared, but I just felt confused.

"When the people see you and feel your spirit, they'll open up their hearts enough to let you in, and then you've got them." Yet that one woman wouldn't even give me a glass of water when I asked. The next woman I asked brought a glass of water to the door and then drank it in front of us. My MTC teachers had said we could get in and teach any night we wanted, in any culture in the world.

Door after door after door after door, the answer was no. Door after door, the rejections seemed to say, "Your faithlessness will damn you to hell." It was all too fast. I wasn't supposed to be a failure *instantly*. I expected not to be great, but I didn't expect I'd be awful, right from the start.

I looked at eight or nine black and white death posters for someone named Luigi Esposito which lined the outside walls of the next building. We had to step over the legs of a man sleeping on the sidewalk beneath one of them. Dirty children in the streets ran around us as we walked to the following building. A five-year-old with a torn shirt was smoking a cigarette butt he'd found in the street. Two teenagers were kissing in an alley, their hands exploring each other's bodies. I saw a couple of hypodermics near the curb. A rat ran along the sidewalk.

"Ooh! Ice cream!" said Elder Williams, stopping in front of a little shop. He glanced at his watch. "Time for a break." We went in and Elder Williams studied the several varieties at length. It felt sinful to be in here, that we were indulging when we should have been working, but I tried to pretend I was at Baskin-Robbins back home. As Elder

Williams leaned forward to continue his inspection, I looked around the shop, not more than eight feet wide, and tried to forget being a missionary and just enjoy the experience. I was in Italy, in a gelateria. How many people back home in America would just die to be here?

"There!" said Elder Williams, pointing to a container so the man behind the counter could dig some of the chosen flavor out with a wide, flat knife. I didn't know the word Williams used, and I couldn't recognize the color as relating to any specific flavor. Even after the man patted more ice cream on the cone several times, it still wasn't as much as he could have gotten with one scoop. Didn't they have scoops in Italy? "Elder Anderson? Which one? I'm paying."

"Vaniglia," I said. That was nice of him, I thought, to—

"You can't have vanilla," he said. "You're going to waste your life away. God needs missionaries that are bold. Pick something else."

I reached in my pocket for my own change but then stopped, feeling completely stupid. "I think I'll pass," I said. "I'm not much in the mood for ice cream."

"Suit yourself."

We stood out front for ten more minutes as Elder Williams slowly licked his ice cream and ate his cone.

A few buildings later, we did finally get into someone's apartment to talk for a few minutes. It felt good to sit down, and to realize we'd finally found our "Golden Contact" of the day. But though I couldn't quite catch what was being said, I eventually got the impression the man was living with a woman who wasn't his wife, and although he wasn't overly interested in our message, he accepted one of our pamphlets. Mostly, I finally realized, he wanted to talk about his cousin in Chicago, who he was sure we knew since we were also Americans. The whole experience felt like a dream, as if I was watching everything through very thick air. I felt like a dog who could only understand a few human words now and then.

I didn't talk much the rest of the evening, hardly any during that visit and almost none to Elder Williams between door approaches, mostly because he only spoke Italian, and I hardly ever knew what he was saying. Once, as we came out of another decaying building, I struggled in Italian and asked, "Where are you from, Elder Williams?"

My companion didn't even turn to look at me as he answered curtly in English, "I'm a missionary, Elder Anderson. I don't want to talk about things which don't concern me now." I nodded, and then we walked on to the next building in silence.

The day had felt two weeks long, and I had almost 700 days more to go.

Climbing six flights of stairs at the end of the evening made me decide to start a serious search for ten lire pieces, but finally I was back in my room and trying to unpack my bags. I had two suits, four ties, an extra pair of good shoes, a pair of tennis shoes, five short sleeve white shirts, five long sleeve white shirts, ten pairs of garments—what other people called Mormon underwear—one pair of blue jeans, one red plaid shirt, several pairs of socks, my instamatic camera, a bathroom kit, a wind-up Big Ben alarm clock, a tiny sewing kit in a Tupperware sandwich box, my scriptures, my *Italian for Missionaries* book, a pack of air mail envelopes and some thin paper, and five empty journals. These were all the belongings I would have for two years, all I would need. It only took a few minutes to find a place for everything. As I was finishing, the door to my room closed. Then it opened again, but there was no one nearby.

"Elder Williams!" I called out. "Come here!"

"What's wrong?" he asked, coming into the room.

"The door opened and closed by itself."

"What? Don't be ridiculous."

"I saw it. It—" Then I stopped when I heard a burst of laughter from the hall. Elder Williams started laughing, too. "What's going on?"

"When you jump on the floor out there, it makes the door open and close. We did it to Lysenko last month, and he almost flipped out. Thought a spirit had come into the room! As if they needed doors!" They all laughed, and I finally did, too. It felt good. I felt my muscles untense, and I thought that after some rest, I'd feel better about everything. It was nice to see that Williams wasn't going to be serious all the time.

"I guess you'd better get studying, Anziano Anderson," he said a minute later, coming over to finger my lesson book. "When are you going to pass off your first discussion?"

I closed my eyes for a moment and then answered, "I guess I can pass off G tomorrow."

"You guess?"

"I'll definitely pass off G tomorrow," I corrected myself.

"Good, and we'll get C on Monday, okay?"

"I suppose."

"You suppose?"

"Yes, I'll pass off C on Monday." The mission program said I had to recite from memory all eight of the missionary lessons and a couple of dozen scriptures, all in Italian, by the end of two months, most of the lessons taking from forty-five minutes to an hour to recite, though G, the baptismal challenge, only took a few minutes. I would have two months to pass them all off the first time, but then I'd have to keep passing off the lessons regularly each month thereafter.

At 10:00, I dropped into bed, exhausted from the train ride this morning and from walking all over the city. I hoped I wouldn't get any blisters because I knew I'd have to keep walking tomorrow anyway. Despite going on "splits" with the elders back home a few times when they had teaching appointments, today was my first real day of missionary work. They'd told me in the MTC that my only limits would be the ones I placed on myself. I tried to think about the day and analyze it so I could find something specific to improve on, but I was too tired. I fell asleep almost instantly.

The alarm rang a few minutes later. It was pitch black as the ringing continued for a solid minute, coming from somewhere on the other side of the room. I sat on my bed, not knowing where the clock was to turn it off, and I couldn't remember where the light switch was, so I just waited. Suddenly, the light bulb above us flashed on, and I looked at the clock beside my bed. "5:30!" I exclaimed, unable to add anything more profound.

"I thought you'd need the extra half hour to study," explained Elder Williams.

"They told us in the MTC that we got up at 6:30 out here instead of at 6:00 like in Provo."

"They were wrong. You can't trust anyone in the MTC. They don't call it the Mental Torture Chamber for nothing." Elder Williams laughed at his cleverness and left to go to the bathroom. Wondering why he got to joke and I didn't, I sat on my bed another minute and tried to decide if I was being robbed of an hour's sleep or just half an hour's, and if that distinction mattered. Then I trudged over to my desk and opened my discussion book.

"I'll fix some breakfast for you," said Williams a moment later, sticking his head into the room.

I tried to smile and turned back to my book, trying to get the white blotches to clear away from my eyes. "Credi che sia possibile seguire veramente il Salvatore senza osservare i commandamenti del Padre?" I blinked a few times and looked at the page another time.

At lunch, I studied my discussion again, knowing I had to pass off G before we went back out later. G was the shortest discussion, and I'd read it three times since we'd come in fifteen minutes earlier. "Signor Rossi, are you sincere in your desire to follow the Savior?" (Wait for response.) "Do you feel it's possible to truly follow the Savior without observing the commandments of the Father?"

I looked away from the book, repeated the last several lines, waited a moment, and tried to repeat them again but couldn't. I glanced over at my companion but knew it was useless to ask for a break from studying. I looked at the next line in the book and tried again.

A few minutes later, I heard Elder Williams say, "Elder Anderson, what are you doing?"

"Huh?"

"I said what are you doing?"

"Oh. I guess I fell asleep for a minute. Sorry."

"Come on, Anziano. Show a little dedication. Don't be like the apostles who fell asleep in the Garden of Gethsemane. You're here to work, so work." Then he turned back to his scriptures.

I turned to my discussions, mad at both my companion and myself, and memorized another line. "The Book of Mormon is the history of the relationship of the Lord with the ancient inhabitants of the Americas." I passed off G right after lunch and immediately began studying C. Elder Lysenko came in and handed me two pieces of milk candy he'd gotten as change. "Milk first," he whispered, "and then meat. You'll get there."

That evening, we talked to a man named Gennaro at his door for a few minutes. He wouldn't let us in, but he did buy a Book of Mormon for a thousand lire, and he gave us each a tiny wooden inlay design of Vesuvius, made nearby in Sorrento, he said. I thought it was lovely and planned to send it to my mom for Christmas, but not long after this exchange, we stepped over a man passed out in a doorway with a hand-written sign propped next to him which said, "Reduced to this state by my wife." He held onto an upturned hat to accept donations even as he slept. Elder Williams tossed in his wooden inlay Vesuvius, laughing, but I didn't want to part with mine. Then I worried the rest of the evening about being too judgmental. We didn't get in to teach.

The following morning, I was still unhappy about having to wake up at 5:30, but I could still see our tiny classroom at the MTC, with signs proclaiming "Catch the Vision" and "Positive Mental Attitude" dotting the walls between posters of Cremona and Firenze. The entire two months there, we heard lessons on positive thinking, watching films like "I Pack My Own Chute" about overcoming fear, and I knew that I needed to do better.

So I smiled as we headed out the door. This was my third day. Sure, I was off to a slow start, but I could make it up now, I told myself. Christ was resurrected on the third day. He resurrected himself. I would, too. PMA. PMA.

I decided to be the first to approach someone, and I picked a man in a suit walking toward us. "Good morning," I began. "Have you ever wondered what our purpose here…"

He didn't actually interrupt me, but he so completely ignored me that I felt too stupid to go on.

"I can't stand it anymore," said Elder Williams. "Why did you stop? You have to endure to the end. If you give up before you finish, what kind of man are you?"

I looked back at him.

"Everything you do out here is a symbol of your life," Elder Williams went on. "You can't keep giving up. Do the next approach."

I did the next one, and the one after that. Elder Williams set a goal for me to talk to at least six men each hour all morning. When Elder Williams said "goal," however, it meant commandment, so I did it.

"Why don't you guys go back to America?" said one of the men I stopped.

"I'm busy," said another.

"Go bother someone else," the responses went on.

"I'm Catholic."

"I'm not interested."

"I've heard you before."

"I'm Catholic."

"I've got a cold."

"I'm late for a meeting."

"I'm not interested."

"I belong to the Neapolitan Catholic Church." Was that different from the Roman Catholic, I wondered?

"I'm running an errand."

"My dog is sick." I think that's what he said.

"I'm Catholic."

I finally turned to Elder Williams with a wry smile. "At least they're talking to me now."

"Why do you let them get away with that?" Elder Williams finally demanded. "You are so insecure, it's disgusting. Those are stupid reasons. Watch."

He stopped a man by almost blocking his path, handed him a pamphlet, and asked, "Have you heard of the Mormons before?"

"Yes, you have long beards and lots of wives."

"We don't have beards, do we?" Elder Williams motioned to his face and mine.

"You're too young to have beards," the man replied, a little condescendingly.

"We shave every day."

"That's very nice, but I'm really not interested." He started to move, but Elder Williams touched his shoulder.

"How do you know, if you don't know what we believe?" he asked him.

"I—"

"Just answer a few questions first, like do we believe in babies dying without baptism going to limbo?"

"I don't care. Really. Thanks, anyway, but—"

"You don't care? I know you don't believe that. How could you not care about a poor little baby? Now, you've probably heard all your life that a baby who dies without baptism can't go to heaven, but how can a baby be responsible for his own baptism? We believe God automatically brings young children who die without baptism into His presence."

"Look, I'm Catholic. I was born Catholic and I'm going to die Catholic. I'm just not interested." And he started to walk off.

"Is that what you're going to say to God on Judgment Day?" Elder Williams called after him. "That you were too steeped in tradition to recognize the truth? That fitting in was more important? What do you think He'll say to that?"

He was almost shouting by the end since the man was still walking away. Elder Williams smiled and turned to me. "See?" he said.

I realized my mouth was hanging open and so closed it. I was wondering how he could possibly see that exchange as effective, but what I said was, "Isn't that a little pushy, though?"

"Of course it's pushy. You have to shake people up. Knock them out of their rut. They're not going to thank you on Judgment Day for not being pushy. They're going to point their fingers and say, 'You could have helped me, but you were too ashamed of the gospel.' It's our job to make sure no one can point their fingers at us. Judgment Day is closer than we like to think. That man has had his chance."

But I wondered. Were two minutes on the street, in a crowd, talking with a stranger, really a "chance"? I doubt I would have responded to such a flimsy chance. Even with years in the Church, I felt I was barely facing its challenge. I wished I had died before I was eight, before the age of accountability, since that might have been my only chance at the Celestial Kingdom. The only thing I was any good at was being "nice," and I had been relying on that to make up for my lack in other areas, but apparently my niceness was more an escape from responsibility and confrontation than anything truly altruistic.

Forcing myself to think happy thoughts, I helped Elder Williams stop several more people the rest of the morning. Williams wrote down two addresses, and finally it was almost 1:00. As we were walking toward a bus stop to head back to the apartment for lunch, I saw two guys on a Vespa scooter in the street, waiting in traffic. The two young men, about seventeen or eighteen, I guessed, were chatting with each other, and suddenly one turned his head and pecked the other one on the lips. I was so surprised I just stopped and stared. A huge thrill shot straight through my chest. Elder Williams turned to see what had caught my attention.

"Finocchi!" he shouted at them. "Repent before you bring destruction on yourself and this city!"

One of the guys brought his cupped left hand over to his right side and then brought his right arm up so that his inner right elbow hit his left palm. We'd been warned against making that gesture back in Culture Capsule.

Elder Williams shot them the horns, another gesture we'd been warned against, and continued to call them to repentance until they drove off. I wanted to ask him to stop but was afraid he'd suspect me. When they were gone, I did finally ask, "Do you think that did any good?"

"Doesn't matter," he replied. "Now they know from *us* that they're sinning. It's on their heads now."

I hoped it wasn't true. I knew *I* was responsible because I had the gospel, but I felt sometimes that I wanted to avoid telling other gay people about it. If they weren't responsible yet because they hadn't heard the truth, then why not let them be? Let them have a little peace. Why ruin both their lives and their eternity? Maybe that was part of my own special mission, to protect gays from the responsibility of knowledge.

But then, maybe I was being falsely nice again. All I knew was that they'd looked happier than I ever felt, and it seemed a sin to take that from them. I saw them kiss again in my mind and hoped the two really cared for each other. I hoped they'd be spared hell because of their ignorance, but I knew that I had to beat this curse myself or I'd be damned to the horrors of a concentration camp existence in Outer Darkness for eternity.

We didn't teach any lessons during the evening, but Elder Williams called a few more people to repentance and shifted the responsibility for their salvation and exaltation onto their own shoulders. "Your favorite T.V. show is on?"

he said derisively to one man. "Is that any reason to lose your soul?"

"You're eating dinner? What's more important, feeding the body or feeding the spirit? Man does not live by bread alone."

"You're not interested? You're going to tell God He's boring?"

I cringed as he talked, but he was, after all, my senior companion. The mission president had assigned me to him for a reason. Elder Williams was my trainer, and I had to let myself be trained.

"Do we *have* to be rude?" I asked weakly after one approach.

"Is it rude to tell the truth?" Elder Williams returned. "We're not rude. We're right."

"But say someone is staining some shutters wrong," I said, remembering an incident with my father. "You don't have to say, 'You're ruining those shutters! They'll be ugly now! Why are you so dense?' Wouldn't it be better to say something like, 'Oh, maybe the directions weren't clear. See, if you let it run like that, it stains in streaks, and you can't ever get rid of the streaks.'"

Elder Williams looked at me coldly. "No," he said, "I don't think your way is better. Which way do you think would leave a stronger impression? We've only got a few seconds to make a lifelong impression. You don't make an impression by being soft. Besides, this is a bit more important than shutters. Would you say to someone, 'Oh, excuse me, but you're pointing that nail gun at my head. It could possibly harm me if you aren't careful'? Or would you say, 'Get that damn gun out of my face, idiot!' Even that is only life and death. *We're* talking of eternity."

I didn't say anything.

"And Elder Anderson?"

"Yes?"

"Don't try to tell me how to do my job. You had better learn your place. You do what *I* say."

I thought about repeating one of the gestures I'd seen earlier. Or pointing out that Elder Williams always pronounced "carita'" wrong, accenting the first rather than the last syllable. Even I knew that much Italian.

But I couldn't bear to be purposely rude. I felt I was being ordered to sin, and something inside of me simply wouldn't permit it. "No, thanks," said a man at the next door I knocked on. "It's good that you offer something to people who need it, but my family and I are quite happy as we are."

"Well, if you know of anyone who might be interested, here's our card," I said, smiling and handing him a little white ticket. "Good evening." Then the man closed the door.

"Elder Anderson, do you want to bring the statistics down for the whole mission? You've got to do better than that. At the very least, don't leave without getting the name and number of one of his friends. Stop being such a wimp. The Lord's called us to be warriors, not pansies."

For a while, I was too nervous to pay much attention to the rest of his approaches, but he did catch my ear again when we finished another building without success and he said, "I wish it wasn't against mission policy to dust our feet. Sometimes, I'd like to see if it would really cause something to shake these people up." He lifted one foot and held his hand over his shoe a moment. "Maybe just a little dust," he said, swiping his shoe with just two fingers. Then he laughed and we walked on to the next building.

I stole a glance at my watch. Only 8:00. We still had another hour of tracting to do. I managed to smile when Elder Williams looked back at me, and we started up the stairs to the next door.

The following days passed in much the same way. I studied my discussions every minute in the apartment and worked every minute outside. I studied my companion's "rudeness" to see if there were some underlying truth I was missing, but I kept missing it. Yet my lack of understanding or obedience to my trainer's orders meant that hour after hour of work brought us no results. We were occasionally able to get an address from someone on the street, but the address was rarely correct. "Another bung," Elder Williams would say. We did teach a couple of lessons a week, but the people were never interested enough to want to hear a second lesson. "Not golden contacts," my companion said. But at least he wasn't blaming me every time.

We did teach one family of five three lessons over six days, and I was getting all psyched up for my first baptism. Five people. I could hardly believe it. Maybe I did have some faith. Thank God. Thank God.

But then during our fourth lesson, the father interrupted us once and said, "Wait a minute. You mean you're not Catholic?" and then escorted us to the door.

A few days after that, we were on a bus when someone grabbed my Book of Mormon and tossed it out a window. Elder Williams lunged toward the man, but I held him back. "It only cost a dollar," I said. "It's not the end of the world."

"He'll see the end of the world if he tries that with *me*."

We climbed off the bus at the next stop and walked back to look for the book. It wasn't easy, with cars parked everywhere and trash covering half the sidewalk.

"Why didn't you stand up for yourself?" Elder Williams demanded. "It's like you're condoning what he did."

I shrugged. "His actions are irrelevant," I said. "I only have to worry about mine. And believe me, that's more than enough. I don't have the energy to worry about him."

"Maybe that's your problem. You need to accept more responsibility. If you'd realize these people's souls *are* your responsibility, you'd find a way to be more successful."

I nodded slowly, thinking about it. "Perhaps." But really, the incident hardly even bothered me. So what if some man didn't like us? It wasn't as if he knew any better.

We walked all the way back to the next stop but never found the book. "Maybe it was God's way of getting it into the hands of someone who needed it," I suggested.

"Maybe someone just threw it away. You'd better be more careful in the future. People don't donate to the Missionary Fund to have their money thrown out the window."

It hardly seemed like my fault, and yet I wondered why at other times I was all too willing to feel responsible for other people's actions, like whenever they said no to my approaches. I wondered why this time I hadn't felt guilty and if Elder Williams was right that I should have. But I couldn't figure out why *I* was the one responsible for what a stranger fifty yards away did with a book he found on the street, and Elder Williams wasn't. Why was it always me?

That evening, an old woman let us inside and insisted we drink some sour milk and eat some hard bread with her as we talked. She was old enough that we felt we could stay without the neighbors gossiping, so Elder Williams tried valiantly to go through lesson C, but it was clear the woman just wanted some company. I had brought my X-15 camera in my jacket pocket for the past couple of days, taking pictures of Elder Williams on a crowded bus, of Elder Williams in a tiny elevator, and of Elder Williams talking to a man in front of a seafood booth on the street. He'd grumbled a little about my worldliness, but I could tell he felt important to be in so many pictures, so I wondered if I should ask the old woman if she'd like to be in a picture, too.

She stood up when Elder Williams paused, and she went to a little cupboard in the kitchen, coming back with an overripe pear sliced in two. "I don't have any dessert to offer, but take this." She held the pieces out to us, and we took them, though I knew I was going to make her go to bed hungry.

As Elder Williams bit into his pear, I asked, "Signora, you are so sweet. Could I take a picture of you?"

She smiled and began pulling back her hair and checking her buttons.

I handed the camera to Elder Williams. "Would you mind?" I asked. "The flash bulb's already on it."

The pear sticking out of his mouth, he wiped his fingers on his pants and took the camera. I moved over beside the woman and put my hand on her shoulder, towering over her, as Williams clicked the shutter. "I want to remember all the nice people I meet," I told her, and she smiled again.

But before she could say anything more, Elder Williams said, "Thanks for the pear and everything, but we really need to go. We have another appointment." I tried not to look surprised as I moved back over to him.

"Well, it was delightful to have you come by," she said, standing and leading us to the door. "Stop by again if you're in the neighborhood. It's nice to see clean, decent boys."

Elder Williams shook her hand officiously but I held it a moment, wishing I knew how to make another person feel better. Then we left, though as usual we had no other appointment. "At least I managed to get through concept four before she grabbed the pear," Elder Williams said.

"That means it was over half the lesson, so we can count it as a complete lesson on our stat sheet."

"At least her salvation is her own responsibility now," I added, though Williams missed the sarcasm.

"Yep, it's been a pretty good evening so far." He brushed his fingers against his pants again, trying to get the last of the stickiness off.

The next Sunday at church, I had a little self-indulgent thrill of my own when I realized I knew Italian at least as well as some of the other missionaries out for seven or eight months. A sister missionary I liked gave a talk and explained how she'd always loved a particular doll as a child and had carried it everywhere with her. Only she didn't use the word "bambola," which meant "doll." She kept saying, "bombola," which meant "gas canister," like the ones which supplied gas to our stoves. "I used to bring my little gas canister to school with me," she said as the Italians looked on, mystified. "I used to dress my little gas canister up every day. I brought my little gas canister to the store, and I brought my little gas canister to the park. I loved my little gas canister."

Elder Williams couldn't wait till she finished speaking so he could point out her mistake, but I put my hand on his arm. "Don't embarrass her," I said. "At least she gave a talk from memory. She didn't read it. Let her be happy with that." He shrugged, but he left her alone.

A few days after that, it came time for me to pass off H, the lesson on the commandments. It was two days earlier than I felt I would be ready, and I really didn't want to do it, but Elder Williams pushed and pushed and pushed until I gave in. "It's my responsibility to see that you pass off in time," he said. So he did take *some* responsibility, apparently, but while he was "responsible," I was the one doing the work.

It took me three full hours to recite the forty-five minute lesson. I felt totally inadequate all over again. Every time I paused when I forgot the next word, there was an awful silence in the air. I could hear the elders in the next room discussing a Church member they didn't like. I could hear the cars going by on the street below, pausing, shifting gears, grinding forward, while there was absolute silence in our room.

"Se dimostriamo la nostra fede…uh, la nostra fede…" I tried, "uh…nel…fede in…uh…la nostra fede…uh…" What *was* that next word? "La nostra fede…"

Elder Williams sighed heavily. "Obbedendo."

"La nostra fede obbedendo a questo commandamento, il Signore ci benedira'." We never actually talked like this, and many words throughout the lesson I still didn't know. "Um…um…ci benedira'…uh…Noi…um…"

A neighbor was playing the radio, and some man singing with a beautiful voice was asking someone what they were doing that evening. "Tu cosa fai sta sera?" If we'd put the discussions to music like the ABC's, I'd probably learn them well enough. I heard that some Orthodox Jews learned the entire Torah by putting it to music, cantillations I think they called it.

"Ci benedira'," I repeated, closing my eyes to block out the poster of Moroni kneeling over the golden plates. "Uh...um...Noi vogliamo...uh...Noi crediamo che... um...Noi..."

Elder Williams sighed deeply again. "Noi le portiamo."

"Noi le portiamo la nostra testimonianza, Signor Rossi, che la legge della decima e' un vero commandamento del Signore." Good grief, a whole sentence. I was rolling. "Egli...uh...Egli..." Oh, God. "Egli vuole...um..."

Diana Ross was now singing next door. "Upside down. Boy, you turn me, inside out and all around."

"Egli...uh...Egli dice che...um...Egli..."

"Egli ci."

"Egli ci benedira'...uh...ci benedira'...se...se noi...uh..."

"Oltre."

"Egli ci benedira' oltre ogni misura, se...uh...se noi...um..."

Elder Williams refused to give me any more cues, and after I struggled with different possibilities, then gave up when I realized they were wrong, and paused interminably again a couple more times, he finally gave me one single word to start me going again, and off I went for another sentence or two before I got stuck yet another time. Then I listened to the cars again, and to voices in the street, and tried and tried to remember the next few words. After three or four unsuccessful guesses with one or two minutes of silence in between, Elder Williams magnanimously gave me another one-word cue. He never let up, and the lesson dragged on and on until I finally pushed out the last few words and closed my flip chart of pictures in relief. Three torturous hours, but at least it was over.

"Do you really think that was good enough for me to accept?" Elder Williams asked in disgust as soon as I closed my binder. "You'll have to do it again. It's your responsibility to learn these lessons on time, Elder. Every day behind you get, you're responsible for the people you could have taught if you'd been prepared."

I said nothing, trying to suppress an almost uncontrollable urge to throw my discussion binder in his face. No. I wanted to *hit* his face. I wanted to punch it. I wanted to push him off the balcony. I left the room and stood in front of the sink in the bathroom. I stared at the drain for several minutes, afraid to move, and then I slowly looked up into the mirror and stared for another minute.

I *honestly* could have killed him.

Was being a murderer worse or better than being gay?

Elder Williams had *known* for over two hours he wasn't going to accept my H, for maybe almost three hours, from the very start. And he'd *still* forced me through it. That could not be the Lord's way. If it was, then I didn't want to follow a God like that. I looked up, half expecting to be struck down.

But if God didn't approve of Elder Williams's approach, that meant leaders weren't always right, which meant I'd have to decide when they were and when they weren't. I wasn't at all sure I was qualified to make those decisions. But better to make a mistake than to live like the creep he was. I washed my face and went back to my room to study, going directly to my desk without looking at my companion.

A few days later, it was the start of my week to cook, so I was able to study less, which should have been a relief, but still almost every day was a disaster. The worst was when I tried to prepare stew. I had no idea how long it would take to chop and peel everything, and I certainly had no idea how long it would take to cook. By 3:00, the others demanded food, and we ate warm, raw stew for lunch. Lysenko and Griffith didn't talk to me as they left the kitchen.

I had one carrot left over, and I remembered a time when I was thirteen, still a deacon, and we visited the family of our former bishop in Salt Lake for Christmas. Two of the bishop's sons made snowmen, placing them right next to each other. Instead of putting carrots in to make noses, though, they'd used the carrots to make penises. One snowman's penis was sticking into the backside of the other snowman, while the recipient's penis was pointing straight out into the air, a smile on his face made with two twigs.

"Get it? Get it?" asked the older boy, laughing. "It's the Abominable Gayman of Mt. Olympus!"

Then with an extra carrot he still had in his hand, he goosed me and laughed even harder.

I was mortified, but when I got back home to Mississippi, I tried sticking the blunt end of a carrot up my butt, to see what it would be like to have a man's penis inside me. I felt terrible shame afterward, realizing I had learned to be this base while on the mountain of the gods in the city of the saints. But every six months or so, I succumbed to the temptation again, each time crying afterward as I realized that I really and truly was an abominable gayman.

Even now, I looked at the carrot longingly, wondering if I dared sneak it into the bathroom. But I shook my head and cut it up furiously, putting it in the fridge so it wouldn't be a temptation anymore.

I tried to see myself living this way for the next two years. Did I really want to do this work, even if I found I was capable of it? I couldn't stop caring about purging myself. If I didn't do it, I was going to hell. I *cared* about that. And really, was Elder Williams preaching for the benefit of the Italians, or just to make sure *he* was guiltless?

But what if I was more effective *not* preaching? I could take the guilt from all those people with me on Judgment Day. If I was going to hell anyway, why not at least let them get off the hook?

I tried to focus on my work and not think, but the foreign pages in my book kept burning my eyes, and I could hardly concentrate. I'd managed over these first five weeks to pass off six of the eight missionary discussions, passing off H a second time in just an hour and a half. Now I had to memorize the two I hadn't even started in the MTC, and I was already so tired of studying that I didn't care if I ever passed off another discussion in my life, much less by next week.

My attitude was as weathered as the side of our building. I stared at the wall in front of my desk, listening to the neighbor's radio.

"Come on, Anziano," Elder Williams said. "If you're faithful for seventy years and then stop going to church, you're still damned."

"Is taking a break the same as giving up? Even the Lord rests once a week."

"I didn't make the mission rules. God did."

"Not the Church?"

Elder Williams shook his head. "Ooh. You're treading on shaky ground." He stepped back from me as if he expected me to be struck down for saying something so blasphemous. "You need to learn that discussion because it's a rule, and because by being obedient, you'll gain a stronger testimony. There's no time to rest. You can't take a break from righteousness. You've got to push yourself more and *do it*. The Lord doesn't give commandments we can't follow. Remember what Nephi said. Now get to work."

I tried to remember the Italian curse word I'd seen scrawled on one of the walls in the hallway, but I couldn't, so I turned back to my lesson book. I was only a few days behind schedule. Who cared if it took two months and three days to finish memorizing everything? Three days couldn't really make that much difference. Then again, to reach the highest degree in the Celestial Kingdom, I had to be more than just good or adequate or average. I had to push myself to the limit. Maybe three days did make a difference.

I wrote long entries in my journal each morning and sent detailed letters home each week, despite Elder Williams reminding me that I had "better" things to do with my time. When I jumped once after a roach flew onto my desk, Elder Williams laughed and talked about a sister missionary who'd been sent home several months ago when she had a nervous breakdown because of all the roaches in her apartment. Her companion had found her sitting in the middle of her bed, wrapped in a blanket and mumbling something about all the "bats" flying around.

I didn't find the story particularly funny. Still, I tried to make it sound funny in my letter home, but I knew some of my depression had seeped through when I received a letter from my mother which said, "If you come home early, we can hide you in the attic." I knew she didn't want me to come home, but the letter served its purpose, making me smile for a moment.

Now it was Sunday afternoon again, and as Elder Williams and I walked down Via Roma toward the church, I tried to relax. I wanted more than anything to go back to the apartment and crawl into bed, to be alone and forget about the rest of the world. I'd never thought a missionary could ever want to stay home from church.

We turned toward Piazza Dante and kept walking. The Church here rented out a third-floor apartment in an old building for our Sunday meetings. The chapel was a living room with a piano in one corner, a homemade wooden podium in the front of the room, and metal folding chairs for pews. The number of classrooms was limited, since one of the four bedrooms had to serve as the branch president's office where he could do personal counseling with the members. Still, having only three other rooms wasn't much of a problem because in this city of probably three million people there were barely sixty members each Sunday. We tried to make the chapel feel like a refuge from the world, but twice since I'd been here, the meetings had been disrupted by the sounds of communists or strikers protesting in the square nearby.

"Oh, ciao, Anziani!" Sister Colombo said cheerily as she hurried past us and into the massive gray building which housed the church.

It didn't seem fair that the Church should make the lives of other members happy and mine miserable. I wanted to be happy, too. But if it could make *some* people happy…

Elder Williams and I arrived in the chapel as the men were singing the opening song for Priesthood meeting, the women in the largest of the bedrooms for Relief Society, and the children in two of the others. We slid into some empty metal chairs in the back row. "The harvest is great and the laborers are few," the men were singing, "but if we're united, we all things can do. We'll gather the wheat from the midst of the tares, and bring them from bondage, from sorrows and snares." A couple of elders from the Napoli Three district gave us an irritated glance for being late, and I felt miserable yet again.

Shortly after I arrived in Naples, I'd written a letter to a non-member friend in Mississippi, mentioning just a few of the problems I was having, and she'd written back, asking why I didn't simply come home. The question of course wasn't whether I was miserable or not. The question was whether or not it was *right* that I be here. Once in ninth grade, some kids were joking about one of the girls trying out for cheerleader. "Don't vote for her," they spread around. "She's a Spic." "My great-grandfather was half Mexican," I told them, "one quarter Indian, and one quarter black. If she can do the jumps, I think I'll go ahead and vote for her." The other boys shut up, but the girl still got almost no votes. But that wasn't the real issue for me. The issue was taking her side, even though I had to lie about my great-grandfather to do it. And I didn't care that I was teased the rest of that year. Well, I cared, but that wasn't what was important. Doing the right thing was important, regardless of misery.

But this was a new level of misery, and it was going on for too long. I didn't know if I could do it, right or not. How could I feel anything but absolute and utter misery when I knew God was disgusted by my very existence? I'd heard a missionary back home talk about his first year at Brigham Young University, where a fellow student had been put through electric shock therapy to rid him of his homosexuality. When it didn't work, he was simply kicked out of the school and out of the Church, the way I'd be kicked into eternal deportation with other lost souls if I didn't change.

One of my MTC teachers had told us the story of the blacksmith who threw away pieces of iron that couldn't take being heated and cooled, heated and cooled. "They'll never be good for anything," he'd said. Our missions would test us the same way.

The Priesthood lesson began, but I hardly paid attention, glaring at the back of the chair in front of me, my teeth still clenched.

Everyone at home thought I was so good, but I was tired, so very tired, of getting shouted at by portieri, of having my companion speak so fast I couldn't understand him, and of carrying trash down six flights of stairs only to find someone else's scattered in front of the building the next morning, where they'd thrown it from their balcony. Yesterday, a good-looking guy I was debating myself over approaching spit on me when I finally did approach him.

Elder Lysenko didn't even bother trying to love his mission. He told me he was here because his father promised to send him through school if he stayed for two years. And yet Lysenko seemed to fit in okay. Maybe my real problem was realizing I was never going to fit in anywhere.

But hadn't the Church rescued me from the time when I would get nauseated whenever I had to speak in public, even if that only meant answering a question in class at school? I had played the role of a missionary in our stake's production of *Saturday's Warrior*. I had won first place in the stake speech contest for the category of sixteen-year-olds. The Church made me try scary things, and that was good.

It was those experiences at church that helped me become student council vice-president as a senior in high school. No one had run against me, but I wouldn't have even bothered running myself if it weren't for the Church.

You could like the Church without liking missionary work.

At thirteen, I had been a weak, introverted nerd that everyone hated. I became active in the Church at fourteen, and by the time I was a junior, I was actually fairly well liked. As a senior, I was voted Most Courteous. People seemed to like me, and I finally felt human. Didn't I *owe* the Church something for its help?

I might end up a failure soon enough, but I couldn't let it happen *yet*. Not just yet. Being a failure *so far* wasn't the same as being a failure *for good*.

Besides, it was clear I could never purge these gay feelings out of my system if I didn't stick it out. "Abomination." "Evil." "Perverted." "Sick." I closed my eyes, afraid to have anyone see them while I was thinking. Oh, God, I didn't *want* to be evil. I would do anything not to be haunted any more by this horrible, horrible secret.

In Boys State at the state capitol in Jackson, I'd heard the other guys joke about salt peter, and I tried to find out in the library later what it was and where I could buy some. I even called a pharmacy, but the pharmacist hung up on me. I'd wanted to bring a two-year supply with me, and I looked in my Italian dictionary in the MTC but couldn't find a translation, so even if I ran across it here I wouldn't know.

I knew that if I didn't find a way to make this mission a success, I'd be such a failure that I'd never be able to resist temptation. Sooner or later, I'd have sex with a man. Then I'd lose all sense of right and wrong, keep having perverted sex, and end up alone, in the gutter, with a totally wasted life.

Half an hour later, Priesthood meeting was over, and Sunday School began. The women came in from their Relief Society meeting and we all sat together in the chapel.

I barely understand what anyone said, still struggling with the language every day. Once, while giving part of the first lesson to a man, I'd explained seriously to him that, "Joseph Smith went to pray in a cookie." Another time, I'd asked a woman very politely if her pencil was at home, rather than her husband. Yet another time, I'd said very solemnly as I bore my testimony, "I know that this is the true church of God on the head." Then, just a few days ago, I'd taught as doctrine that, "While Joseph Smith was praying, a hill of light fell on him."

I started to smile now as I remembered. I'd caught Elder Williams making a couple of funny mistakes with the language as well. I realized, too, that despite the trash everywhere, there were still some spectacular views here from the hillsides. And there had been that old woman who invited us in on a particularly cold day last week and given us two old sweaters to wear under our jackets. Misery was on a spectrum, and if I could just move the needle once in a while, maybe two years from now when this mission was all over, I'd be able to smile back on the whole thing.

Maybe. But I would *never* tell other teens about to go on missions how "wonderful" it all was. Was that how God had tricked us into coming to Earth?

"Well, go on," my companion urged me, interrupting my thoughts.

"What?"

"He just asked you to give the prayer."

"Oh!" I quickly walked up to the front of the room and mumbled a short prayer, trying to sound sincere.

Sacrament meeting immediately after Sunday School consisted of ten-minute discourses given by three Italian members. I paid attention as best I could and wrote down two new words to look up when I got home.

Another hymn, one more prayer, and then the meeting was over. Everyone usually stayed in the chapel another fifteen minutes, talking, joking, and sharing experiences of the past week. Since I hadn't made any friends yet and my companion had to pass off the D to me, we both decided to go back to our apartment instead of talking to the other members.

The air was cooling off, and we walked briskly back to the apartment. The city looked much better at night. The dirt was far less visible on the narrow, black-bricked roads and on the old, shabby apartment buildings, and we rarely tried to stop and talk to people on the street in the evening. We hardly had to do any work at all on Sunday because church started so late, and I was beginning to feel a little better since I knew I wouldn't have to interact with any more people that day except my companion. Well, one more day down, only 646 more to go.

I thought about Anne Frank, and how she'd died just a few weeks before liberation. If she'd known ahead of time how close she was, would she have had the strength to hold out? I didn't know how long my test of Earth life was going to be, but I did have a specific date for the end of my mission. And while my unhappiness in no way compared to what Anne had gone through, I prayed God would cure my typhus if I hung on a little longer. I was going to have a good life. I was not going to live out my days confined to a couple of hidden rooms, or to overcrowded, filthy barracks. And I was not going to spend eternity in Auschwitz for who I was.

But I would have to work for my freedom.

I felt a chill as I thought of the phrase, "Arbeit macht frei," but I believed the words when the Prophet said them. They weren't just a trick.

I saw a man in his thirties coming down the street toward us. He wasn't well dressed, but he was neat. Maybe I should surprise Elder Williams by stopping him. My companion knew I didn't enjoy referral taking, but the man looked nice enough, and we were low on referrals for the week. Then again, I thought, why bother? Take at least one day off, I told myself. I was so tired.

But I needed to be good, I told myself firmly. I had to at least try.

"Good evening," I said to the man, changing direction to walk alongside him.

"Good evening."

"We're from the Church of Jesus Christ of Latter-day Saints, and we have a message about families we'd like to share with you."

"No, thank you. I'm not interested."

I turned around and started walking back toward our apartment. I still wasn't great with those approaches, but I was getting better. I managed at least to finish my approaches now. It was something.

"Good work," my companion said. He didn't add anything else, and I was grateful. I still felt drained from the experience. Sheesh, how was I ever going to survive if something that small was always such a major ordeal for me?

A minute later, we were back at our building. "Race you to the top, Elder Anderson!" I almost felt up to a race anyway, so I started sprinting up the stairs. Elder Williams had been there longer, though, and was in better shape. He held the door open for me when I reached the apartment a few moments after he did.

He stood by his desk, briefly reviewing his lesson before reciting it to me. I sat on my bed, resisting the temptation to kick off my shoes and lie back. I knew the rule about not studying on our beds, though, so I stood up and started for my desk. I suddenly felt dizzy and reached to brace myself on my bed. Our bedroom door closed.

"I guess the other elders came back, after all," Elder Williams mumbled. "Must be jumping in the next room to surprise us."

Elder Williams's desk lurched, knocking off a couple of books. The door closed and opened again, and my chair wiggled toward my bed. A low groan deep below quickly became a tremendous and continual grating noise, and the lights flickered. I fell onto my bed. The magazines slid out from under it, and the foot of my bed hit the floor.

"It's an earthquake!" shouted my companion. "Let's get out of here!"

We stumbled down the hall toward the door, the awful sound of concrete scraping against concrete hammering into our ears. Above the roar of the shaking, we could faintly hear screaming and yelling coming from below us in the building and out in the streets. We reached the front door and pulled it open. Plaster and bits of cement littered the stairway and more kept falling. The stairs shook and twisted.

"They'll collapse!" Elder Williams shouted. "We have to stay here!"

We left the door to our apartment open, trying to stand in the doorway. I was facing the inside of our apartment and stared as lightning-shaped cracks opened in our walls and pipes jutted out. I could see part of our kitchen, and I watched as the refrigerator door swung outward, flinging a carton of milk into the hallway. The lights flickered again. A moment later, the shaking ceased.

For a few seconds, there was silence. Then moans and screams from below reached our ears. Accidentally pushing me into the wall, my companion started for the stairs. "Let's get out of here before it starts again!" he said, already on the first step.

I put my hand on the wall to catch my balance, and a plate-sized section of plaster came off and dropped to the floor. I quickly followed my companion into the hall.

We had only descended two flights when we were stopped by an old man. He had hurt his leg and needed help getting out of the building. We led him down the stairwell, avoiding the debris and the other people hurrying past us. On the second floor, a woman grabbed me and dragged me to her apartment.

"My son!" she sobbed. "Help him!"

My companion kept on down the stairs with the old man. "Never leave your companion for any reason, under any circumstances." I'd had the message drilled into me so often that even now I expected to be struck down for allowing our separation.

I followed the woman into her apartment. Lying face down in the hall was a young man of perhaps fifteen or sixteen. A fallen painting was on the floor beside his head. The mother's arms flung about wildly as she spoke almost incomprehensibly fast. She tried to get some water for her son but then became more upset because the pipes were broken.

I felt a lump on the boy's scalp, making him moan. He turned over, tried to open his eyes, and immediately tensed, his eyes now bulging. I kneeled, lifting the boy to rest against my legs, and softly began singing the words to a children's hymn I'd learned in the MTC, one I didn't even remember the words to in English. "Disse il ruscello un di'…" I felt a little awkward, since the boy was almost my own age, but the song comforted us both. When he relaxed a bit, I helped him sit up, still kneeling next to him. He held onto my arm.

Then his mother rushed over. "Are you all right?" she asked, hugging and kissing the boy, who continued to look at me.

He nodded slowly. "My head," he said, hugging her back.

There was a slight rumbling and the building quivered. We heard more screams accompanied by a thud and the sound of glassware crashing to the floor somewhere above us. I crouched over the boy's head to keep anything else from hitting him. The tremor ended a few seconds later. Grabbing her son, the woman tried to lift him. Not thinking she was strong enough, I took the boy and lifted him to his feet, telling him to put his arm across my shoulders for support. There was another tremor which lasted only a second, and we walked quickly out the door and down the stairs.

The streets outside were crowded with shouting, screaming, and crying people. I sat the boy down on the hood of a car stopped in the street. He looked at me gratefully, and I nodded slightly, looking at him just a moment longer. Then I turned around to look for my companion, but someone grabbed me from behind and twisted me about. The mother hugged me and kissed me on the cheeks. "Grazie! Grazie! You boys are angels!"

I hugged her for a moment and then broke off to look for my companion. I found him a few seconds later, searching for me in the crowd. "You all right?" he asked.

"Yeah. I just had to help someone get out of the building."

"You know the mission rules say not to place ourselves in unnecessary danger. That's why we can't go water skiing or mountain climbing on our missions."

I stared at him blankly. I felt as if I couldn't even understand English any longer.

"It doesn't matter. You're okay. Let's go check on the church."

We made our way back to the church and found that two members had fainted and another had fallen down the stairs during the quake, badly bruising her leg, but everyone was mostly okay. The floor of the church had cracked, one part sinking a few inches below the other side, but the place was still standing. I followed my companion back out the building, feeling dazed, as if I were in a dream.

The air still felt thick when you didn't understand much. I was a smarter dog now, but human speech was still beyond me.

We found Elders Lysenko and Griffith, who were fine, and we split up to walk a few members back to their apartments, agreeing to meet the next morning in front of our building and decide then if we could go back inside or not. As Elder Williams and I walked with some of the members to their homes, we saw a few collapsed buildings on the way, people trying to pull away chunks of cement to find the bodies underneath.

One member lived just behind an old folks home, but she could see from far off that her building was still standing because the old folks palazzo was gone. Some men were trying to lift a huge block of cement off of a tiny car. A teenage couple had been making out, they said, but the cement was too heavy to budge. No one could be alive underneath it anyway.

Several people sat in the streets crying, holding an injured arm or trying to wrap a cut with a handkerchief. But most people seemed okay, just frightened. With the streets of Napoli crowded even on good days, they were absolutely packed right now, so it took us a long while to work our way back toward our apartment. We knew we couldn't go inside, but it was comforting to be back in our neighborhood. It somehow felt like home now though it never had before. Stopping finally in Piazza Dante, Elder Williams and I found a few inches between cars and other people and prepared to spend the night. It was late November and getting chilly.

"I guess this changes our plans to get referrals tomorrow morning," I said, letting the slightest smile onto my face.

"Yeah." Elder Williams paused for a second. "I hope my parents aren't too worried. I know they'll hear people were killed."

It struck me that this was the first time he'd mentioned his parents since we'd been together. The desire instantly sprang up to ask if what went on at home was relevant.

"We'll try to call them tomorrow," I said. "We should at least be able to get through to Rome and tell the mission president we're okay."

For the first time, I realized that I should have been killed. To die as a missionary would have assured me the Celestial Kingdom, my only hope of ever achieving godhood, yet God hadn't let me die.

Maybe He didn't want me. Maybe I was only destined to be an angel, something lower, though I had my doubts I'd even achieve that height. To spend my whole life trying to learn how to become a god, and then to end up in the lowest order of heaven, if I was lucky, if I never succumbed even once to the temptation of sex. It seemed so fruitless.

But somehow, despite that possibility because of my survival, I felt stronger, as if I'd survived because of something I'd done, though that wasn't true. I felt glad to be alive, even having missed out on that slot in heaven. Maybe working my way there would be harder, but I was glad to have a chance to keep trying. I felt that I wanted a chance to be nice, even if there wasn't much hope of my ever being good. Maybe nice was good enough, after all. I would have to make it be. It suddenly felt like the only important thing.

"You think your parents are worried?" asked Elder Williams.

"I don't know. They don't get excited too often."

"This might almost be enough to shake them up then?" Elder Williams smiled.

"Maybe." I laughed. But then I wondered who this quake was meant to shake up. Was it the unrepentant sinners? And by that, did God mean the Catholics who weren't listening to us, or only those who were committing particularly bad sins? I'd have to keep a lookout for those guys I'd seen on the scooter. Had they been killed? Or was I the one who had brought the destruction, being a Mormon and still sinful? Maybe God hadn't killed me because if I died as a missionary that would end up blessing rather than cursing me. I looked up at the gray building where the church was located. It had a new, large crack running up its face.

"Elder Williams," I said then, "you never did pass off that discussion."

"What?"

"You don't want to get behind, do you? Besides, maybe someone will overhear you and get interested."

"Well, okay. I'm not real sleepy, anyway." He paused, looking around briefly at all the people sitting nearby, and then he took a deep breath and began discussion D. "Signor Rossi, have you ever asked yourself questions such as, 'Where did I come from?' 'Why am I here?' 'Where will I go when this life is over?' Before we were born…"

I looked about me as he continued talking and watched the Italian people huddled together against the cool breeze. The statue of Dante had fallen over in the middle of the square, and a large bell had fallen off a nearby wall and onto a parked car, not Brother De Luca's car, I noticed, though he usually parked right there each Sunday.

I could hear a man trying to calm down his wife. It was hard to believe I could understand what he was saying to her. He must have been speaking slowly, perhaps even patronizingly, but at least I could follow. "We'll find your sister tomorrow. If her house is wrecked, they can stay with us for a while."

"But what if—"

"Everything's going to be all right." He put his hand on hers, and though she didn't look fully comforted, she did relax a bit. I wished there were something I could say to help them or the thousands of others that needed comforting now. What was the appropriate way to help? What should a missionary do?

But I didn't want to do what a missionary should do. I wanted to do what *I* could do. Instantly, I knew I shouldn't have asked Elder Williams to pass off in public. And I knew also that I was facing a long battle for the next twenty months, a battle deciding just what I was capable of, or even what I really *wanted* to be capable of.

I was different, for whatever reason. I couldn't be what everyone else wanted me to be. Their standards just weren't going to work for me. Most of them might, but I had to make up some of my own standards, too. Perhaps mine were only Terrestrial ones, but that was just how it was going to have to be. Of course, if we'd all lived with God in the premortal existence before coming to Earth, I'd already seen firsthand what it was like to be a god. Maybe, I thought, I wasn't here on Earth then to learn how to be a god, but to learn how to be human.

I used to be decent, or at least more decent, before I became so preoccupied with being good. Yet as I tried to think of a way to help all these frightened people, my mind was blank, and I wondered really if I was capable even of Telestial level niceness.

Back home, I'd read bedtime stories to my little brother and even played catch with him, a game I would never have liked on my own, but I wanted him to feel a connection with an older man that I'd never felt with my father. And when Dad had laughed at him once for crying over a loose tooth he was afraid would hurt to come out, I'd taken him to his room and hugged him for a few moments and then lightly pinched him, explaining that it wouldn't hurt any more than that. He cheered up right away and laughed later when the tooth came out.

I looked at the couple again. The man was leaning against a car, and the woman was leaning against him. Sleeping nearby was a boy of about ten. The man noticed me looking at him, so I smiled and nodded my head. He smiled slightly and looked away.

I looked away, too, a little scared. If I screwed up, would God wait until after I finished my mission, and then strike me down when it would send me to hell?

And for just a second I wished the ceiling could have caved in on me, after all. But then I remembered the sixteen-year-old boy, lying face down before me. I saw again the look in his eyes when we made it out, and I, too, felt grateful. Not that I had really helped him any. The building was still standing. He'd have been fine without me. I simply liked being around to see that.

I had liked the look in the eyes of those two young men on the Vespa, too. There was goodness in that look as well. Even if there was sin, there was goodness mixed in with it, and it couldn't be right to condemn it completely. But where were we supposed to draw the line in all of these things?

Were the Church's rules iron bars to enclose us or paths to guide us, and did God mind if we strayed off the path to get a closer look at some things along the way? According to Lehi's dream, He did. But I had to make myself believe it was God's plan that we think for ourselves, despite the dangers. Perhaps that was like building a house in an earthquake zone, but it seemed to me every area worth living in had its own dangers. We had hurricanes back home. Maybe taking a spiritual risk was the only way to attain spiritual greatness. Or even spiritual adequacy. I was too tired to think about it anymore.

Elder Williams finished reciting the lesson. Though hardly paying attention, I had noticed him make two mistakes. He wasn't perfect, either. But maybe that was okay. "You did good, Anziano," I told him. "I hope I can learn the lessons that well."

"You will, Elder."

We lay down then, and despite the frightened voices from the others nearby, we tried to get some sleep.

The Napoletan Bump Syndrome

We walked into the foot doctor's office and sat down on the only two chairs in the small waiting area. The room was probably just eight feet wide. Cigarette ashes littered the floor in front of us. Picking up a *Gente* magazine from a small table, I sighed nervously and turned to my companion.

"Oh, I don't know, Elder Gibson. Are you sure about this? I really hate doctors."

He put down an *Oggi* magazine he was flipping through. "Elder Anderson, you've been limping around Napoli all January. Your foot isn't going to get any better by itself."

"I guess not."

"Can what the doctor will do be any more painful than having to limp all the time?"

"I don't know. All those stories you've told me about Italian doctors—"

"Oh, that reminds me! Oh…I'll tell you later."

"Thanks, Elder. I appreciate that, you flipper."

"Oh, have a good attitude, Elder Anderson. Look at it as a great journal entry."

A young, blond-haired man in a white lab coat pushed back a curtain and came into the room to look at us. "Who's next?" he asked.

"I am," I replied as my companion pointed at me.

"Come on in here then," he said, going back into a small cubbyhole. I stood up to follow.

"Have a nice time, Elder," said Elder Gibson. He picked up his magazine again and began reading.

I sat down in what looked like a dentist's chair, and the man pulled the curtain over to shut us off from the waiting room. He was slim, about twenty-five, and kind of cute. I hated that I noticed, especially at a time like this. Slipping off my left shoe, I briefly explained my problem to him. I had a strange lump, clear and hard, growing into the bottom of my foot. At first it had just been bothersome, but now it hurt to walk on the brick roads of Naples, and pressure on my foot made me wince.

I wondered if maybe this was my punishment for the time last month when I'd let my mind stray as we passed that prostitute up by the Ospedale Cardarelli. I hadn't even noticed her at first, off to the side of the road near a small campfire. Then Elder Gibson nodded at her and said to me, "Well, you know what they say. You should enjoy your work." I'd had to fight with my mind for the next two weeks, trying to get control of my thoughts, and it hadn't always been easy.

Not that I was thinking of the prostitute, of course. My mind kept going instead back to that absolutely gorgeous guy who was about to buy some of her time. Why did he need a prostitute? I could still see that natural tan, those firm arms, that trim waist, that hairy chest…oh, stop it, Elder.

I'd tried not to think about him, but at night twice I'd awakened from a thoroughly satisfying dream about the man, feeling afterwards terribly guilty that it was a wet dream. Those dreams weren't exactly voluntary thoughts, but somehow I knew I was guilty for having them.

The real trick was changing my garments before anyone saw what had happened. "Mormon underwear" were shaped like long shorts and a T-shirt all in one piece, like old-fashioned union suits. The garments made of a silky fabric that hardened into a crust where my semen had dried, making a noticeable shift in texture on my groin and stomach. If I woke up shortly after the dream and the semen was still wet, I put my hand inside and felt the sticky substance, pretending it was from the man in my dream. But then I'd get another erection and feel guiltier than ever.

Still, now I felt I was more in control of my mind, and I was in the process of repenting of my bad thoughts. And Heavenly Father wasn't vindictive. Besides, everyone who came to Earth sinned at one time or another. There wouldn't be much point to having the Atonement if it couldn't help us get ourselves spiritually healthy without physical torture. No, this lump was just another earthly trial of many I would have to face on my mission, trials which I knew were supposed to help me grow.

"Race you to the top of the stairs," Elder Gibson had said as we were tracting out a building in one of the slummier parts of the Napoli Two district a few weeks earlier. Gibson liked to race, allowing the winner to ring the doorbell as soon as he reached the first door on the top floor, so that he'd be recovered but the second person might still be panting when the resident opened up. Then the loser, still gasping, had to give the door approach.

"Fine. I'll see you in a few minutes," I said. Avoiding the rough, wooden beams placed in the stairway to support the earthquake-damaged building, I began slowly climbing the black stone steps of the dingy apartment building. Some of the steps were cracked or chipped. My last companion had taken a huge chunk of the black stone, almost half a step, two inches thick and a foot and a half long, and sent it home to America in a box, as a souvenir. He said he always wanted to remember those black stone steps of Naples.

Even if my foot was feeling fine, I didn't feel like tripping as I had a week earlier on another broken step and tearing the knee in my suit pants. We'd kept working all evening with my bloody knee greeting everyone at the door, because Gibson thought it might make someone let us in out of sympathy.

"What's the matter? Cat got your feet?" Elder Gibson laughed when I refused to race. He peered down at my feet as if expecting to see something.

"No, I just don't feel like running."

A couple of weeks after the bump had first appeared, I had started trying to carve it out myself with my scissors, picking at it each night before I went to bed. It was odd afterward to see a hole in my foot maybe a fifth of an inch deep that didn't bleed. I wondered if the lump would keep eating its way into my foot, so I dug until I got out the "core" of the lump, hoping that was where whatever was causing this lived. No matter how successful I thought I was, though, before long the bump was back, and soon it became painful. Within another week, I could no longer hide the pain.

"What happened to your foot, Elder Anderson?" Elder Gibson asked me two weeks after our interrupted race. "For the last couple of days, you've been limping a lot."

"I think I sprained my ankle. It'll be better soon."

"Just how did you sprain it?" Gibson asked slyly, as if that should somehow be a provocative question.

"Huh?" I had hoped he'd find a sprained ankle less interesting to talk about than the growth on my foot.

"I remember a couple of years ago in high school," he said, "when I saw this beautiful girl at a football game. When she was leaving, I ran after her to see if she'd be meeting one of the players or would be leaving alone, and I slipped and twisted my ankle. I was wondering if your hormones had anything to do with your injury, too."

With those words, my guilt came rushing back. Was there always a reason for why bad things happened to people? President Kimball, the prophet, had been inflicted with throat cancer. Surely, it wasn't for sinning. Then again, even he couldn't be perfectly sinless. But I thought sinners often led great lives on Earth and simply had to pay in the hereafter. It didn't seem fair that I had to suffer both now *and* later. Maybe my sin was just too horrible. I wanted so badly to talk to someone about it, but did I dare tell Gibson anything about my fantasies? I didn't have to mention gender, but he at least seemed willing to discuss sex on some level. He wasn't the type I'd probably ever become great friends with, but he was here, and he was all I had.

"Well, maybe I did let my mind wander a little before," I ventured.

"Yeah, and…"

"And so maybe I'm being punished?"

Elder Gibson stopped. "Oh, for goodness' sake, Elder. Everybody thinks about sex sometimes. You don't see four billion people limping, do you?"

"But I'm a Mormon, and a missionary. Maybe the Lord expects more of me."

"You don't see five million Mormons limping, either. Or 30,000 missionaries. What makes you so special?"

I laughed but without much humor. "I don't know. I guess I've always felt I had to be better than everyone else, that I had to be perfect. I get depressed every time I think I've done something wrong."

"You must get depressed a lot."

I laughed again.

"Don't sweat the small stuff, Elder. A little fantasizing is probably healthy. Certainly no less healthy than totally repressing yourself. Don't fight so hard."

Maybe he was right. But was a sexual fantasy really "small stuff"? For him, maybe, thinking about girls, it was no big deal, but wasn't it worse for me?

Or was it? Why *did* I think I was so special? Was it that I genuinely cared more about doing what was right? Or did I simply have an ego problem, trying to make up for feeling inferior in other areas?

"Elder Lysenko seems healthy enough, doesn't he?" said Elder Gibson.

"Yes. So?"

"Did you know he was almost sent home twice for sneaking pornography into his suitcase?"

I stopped and looked at him. "Really?"

"I guess I shouldn't say names, but…" and he smiled impishly, "Elder Williams was caught kissing a girl he was teaching, and Elder Ramsey confessed to having sex before his mission. He was supposed to take care of that before coming out here, so he lied to his bishop. There's a lot more of that than you think."

"Did you ever do anything you had to confess?" I hoped he wouldn't ask me anything in return.

"No, darn it. I just thought about it. You?"

"No, I guess I never had the nerve." I'd had to confess to masturbation but nothing else.

Elder Gibson laughed. "Do you regret it?"

I smiled. "Sometimes, it seems like these other elders get to do things as teenagers and repent. Then they're just as good as those who fought every day not to give in."

"Remember your parables, Elder, about working in the garden. The same wage for all, no matter when they start working."

I smiled wryly. "Now I'm guilty of jealousy, so I'm still worse off than they are."

He shrugged. "Everyone is jealous of something once in a while. And we're all overly proud of something, too, even if we generally feel insecure about other things."

"We don't *all* commit *every* sin, do we?"

"I wonder sometimes," said Elder Gibson. "If thinking of adultery is committing it in your heart, have we committed every sin at least mentally? I know I've thought of murder."

"What?"

"You've never wanted to kill someone, even for an instant?"

Just myself, I thought, but what I said was, "No." Then I remembered a fleeting thought from Napoli One, when I considered pushing Elder Williams out a window. "Well…"

"Yeah, I thought so." But then he shrugged again. "Still, I guess you're right. Elder Thomas said he used to be a loan shark before his mission, and Elder Mabey sold drugs to raise money to come out here. I've never even thought about doing either of those."

"But even if everyone does it," I said, "that doesn't make it right. We can't let that excuse our doing something wrong, or even thinking something wrong. If there's something bad about our character, don't we have an obligation to fix it, to cure it, no matter what other people do?"

"I guess so. If it can be cured. I wonder sometimes how much is curable. If you break your arm, it heals. But if you don't even have an arm in the first place, what do you do? I wonder if there might be spiritual handicaps like that. Certainly, there are mental ones."

While I was trying to figure out how homosexuality fit into that, Elder Gibson pointed. "And here come a couple of mental handicaps now," he said, laughing. Two sister missionaries were walking down the street.

We rarely ran into other missionaries while we were out, but it was always fun to take a break and chat for a minute. One of the sisters approaching us, Sister Weekly, was pretty and the other rather average. The elders had been talking about the pretty one for months, ever since she'd arrived, wondering why a pretty girl would go on a mission rather than get married, since girls didn't *have* to go like we did. She'd grown so tired of the question that she eventually stopped wearing make-up and bought a couple of unflattering dresses, but in the last couple of months she'd readopted her beauty and in fact started capitalizing on how she could make men feel, deliberately carrying heavy books or dragging a heavy streetboard display and getting men to help her. Once they were talking, she'd keep using that energy until she could arrange teaching appointments with the whole family. She and her companion had been responsible for the baptism of a family of four last month.

Technically, sister missionaries weren't supposed to approach men, but no one wanted to complain about the baptisms. I noticed that today she was limping, too, and I wondered if she too were being punished for her sexuality. As she came nearer, though, I saw that the heel of one shoe was broken.

"What happened?" asked Elder Gibson, laughing. "Someone slam their door on your foot?"

Sister Weekly smiled pleasantly. "It's a new approach," she said, "to look like I need a lift."

"You're not going to get in a car with a stranger, are you?" I asked.

"No, but I'll get cab fare and promise to bring it back, along with some home-baked cookies. I'll get an address and a teaching appointment out of it."

Elder Gibson laughed. "Elder Anderson's been limping for days, and no one's offered him a ride yet."

"Maybe you're not hanging out in the right areas," Sister Weekly suggested.

"Maybe I'm not pretty enough," I said.

"Oh, you're pretty enough," said Gibson, pinching my check. "You're just not vulnerable enough. You keep up that defensive shell all the time." He laughed.

We chatted for a few more minutes, about nothing in particular, pretending we weren't wasting time, and then we separated to get back to work, Sister Weekly limping away attractively.

I limped unattractively with Elder Gibson to the tram station, Gibson laughing and limping too for a bit but giving it up when no one paid any attention to him, either. We took the funiculare down the hill from Vomero to the lower part of Naples and began working the area near the water. No referrals, but at least it was a change in scenery, and riding the hillside tram gave me a few minutes off my feet.

After about half an hour, I noticed two American sailors walking together. One kept slapping the other on the back, and they seemed very friendly. I wondered if they were gay. I'd heard that gays tended to join the Navy more than other branches because they got to be alone together out at sea for months. I wondered what it would be like to—

Then I stepped on a cracked piece of pavement and remembered not to fantasize about sin. Perhaps that earthquake that killed 3000 people a couple of months ago wasn't the result of my being gay, but clearly this bump was. Why else would God keep reminding me of it every time my mind strayed? And yet everyone thought about sex, Elder Gibson said. The bump was just a natural growth.

Natural or unnatural, however, something had to be done about it.

Still, it took me a few more hours to work up the courage to say anything. "Elder Gibson, you remember that clinic we passed on our way to the tracting zone tonight?" If Elder Gibson were right and my foot wasn't a punishment, I had to find the nerve to take care of it. Perhaps I'd been hoping it was a punishment so I'd have an excuse not to find a doctor. My avoidance was childishness, not penance. I was glad I'd finally said something.

"You mean the clinic with the skull and bones on the sign in front?" he asked.

"It was a red cross."

"Oh. Yeah, I saw it. Why?"

"I was just wondering. What do you suppose the doctors are like here?"

Elder Gibson's eyes widened, as if he couldn't believe the question he was hearing. Then he laughed. "Let me tell you what happened to Elder Moskowitz in Sardegna!" he said. I thought I saw a glimmer in his eyes. "He had appendicitis, and now he has a scar ten inches long! Oh, the poor guy!" He laughed again.

"Does stuff like that happen often?"

I had expected at least one horror story, but Elder Gibson then related another incident that had happened while he was in Sardinia. An elder had fallen ill, gone to the local hospital in Sassari, and been quarantined for having typhoid. He got sicker daily until the other three elders in his missionary district finally convinced the doctor to let them take him to Rome. The Roman doctor diagnosed the elder as having a simple virus. With that news, the elder began feeling better instantly, and within twenty-four hours, he was back to his old self again. Elder Gibson laughed as he finished the climax of his story.

"Well, at least that kind of thing only happens in Sardegna." I started walking up the dimly lit stairs of an old building.

"Haven't you heard what happened to Sister Parker?"

"Maybe some other time. Let's do some work." I completely avoided the subject of doctors for the rest of the evening, although it was almost all I thought about. I hardly wanted to trust an infallible doctor, much less one that might make a mistake. But apparently I couldn't cure the bump without help. I'd have to trust someone whether they deserved that trust or not.

Maybe, though, trust was like faith. Perhaps my trust alone would cure me. Elder Moskowitz might have a huge scar, but he *was* cured. Of course, having faith in the wrong diagnosis almost killed the other elder. Funny how just believing you were ill could actually make you ill. I wondered if I'd willed this growth on my foot because I *wanted* punishment. God. I hoped I wasn't that sick.

I tried to think of pleasant thoughts, so Elder Gibson and I talked of our favorite movies as we tracted out several buildings near Via Salvator Rosa. In between movies, we let a few more people know about the Church. Not many were interested, but we did teach one lesson and leave a Book of Mormon with a family.

Later, limping back to our apartment on Via Nicolardi, I tripped over a broken piece of cement tile that was protruding from the cracked sidewalk. Gritting my teeth to keep from crying out, I knew I couldn't go on much longer. Still, I remembered Elder Gibson's last story. What *had* happened to Sister Parker, and where had she been? Even if going to a doctor would result in more pain, though, maybe that was the price I would simply have to pay for a cure. No matter what had actually caused the thing, it was obvious that prayer and hope alone weren't going to get rid of it.

I thought about doctors all the next morning as we walked slowly up and down the streets talking to people. About halfway through the morning, I pointed to a park, pretending to want to take referrals but really hoping to find a bench, and expecting some other punishment for the deception. As we walked through the entrance, I spotted an empty bench, but standing between the bench and myself was a man with a handful of pamphlets, trying to talk to anyone who ventured near.

"Let's go," suggested Elder Gibson, smiling and fingering his nametag momentarily as if he wanted to remove it and pretend he wasn't a missionary.

We walked over and introduced ourselves, and the man in turn introduced himself and told us the name of his church, which was one I'd never heard of before. He began explaining some of their beliefs, that women should stay at home, that education was dangerous because it led to doubting and questioning God, that all birth control was evil, that only men should read the scriptures and not women so that there would be no religious discord in a family, children should never be allowed to watch television, and finally, if a woman ever committed adultery, she should be physically thrown from the house and never spoken to again, as an example for the children. The same was true of unwed daughters who ever practiced fornication.

I didn't want to talk. I only wanted to get to the bench. But here was a man interested in religion, so I had an obligation to try to reason with him. I couldn't let my personal weakness detract me from my purpose. "What about the men?" I asked. "Don't they need to set an example, too?"

"No man would ever fall without being seduced by a woman," he replied, "so she is ultimately responsible for the sanctity of the home."

I was less than convinced, knowing no woman was ever going to seduce me. "Aren't men responsible for their own sins?" I asked, "Especially if they're the only ones reading the scriptures?"

"Men only fall when wicked women seduce them," he repeated.

"You act like sex is a disease you have to ward against." Gibson laughed. "Is sex what's wrong or is infidelity?"

"Intercourse is too sacred to talk of in public."

"Too sacred or too dirty? Sex is a good, positive thing, and it's a part of each of us. We'll only be healthy when we accept it instead of trying to cut it out of our souls." Then he turned to me and added in English, "It's the main reason we all want to make it to the Celestial Kingdom, isn't it?" Only those who became gods were allowed to have sex throughout eternity. Everyone else, I realized, must be forced to wear some kind of eternal chastity belt.

I giggled like an idiot.

The man raised his right arm toward the sky and pointed at us with his left hand. "Lord, cleanse these unbelievers of their wicked, sickly ways. Oh God, take the evil out of their hearts. Let them be made whole!"

I had never been exorcised before, and my mouth hung open, but no pea soup came shooting out. I looked at Elder Gibson. "Whew!" he said, smiling. "I still feel the same." He punched me in the arm and we continued on through the park, talking to a couple more men before finding a bench.

"There sure are a lot of sick people out there," Elder Gibson said.

I was disappointed I did feel the same after the man's prayer. If that guy had faith, why couldn't he have cured me of my homosexuality? People did get well sometimes from faith healers, not because the healers were of the right religion, but because of the faith involved. I'd seen it once as a boy out in the country in Mississippi visiting my grandparents, when an old woman stopped by, and my grandmother mentioned a sick neighbor on a nearby farm. The woman prayed, and after she left ten minutes later, my grandmother called her friend, who said she'd started feeling better about ten minutes earlier.

"The Savior is supposed to be the Great Healer," Elder Gibson went on, "but half the people who claim to be following Him go around making everyone sicker."

I nodded. "At least there are a few of us out here teaching the right things." Even if we didn't have the faith to back them up.

We rested for maybe five minutes before Elder Gibson stood. My foot often seemed to hurt worse after resting, throbbing now. I almost decided I could at least have a doctor look at my foot, if that story about Sister Parker hadn't happened in Napoli. Finally, during lunch back at the apartment, I asked Elder Gibson to tell me the story he'd wanted to relate the night before.

"Oh, it's so funny," he said, almost choking on the water he was drinking. "You'll love this. Sister Parker had this wart thing on her foot, so she went to have it cut out."

Uh oh.

"So she went somewhere downtown in Napoli to this doctor. Well, she didn't know they wouldn't use any anesthetic, so when the doctor started cutting away, she yelled out in English to this man, 'You bastard! You horrible monster! You stupid asshole!'" Elder Gibson stopped to laugh for a moment. Tears started to form in his eyes. "She doesn't have a wart anymore, anyway!"

Well, that was it. Forget it. I'd limp for the rest of my life.

But three days later, we were taking more buses and tracting out fewer buildings each day. We were in our second building of the evening, and I was praying desperately that we could get in and teach so that I could sit down, hating my motivation, and knowing I couldn't let the growth continue to corrupt both my body and spirit. I knocked on the first door on the top floor, determined to give a good approach.

A young boy, perhaps six, opened the door. "Is your father or mother at home?" I asked.

The boy ran off, leaving the door open, and returned a moment later with his mother. Gibson and I introduced ourselves, and the woman quickly told us she wasn't interested. Then, turning to the boy, she said, "Don't you ever open that door without asking me first!" She slapped him across the face and kept slapping as she slammed the door. We could hear the slaps continuing for a minute after that, too, along with the boy's cries.

The woman was right, of course, about the danger in opening to strangers, but surely there was a way of conveying that without causing danger herself. I felt responsible for the beating since I'd been the one to knock on the door, as if allowing my foot to get worse were responsible. I started limping toward the stairs, not wanting to do the other two apartments on this floor, but Elder Gibson just stood in front of the door. He was trembling a little.

"Elder?" I asked.

He finally pulled himself away from the door and then sat on the top step of the stairs. I sat beside him. The chance to rest my foot was countered by the sin of an unnecessary break, but I tried to relax and empty my mind.

"Why do people beat kids?" Elder Gibson asked. "Isn't life hard enough without that?" So much for relaxing.

"It is for me," I said.

"You were never beaten?"

"I think I was spanked about five or six times."

He looked at me. "Hell, I've been hit that many times in one day." He closed his eyes. "Sometimes, months would go by. I'd think my dad finally wasn't going to hit me again, and just as I was about to trust him, wham."

I didn't know what to say and so remained silent.

"My parents were always active in the Church, and it took me a long time to realize my dad wasn't supposed to be hitting me. Then I got mad at the Church for not stopping it, and it took me a while longer to realize that there was no way the Church could know about it."

"You never told anyone?"

He smiled. "You want to know something? You're only about the third person I've ever told. I know we're not close, but I felt I could tell you." He breathed out slowly. "I guess we all have some deep, dark secret inside us. I was always the class clown. I suppose I use humor sometimes as a shield. It does help keep me sane." He laughed. "Or just insane enough to survive."

"How does your dad treat you now?" I asked.

"He hadn't hit me in a few years before I came out here, but he still yelled once in a while. The rest of the time he acted like nothing was wrong. I got to where I hated to see him smile. It seemed like such a deliberate lie. It makes it hard for me to trust people." He shook his head. "I hope I can be a good father one day."

I nodded. "You will be."

Gibson laughed. "My last Father's Day at home, I gave my dad a card. It had a picture on the front of a man taking a vitamin and it said, 'Prepare yourself, Dad. Your son is about to give you a compliment.' Then on the inside, it said, 'You have a terrific son!'" He laughed again. "I can only give a card if it portrays my honest feelings!"

Laughing, we stood up and finished tracting out the building. As we stepped outside later, I winced when I put my foot down on an uneven section of the sidewalk.

"You sure your ankle's okay, Elder Anderson? You've been limping for over a week now."

"No, it's not," I said, sighing. "Something's growing on the bottom of my foot, and it hurts like heck."

Elder Gibson stopped, spreading his arms wide, a look of joy on his face. "You've got a Napoletan bump," he said. He patted me on the back. "You've been initiated. You're a Napoletano now."

"What?"

"Haven't you noticed? Everyone gets sick here. You saw that old man down by the castle yesterday with that big lump on his cheek. And that woman last week with the bump on her forehead. And that couple today, the man with the hunchback and the woman with gnarled hands? Everyone catches something here." He laughed.

"What have you caught?" I tried putting my weight on my good foot, but this caused the blood to rush through the other, making me wince again.

"I had bronchitis the first time I was in Napoli last year. Everyone catches something. Like Sister Parker. She had a Napoletan bump, too."

"Well, if I go somewhere else, like Rome, will my Napoletan bump go away?"

"I doubt it," he laughed. "You'll have to go to a doctor."

"Mica tanto!"

Elder Gibson kept joking about my foot for the next two days, and he told everyone else in the district about it, too. They didn't joke, but they suggested that maybe it really would be best to go to a doctor. This was a temporal world with temporal problems, and God didn't want to step in and take over. It was up to us to suffer or adapt or take care of the problem. I didn't find their wisdom comforting.

But finally, I looked up several foot doctors and picked out the one closest to our apartment. I wanted to be able to come home and rest as quickly as possible after my visit, especially since I would be walking home.

Now, here I was sitting in a tiny room in the doctor's office, separated from the waiting room by a curtain. I didn't feel well. My stomach hurt.

"What medical school did you graduate from?" I asked weakly, trying to smile, hoping some friendly chatter would soothe me.

The man smiled back with an expression I'd seen on my mom's face when she knew something was beyond my comprehension. "They don't have schools for this here," he said softly.

I felt as if my heart literally skipped a beat. No wonder he seemed so young. But maybe he was smart. Maybe he'd studied on his own and knew what he was doing. You didn't always need an authority to tell you that what you were doing was right.

He lifted my foot and studied the growth, prodding it lightly and looking up at me to see my reaction. He was very gentle, even while making the growth hurt, and it was somehow soothing to have this young man holding my foot, touching me. Then he opened a bottle and began applying a liquid to the bottom of my foot, pressing harder on the bump and making me stiffen. Maybe this was going to hurt more. I felt a little queasy.

I was suddenly glad I had managed to kick out those sexual thoughts that had crowded my mind earlier in the month. Times like this made me glad I was on the Lord's side and at least trying to follow Him.

"Actually," the man told me, "this kind of thing usually doesn't cause problems. Yours is infected, though. You tried to treat it yourself?"

I nodded sheepishly.

"Trying to get rid of it is what caused the problem, but I'll see what I can do."

He opened a drawer, displaying an array of knives and cutting tools. Picking up a sharp-looking scalpel, he studied it for a moment and then grasped my foot. "I know a plantar wart seems like a problem, but it's not. If this ever comes back, just leave it alone. Okay?"

I nodded silently, trying to slide further down in the chair to lower my head, hoping to keep from fainting. Already green blotches began floating in front of my eyes.

The scalpel cut into my foot. It didn't hurt as much as I expected, but I felt sick, as if I might throw up. I hoped remembering this day would keep me from ever committing another sexual sin.

But Elder Gibson said I shouldn't worry about fantasizing. Then again, who was he to absolve me of guilt or sin? The scriptures said that those who obeyed the Word of Wisdom would "walk and not faint." But if I'd had a severed spinal cord, faithfully obeyed the Word of Wisdom and found I still couldn't walk, would I feel I was nevertheless somehow at fault? Perhaps the Church beating me up because of something I had no control over was a form of spiritual abuse. And yet maybe I really did need a "spanking" once in a while, and the Church was right to pummel me over this.

Of course, the Church didn't need to beat me if it could teach me to beat myself.

"This will stop being a problem on its own if you don't mess with it," said the doctor, bringing me back to my physical pain.

The best thing to do was concentrate on my health and listen to the doctor, so I could get back to working again. I had enjoyed picking on the bump with my scissors. The sensation had been painful but oddly comforting, giving the illusion of control. But if it was hurting me and keeping me from being healthy, it was a sin.

I had just started to pray when the doctor cut deeper. I moaned, not for any pain in my foot but because of the queasiness in my stomach. The green blotches in front of my eyes started gathering together. Feeling I was about to lose consciousness, I fought to focus and saw Elder Gibson come through the curtains and kneel beside me to hold my hand.

The splotches faded. I felt suddenly damp with sweat, but I smiled up at my companion as the doctor finished cutting and taped a bandage on my foot. He smiled at me and winked, and I felt the blood rush back to my head. He patted my leg gently. "You're fine now," he said softly.

Elder Gibson paid the man and then nodded for me to get up. "Come on," he said. "I know this great little gelateria with a fantastic new flavor that'll cheer you right up."

"What is it?" I asked, standing and feeling surprised not to hurt.

"I call it Sinful Passion," he said, raising his eyebrows like Groucho Marx.

Oh, good grief, I thought.

"Maybe we can sit on that brick wall overlooking the city up by Ospedale Cardarelli," he went on.

"Where the prostitutes work?"

He shrugged. "Ice cream's the best I can offer, I'm afraid."

I smiled. "It'll do."

He motioned, and I followed him out the door and back out on the street.

The Rift

"Elder Anderson, if you ever turn that light on again before I'm up, I'll break your fingers." Elder Mosby glared at me from his bed, his voice low and menacing. He meant what he said. Stunned, I turned off the light and left our bedroom.

It was 7:00. I'd already been generous in leaving the room right at 6:30 when we were supposed to be up. And earlier in the mission, we'd had to get up at 6:00 every day. Elder Mosby had been in bed until 7:00, and I'd already eaten breakfast and taken my shower. There was nothing left for me to do but get in my required two hours of study this morning before we left for work.

I stood in the hallway looking at my door as the other four missionaries in the apartment bustled about. Two of them were wrestling in their underwear, bouncing on the bed and floor. It seemed a little juvenile. Sometimes, when one or the other bent over while wrestling, the Mormon undergarment he wore would be pulled tight over his behind, pulling the slit open and revealing the crack in his behind. One of the elders was good looking, so after my first couple of glimpses of their wrestling, I made a point of never looking into their room when the bumping and grunting sounds of their playing started. At night as I went to bed, I tried not to fantasize about one of them pinning me down.

The other two elders in the apartment were our zone leaders. Only the two mission assistants up in Rome were higher ranking, and the zone leaders here were in charge of all the missionaries in Naples, frequently reminding us that they were the ones God had chosen to guide us. How could they just let Elder Mosby stay in bed all morning? If I was so much as two minutes late coming out of my room, they'd stick their heads in to check on me.

There was a tiny closet at this end of the hall where we stored ten years' worth of *Ensign* magazines from the Church. I went in the closet, turned on the light, and closed the door. There were still a few issues here I hadn't read. A couple of articles had been torn out of a few of the magazines, which irritated me. Since almost every missionary apartment had a complete set, I couldn't imagine why it had been necessary to damage them, and I wanted eventually to have read everything the Church ever published, without even the tiny gaps these missing articles might leave. Reading the *Ensign* would still count as study time, even if it wasn't technically the scriptures. I pulled down an issue and began reading. There were no articles on how to get along with a difficult companion.

One article was about communication in marriage, but I wasn't sure the same rules applied to companions. Our goal wasn't to be together forever or to love each other but only to work together for a couple of months. Sometimes, not communicating seemed better. If Mosby had been angry at me about the light but had said nothing, would we be worse off than now? I certainly would feel better not worrying about broken fingers. Then again, if he could have communicated without the anger, simply said that he knew it was against the rules but he was going to sleep in, and would I mind studying elsewhere, there wouldn't be a major problem, either. So how could I communicate to my senior companion in a non-threatening way that I didn't like being threatened?

Devotional was at 9:00, and though I didn't know when he finally got up, Elder Mosby sat in the kitchen smiling and eager to go over the day's plans. "Let's go take referrals in the ghetto today!" he said excitedly. Maybe he was okay now that he'd had enough sleep. We'd both gone to bed by 10:15 the previous evening, however, so unless something had kept him up, I didn't know why on some days he seemed to need extra sleep. "I always like working in the gut." I nodded agreeably and as soon as the others all said their plans, the meeting was over.

Elder Mosby and I caught a bus down the hill into Napoli. I noticed a nice-looking man halfway across the bus, but I felt it was wrong to approach someone because of his looks, so I tried to psyche myself into asking a heavy-set man near us, but I ended up not talking to anyone. We got off the bus on Via Roma, not far from Piazza Dante. On one side of Via Roma was a crowded, poor section of Naples, and on the other side was a very old, crowded, and even poorer section, the ghetto. It wasn't a frightening place, like a ghetto might be in America. It was just dreary. One-room, cracked, decaying apartments lined many of the streets, blending into each other. It was amazing that any of them were still standing after that earthquake a few months earlier. I always tried to keep an eye open for places to hide if another one struck. We'd had several tremors, and the threat was always there that everything would come tumbling down around us.

While riding down from our area, I looked over as usual toward Vesuvius. It was really rather pretty, comforting in its beauty despite its threat. Still, I wondered how a million people could want to live so close to an active volcano. Herculaneum, on the Napoli side of the volcano, had been buried under six stories of ash. A stronger eruption, or a stronger southerly wind, could have easily sent the flow on to Naples.

On the other side of Napoli, the ground under Pozzuoli was rising because of magma, and I'd heard that a new crater might form there, that in fact Pozzuoli, with 80,000 people, was right in the middle of an ancient crater that was twelve kilometers wide, that 200,000 people lived in the caldera. The area was called Campi Flegrei, which I thought sounded pretty until I realized it meant Fiery Fields, and it had undergone periodic eruptions throughout the last several centuries. Another strong earthquake like the one we'd just had could set off any of these volcanoes, even though the earthquake by itself would be awful enough.

How could people live here without knowing if two months down the line their homes and businesses and even their lives might be taken? Coming from Biloxi, I'd heard similar questions, of course. How could we live right on the coast when a category 5 hurricane like Camille was sure to strike again sooner or later? But unless you lived right on the beach where the storm surge hit, you could survive a hurricane. Even a tornado could pick and choose houses. But a superheated ash flow like that of Mt. St. Helens or

Vesuvius just wiped out everything for miles, even if a million people lived in those miles. I hoped if Pozzuoli blew up, it wouldn't be while that nice Elder Collins was stationed there. Looking about me now, I realized that the biggest reason people stayed was because they were too poor to leave.

The dirty walls and heavy doors in the "historic center" of Naples joined the black, stone streets without any sidewalk to buffer the transition. People milled about, selling fish or bread, dirty children played in the street, and laundry was draped across every road, window after window, thousands of pieces of clothing dangling in the air. Inside the apartments were often clean, neat people who managed to make their tiny living spaces reasonably beautiful. It seemed strange they had so little concern for the outside, although they probably saw it as hopeless. By setting the inside apart, they could pretend they didn't really live here in both the dirt and the danger.

"Good morning, sir," I said now to a man walking toward us. "We're from the Church of Jesus Christ of Latter-day Saints, and…"

He was already past by the time I finished. "It's a shame the Church has such a long name," I said to Elder Mosby, smiling. He didn't answer.

We kept on, roaming the streets and stopping any man who dared look at us. One man nervously gave us an address I knew wasn't real, but I accepted it and promised to come by. Then he hurried away.

One road we turned onto ended in a desolate, two-story apartment complex which looked four hundred years old. The faded yellow walls were cracked, the railing was missing in places, and trash was everywhere, as was the rule in Naples. Two teenage girls leaned dangerously over the balcony and waved sweetly at us. I nodded, and Elder Mosby waved back.

Then four little boys about six years old came up to us and began speaking in dialect. I couldn't understand Napoletano, and the people here slurred so much even when speaking standard Italian that I had a hard time, so I just smiled and looked on as Mosby joked with the children. Suddenly, though, Mosby's face grew dark, and he hissed at one of the boys, "Tu sei un buco di tua madre!" The boy looked devastated, the others looked mad, and soon they all ran off.

I had never heard the expression before. "You're a hole of your mother?" I asked. "Why did you say that?"

"They were making fun of us in Napoletano, thinking we couldn't understand them. I wasn't going to let them get away with that."

"What did they say?"

Mosby turned and glared at me. "You don't have to know everything, do you, Elder Anderson? I'm your senior companion. You can show me a little trust."

"Well, sure," I said. "I was just curious." Of course, the fact was that Mosby was famous for misunderstanding Italian. Once when a man had asked us jokingly if we understood what he was saying, Mosby had defiantly replied, "Si', capisciamo bene!" With that poorly conjugated proof, the man walked off laughing. Mosby had been so furious that I never did point out his error, that he had conjugated a very common irregular verb as if it were a regular one.

Another time a teenage boy on a bus had nodded toward Mosby's watch as Mosby held onto a bar over our heads. "Ora?" the boy asked, wondering what time it was. But Mosby just smiled and shook his head. "No," he replied. The teenager looked shocked. I could see in his face the thought, "These guys won't even give me the time of day!" But there was never an opportunity to whisper to the guy that Mosby had thought he'd said "oro," asking if the watch were gold. I either had to let the guy leave with a negative impression of us, or I had to face Elder Mosby's uneven temper, so I decided the boy would never have been interested in the Church anyway, and that it didn't matter. Besides, Italians should realize we didn't always understand everything.

I still had plenty of problems myself with the language, but Mosby had been out here ages longer than I had and was only just now a senior companion for the first time. I expected some of his stress was related to finally being in charge, so I wanted to be understanding.

With my last companion, kids had once jokingly pointed to me when I had my hands in my pockets, asking if I was playing with myself, if I were "going fishing." I hadn't understood but my companion had, and we'd laughed about it after he explained it to me. Another time, a couple of kids had yelled, "Finocchi!" at us and from a distance added that we were always together, so we must be married. My companion had explained that "fennel" was the slang for gay, and we'd laughed over that, too, though it had certainly made me nervous as well. I hadn't recognized "finocchio" from the kids today, but they might have slurred it or used another term, or Mosby might simply have thought they said it. Maybe he already suspected I was gay, and hearing other people say it made him feel he was suspect, too.

I looked at my watch. It was only 10:45. It was going to be a long day. When we'd first become companions only two weeks ago, Mosby had treated me to a stone oven-baked pizza, and the next day, he'd treated me to ice cream. He was pleasant and seemed willing to be friends, which was a rare event out here. Most elders seemed to want to be right or better or more important than others. I relaxed and thought maybe I'd have a pleasant experience this time, someone who could help me concentrate on the work rather than on surviving the relationship.

Yesterday, though, a couple of hours after lunch, we were standing at a bus stop waiting for the bus, and I was trying to work up my nerve to talk to a man standing closer to the sign. He was on the other side of Elder Mosby, and without realizing it, as I tried to steel myself for the approach, I was slowly inching over toward the man.

But that meant I was also getting closer to Elder Mosby. In a cold voice, he finally asked, "Why do you keep trying to get next to me?"

My mouth fell open, and I moved away a few feet, giving up approaching the other man. Did Mosby think I was making a pass at him in broad daylight in public, when we shared the same bedroom? At first, I thought he must have finally realized I was gay after all and felt uncomfortable, but his reaction seemed so odd. Was he really afraid of *me*? It was almost as if… as if he were afraid of himself. I wondered if he might be attracted to me, if maybe he was scared I might be gay because then something might happen between us.

But it wouldn't, would it? I was quite determined to beat this thing, and if he was a missionary, he must be, too. If he approached me, I'd—

Wait a second. Just minutes before we went to the bus stop, we'd been in another gelateria, and Elder Mosby had put his hand on my shoulder after handing me an ice cream he'd bought for me. I'd pulled away instinctively despite liking the contact, and he'd been rather quiet after that. Had all these treats been his way of subconsciously courting me? I wondered. Perhaps I was reading too much into the whole thing. But that did seem like the moment when he began acting strangely again.

This was a five-week month, too. At best, I was still going to be with him three more weeks before transfers. I just hoped his paranoia at the bus stop wouldn't lead him to say anything to the other elders. I'd still never done anything gay in my life, and I was hoping my mission would cure me. I didn't need the others gossiping about me or trying to get me sent home before that happened.

Mosby hadn't said anything to the others last night, and today his thoughts clearly seemed somewhere else. But even so, he appeared set on giving me other worries. How could we pass the day productively without having him curse little children or doing anything else too weird? He obviously had a lot of tension building in him for some reason, but did yelling and cursing have to be the only way to relieve that pressure?

Perhaps, if his yelling prevented a total breakdown. After all, in places like Naples, it was good to have small earthquakes or small eruptions. It let off the pressure gradually instead of letting it build up. And the pressure was there naturally. It was going to need release sooner or later. I wondered if it wouldn't be good to yell and punch a pillow every night for no real reason, or to deliberately set charges and intentionally set off earthquakes on a regular schedule before too much tension built up.

I thought about masturbating when I was back home in America. When the bug spray man would come to our house, I'd fantasize about him for hours afterward, starting to fondle myself and then forcing myself to stop, trying to make myself go back to my studies or whatever. But before long, I'd lose myself on the page and pretend the exterminator had brought in a spray can of anesthesia, knocked me out, and "taken advantage" of me without my being aware of it, except of course since I was fantasizing I got to watch the whole thing in my mind. I'd start fondling myself again, then pray and force myself to stop, and this would go on and on until I finally realized I'd have to go ahead and masturbate or never be able to concentrate on anything else.

Some months, I didn't even put up a battle, just masturbating at the first urge so I wouldn't waste half the day fighting it. I did get a lot more accomplished during those months, but sometimes, I ended up masturbating twice a day. That just couldn't be right. It proved that giving in didn't help but only made things worse. So I repented and started fighting the temptations again.

Damn. I had an erection now. I glanced down to see if it were noticeable. Not really. I glanced at Elder Mosby, but he was ignoring me anyway.

"Come on, Elder Anderson," he said a moment later, motioning toward some stairs. "Those girls are waving to us."

"You think we ought to be talking to teenage girls?" I asked. It was clearly against mission rules.

"Don't you like girls?"

Uh-oh. Was this a test? Did I have to break the rules to prove myself? "Isn't that the reason we're not allowed to talk to them?"

"You do what you like. I'm going up."

He could hardly tell the other elders about this, since he was the one breaking the largest rule of leaving his companion, but it could still lead him to drop hints and start rumors. So I followed him, and soon we were on the cracked balcony, talking to two young teenage girls. One was blond, like Mosby, and said her name was Paola. She was fifteen. The dark-haired girl was fourteen and named Sofia. "Like Sofia Loren, from Pozzuoli." The two teenagers were cousins. We talked about America and about American sailors who came to Naples, and then they invited us to their apartment.

"We really aren't supposed—" I began.

"Sure," said Elder Mosby. "I could use a glass of water."

I followed the other three reluctantly, praying for a way out of all this. I was supposed to be a missionary spreading the gospel. I was here because I thought it was what God wanted of me. I wanted to do everything I was supposed to. And as much as I hated stopping people on the street to see if they were interested in the Church, that was about all we could do in the mornings, so I wanted to do it. It wasn't bad enough that the job itself was so difficult, but extra obstacles had to come along every step of the way. Why did being good have to be so much harder than necessary?

The two mothers were in the apartment, fortunately, and as we all sat around the table, drinking water and talking of America, one of the women asked Elder Mosby, "Don't you think Paola is pretty?" The girl smiled sweetly, and Elder Mosby grinned. "Why don't you marry her? You both have blond hair. It'd be a perfect match."

Then the other woman spoke up. "And why don't you marry my daughter? You both have dark hair." Sofia smiled at me, and then the two girls smiled at each other.

Please. I had a girlfriend back in America who I didn't even want to marry. But Elder Mosby looked excited, enjoying the flirting. He must not be gay after all. Maybe this flirting would at least satisfy him enough that he wouldn't have to worry about me for a while.

"Aren't they a little young?" I asked. I hated to say anything at all, but Mosby was just sitting there grinning.

"Oh, but you boys can't be more than nineteen or twenty yourselves, and you know girls mature faster than boys."

The one woman nodded toward Paola's breasts. "You can't keep a pretty girl locked up in the house forever. You just try to marry her off to someone respectable."

"Well, we have to finish our missions first," said Elder Mosby, still grinning, "but we'd certainly like your names and address so we can come back later." It looked like he winked, but I couldn't be sure.

Paola's mother's eyes lit up, and she hurriedly found some paper but very slowly and awkwardly wrote down the information. "Ours are good girls," she said. "You'll like them."

"Of course, we're only supposed to marry Mormons," said Mosby, shrugging.

The two women looked at each other carefully. "Maybe," said Paola's mother. "Maybe."

We finished our water and stood up, Elder Mosby shaking everyone's hands warmly and making a show of putting the address in his pocket before we left. Back in the street, he turned to me triumphantly. "See? And you didn't want to go. Now we have a referral to give the sister missionaries."

"Uh huh." We walked on in silence as I wondered how he could possibly see that experience as effective missionary work. The Church had once used missionaries coaching baseball to pressure teens into joining, but there was no "propose to baptize" campaign that I knew of. Yet then so much of our pressuring people seemed slightly unethical. I wondered if the ends justified the means. Because we were bringing people the greatest gift, was it okay to trick them a little? If what we had was so great, why did we need any kind of pressure at all? Was this why so much resentment built up in converts that the majority stopped attending church before they'd even been members a year?

We were certainly misled as missionaries, told these would be the "best two years" of our lives, that we'd constantly be having spiritual experiences. Why couldn't Church leaders tell us the truth and let us emotionally prepare ourselves? If the mission was miserable but still worth doing, why not be honest about it? If they could only get young men to go by lying, what did that say about the morality of the leaders? Or about the caliber of missionaries that were serving?

I looked at Elder Mosby. Last week, he'd told me that as a child, after one of his friends teased him about Mormons having horns, he'd glued two rose thorns to his scalp near the hair line and then gone over to his friend's house. He pulled his hair back and showed him the horns, and the little boy had begun screaming hysterically. It seemed a funny story last week, but now...Hopefully, Mosby felt he'd proven his manhood with those girls, and things could get back to normal, whatever that was.

We kept walking and eventually ended up at a little piazza where half a dozen streets converged. One man was selling used shoes, a couple of people were selling fruit, and several cars whizzed by.

Two teenage boys, probably the same age as the girls, walked up, smiling. "Americans," said one boy. "Waat taim eez eet?" He turned my wrist to look at my watch. "Ah, eet eez eelehveen and half." He smiled again.

I wasn't much in the mood and didn't expect these teenagers to be terribly interested in the Church, but they were friendly, and they were talking to us, so I asked if they'd like to hear our lessons. "Sure," said the first boy in Italian. He pulled out a piece of paper and motioned to show he had no pen. Elder Mosby reluctantly offered his. He was looking around nervously, shifting his weight from foot to foot. What was his problem? The teens seemed to just be pretending interest so they could talk to Americans, but there was no harm in that. Public relations was also part of our job, wasn't it? The boy handed me the paper with his name and address, and I accepted it, smiling.

"Well, we'll certainly try to stop by—" I began, but suddenly, Elder Mosby had the boy by the collar.

Mosby grabbed his pen out of the boy's shirt pocket, screamed curses at him which I didn't understand, accused him of stealing his pen, and then spit in his face. Finally, he marched off, leaving me behind.

I stood in shock, watching the boy wipe the frothy spit off his face. The boys looked at me, my mouth still hanging open, and walked away. One boy put his arm on the other's shoulder. Maybe they were gay and Mosby had sensed it, but they didn't seem gay to me, and males here in Italy often touched each other like this. They were reasonably cute, but even I hadn't much noticed that, given the stress of the morning. If Mosby was gay, though, and really fighting with it right now, maybe he'd noticed.

Good grief. Did everything have to be about sex? Maybe Elder Mosby was mad because the boy was trying to be a smart aleck and steal his pen. Still, why not just smile knowingly and take the pen back? Of course, Mosby's problem might simply be temper and not sexuality. Heavenly Father, why couldn't You just put me with someone normal and let me do the work?

I was still staring at the two teenagers, and the one who hadn't been spit on looked over his shoulder at me. I should have apologized, but how did one apologize for something like that? Did the Church realize that this guy was out here representing for many people their only impression of the Church? Surely, other companions had said something. Of course, Mosby hadn't broken any of the major rules, the ones dealing with sex, and the Church tried to be lenient with people who only broke the "lower" ones. It was too damaging to send an elder home from his mission. He'd probably become inactive and leave the Church. Clearly, Elder Mosby needed to be out here on his mission every bit as much as I did, to work out whatever his problems were. He needed all the spiritual help he could get.

That didn't mean I shouldn't report him, though. He also clearly needed some kind of counseling. I probably did, too, but at least my problems were still reasonably bottled up inside me. But then, I'd had elders reporting on me my whole mission for every little thing. I didn't want to feel like a spy now, too. And what if I reported Mosby, and when the President asked him why he acted this way, he said it was because he felt nervous being around someone gay?

We roamed some more and ended up at the funicolare. We took the tram almost straight up the hillside to Vomero and began walking around there. This middle-class area was so much more pleasant. We didn't stop many men, and I tried to enjoy the beauty of the area and relax. I could live in a place like this. Only I could never truly imagine a life after my mission, with a career and a family. I'd only had one year of college and still had no major. And with no desire for women, the future seemed even drearier than the present.

But this area was relatively clean and on days when the smog wasn't too thick, we could easily see Naples, the bay, and Vesuvius. It was all so beautiful from a distance. I could pretend the bay wasn't polluted, that trash wasn't six inches deep in the city below. And up here on the hill, Vesuvius didn't seem like much of a threat. Unless this hill were instead just the slope of another volcano.

All that teeming multitude down below was going about life without any apparent concern for the continual danger they were in. The people here believed in San Gennaro's blood, kept as powder in a vial and paraded through town once a year, for almost 600 years now, turning into liquid blood on that one day, the miracle assuring people that the martyred Gennaro was still protecting the area. The Catholic Church wouldn't let the powder be analyzed, but whatever it was, it did change every year on that day. And Naples hadn't been destroyed in the most recent earthquake, and Vesuvius was still sleeping peacefully, since 1944.

That seemed more like coincidence than a miracle, however, a superstition that was going to lead many of these people to their deaths one day. Of course, God *could* stop a volcano if the people had faith, but the Mormon Church taught that faith was a belief in something true, not just a strong belief. As much as a child might believe in Santa Claus, it could never be called faith because Santa Claus wasn't true. So even if people believed they had faith, if they believed something that was false, it wasn't going to save them.

To have your whole city, your whole life, based on a vial of powder, or even based on the denial of tectonics, seemed so pathetic. Then again, droughts or blizzards or floods or forest fires or something terrible happened almost everywhere. Maybe it was to help us remember that eternity was more important than this life, to help us not mind suffering and dying so much.

I didn't feel like talking to anybody on the street any longer, and Elder Mosby hadn't stopped anyone in over half an hour. Yet it made life feel meaningless not to at least try, so I finally stopped a man in his 50's. He wasn't interested. Elder Mosby said nothing, and we walked on in silence.

Finally, finally, it was almost time for lunch, so we took a bus to the Ospedale Cardarelli and waited there for another bus to take us back down to our area. But Elder Mosby started shifting about again, looking very uneasy. "We can't wait for a bus," he said abruptly. "We've got to get back to the apartment *now*." He started walking.

"Why?" I asked, following.

"I've got to take a shit," he said, "and I can't wait."

We'd probably be home in five or six minutes by waiting for the bus, faster than we could walk to Via Nicolardi. I tried not to look surprised. We walked only a few yards further and were near the site where the prostitutes built their fire every night. There was a low stone fence along the road, and past it, the hill sloped downward, covered in trees here, and we could look down below at Napoli, and past Napoli to Vesuvius. It was a beautiful view, even if I did now always associate it with prostitutes.

Elder Mosby hopped the wall and pulled down his pants. Then he pulled on the sides of his garments to open the slit in the back, and he crouched down. He looked at me a little challengingly and I turned away.

I was worried, though, about the "public relations" aspect again. No one could see him from up where I was, but about half a million people could see him from the buildings along the bus route down to our area, and then from Napoli below. Still, if he really had to go, I suppose there was no choice. A few minutes later, Elder Mosby grabbed some leaves from a nearby bush and soon rejoined me.

"If you ever tell anyone about that," he said in a low voice, "I'll kill you." His face was impassive and his eyes stone cold.

I believed him. But I tried to keep my voice calm as I replied, "You know, it may be that most people won't find your going to the bathroom a topic they care to dwell on."

I wasn't sure what his reaction would be to that, but he turned away and looked down the hillside, staring into the woods for several moments. Finally, he looked back again at me coldly and then turned to look up the road for the bus.

What in the world was going on in this man's mind? As a missionary, I was supposed to be spending my time figuring out more effective ways to spread the gospel, but my every second was filled with finding some way to understand the missionaries about me just so I could survive.

Soon we'd be back home for a two-hour lunch break, but then we'd be out working for six more hours before time to head back to the apartment. Maybe I could talk to the zone leaders about a "work visit," changing companions for the evening. I'd be with someone who criticized my every technique, but it had to be better than this. And the zone leaders needed to see Mosby in action. Of course, he might behave perfectly and save it all just for me, but if he did behave well tonight, that would still be a good thing, unless he felt betrayed by my asking for a work visit and suspected I was talking about him behind his back.

At least three more weeks with him before transfers, I remembered, and maybe neither of us would be transferred even then. If we did get separated, someone, or eleven someones, would have to be with him for the eleven remaining months of his mission. And I had seventeen more months of my own mission. How many more companions like this would I have? None of them had been real winners yet. I wondered if we really needed to have companions in the first place. Would all this prepare me for marriage, if I managed to get married at all, or would it ruin me for it?

I looked up the street, hoping to see the bus. Not yet. I saw a man about thirty, with a moustache, leaving an apartment building and walking toward us until he turned a corner. He looked so calm, so confident. I wished I could have someone like that for a companion. To just have a real friend for once. In fact, I wished—

I felt an erection beginning, and I tried to focus again on the present. God had put me with Mosby for a reason. I had to find a way to connect with him if we were to be at all effective in spreading the gospel. Maybe I could tell him a story that made me look vulnerable and see how he reacted. I looked over the wall at the view and then back up the street for the bus. Then I looked out at Vesuvius again. It really was a lovely sight.

"What are you thinking about?" asked Elder Mosby suspiciously. I realized I shouldn't have been looking over the wall in the direction he'd just come from.

"I was thinking about Santa Claus," I said, hoping to divert him. A memory from a few years ago had jumped suddenly into my mind.

"Huh?"

I thought maybe I could get him to think about normal things again, so I kept on. "I believed in Santa for a long time."

"So?"

"My parents hired a man one year to come to our house so we could catch him in the act of putting down gifts, so I believed for years."

Elder Mosby had a superior smile on his face, but it was better than the suspicion he had earlier. "How old were you?" he asked.

Here was my chance at being vulnerable. Did I dare be honest? I might never live this down if he made an issue of it. "Thirteen."

Elder Mosby's eyes widened and he burst into laughter. "Oh, my god," he finally managed. "You really were a dork, weren't you?"

I wondered if being trusting was a sign of innocence and something necessary for faith, or if it only meant I was being naïve. How did one reconcile the need to be trusting with the necessity of not being gullible? "When I was twelve," I continued, "I even asked my mom, 'Is there really a Santa?' and she said yes. I didn't think my mother would lie to me when I was asking for the truth."

I'd even said publicly at school that I still believed, in front of my entire eighth grade class. When I found out the truth a year later, I vowed I'd never lie to my children, I'd never set them up to feel betrayed, and I'd never teach them that what they thought was faith was really nothing. What message would that send to them about believing in the Church?

How could any child ever trust their parents after that kind of humiliation? I was going to be a good father, if I ever had the chance to be a father.

"You believe everything anyone tells you?" asked Elder Mosby.

"I don't believe my parents would lie to me now," I said. "I believe the prophet wouldn't lie, that the apostles wouldn't lie. I guess they're the only people I really need to trust."

Elder Mosby didn't say anything, so I looked expectantly at him for a few moments. Then I thought about the time I was eight and I'd lost a tooth and put it under my pillow. The tooth fairy had never been a big deal in our family, so I didn't really believe, but I was going to stay awake that night and find out for sure. But when I left my room for only a minute to go to the bathroom, well before bedtime, and came back to check, there was a quarter under my pillow. I couldn't believe it. And my mother was way down at the other end of the hall sewing. She *couldn't* have done it. So I believed in the tooth fairy for another year.

I shook my head. What possible good could come from teaching children about the tooth fairy? Why did parents lie for such stupid reasons? On the surface, it seemed sweet, but the reality was that kids were being taught not to believe even in God. It was hard enough to believe without parents deliberately opening a chasm in their children's ability to believe. It was like crying wolf. Even if parents told the truth after that, how could anyone know?

God was different, though. People wouldn't lie about God. I believed, and I had faith, and my faith was somehow going to get me married and raising a family of my own. I could believe what the Church said. I was going to be a good father.

"Why do you keep looking at me like that?" asked Elder Mosby.

Oh, my god. He was going to drive me crazy. I was going to go crazy.

"If you keep looking at me like that, I'm going to break your glasses."

Heavenly Father, I prayed. Can you hear me? Can you help me through this?

"The bus!" I said, pointing down the street. "Look! The bus is coming!" If we could just get home and have a little break from the tension, maybe I'd be okay. Maybe he'd be okay, too. I looked at my companion, hoping he was sufficiently distracted from his threats for a while.

But Elder Mosby smiled suddenly and clenched his fist. I stared at him. Oh, my god. He was going to push me in front of the bus. The man was cracking up. Looking at Elder Mosby's balled fist and tensed jaw, I knew I had to do something fast, do something now.

If I got killed out here, I wanted it to be for my principles so I could be a martyr and go to the Celestial Kingdom, not because my companion had a split personality. What was I going to do? Elder Mosby raised his arm, and as I braced myself, he playfully punched me in the shoulder and winked. "I can't wait to tell the others about our referrals," he said.

"Uh huh." I wondered if I was the crazy one. Surely, I was misreading a lot of cues. But I didn't think I was that out of touch yet. I looked down the road and avoided looking at my companion. What in the world was going on inside of his brain? I'd heard a little about manic-depressive disorders. Maybe Mosby had that. Or perhaps he perked up because he would no longer have to be alone with me.

Constantly trying to second guess was exhausting. I'd always expected a mission to make me emotionally healthier. Church leaders often spoke poorly of psychiatry and psychology, claiming they were too secular and rationalized sin, that all anyone needed in order to have a sound mind was to live the gospel.

But how could someone live the gospel in the first place if they didn't have a very sound mind? And in a world like this, with people like this, how were we supposed to ever develop a sound mind to begin with? Just what were we supposed to *do*? I'd been going to church weekly, plus praying and reading the scriptures daily, for years. It just wasn't enough.

"I'm hungry!" said Elder Mosby. "I can't wait to see what the other elders cooked for lunch." Smiling, he climbed aboard the bus as it pulled in front of us. I was so tired of the whole mess. I wanted to turn while Mosby wasn't looking and run, but I didn't know where to go. And a mission was where God wanted me.

But I was going to have to relieve some tension somehow. Maybe I'd have to take up wrestling with the other elders after all.

Instantly, though, I imagined one of the elders bent over, with his behind stretching out against his garments, a big, floppy protrusion in front, and that familiar pressure below my belt started again. This was just not going to work.

Elder Mosby was already on the bus, though, so there was no more time to waste thinking. Forcing a smile, I followed up the steps behind him and we headed on home.

Coping with the Camorra

"What about Mountain Meadows?" asked Signor Cuomo, pointing his finger at us. "You Mormons are nothing but a bunch of murderers."

I was shocked at the accusation, even more shocked that someone in Naples had heard of the Mountain Meadows massacre, in which a group of Mormons had ambushed and killed a group of 120 non-Mormon pioneers traveling through southern Utah in 1857, one of the blackest marks in Latter-day Saint history.

"It was one incident out of our entire 150-year past," said my companion, Elder Walker. "Not every Mormon is perfect, but we have a pretty strong track record of good deeds."

"What about your prophet Joseph Smith destroying the printing press of a newspaper that published bad things about him?" Signor Cuomo went on. "Success went to his head. He thought he could get away with anything. I thought you Americans believed in freedom of the press."

"Come on, Elder Anderson," Elder Walker told me, standing up from the sofa. "This guy's heart is too corrupt for us to bother with." He walked to the door, and I followed.

Elder Walker didn't wait for Signor Cuomo to open the door for us. He opened it himself and we walked out into the apartment building hallway. "How many of your leaders were in jail in 1890?" Signor Cuomo continued, but we ignored him and walked down the stairs and out of the building. We thought we'd hit the jackpot earlier when Signor Cuomo seemed so eager to let us in after we knocked on his door. Missionary work was generally kind of slow, so we were excited at his openness. But then he'd jumped us.

Elder Walker didn't say anything for a few minutes. He headed over to the next building and just leaned against the wall for a moment. Then he turned to me.

"Thanks for getting us in that door," he said acidly. "That was sure a waste of time."

I was too surprised to answer. The man clearly hated Mormons and would have asked us in just as quickly if Elder Walker had done the door approach. It seemed an unfair attack.

"Well, let's see if we can find someone better in this building," I suggested, motioning to the doorway of the next palazzo.

Elder Walker shrugged but marched on into the building. We continued tracting for another hour and a half, until just after 9:00, when it was time to start back for our apartment.

Walking to the bus stop, we passed a piazza where a burned-out bus sat forlornly in the darkness. A few days earlier, a man protesting the "corrupt" government's slow response to help earthquake victims from the November quake had poured gasoline on the bus and set it on fire while people were still inside. Everyone had scrambled out the windows and doors, and luckily no one was hurt, but it had certainly been unnerving to hear about.

Back at the apartment, Elder Walker soon cheered up when two of the other elders talked of their success tonight in teaching a lesson to an elderly couple. "You're never too old to repent and turn to God," said Elder Walker proudly, as if he'd been the one to teach the lesson.

I wasn't sure the couple were big sinners just because they weren't Mormon, but I didn't say anything. I listened eagerly to the elders' stories, too. Then I had a few cookies with milk, brushed my teeth, and went to bed.

The next morning as Elder Walker and I stopped people on the street to try to interest them in the Church, I thought more about what Signor Cuomo had said the night before. Church leaders always brushed off any comments about the Mountain Meadows massacre, though there were serious allegations that the order to attack came from Brigham Young himself. Even if that were the case, though, and he'd thought the innocent farmers were a legitimate threat, he had verifiable reason to worry. There was the Haun's Mill massacre earlier where Mormons had been the victims, and the Saints had been driven out of state after state, finally ending up in the desert. The governor of Missouri had even issued an extermination order, legalizing the murder of any Mormon in the state. That law had stayed on the books until 1976, just five years ago. Still, it seemed more likely that the accusation of Brigham Young's involvement was pure hatefulness, a spiteful attack on a successful man. The Church was not a lawless organization. If anything, we were overly law-abiding.

I never so much as broke the speed limit back home. But that didn't mean I was totally innocent. I was in near constant danger of committing a felony. As a gay man, if I ever had sex with another man, both anal and oral sex were felonies in many states in the U.S. Even married couples could get five years in prison for oral sex. I'd never done it, of course, but I'd thought about it plenty. It was a secular as well as spiritual crime. I needed to beat this gay thing and become law-abiding in my heart as well as in my actions, or my actions would one day get me in big trouble.

Elder Walker stopped for a moment at a sidewalk newspaper kiosk to buy some gum. I thought gum-chewing looked nasty, but he was my senior companion, so I wasn't about to say anything. While we stood there, I glanced at the newspaper headlines. Something about the Camorra, which I'd heard was the branch of the Mafia here in Napoli.

If I understood the history correctly, the Mafia had originally started in Sicily, a vigilante group to protect people against bandits. After the Mafia became successful, however, "protection" had eventually developed into extortion, and organized crime was rampant now in most of southern Italy, including Naples.

I didn't have that much experience with crime, a bit as a victim, of course, like most people. A couple of months ago, our apartment had been burglarized. We didn't have much worth stealing, but Elder Harter's cassette recorder and camera had been taken. My instamatic was hidden at the bottom of my laundry bag and was safe. The police could do nothing for us, so Elder Harter and his companion went to the black market to look for his camera, and they found it, same serial number and everything. He bought back his hundred-dollar camera for thirty dollars and felt he'd made a good deal. He didn't trust the police to help him if he reported the men stealing it and so just took care of it all himself.

Another time, Elder Walker and I had taken the funicolare up the hill but had gotten off at the wrong stop, at 8:30 one night in a poor neighborhood. I'd never felt worried for my safety before, but I did feel a little uneasy that time. Then an old woman came up to us with a concerned expression and said in English, "These streets no good for you! These streets no good!" I was sure she knew what she was talking about and we left quickly.

All in all, though, my experience with crime was pretty minor. The only serious incident was when I was about ten and playing with my eleven-year-old cousin Lisa out by the garage of my house. It was raining lightly, we got in an argument over something, and she pushed me. Because the cement was slick, I slipped and hit my head hard on the concrete. I remember thinking, "She's killed me!" and I wailed in grief as much as I did in pain. But I remember seeing her face, cold and impassive. She couldn't have cared less if I died. I was probably overreacting to a childish incident, but I made sure never to be alone with Lisa again. I'd be friendly when our families got together, but I knew I could never trust her after that.

Now I wished maybe she'd been successful in accidentally killing me. It would have saved me from committing unforgivable sins with other men. And I'd certainly heard the other elders say things before like, "The only rehabilitation for gays is execution." I wondered if they were right.

I remembered my only other childhood encounter with crime. I was about eleven, and a friend of mine, Adam, came over one day to tell me horrifying news. A man in a car had stopped and asked Adam for directions. As Adam was explaining, the man got out of the car and unzipped his pants and flashed him. Adam had run away in horror, certainly justified, but all I could think when he told me that story was, "Damn! Why couldn't that happen to me?"

Obviously, molesting was a terrible crime, and the fact that I wanted to be molested clearly made me a horrible person as well. I remembered walking past construction sites in my neighborhood and seeing rough, manly men go into portolets. Even at the age of eleven, I was plotting ways to go into an occupied portolet and hoping to be molested. What a sick, sick person I must be. Tempting a person to molest had to be as big a crime as molesting itself. I hadn't ever tried to entice a man, but God knew I'd wanted to, and that had to count against me as well. It just proved that gays were bad, bad people.

One Sunday back in the summer of 1973, the same day I turned twelve and was ordained a deacon, someone had set the stairwell leading to a second-story gay bar in the French Quarter on fire. New Orleans wasn't far from Biloxi and we'd visited a few times when I was a kid, though I didn't remember seeing the place. Thirty-two people had died in the UpStairs Lounge that evening, not from smoke inhalation but from the actual flames themselves. I still remembered the awful photo in the paper the next morning of a minister who burned to death halfway out a window.

I also remembered one reporter who arrived at the scene just after the fire had been put out, saying he wondered what all the fuss was about. He could see by looking up into the windows that it was just a mannequin factory. Then he realized that all the stiff figures he could see in the building weren't mannequins.

Even at such a young age, I followed the story for weeks. Families of some of the victims refused to accept their son's or husband's bodies, ashamed to have everyone know their family members were gay. Churches refused to bury the dead because they had died "in the midst of their sins." Even in my hometown in the days after the fire, kids were making jokes about it. "Did you hear about the weenie roast in New Orleans yesterday?"

I knew even at the age of twelve I was gay, and that experience in New Orleans proved absolutely that I could never let anyone else know my secret. I knew it was a crime just to be gay, even if I didn't act on my feelings. Other than that, I really tried hard not to break the law. But out here on my mission, I'd committed my first actual crimes. When I'd moved to a new apartment after the earthquake, by law I was supposed to register my new address with the Questura since I was an alien, but the line had been so long my companion and I just decided to forget it. I could be stopped by a policeman at any time and forced to show my documents, and I wouldn't be able to. And another time I'd once bought what I knew was a pirated music cassette so I'd have some Italian music to listen to after my mission. I'd later gone out and bought a real copy of the same cassette, so the artists would get the money, but I knew in my heart I'd still supported piracy. There was no way to take that back.

None of this compared to what two other elders had told me, however. Elder Turnley said he'd earned money for his mission by cashing counterfeit checks. And Elder Snow had sold bicycles he stole to "earn" money for his mission. I thought they were joking at first, but they were serious. Certainly, most of the missionaries had earned their money honestly, but I couldn't understand how these two could reconcile committing such major sins, even crimes, to "serve God," but people seemed able to rationalize almost anything. I knew I felt close to rationalizing homosexuality at times. There were days when it just seemed right. But I tried to repent of those feelings as quickly as I could and get back on the straight and narrow.

"Come on, Anziano," Elder Walker interrupted my thoughts. "It's your turn to approach someone."

I steeled myself for the job and stopped a man about forty, wearing a tweed cap. The man wasn't interested, but even though it was Walker's turn now, I stopped another man, too.

"We're with the Church of Jesus Christ," I said, "and—"

"Hey!" Someone shouted right behind me, and I saw a man about twenty-five jump suddenly on the sidewalk a few feet in front of me, as if he knew the person was trying to get his attention but wanted to ignore him. He started to quicken his pace, but then all of a sudden the man who had shouted and two others ran up to the young man and grabbed him.

They had guns, and one of the men hit the twenty-five-year-old in the head. A car screeched to a halt in the street just beside them, a young, dark-haired woman in the front seat next to the male driver. She looked worried.

One of the men ran over and opened the back door, and the other two men continued beating the twenty-five-year-old as they dragged him toward the car, hardly resisting. I couldn't believe it. I was witnessing a kidnapping. They were common enough in Italy. I knew I should help the man, but the kidnappers had guns. What could I do? Yet if I did nothing and he was killed, I would be partly responsible for not trying to help. I remembered hearing about a woman in New York who'd been stabbed to death while fifteen neighbors heard her screams and not even one of them so much as called the police. I didn't know what I could do against guns, but I had to do something.

I took out my appointment book and my pen, and I casually walked down the street a few feet so I could read the license plate. Very nonchalantly, I wrote down the license number and tried to memorize the make of the car. At least I could give the police someplace to start.

With a last punch, the men threw the twenty-five-year-old into the back seat and climbed in after him. Then the car squealed away.

"And so the undercover police make another arrest," said Elder Walker.

"That was the police?"

"Sure. I've seen it a dozen times. Probably picking up someone in the Camorra." Then, as if nothing had happened, Elder Walker stopped another man on the street and asked him about the Church.

I was still unnerved, but I managed to get back to work. We walked the streets the rest of the morning, stopping in a bar once for some mineral water, and then made our way to the bus stop to head back to the apartment for lunch at 1:30.

In a little piazza near the bus stop, we could see a large crowd gathered, maybe twenty or thirty people. They were surrounding a car where some police were moving about. Suddenly, there was a collective gasp from the crowd, and they moved back, giving us a glimpse of the front car door, which was open. A human head fell out of the front seat and onto the pavement. A woman screamed, and the police tried to get everyone to move back.

I felt sick, and Elder Walker pulled me away as the bus drove up. "What a cool story to write home about next week!" he said. We squeezed onto the crowded bus and headed back up the hill toward our apartment.

Elder Walker told and retold the story of the arrest and of the beheaded man during lunch. Was it natural to become insensitive after being confronted with crime so often? I remembered seeing photos of World War II refugees walking past corpses along the side of the road, as indifferent as if they were walking past clumps of weeds. They'd seen so much horror that a few more dead bodies didn't mean very much.

It was the same fear I had about my homosexuality. After living with the guilt for so many years, would I finally just become numb to it and fall into sin? And would sinning with one man make it easier to sin with the next, and the next after that? Would I eventually become so desensitized to the horror of homosexuality that I would no longer find it offensive? It seemed to me my only chance of survival was to continue to find all sin, all crime, repulsive.

That evening, we tracted without success, and the following morning, we only got one referral. In the afternoon, we headed back out to our tracting zone. It consisted largely of groups of INA Casa buildings, housing projects for the poor. There was practically no one on the bus when we got off, and virtually no one on the street. It looked like a Sunday afternoon, though it was only Thursday. Not a single person was home in the first five-story building we tracted out. That seemed odd. Walking past a few stores to the next building, we noticed that all the businesses were closed, metal grates pulled down over the doors and windows. No cars drove down the street.

"Is it a holiday?" I asked Elder Walker. "Where is everybody?"

"Damned if I know."

It again made me think of Sundays back home in Mississippi. Like many cities, Biloxi had laws prohibiting most stores from being open on Sunday. It was clearly due to the largely Christian influence, Sunday being a day when no one was supposed to buy or sell. It was the same in Salt Lake, I'd discovered, when the Mormons successfully found power in numbers. Any time a Christian majority made laws, they often forgot that not everyone was Christian. I'd always though it unfair to have stores closed on Sunday. I'd never known any Jews, but I still wondered where that left them. They couldn't buy or sell on Saturday, their Sabbath, and they couldn't buy or sell on Sunday, which was permitted to them by their religion but forbidden by law.

Mormons proudly broadcast their belief that one day they would produce a theocracy to rule America, but I still believed in the separation of church and state. If there was to be free will, you had to be able to sin without it also being a crime. Even if you were a majority, it seemed an abuse of power to want a theocracy. I didn't say that out loud, of course, but we were told that even in the Millenium, after Jesus came back, not everyone would be Mormon. So how could we make laws forcing people of other religions to follow our rules? It seemed as much like extortion as the Mafia asking for protection money.

I knew that even Church leaders weren't exempt from abusing their power. I remembered that the Doctrine and Covenants said in section 121 that "we have learned by sad experience that it is the nature and disposition of almost all men, as soon as they get a little authority, as they suppose, they will immediately begin to exercise unrighteous dominion." I'd never really seen it before coming on my mission, but my leaders out here were often bullies, and seeing that made me wonder if it were happening with the Church in general. Elder Boyd K. Packer seemed particularly harsh in his talk condemning masturbation, which was turned into a pamphlet and handed to every teenage boy. I thought I would die of embarrassment.

Even if we as a Church managed to stop bullying non-Mormons, was it okay to still bully members of our own religion? I remembered while reading the Book of Mormon, thinking that if Nephi had said to me some of the things he said to his brothers, I'd have been mad at him, too. He may have been right, but his psychology was all wrong. He was being overbearing.

But maybe it wasn't really bullying. Perhaps we needed to be chastised for our sins.

Still, I couldn't help but wonder how much of what they said was what God told them to say, and how much came from their own hearts. Some of them seemed to enjoy chastising a bit too much.

I was tired of thinking about it for now. I tried to forget about spiritual accusations and focus on the work at hand.

We tracted out a second building without a single person answering the door in this building, either. Something was definitely going on. Was there a gas leak or something?

"There were plenty of people in our part of town," I said. "Should we go somewhere else just for the day?"

"This is our tracting zone," said Elder Walker. "We prayed about it before selecting it, and we blessed it when we started working here. We need to stick to our plans and not let little troubles sway us."

In the third building of the afternoon, on the fourth floor, we saw a tag on a door that said, "Brigatte Rosse." They had kidnapped and killed the former prime minister Aldo Moro not long before I came on my mission. That and the train station bombing by an unidentified group in Bologna that killed seventy-five people just two days before I entered the Missionary Training Center was about all I knew of Italy before coming here. The door tag today was most likely a sick joke, as the Red Brigades probably didn't advertise their presence, but we skipped ringing that doorbell just in case.

I noticed in all three of these buildings, in the windows on the landings between floors in the stairwells, there were little altars set up, with pictures of young men who'd apparently been killed, along with a few flowers and a picture of the Madonna. It took me a while to realize all these young men had probably been killed selling drugs.

In the fourth building, no one answered on the fifth floor, and no one answered on the fourth floor, but on the third floor, we heard some movement behind one of the doors when we knocked. Even though no one answered, we were so happy to find signs of life that we knocked again.

After a moment, the door cracked open just a little, and we could see one eyeball through the crack. "Che volete?" asked the woman inside, a little harshly.

"We're missionaries with the Church of Jesus Christ," I began, but stopped when the door suddenly swung open all the way.

"Oh, my god!" exclaimed the woman. "What do you think you're doing out there?"

"Well, we have a message about—" I tried to go on.

"No, I mean, what are you doing out there *today*? Don't you know what's going on?"

Elder Walker and I looked at each other. "No," we said together.

The woman reached out and grabbed us, pulling us into her apartment quickly before shutting and locking the door behind us. "There's a gang war today," she said. "One part of the Camorra is mad at another part for that beheading yesterday, and the godfather of the one part said they'd kill anyone they see out in this area today."

"So that's it..." said Elder Walker. I could see he was excited to have something else to add to his letter home.

"How long have you boys been on the streets today?" asked the woman.

"About an hour and a half in this neighborhood," I said.

"Oh, my god. Well, you can't leave till it gets dark, so you may as well sit down and relax. I'm Signora Zamparelli. Can I get you anything?"

"Some water would be nice," I said.

"You have any orange soda?" asked Elder Walker.

Soon Signora Zamparelli came back with our drinks, and she sat in a chair while we sat on the sofa. "I don't really even want to turn the T.V. on," she said. "I don't want anyone to hear that I'm home. But you young men obviously have something to say or you wouldn't be here. Why not tell me a little about your Church? I'd like to hear some law-abiding young men talk for a change."

We taught her our C lesson, about the restoration of the gospel, and since it wasn't dark yet, we continued on with D, about the plan of life. Signora Zamparelli seemed very receptive, and I was sure we'd hooked her, but at the end of our second lesson, she said, "It's dark now. You'll be able to get home safely. You boys need to be more careful in the future. You don't want to be killed just for being in the wrong place at the wrong time, do you?"

"I don't want to be killed at all," said Elder Walker, laughing.

"Well, you go right home now," she said as she gave us a little hug and then quickly shut the door behind us.

We walked down the stairs and straight to the bus stop without trying to tract out any more apartments. "Well, the Camorra did a good thing tonight," said Elder Walker. "Got us to teach two lessons in one evening. That's only happened a couple of times in my whole mission. And Signora Zamparelli may not come around soon, but she'll come around eventually. Not many people can hear two lessons in one night and not be moved. You did good, Elder Anderson."

"Thanks," I said, though I wasn't sure I'd done anything more than usual.

A nearly empty bus stopped by just a few minutes later, and soon we were back in our neighborhood, where life was still bustling about without threats. It was way too early to go back to the apartment, but Elder Walker seemed to feel we'd gotten in our quota of good deeds and was calling it a night. We stopped at a gelateria and got an ice cream cone, and we licked our ice cream carefully as we slowly walked back to the apartment.

We were sinning by not staying out another hour or so, but we were also more successful than usual. Did becoming successful always lead to being lax with the rules? I remembered King David after he rose to the top. He ended up having Bathsheba's husband killed so he could marry her. What if I became really successful in my mission as I hoped? Would I become arrogant and then let my homosexuality take over? I wanted to be a success, but I also wanted to be good. Surely, you could do both. It was hard to know what to pray for anymore.

"It'll be nice to have the apartment to ourselves for a little while," said Elder Walker as we unlocked our door and turned on the light. He went immediately to our bedroom and stripped down to his garments. I put on my blue jeans, which I used as pajamas.

"Why don't we try to get in a little extra Dual Study since we have time?" I suggested. "We could read an article from the *Ensign* or something."

Elder Walker gave a little scowl but then shrugged. "Okay," he said. "You pick something out and read. I'm going to lie in bed and rest my eyes, but I'll be listening."

I flipped through several issues looking for something appropriate to what we'd been experiencing lately, and I finally found an article on how to be "in the world but not of the world." I started reading out loud, but I hadn't finished the first page before I could tell from Walker's deep breathing he was asleep.

I turned back to the article and kept reading out loud. Maybe Elder Walker couldn't hear the words, but I needed to hear them. I kept reading the article, letting God talk to me through the Church magazine. We were lucky to have authorities in Salt Lake give us spiritual messages each month to help keep us in line, men who were successful at being Latter-day Saints. Maybe if I survived all the trials God had in store for me, passed all the tests in my way, I'd become a General Authority one day, too. It wasn't so farfetched. If I was supposed to be able to become a god one day, surely it wasn't expecting too much to be a seventy or an apostle. Then I could find a way to reach other gays and really help them, more than the current General Authorities were helping me now. Maybe no other gay man had ever made it that far before, so no one felt any special reason for outreach.

I'd give a great talk on the subject one day at General Conference, perhaps write a manual about it, and the talk or the manual would be read by missionaries and other members all around the world. Rather than make gay members feel other members wanted to murder them, I'd make them feel understood, and show them the right way.

I finished reading the last few paragraphs of the article, feeling energized. Then just as I closed the magazine, I heard the key turn in the front door. Two of the other elders were home. I went out to greet them and tell them of our success this evening, and they grudgingly praised us for our work.

I brushed my teeth and got ready for bed, but once in bed, I found myself gently caressing my penis through my garments. I did it automatically on many nights, a way of comforting myself before going to bed. As if sin could ever be comforting.

But I was going to do it tonight regardless. I couldn't be expected never to sin at all in my life.

So my success *was* in fact making me feel above the law, I realized sadly. I sighed and stopped touching my penis. Then, lightly caressing my chest and rubbing my nipples through the embroidered religious symbols in my T-shirt, I pulled the covers up tight to my chin and listened to Elder Walker's light snoring nearby, thinking about young men with guns shooting into the night.

The Letter

"Dear Robert," the letter began, "There's no easy way to tell you this. But at the Single Adult conference in Pensacola last month I met Jerry. He lives in New Orleans but he's been driving here to Biloxi twice a week for the past month to see me. And, well, we're getting married in the Washington, DC temple in two months. When you know it's right, there's no reason to wait. I don't know if my parents will be able to afford to come, but they can come to the reception at the church in Biloxi.

"Robert, I really want to thank you for keeping me pure. Other guys I went out with before always tried to get fresh. But you have such a strong commitment to the gospel. You were always a perfect gentleman. Thanks for your friendship, and may the Lord bless you on your mission in Italy. Love, Rachel."

I sat staring at the letter in my hands, listening to the sound of cars driving past my apartment in Naples. It was warm, our windows were open, and a couple of flies buzzed about the room.

My girlfriend was getting married. It was the thing every missionary dreaded. Even more than the fear of not baptizing, we worried about the girlfriend left alone back in America finding another guy. And mine just had.

"Pronto, Anziano Anderson?" my companion, Elder Walker, asked, striding into the bedroom. It was almost 3:30, time to leave the apartment for the rest of the evening. I was grateful we had a teaching appointment set up for 7:00. I needed something good after a letter like that.

"You say the prayer," Walker told me, folding his arms and bowing his head.

"Please help us to be in tune with the Spirit," I prayed, "and help us be able to touch the people we come in contact with."

"Why didn't you pray that Massimo would be ready for the baptismal challenge?" Elder Walker said after I finished. "You set your goals too low all the time."

"Gee, we're challenging him tonight?" I asked, surprised. "It's only his second lesson."

"You always have to be prepared. Weren't you a Boy Scout? I made Eagle at 16."

We had plenty of time to kill before 7:00, so we spent the first couple of hours walking along busy streets, stopping people in their tracks and asking if they'd be interested in hearing about the Mormon Church. No one was.

It was hard for me to get in the proselytizing mood, my thoughts turning back to Rachel. I had never loved her, though I had liked her well enough. I had never loved any girl. The only person I ever even had a crush on was Johnnie, when I was in the 11th grade and had to take P.E. with the 9th graders because of my class schedule. He was so attractive and masculine I just couldn't stop looking at him. I watched him change clothes every day in the locker room, and he watched me, too, probably worried that I was looking at him.

I could still see even now the lumpy bulge in his white, white briefs. I tried not to let him get too close, afraid he'd see the red rash of my jock itch that I was too embarrassed to seek treatment for. I did see him glance at my crotch a couple of times, but was it to see my own bulge, or was he disgusted at my jock itch? I wanted him to be attracted to me, and yet I wanted to spare him the torment of having the kind of abominable nature that I had.

We looked at each other in the locker room every day for nine months, and never spoke one word to each other. The only time he ever even said anything about me was the time during softball when instead of paying attention and catching a fly ball, I was looking at him and let the ball hit the ground three feet from me. Then I heard Johnnie say to another teammate, "He just *stands* there!" I was mortified. I needed him to hug me, but of course, he was looking at me like I was an insect. I tried to play better from then on, to "win him back," but we still never spoke, until one day when I managed to say hi to him in the hall. I even wrote about it in my journal. "Today I said hi to Johnnie." Pretty pathetic.

I wondered what he was doing now.

Wait a minute. My girlfriend had just dumped me, and I was wondering about a boy? What was wrong with me? Why wasn't I remembering the times I'd spent with Rachel? What if no other girl ever showed an interest in me? What if I could never manage an interest in them? How could I follow the commandment to have a temple marriage and get to the Celestial Kingdom without a girl? I might be going to hell, or at least only to one of the lower kingdoms of heaven, and all I could think about was Johnnie?

"Look lively, Elder," said Walker. "You haven't talked to anyone in ten minutes."

I saw a couple of gypsies standing by a store entrance with their hands out and ignored them. I remembered that as a kid, I'd watched Lon Chaney in *The Wolf Man* and wondered why everyone hated the gypsies. It seemed an unfair prejudice. But once, a couple of months ago, I'd been stopped by a gypsy woman who asked for money, and I'd given her a five hundred lire note. She hit me in the chest and said, "That's not enough. I want more." Though I was astounded at her brazenness, I resisted the demand.

Another time, maybe a month after that, I'd seen a gypsy woman begging with two young gypsy children. They were all in rags, the two-year-old looking near death as he slept almost too soundly in his mother's lap while she sat on the sidewalk. The five-year-old boy was up and stopping different people, asking for money. I watched as he stopped two businessmen talking. One was eating an ice cream cone and obviously felt too guilty to enjoy ice cream while this boy was suffering, so he reluctantly gave the cone to the boy. The boy was overjoyed and ran to show his mother what he'd received. She grabbed the cone out of his hand, threw it on the ground, and pointed her finger in the boy's face. "You don't take anything but money!" she told him fiercely.

I lost all respect for gypsies after that, and it made me leery even of just "regular" bums. Still, I remembered King Benjamin in Mosiah talking about the necessity of giving to beggars without judging whether or not they really needed the money or deserved it. It wasn't our place to make that call. We simply needed to give. It wasn't enough to help only those people we liked. We had to give to everyone who needed assistance. I found a two hundred lire piece in my pocket now and handed it to one of the gypsies without comment.

Then I got back to my street contacting, looking for men who might be interested. It occurred to me for the first time that perhaps we weren't so different from those looking for marks to hit up for money. But I tried to put the thought out of my mind and get back to work. "Excuse me, sir," I said, stopping a man about forty, who'd made the mistake of glancing at us, thus signaling his vulnerability. "We're talking to people about their families today. Do you have a family?"

"Yes," he said uncertainly. "Two girls."

"How old are they?"

"Nine and ten."

"Do you find it hard raising children with good values in today's world?"

"Uh, sometimes." He still looked nervous, as if trying to think of a way to escape.

"We have a program called Family Home Evening we'd like to talk to you about sometime. It helps bring the family closer together and helps us face the problems and temptations of the world. Do you think we could get your address and phone number so we could arrange a time to come by some evening?"

"Sure." The man gave us his address on Via Roma and then hurried away past a tobacco shop. I couldn't tell if he was really interested or not. After all, he didn't have to give us his name and address but did. Maybe if I couldn't save my own soul, I could help save his. Perhaps there wasn't much difference in being open to helping the poor and being open to hearing the gospel. Both required a certain willingness to suspend judgment.

"Elder Anderson, shouldn't you be concentrating more on the gospel itself rather than just on programs?"

I looked at my companion a moment and then kept walking. Was he kidding? It was the first referral we had taken in two days, and he was complaining? I could never get over how negative everybody was out here, always ready to find fault. There was very little suspension of judgment among the other missionaries.

But when "Be ye therefore perfect, even as your Father which is in heaven is perfect," was a commandment, not just a guideline, every flaw could be the one to block eternal happiness.

Still, it was hard to worry about my hundred minor flaws when there was only one that was really going to damn me. I had to get married and have a family. It was the main purpose of Earth life.

Should I try to win Rachel back? Send her a letter so full of interesting, humorous, spiritual news that she'd give Jerry a second thought and wait for me after all, as she'd promised? Maybe other girls could sense something was wrong with me and would never go out with me. What if instead of having a scarlet letter A for adultery on my chest, I had a pink G for gay on my forehead? I didn't think I was obvious, but perhaps there was something that marked me. I wasn't supposed to worry about girls while on my mission, but how could I help it? Perhaps Rachel was my only hope for salvation. I remembered how I'd first approached her at a church dance. She'd been talking to a girlfriend and laughed in a sweet, innocent way.

"I just love *Xanadu*," Rachel had gushed to her girlfriend. "It's so deep!" I had zeroed in quickly after that, almost targeting her because of her innocence. It seemed so calculated. Would I have to act that predatory again to find another girl who'd be innocent enough to date me?

Elder Walker and I ended up going all the way down to the water's edge, the time between approaches growing longer and longer. Finally, around 6:30, just as we were getting ready to head back up the hill, passing by the dark, black castle, Piazza Municipio, we ran into Francesca, the daughter of one of our local members.

"Ciao, Francesca," I said. "Come stai?" We could use the familiar "tu" with her because she was only fourteen. Any older and we'd have had to use the formal "lei" to keep an emotional distance. She was so pretty, though, we probably should have used "lei" even with her.

"Oh, Anziani!" she said. "I'm late. My father told me I had to be home by 6:30 no matter what. I just missed the 109 up to Colli Aminei and my father is going to kill me!"

"Too bad," said Elder Walker. "You should've started back earlier. It'll be another twenty minutes before the next bus comes along."

We needed the 109, too, but it was still half an hour before our teaching appointment, so the wait wouldn't kill us. I thought Elder Walker's insensitivity was going to irritate Francesca. The teenage years were always hard on Church members, and I didn't see any point in giving her any additional reasons to feel disenchanted with the Church. Francesca was a physically beautiful girl, one of the prettiest I'd seen since coming to Italy, and she would certainly be in a position to face lots of temptations in the coming years. I wanted her to be strong, to be able to resist all the approaches she was sure to get.

"Oh, you're right, Anziano," she said. "I was talking to friends and forgot the time. What will I do now?"

"Well, we'll wait with you," Elder Walker offered magnanimously.

"Thanks, Elders."

A taxi drove by then and I had an idea. "Would it help if we shared a cab up the hill?" I asked. "We're going that way, too."

"Oh, yes! What a great idea!" she said.

"Elder, could I talk to you a minute?" said Walker. He pulled me aside. "We don't have money for a cab. You know our budget. We can't afford luxuries."

"I'll pay for it," I said. "I have five mil on me. She can pay a mil. That ought to be enough." It wouldn't hurt me to go without gelato or biscotti for a couple of weeks, anyway. I had lost fifteen pounds so far on my mission but could afford to lose a couple more.

Then I realized I had ulterior motives for helping, and I felt ashamed. I was thinking that by the time I finished my mission and then college, Francesca would be just old enough to marry, and maybe she'd remember me if I came back. It was like the time one of my classmates in high school complimented me over and over about how intelligent and creative I was, getting me to feel all good and self-satisfied, and had then asked me to write a book report for her. The compliments evaporated into nothingness once I realized they were just there to set me up. How nice was I truly being to Francesca if I was really only thinking of myself?

Francesca quickly found a cab for us and we climbed in, getting up the hill even with traffic in just a few minutes. As we left the center of the city, the buildings became newer and cleaner. The city felt happier. After we dropped Francesca off, Elder Walker turned to face me. "That was a total waste of money. She was still late. She'll still be yelled at, and we aren't supposed to be seen alone with pretty girls."

He was right on all counts, and I felt ashamed again.

"And there you are, trying to flirt with that young girl. Sheesh, Elder, if they ever made a movie about your life, it would be the worst kind of B-movie. So second-rate."

"I wasn't flirting," I said petulantly, adding with a tone of recklessness, "She isn't my type."

"Yeah, right. And besides, we're supposed to be frugal with our money. It's not ours anymore, even if we earned it before we left home. It's the Lord's now."

"Okay. Okay. I won't do it again. Let's get on up to Vomero now so we can teach Massimo."

We were back in his neighborhood a little early, so we stopped at a gelateria for a few moments to take a break. I didn't buy any ice cream but Elder Walker did. Watching him eat reminded me of being in the high school cafeteria watching Johnnie eat, which I did out of the corner of my eye almost every day at lunch. I should've invited him to church sometime, but I was too afraid to talk to him. I kept looking for some sign that he might be open to talking to me, yet I'd never seen it.

Then one day, miraculously, Johnnie stopped me in the hall. "Hey, Robert. Want to go to church with me Sunday?"

It was supposed to happen the other way around. *He* wasn't supposed to bring *me* to a *Baptist* church. "Yes, I'd love to," I said, blushing. But Johnnie seemed not to notice and smiled at me.

We sat together at his church the following Sunday, and when the preacher asked if anyone wanted to be saved, I almost walked to the front of the chapel. It would make Johnnie happy. I resisted, though, and wondered if I could ask Johnnie to return the favor and come to my church next. Maybe I really could save *him*.

But I never did. We said good-bye in the parking lot when my mom came to pick me up, and at school, we resumed our staring at each other in the locker room in silence. We never spoke again. Did he miss his opportunity to join the Church because of me?

Soon we were at Massimo's apartment and knocked. He let us in and we all sat down. He was even willing to say a prayer before we started. Most guys were afraid to. Massimo was probably twenty-four, with straight black hair that came halfway over his ears and fell just a little below his collar. He had one mole high on his left cheek, but it looked good on him. I was glad I'd done a good approach when we knocked on his door last week.

We went through the D discussion, about the purpose of life. When we got to the part about marriage and I showed the flip chart picture of the Washington DC temple, I ad libbed, "And this temple is where my girlfriend is marrying her new boyfriend in two months."

"What?" said Massimo. He looked at me to see if I was serious and then laughed.

"Do you have a girlfriend?" I asked, again deviating from the script. I wanted him to say no. I didn't even know why I was bringing it up.

"I have a lot of girlfriends," he said, still laughing.

"You don't have sex with them, do you?" Elder Walker interjected.

"Of course," Massimo replied, looking puzzled. "It's one of the great pleasures in life. One of the few I can afford. You're not telling me I'd have to give that up, are you?"

"Well, yes," said Walker. "We believe in the Law of Chastity, but that's another lesson. Perhaps we could come back in a few days to teach that one."

"Hmm, I don't know. I don't think that one interests me. Why don't you leave me a pamphlet or something, and I'll give you a call when I'm ready to have you back over."

Massimo prayed again before we left, but with less enthusiasm this time. Once we were back on the street, Elder Walker said, "Why did you have to bring girlfriends up? You spoiled everything. He'll never call now."

"Well, you didn't need to blurt out he'd have to be celibate from now on until he got married. We could have built up to that over several lessons. There's a reason the Law of Chastity comes in lesson H, not D."

"Don't contradict me, Elder. I'm the senior companion here."

While I knew I was right, I couldn't get over the fact that we seemed almost like con men, forcing our mark to go down the path we had ready for him until he did everything we wanted. Was that why our scripts were so carefully plotted out? We started with lesson C and worked our way up to J. Why there was no A or B I didn't know, but we almost always went in order, though we could throw in G, the baptismal challenge, at any point we thought appropriate. And each individual lesson was meticulously designed as well. All carefully thought out by minds in Salt Lake, to gain the best psychological advantage? I shook my head. I knew I was being evil to think that way. If a person were truly open to the gospel, he'd be open no matter what order the concepts were presented in.

Elder Walker and I were already in our tracting zone, and since it was only 7:45, we had a good while before it was time to head back to the apartment for 9:30. We got out our tracting book and looked for the last address we'd been to, and we started knocking on doors in the next building on the list. We put an X by the address if we got a no, a dot beside it if no one was home, and the letters CB for "call back" if the person told us to come back at a better time. We got mostly X's and dots the rest of the evening.

A striking guy about seventeen opened the door at one apartment and said his parents weren't in. I wanted to go in and teach him anyway since he seemed reasonably interested, but Elder Walker just wrote "CB" and we moved on. I doubted his parents would want to hear us. It would have been nice to get at least one lesson in, though, plant a seed, before his parents found out. He seemed so open, so nice.

The teen was the same age as Johnnie, I realized, and I thought of him again, and of Rachel. How was I going to do it? If I married, I'd at least have some kind of sexual outlet, no matter how inadequate. And if I was married, I could start learning how to like women. But all alone, how could I manage? What if one day back home I ran into a cute guy like I had this evening, or like Massimo, or like Johnnie, and he asked me out at a time when I was vulnerable to his approach? Would I have the strength to say no?

All I could do was live one day at a time, like an alcoholic—just try to be good today and worry about tomorrow tomorrow.

I decided I could be good tonight. When we started back for the apartment, we usually turned off our missionary personalities, but I wanted to be an A-list missionary, at least for today. There was a young man about twenty-five waiting at the bus stop with us, so I worked up my nerve and nodded at him.

"Heading home?" I asked.

The man smiled. "No. I'm heading out. Time to party."

That kind of threw me, but I persisted. "What kind of fun do you like to have?" I was trying hard to think of a way to turn the conversation around.

"Elder," said my companion warningly.

"Drink and meet girls. What else is there?"

"Do you like sports?" I asked. "Our church tries to organize teams to play each other." That was not nearly as successful in Italy as it was in America, but I didn't have to say that just yet.

"Soccer?" asked the man.

I nodded. "I could give your name to our congregation's captain and have him call if you'd like."

The man thought for a moment. "Sure, why not?" he finally said, and I wrote down his information. His name was Nuccio, and he lived here in Vomero.

His bus pulled up then, and as he got on and turned to wave goodbye, my eyes accidentally fell upon his slightly protruding crotch. I had an instant vision of him in a jock strap, getting ready for a soccer game. It might as well have been a G-string, though, for the way it affected me. It made me think of the day in high school when I was a senior and no longer in Johnnie's gym class, and I saw that he had earned his letter jacket, and how that had almost tempted me to try out for the basketball team.

But though I missed seeing Johnnie in the locker room, I knew my limitations, and I'd decided it was best not to tempt myself with more visions of crotches, his or anyone else's. I smiled now and waved back to Nuccio, grateful the darkness and the distance made it impossible for him to see the growing bulge in my own pants.

I should have been happy with the referral, even if it wasn't for a teaching appointment, but everything good I did seemed tainted. I was like Midas, but instead of turning everything into gold, everything I touched became a sin. I'd never be able to get married. Who would want someone like me around? I was trying to live one day at a time, but I couldn't be good even for one hour.

Staring at the ground, I waited in silence until our bus came a few minutes later.

We were back home by 9:25, and I went to the kitchen, eating just two cookies with milk, rationing out my last roll of Bucaneve biscotti until next month's check came. I chatted with the other four missionaries for a few minutes and then went on to my room, sitting at my desk and rereading Rachel's letter.

"Dear Robert, There's no easy way to tell you this…. We're getting married in the Washington, DC temple in two months. When you know it's right, there's no reason to wait."

Well, it certainly wasn't right with a gay man. She was making the best decision, and I was glad for her. I'd just have to work out my own problems by myself.

I was about to put the letter away when I read the next line again. "I don't know if my parents will be able to afford to come, but they can come to the reception at the church in Biloxi."

Mormon weddings were pretty cheap as a rule. There was no charge for a temple wedding. The trick was getting there. More temples had been built in recent years, but still the closest to Biloxi, Mississippi was the one in Washington, DC. There was also no charge for the gym or "cultural hall" at church where the reception would be held. The only cost was decorations and refreshments, all usually done by the family, not by professionals. But Rachel's family wasn't well off, and gas even at 80 cents a gallon, much cheaper than here in Italy, was going to add up for a trip that far.

I thought for a moment. I still had $30 in U.S. currency left over from when I first arrived. I'd kept it as emergency money, or something to have on hand when I got back to America after two years. But it sounded like Rachel's parents could use it.

Giving away money twice in one day. The news must really have shaken me. I was normally such a cheapskate. And I wasn't quite sure how I was going to get anything out of this. But even if this might be something I could finally consider truly altruistic, it still was helping someone I liked, not a total stranger, so it still probably didn't count for much.

I shook my head. Did everything have to get me Celestial marks? Heavenly Father, please help me to get through this life, I prayed. Please, God, help me.

Then I shook my head again. I was every bit as much a beggar as the people who stopped us on the street every day. I just hoped God was more generous than I was.

I opened my desk drawer and pulled out a blank greeting card with a picture of Vesuvius painted on the front, designed by a member of our church branch. I'd bought a few from her a couple of weeks back, to give her encouragement.

I wrote out a congratulatory note to Rachel, put the $30 in the envelope, and added, "To help your parents with gas for the trip."

I was probably going to hell, but she wasn't. That was something. All I wanted from God was to get an A on my Earth exam, though my faults seemed too great for that. I simply wasn't destined for greatness or happiness myself. But I could still make life a little nicer for others. Maybe that was all I was capable of. It would have to do for now.

I read another chapter of the Book of Mormon, got down beside my bed and prayed, and then got under the covers. I tried to fall asleep, but I couldn't stop thinking about Johnnie.

The Shepherd Boy

I always ate my Corn Flakes first thing when I woke up at 6:30, letting the other missionaries take their turns in the shower. I ate slowly, reading and rereading the cereal box. "Pour in bowl. Add milk. Do not boil." The story was that the Italians had initially thought Corn Flakes were another kind of pasta and so had to be alerted not to boil them. It seemed funny to think that what was "common sense" for one group was hard-learned behavior for another. Reading the warning every morning made me feel a thrill that I was no longer in Biloxi, Mississippi, but instead in Quartu, on the island of Sardinia, off the mainland of Italy. Even though life was often dreary here, I at least had that.

Eating slowly, I opened my Book of Mormon in Italian and began reading. I was getting pretty fluent by now and longed for the day when someone would mistake me for a native. People spoke much more clearly in Sardinia than in Naples, so I understood more and more every day, about 90 to 95% of most conversations, and I made myself learn ten new words a week. "Kettle" and "bookcase" were two of my latest. The real trick was finding ways to use them so I didn't forget them.

I wasn't a very good missionary, despite believing so strongly in the Church. I simply wasn't aggressive. If people didn't want to change their lives, if they were happy as they were, why bother them? It was a miracle really that Elder Collins and I had found and taught a family of four while doing work visits together, since he wasn't even my regular companion. Although the DeAngelis family was scheduled for baptism in a week, my second set of baptisms so far, I still felt like a failure. Life would be hard for Mormons in a Catholic country. Was I really doing them a favor?

I'd thought often enough how much simpler my own life would have been if two sister missionaries hadn't knocked on my family's door eleven years earlier. The Church said people were only accountable to live as much of the gospel as they had. The more God gave, the more He expected. Since I was a member of the Church who'd also been privileged enough to grow up in America, the Lord expected the ultimate out of me.

The ultimate was so much, though, that I sometimes wished I'd never heard of the Church. I was good enough to live an average life, and with an average amount of "gospel," I'd have been a good person. But I was average while having "the *fullness* of the gospel." The inequality in that equation made me both a bad missionary and a bad person. I knew I could learn the language, however, and I hoped at the very least that where I failed in inspiring people to study the Church through my spirituality, I might at least intrigue them with my tongue. I even thought in Italian most of the time, and prayed in Italian, too. "O Dio, abbi pieta' di me!"

I hated that I always whined to God, but I tried to act stronger in front of the other elders. No one knew that I was suicidal half the time. I was tempted to sprinkle a little extra sugar on my cereal now to boost my blood sugar level, but I knew a sugar high was always followed by a sugar low, so I resisted, feeling proud of the accomplishment. Then I frowned, disgusted that this was the order of triumph I experienced, holding back on a spoonful of sugar.

By 7:15, the other three elders had finished their showers, and I took my turn. Then at 7:30, Elder Shaw, the district leader, called, "Quiet Hour!" and I went into one of the empty bedrooms to study.

Most missionary apartments were overly cramped, six guys sharing a living room and two bedrooms, but the Quartu apartment was huge. We had a living room and three bedrooms but only four missionaries, so two bedrooms remained empty, one for hanging laundry when it was raining outside.

Missionaries almost never had a chance to be alone. During Quiet Hour, however, we at least enjoyed a little peace. Even if we were studying or praying in the same room, we weren't allowed to speak unless it were necessary. But here in Quartu, I had thought of going to one of the empty rooms to study during Quiet Hour. The district leader had popped in a couple of times saying, "Studying, Elder Anderson?" to make sure I wasn't sleeping or reading yesterday's mail, but I was always diligently studying and was soon left alone.

Only sometimes I didn't study. Some mornings, I knelt and prayed the entire hour. I prayed to find people who wanted to learn about the Church. I prayed for my companion to be nice to me. I prayed to be able to go on splits again with Elder Collins for a day. I prayed for my family back home.

But mostly, I prayed for God to remove the curse of homosexuality from me. Or, barring that, for God to let me be killed before I fell into sin. I prayed so hard I felt sure God would hear and answer me. Somehow, God would find a way to help. I would get meningitis and become brain damaged. I'd be hit by a bus and paralyzed from the waist down. That might not control my thoughts, but it would at least control my penis. God *promised* in I Corinthians not to let me be tempted above that which I was able to bear. I *knew* God would come through somehow. I only hoped I could hold out until it suited the Lord to do so.

This morning, I prayed for a few minutes, but it was hard to concentrate. I stood up and walked to the window. In the square across the street where we played soccer on our day off, I could see a young man, perhaps twenty, my own age, sitting and whittling a stick. His hands looked strong, and I could just see enough of the man's chest to be impressed. I had lost twenty-five pounds since arriving in Italy and did sit-ups and push-ups every day, so I was in surprisingly good shape. After staring intently at the man a few more minutes, I clenched my jaw and lay on the floor, exercising until I was forced to grunt, and stopping only to prevent the others from hearing I wasn't doing something more spiritual.

Finally, it was time for devotional, where the two companionships shared our plans for the day. We all gathered in the living room, which the district leader and his companion used as a bedroom. We put our four chairs in a circle and began. "What are your plans for the day?" asked Elder Shaw. I braced myself to hear something dreadful or boring but then had to suppress a smile when I heard my companion, Elder Barker, tell the others we were heading to Cagliari to rent *Fiddler on the Roof* to show to the Church members the following night. It would help them see how tradition could be changed, that what people so often thought was the only way to do things wasn't necessarily set in stone. Hopefully, the members would feel inspired to allow the elders to talk to their friends about the Church. I was pleased about the trip because it meant not doing missionary work this morning, and I just wasn't in the mood.

"How about a challenge?" Elder Shaw asked. "You try to get referrals on the way to Cagliari and back, and Elder Collins and I will try to get some here. Whoever gets the most gets treated to gelato after lunch by the others."

"Sure thing," said Elder Barker, and I resigned myself to my fate. I'd be a good missionary if it killed me. God willing, it would.

At 9:30, Elder Barker and I left the apartment, and I forced myself to talk to two men on the way to the bus stop, getting one referral. We'd get a couple more in town, and another on the way back. Stopping people on the street to ask their address wasn't so bad once I set my mind to it. It just seemed sinful somehow that the work of the Lord came so unnaturally to me, that I had to work this hard simply to achieve a tolerable competency. I didn't know where my real talents lay, but they were clearly elsewhere. I hoped they'd be reasonably compatible with the gospel, that I could live my own life peaceably somewhere and still in my own way do something that wouldn't utterly displease the Lord.

We caught the express bus to Cagliari, bypassing Quartucciu and Selargius, heading directly through the marsh to the city. Once in Cagliari, we changed buses. I got another referral as we waited, and then we headed up and around the big hill.

The bus was packed today, unusual for Cagliari though it had been common in Naples. I couldn't even reach a handhold and just leaned against the other passengers as the bus churned its way up the winding road. At times, the bus seemed to lurch awfully close to the edge, and I could see down the steep embankment. It was frightening, but I also knew I'd prayed for death so much I had to accept it might be the answer God finally chose to help keep me good. Better to die average now than to die later an apostate.

An elder up in the Milan mission had been killed recently while riding his bike, and everyone talked about him like a martyr with his exaltation secured. I looked out the window and prayed for the Lord to have pity on me, just as I prayed every single day I was out here, hoping the prayers could have some kind of cumulative effect. It was okay if God tortured me till the end of my mission as long as he finally killed me and saved me. I was doomed if I lived to go home. I turned to look at Elder Barker, whose face never showed any anguish of any kind. Must be nice, I thought.

Then the bus turned another corner, and the passengers all seemed to shift to the right at the same moment. The bus slipped ever so slightly, and the rear wheel seemed to skid. I felt a thrill of anticipation as I reached for a handhold, but I was blocked by a large man also reaching. I didn't mind, though. It meant I was more likely to be hurt if anything happened.

Several passengers shouted to the driver, and then the bus seemed to shift violently to the right. I lost my balance and fell onto an old woman, who fell onto a man sitting down. The look in his eyes scared me. Everyone started screaming, and suddenly there was the sickening feeling of falling. The bus had gone over the edge. Immediately, I knew it had been a sin to pray as I had, and I knew I was responsible for whatever happened to everyone else. I just wanted to be free of all responsibility, and I felt my body relax as we fell.

The fall didn't really last long, but each hit on the way down was devastating as each body was thrown on top of everyone else. I couldn't breathe, with a knee in my stomach and someone's breasts in my face, and then I hit my head on the roof before being thrown back to the other side, with another knee in my back. The tumbling and bumping and screaming and suffocating continued for several more seconds, and finally, finally, we were still.

The bus had split open somewhere along the way, and there were a couple of bodies strewn along the descent and several here at the bottom, though most were still lodged in the bus. Some moved and some didn't, and sounds of weeping and wailing rose into the air.

I stood and looked at the scene, knowing I should help but I'd never even taken a First Aid class. "Please! Help me!" shouted a man lying half out a window, trying to crawl.

"My leg! My leg!" shouted a woman, lying near a rock which seemed to have split her leg in two, blood covering the ground.

An old woman crawled on her hands and knees, blood dripping into her eyes from a gash on her forehead. She stumbled over someone's shoe and fell sideways onto an unmoving child. I had done this. We were told to be careful what we prayed for because we might get it. Guilt flooded my bloodstream like adrenalin. I looked for my companion but couldn't see him. He must still be inside the bus.

The scene didn't seem real. How could this be happening? Why wasn't I dead? What could the Lord possibly have in store for me that was better than death? It seemed unfair to tease me like this, to put me in an accident and make me live through it. My head hurt terribly, though, and I felt dizzy. I prayed I might die, after all. But I'd go and try to get help for the others first. There almost seemed to be a voice inside me urging me to go. I wondered if I simply couldn't think clearly or if it were inspiration.

I staggered off, climbing over rocks and slipping down little embankments, as I looked for a road. It was warm enough that I hadn't been wearing a suit jacket, only my slacks and tie, but my name tag had been ripped off my shirt pocket in the tumble of bodies, and my mission rulebook with my residency pass from the Questura was missing, too. I had torn my pants leg when falling out of the bus, but I had suffered only a superficial cut on my leg. My tie felt awfully confining, so I pulled that off and tossed it aside, wondering if I should have used it to help bind someone else's wounds.

I kept working my way downward and to the right, and after a while I came to a little pass that led to a road which bordered the sea. A couple of cars passed, but it was not a busy road, just outside of town. I wanted to flag someone down but felt too tired. Maybe if I could just lie down a moment first, I'd be okay. I crossed the road and lay among the rocks by the water. Not terribly comfortable, but I was so tired, so very, very tired. I vaguely noticed my wallet slipping out of my pocket, but I was simply too exhausted to pick it up right then. Perhaps I was losing blood internally. Maybe I wouldn't ever wake up. I smiled as I closed my eyes.

***

I awoke after what might have been only a brief nap, my head all fuzzy. I couldn't quite remember why I was there. I shook my head, but that made it hurt. I sat still and tried to let my thoughts sift into place. I had something to do, I was sure of it. I stood up and stretched, feeling sore all over. I felt my head, which ached terribly, but saw no blood when I withdrew my hand. It felt as if there should be blood. I must have tripped and fallen among these rocks while on my way somewhere. Or maybe someone had pushed me out of spite. I had an awfully negative feeling about whatever had happened, and I just wanted to get away. I stared at the sea and tried to listen to the waves, but there was a ringing in my ears that made it hard to hear anything else.

It felt odd not knowing what had happened, and I suddenly realized I didn't remember anything at all about my past. I looked at my hands, at my scuffed shoes and torn clothes, and realized I must be some kind of loser. I probably wasn't missing much by not remembering anything. I was clearly a nobody. I almost felt glad I couldn't remember, as if it meant I could forget some terrible sin. I was probably a drifter who'd been fired after being caught stealing at my job. I felt I'd done something wrong, but I also felt there'd probably been extenuating circumstances. Maybe if I couldn't remember, I could somehow regain my innocence and not make the same mistake again. I wondered if I'd deliberately hit my head on the rock to try to forget what had happened. I wouldn't put it past myself. I couldn't remember who I was, perhaps, but I knew the idea of self-mutilation didn't seem shocking. I hoped I could be normal now.

I began walking along the road, not sure in which direction to go. I saw a couple of ships heading into port and wondered if I was coming this way to try to find a job. It was something important, but I didn't think I'd like working on a ship. Maybe I was trying to get on board to go somewhere. Yes. That might be it. I did feel I was supposed to go somewhere.

I felt my pockets. No money. It must not be a ship passage then. But then maybe I'd been mugged back there. Or maybe I was only hitchhiking somewhere. If it was important, it would come back to me if I walked long enough. It hurt too much to concentrate now.

After a while, I stuck out my thumb, but no one stopped. I was too dirty and shabby. I felt this wasn't my normal attire, and yet there seemed to be a certain freedom with it as well. Maybe I'd quit my job deliberately rather than lost it; maybe I'd chosen to be homeless. The idea should have terrified me, I felt, but didn't. Could I have deliberately chosen to be irresponsible? No, I thought. Somehow, I'd been forced out. I could feel there was a job that had no room for me. I could feel I had no place to call home. I was a street person. In some way, though, I knew inside that this was a blessing. I knew I believed in God, that God took care of His children. I vaguely remembered a religious principle about the Veil of Forgetfulness, something about living with God before we came to Earth. We'd been made to forget everything so we could learn anew, or be tested, or something. Maybe I was in some kind of Witness Protection program and had been given amnesia because I knew too much.

So now I was to have a new start. A new start with no money and torn clothes. It wouldn't be easy, but… well, what did I want to do? It felt like a question I didn't often ask myself. I looked up toward the city and knew I didn't want to go back. I sensed I liked it well enough, but somehow there was danger there for someone in my position. I could see mountains off in the distance, and I knew I wanted to get out into the country. Perhaps I could work on a farm. I needed something simple. Something intellectually easy. It would be a long walk yet to a farming area, but it still hurt too much to think about specifics. Walking would be good for me.

I focused on the road, trying to block out the aches all over my body, walking for more than an hour before stopping by the side of the road to rest. After ten minutes, I stood up and walked for another hour. It was clear I was used to walking, as I wasn't overly tired. Whatever job I'd just lost had required me to be on my feet all day. But the bruises hurt, so after a while I rested again for a few minutes.

I saw a truck coming along the road, and I stood and held out my thumb. The truck stopped, and the driver called out. "Where you heading?"

"Inland. I'm looking for work on a farm."

"Well, good luck. I'm going thirty kilometers anyway, up to Senorbi. Hop in back."

I did and tried to relax against the hard metal. I could see we were heading to a higher elevation continually, and every kilometer further we went, I was able to relax a bit more. Were the police after me, too? I felt I not only wanted to leave but needed to in order to protect myself. Maybe it was just fear that whoever had mugged me might come back if I ever remembered his face well enough to identify him. But riding calmed me, so I watched the scenery go by and tried to forget what I had already forgotten. Finally, the driver pulled to the side, and I jumped out of the back before the he moved on up a side road.

I kept walking, but it was almost forty-five minutes before another driver stopped, an old man who drove me ten kilometers, up to Orroli. Then there was another half hour walk, and a twenty-five kilometer ride to Sadali with a huge family stuffed into a tiny car. I was growing hungry by the time they let me out, and another hour of walking didn't help.

The countryside seemed almost deserted. Dozens of stone fences crossed the rocky landscape, made by people trying to clear their land of stones, but there were still plenty of stones about. The land didn't look any too good for planting, and I wasn't sure what to do. I saw a handful of cows and a few flocks of sheep but realized I didn't know much about either. I could pick up stones, however, if nothing else. Hopefully, someone would be happy to have their land cleared some more.

I stopped at the next house I came across, but the man there didn't need any help and didn't know anyone in the area who did. He did give me a piece of bread, though, before sending me on my way. More walking and a couple more short rides brought me to one of the most desolate areas yet. The last driver had told me I was in the Glennargentu region. I was sure I'd never heard of it. This should be as good a place as any for a new start. I felt high up in elevation and transported back in time a hundred years. Life here looked physically hard but also simple somehow, and I found myself smiling. It felt like something I hadn't done much lately.

It was getting late, however, with only a couple of hours of light left, and I was tired of the tiny road. I needed to find someplace even more secluded where I could sleep, and I started off across the closest field. I walked and walked, finding no houses and only one unpaved road, and I kept walking. Finally, as it was just turning dusk, I climbed over another of the stone fences and lay down beside it where it joined another fence. Here, I'd be protected from the wind on two sides, and I just couldn't go any further. I fell asleep almost instantly.

I awoke to find a sheep grazing inches from my face. I sat up slowly and saw three dozen more nearby. Walking among them was a young man about twenty. He had curly black hair and strong arms. He was smiling curiously as he approached.

"And who are you?" he asked, standing a few feet away.

"Roberto," I answered, feeling reasonably sure about that. "I'm looking for work."

"Oh God, not for money, I hope?" He laughed. "I could feed you if you helped me, but that's about it. Nobody has much money around here."

I stood up slowly. "Food is good, and a place to stay. I'll do whatever you want."

The man lifted an eyebrow. "The name's Marco." He extended a hand. "I'm afraid I've only got a tiny little house, but we'll find room. It's a couple of kilometers away. You'll help me with the sheep today. Tomorrow, I can probably find some work around the house for you."

Watching the sheep wasn't difficult. We could walk to a new field and then sit and talk while the sheep grazed. Then we could walk a little further. I sensed I'd actually had a little experience, perhaps with cows, perhaps on my grandparents' farm, but it hadn't been in Sardegna. It must have been on the mainland. And it must not have been an awful lot of experience because I had to listen to every bit of instruction that Marco gave. I tried not to sound too mysterious when he asked about my past, and I tried to get him to talk about himself instead.

Marco, it turned out, had managed to go to school for eight years before his family moved too far away for him to attend. He didn't believe in the Catholic Church but did believe in God. He liked herding sheep because it made him feel closer to David, and to Christ. Sometimes, he wondered if he were really a pagan, though, since he enjoyed everything that was natural so much, and because he'd found an old collection of Greek pastoral poems once and read them while out with the sheep. He could see himself fitting into Greek society as easily as Christian.

He sometimes made up little songs, but he was too embarrassed to sing any for me just then. I felt sure I liked to sing, too. At other times Marco ran across the fields just to feel free, and as he said it, I had a brief flicker of being on my school's track team. "Sometimes," Marco said, lowering his eyes and speaking more softly, "I run naked." He laughed. "Or I'll lie down to get a tan all over. There are a couple of streams, and if the sheep haven't been upstream lately, I'll go skinny dipping." He looked at me. "I hope you don't think I'm hopelessly decadent."

"No," I said, shaking my head slowly. "It sounds fun." I was almost sure I'd never done anything like that, though I felt I'd longed for similar freedom. I looked down at my tattered white shirt and dress slacks. I knew I wished I could chuck those clothes forever, but doing so even for a few minutes to go swimming would be more freedom than I usually enjoyed.

It was nice how many ways we seemed to be sharing the same ideas and feelings. Maybe God had directed me here just to meet him, to learn something from him, maybe even to finally have a friend. I was almost sure I'd never had a real friend. Maybe that's what had gotten me into trouble at my last job. Perhaps if I could develop a true friendship, I wouldn't feel tempted to do whatever it was I'd done wrong before. Knowing someone cared about me would give me a sense of responsibility. So I tried to stop thinking about myself and listen to him.

Marco talked about gathering rocks and putting them in little piles near the fences. He didn't want to make the fences taller or he couldn't get over them. Besides, those fences had been there for hundreds of years. While Marco didn't feel traditions were good for their own sake, it was hard to interfere with some of them. After a while, some traditions seemed natural, and it seemed spiteful to change them.

Shepherding was his family's tradition, and he was proud to carry it on. For the past three years, he'd been living on his own after his father helped him buy some sheep to get started. He worked with his father once a week but spent most of his time alone. He sometimes fantasized about moving to the city but enjoyed being his own boss. "Fantasizing about people is usually better than being with them," he explained.

"Don't you get lonely?" I asked.

"Yes. And don't you? Traveling alone across the country? Where are you from, anyway? You don't sound like you're from anywhere around here. Do you speak Sardo?"

I shook my head. I couldn't remember my own dialect. Only Italian. And yet I was sure I wasn't from Florence. The blow to my head must have made me forget if I had a dialect as well as forget the rest of my name and where I was from.

"I have amnesia," I said, stumbling over the word. "I can't even remember some simple words, like what you call the hair on a sheep."

"Wool?"

"That's it." I repeated the word. "I hit my head. I hope I don't have brain damage." I laughed, and Marco did, too. It was a marvelously friendly laugh, and I realized I was very glad I'd run into the man. Something about the starkness of the area made me feel that anyone who could be friendly here could be sincerely trusted. Of course, without a past, there was little to trust Marco with, but still, I felt content with the idea of staying. Maybe the only way to find where I truly belonged was to have gone so far away. I hoped that both the job and the fledgling friendship would work out.

"When I was a kid," Marco said, "if I tried to tell my mother something but forgot what it was, she'd say, 'Couldn't be important if you forgot it.' It used to drive me crazy, but I think there's some truth to it. Whatever you need to remember, you will."

We arrived at Marco's house a couple of hours before dark. As Marco had said, the place was tiny, stone and plaster with rather small windows, a kitchen and a small bedroom. Just outside was a bathroom, with running water, though that clearly was just within the last few years. But there was no electricity. "Don't need it," explained Marco.

"What do you do at night?"

"Go to bed."

And we did, not too long after sunset, after we'd finished eating. First, we'd had to milk a couple of goats and tend to the garden, but none of that had taken long. Marco's mother had a bigger garden a few kilometers away and canned some of her extra vegetables. There were just a few chickens running around, too, so there would be fresh eggs for breakfast. I felt sure I could adjust, though I also felt sure I was used to a refrigerator. I could remember that word.

I had washed myself before going in for supper, and Marco had offered another set of clothes for me to wear while putting mine in a large bucket. We'd wash them another day. I felt odd wearing Marco's clothes, even Marco's underwear, but I felt even stranger when Marco announced it was time for bed and carried the lantern into the next room.

The bed was not overly wide, though it would hold two. Still, we wouldn't be able to avoid touching. And Marco was taking off all his clothes. All of them. I suddenly remembered something else about myself, something perfectly natural for me though unpleasant sometimes for others. What if Marco accidentally brushed up against me in the night and I had an erection? Marco was so simple he probably didn't even know what homosexuals were. When he found out, I might lose more than my job.

"Turn out the light and get in bed. Morning comes quickly."

I turned off the lantern and then took my clothes off, tossing them on the chair I'd seen Marco throw his on. Then I took a deep breath and slid under the covers. Marco's legs brushed against mine, and while too terrified to allow the contact, I also enjoyed that contact too much to move away.

Neither of us said another word, and although I was tired, I was too nervous to sleep. Marco seemed to fall asleep almost immediately, however. About twenty minutes later, he turned so that his entire leg, from foot to hip, was against me, and his whole arm, too. Several minutes later, Marco turned on his side, letting his knee rest on my leg, and his hand on my chest.

I certainly couldn't sleep now, though I was glad Marco could. Once I got used to it, I was sure I'd enjoy sleeping like this every night. I didn't think I'd ever done it before, but I knew I was looking for a man to share my life with. It was too soon to know if Marco was that man, but it might be pleasant for a while finding out. I sighed happily, feeling comfortable and relaxed for perhaps the first time ever.

I finally did drift off to sleep, but sometime in the middle of the night, Marco changed position again. This time, he turned from his side onto his stomach, but he did it lying face down on top of me. I had an erection in seconds and didn't know what to do. I figured Marco must be so lonely out here that he subconsciously needed the contact and could climb on top even in his sleep. I felt so sorry for his pain that I put my arms across Marco's back and held him. And after a while, I fell asleep again, too.

I woke up later feeling something wet and wondered if there were a leak. The room was pitch black, and Marco was no longer lying on top of me. I reached down and found that the something wet was Marco's head. Marco had taken my penis in his mouth and was moving his head up and down.

"Oh, my god."

"Am I doing it okay? I'm afraid I've never really had any practice."

"It feels wonderful."

"Good. Once we get this wet enough, I want you to put it in me."

"What?"

Marco slid up and kissed me on the lips. "I want you in me. Will you?"

I paused only a moment. I knew I'd found what I was looking for. "Yes," I said.

"I want you in my bed every night. I've been praying for God to send me the right man, and there you showed up in my field. I'm sure we're meant for each other. You must have been praying, too, weren't you? I can teach you whatever you need to know about sheep and gardens. I enjoyed talking with you all day. You're kind, and beautiful, and I'm sure God put us together for the rest of our lives."

I pulled Marco down on top of me, and we kissed furiously and deeply for several minutes. Then Marco pulled away and again took my penis in his mouth. Next, he turned onto his stomach and told me to get on top. I gathered up some saliva and put it in my hand, then applied it to Marco's behind, groping for it in the dark. I maneuvered to aim my penis at the right spot, and I forced myself in as gently as I could. Next time, we might need to use butter. Marco groaned and I sighed. Then Marco pushed his behind up to force my penis all the way in. I knew he was right, that somehow we were meant to be together, away from the world, just for each other. We'd work hard on the farm all day, even harder since there were two of us now, and we'd make love to each other every night. I started slowly pumping away, listening to Marco's grunts of pleasure, and—

***

"Time for Devotional!" There was an abrupt knock on the door, and I turned away from the window where I was still staring at the man whittling on his third stick. I had a huge erection, so I made myself think of a willow tree, concentrating in my mind on the limp branches, until I felt myself grow flaccid.

I'd have to work hard today to deserve forgiveness for thinking all those sinful thoughts, and for wasting an hour of the time I was supposed to have dedicated to the Lord. It was pitiful how desperate I was to sin. Pathetic. I was scum. I hated knowing how horrible I was, but I did know, I did know, and so I had to do something about it. I'd have to start a fast later to try to tame my appetites more fully, exercise some more this evening, memorize an extra scripture verse. And in the meantime, I'd approach more strangers on the street, since that was what I hated the most, risk more rejection by asking more people about the gospel. It was why I was here, after all, to share the gospel and help make people's lives better, to help lead the lost sheep back to the fold. It *was* better to know the truth than to live in ignorance. I was sure of it, or why would God even bother sending the gospel to the earth to begin with? It *was* better, I told myself. It *was*.

I hit myself in the testicles lightly to make myself feel a little sick, to teach myself a lesson about thinking evil thoughts. Fighting the nausea, I pulled my tie up to a firm knot at my neck. I looked with a sigh at the city map and island map tacked to the wall. Then I forced myself to smile and opened the door to join the other missionaries down the hall.

The Happiness Approach

When I was in third grade, my mother told all our relatives I was destined to be a "ladies' man" because I married four of the girls in my class at school. It had started innocently enough. A cute red-haired girl named Susan sitting behind me in class had tapped me on the shoulder and passed me a folded piece of paper. I'd opened it up carefully. "Do you like me?" the note asked.

I turned around and whispered, "Yes," with a big smile.

Then Susan turned up her nose and said, "That note was for the boy in front of you."

But I'd laughed, and after class, I asked if she would marry me. She said yes, and the next day, I brought her a cheap ring.

Though the boys and girls in our school were separated during recess, we began sneaking to see each other, and Susan started bringing along a couple of friends. Soon I was married to Becky, Tammy, and a second Susan as well. And honestly, at age eight, I had still never heard of polygamy in the early Mormon Church.

My mom was tickled at my precociousness, but when Susan #1 invited me to her birthday party and I discovered I was the only boy there out of twelve guests, I began to suspect something was wrong. I got along well with girls, obviously, but apparently it wasn't supposed to be this way. I was supposed to like sports and running around, not enjoy Susan entertaining us with her new ventriloquist's dummy. My being there made Susan happy, made me happy as well, but even at age eight I was also a little concerned.

I wondered as I grew older if those four marriages would be the end of my success with women after I realized I was gay. Susan #1 and I had stayed friends over the years, even though her family had moved from Biloxi to Nashville when we were in the sixth grade. We still wrote, but in the Missionary Training Center, our leaders told us to try to convert our non-member friends and relatives, and after I sent a dutifully zealous letter, Susan had written back quite offended, and we hadn't corresponded since. Had the Church asked me to do something wrong? Questioning was a sure way to apostasy, of course, and I felt guilty, but I couldn't help it anymore.

But I tried to forget about Susan. I always reflected on things like this on our way home in the evening, once I was no longer occupied with proselytizing. I was tired after a full day's work and didn't even bother trying to think in Italian like I usually did earlier in the day.

It was 9:30 in the evening. Elder Barker and I trudged wearily up to our apartment building in Quartu. The full name of this town on the southern coast of Sardinia was Quartu Sant'Elena, and I was surprised by how often people said the whole name. The missionaries just said Quartu and left it at that. I liked working in Quartu well enough, but right now, I just wanted to undress and get in bed. My feet were sore and my neck was aching.

But first we had to run the gauntlet. Our building was five stories tall, the largest building facing the square, and for some reason, all the tough teenagers in the area liked to hang out on the steps of our building, smoking and talking amongst themselves. They never moved out of the way as we tried to get up to the main entrance, just glaring at us and muttering under their breath. They seemed just as unhappy as I was to be there.

Tonight, a boy about sixteen, only a few years younger than we were, sat right in front of the door. We stood staring at each other for maybe forty-five seconds before he finally moved off to the side. Elder Barker went into the lobby and I started to follow, when I felt a hard kick in the leg. I ignored it and went inside, closing the door behind me.

Soon we were back in our apartment one floor up, and I took off my shoes. "Hey, Elders," said Elder Shaw, the district leader, coming into our bedroom. "How'd your evening go?"

"We taught a partial C," said Elder Barker. "Anderson got us in the door."

"Good work, Anziano," said Shaw, and his companion, Elder Dorsey, smiled at me, too.

I nodded but felt stupid. In the Call-Ins to Rome yesterday to report our weekly stats, we got a message from the mission president saying spirituality was low in the mission. Elder Shaw had glared at me then, saying, "You and your stupid songs aren't helping."

Just that morning, we'd sung "Oh, How Lovely Was the Morning" at Devotional, the hymn about Joseph Smith's first vision, but instead of singing the normal second line, "Radiant beamed the sun above," I'd sung, "Oh, how lovely was the morning. Bacon, eggs, and French toast, too." Everyone had laughed at the time, but apparently my irreverence was impacting the mission. Everything I did felt wrong out here. I thought I'd try to have a little fun, which I rarely did. I was normally too concerned about going to hell to have much of a sense of humor.

So I'd been reprimanded for the song, but maybe I was back in Elder Shaw's good graces now for teaching. While a partial lesson wasn't much, we'd take whatever we could get. It should've made me happy, but I still felt empty.

The other elders had cookies and milk, but I wasn't in the mood for a bedtime snack and instead changed out of my suit into my jeans and climbed onto my mattress, opening my scriptures though it was forbidden to study in bed. I read from Alma chapter 41 about how on Judgment Day "all things shall be restored to their proper order.... The one raised to happiness according to his desires of happiness…and the other to evil according to his desires of evil." I wasn't sure where that left me. I certainly had evil desires for other men, but at the same time, I sincerely desired happiness. But Alma went on to say, "Do not suppose…that ye shall be restored from sin to happiness. Behold, I say unto you, wickedness never was happiness." That must be why I was so rarely happy out here, even when the work was going well. I'd simply have to try harder to desire good.

I put the Book of Mormon aside and pulled the worn sheet up to my chin. When I was asleep, I didn't think constantly about my sinfulness. I never dreamed about missionary work either. I usually didn't dream at all. Sometimes, though, I'd dream about my grandparents' farm. Other times, I'd dream about my biology class in college. And sometimes, I'd dream about a good-looking guy I'd just seen that day, but I never felt guilty in my dreams. The dreams were always strangely comforting, until I woke up later and realized I'd been sinning in my sleep.

Tonight was another dreamless evening, and by the next morning, I felt better. After breakfast, a shower, and some study time, I was ready to face a new day. This morning, Elder Barker and I headed to Radio 8 downtown to do our weekly radio show. We did a half hour show once a week at 11:00. We received the airtime for free and did our best to reach a wide audience with our gospel message.

Unfortunately, we didn't really invest a lot of time in preparing the show, despite its potential to reach more people than by going door to door. We usually just read a few chapters from the Book of Mormon, or a pamphlet on the Law of Chastity, or even part of our standard lessons. We might read a chapter from Mosiah about Abinadi's martyrdom, then play "Call Me" by Blondie, read a chapter about the Gadianton robbers in Helaman, and then play "Lonesome Loser" by the Little River Band. We sometimes felt important to be on the radio, but really, it was unlikely anyone was listening to such a bizarre show.

Today, we asked Emilio Floris, a fifteen-year-old member of the congregation, to join us so we could interview him on the air, to show other teens that it was cool to be Mormon. We met him in front of the building and rode up to the sixth floor in the elevator together.

Soon we were in the studio, sitting in front of the microphone. Elder Barker introduced the three of us and then started right in on the questions. "Emilio, how long have you been a Mormon?" he asked.

"My mother and father and I joined the Church two years ago when I was thirteen. My two older brothers who are nineteen and twenty-three didn't join. It's not that they're devout Catholics or anything. They're just not interested in religion."

"Does that cause any trouble in the family?" I asked. Elder Barker gave me a frown for interrupting.

"Not really." He hesitated. "I suppose everyone's a little unhappy is all."

"What can you tell us about Spencer W. Kimball?" asked Elder Barker, getting back to his list of questions with another irritated glance in my direction.

"He's a prophet of God," said Emilio simply, "just like Moses or Isaiah." He paused a second and then added, "Just like Joseph Smith."

"Joseph Smith was the prophet who restored the true church on the Earth," Elder Barker explained to the audience. Then he turned back to Emilio. "Emilio, do you know when the Church was reestablished on the Earth?"

Emilio looked at Elder Barker and then at me and shrugged. "I think it was in 1830," he said. "I'm not sure."

Elder Barker looked at me and rolled his eyes. Then he said into the microphone, "It was 1832, but that's close."

Emilio looked at me and I grimaced, but I wasn't about to say anything. Emilio had been right and Elder Barker was wrong. It was embarrassing that a missionary didn't know the most basic information about the Church he was representing. Just last year, on April 6, 1980, we'd celebrated the 150th anniversary of the Church. But while I'd probably read sixty or seventy Church books as a teenager and most likely knew more about the Church than many of the missionaries out here, they weren't miserable sinners like I was. So what was really more important?

We kept up the interview for a full half hour, playing only three songs at regular intervals when we felt things were slowing down too much. But finally it was all over and we said goodbye to the program director who was always nice to us despite not being interested in the Church.

Down on the street, we thanked Emilio for his help, he thanked us for putting him on the radio, and we shook hands and headed off in different directions. We did a little street contacting for a while, getting one referral, and then we started toward home.

It was about 1:10 when we got back to the apartment, way too early for our 1:30 lunch break. "Hey, Anziano," I said, "I need a new pair of socks. We have a few minutes. Let's hop over to the Upim."

Upim was a small department store on the opposite side of the square from our apartment. "We're supposed to do our shopping on Preparation Day," Elder Barker replied.

"Come on," I said. "We're early anyway." Not working somehow felt like less of a sin if we were at least doing something constructive. "Besides, it's air-conditioned." Upim and the grocery were about the only two buildings in town that were.

That seemed to convince Elder Barker, and we walked over to Upim, sighing as the cool air enveloped us. We made our way to the socks, and I picked out two pairs of black. Just then, I heard a gasp and turned around. An auburn-haired woman was pulling a sandy-haired man away from us in alarm. They talked to each other urgently for a moment as I looked on, confused, and then their shoulders seemed to slump, and they walked back over to us.

"Hi, Elders," the man mumbled sadly in English, with a British accent.

"Hello," Elder Barker replied uncertainly. "You know us?"

"We're Mormons," the man said, "from England. I'm Dan Padding, and this is my wife, Elaine." They both appeared to be in their early twenties.

We all four shook hands, and in the process, we formed an X with our arms. "Oh, non fare la croce!" Elaine said, pulling her hand back. It was a superstition here that it was bad luck to make a cross when shaking hands.

"So you aren't tourists," I said.

"I'm in the military," said Dan. "We have a base here."

"We were baptized about a year ago in England," explained Elaine, "but after six months, we stopped going to church. Later, when we were told Dan had to take an overseas assignment and the military gave us a choice of three bases, I decided we should go where there was no chance of seeing another Mormon. So we came to Quartu." She looked at her husband forlornly. "And yet here you are."

I was impressed by their story. I knew there was no escaping God, but it was both comforting and disturbing to see evidence that it was really so. Sometimes, I thought about running off into the countryside where no one would know where I was, but I knew in my heart that God could always find me.

Elder Barker took a card out of his pocket and handed it to Dan. "Here's the address of the church in Cagliari. You should come this Sunday."

Dan looked at his wife and she nodded grimly. "We'll be there," she said.

They moved off then and Elder Barker and I went to the cash register to buy the socks. "Gee, Anziano," said Barker. "You must have been inspired to come in here."

"Maybe you were inspired to come home early for lunch," I countered.

He nodded slowly. "Yeah. Maybe so."

We went back to the apartment and joined the other elders, who were also back now for lunch. Elder Shaw was cook this week, and he had lunch on the table by 2:15. By 2:30 we were finished. We still had an hour left before time to leave, and since we were forbidden to take a nap, Elder

Barker and I got in a little Dual Study, reading aloud to each other from the Doctrine and Covenants.

After a little studying, it was time to leave. I forced a smile and tried to get in the right mood. It was early yet for tracting, so we did another hour of stopping people on the street, always awkward and an unhappy experience for all involved, but finally it was time to start going door to door.

While we tracted, I couldn't help but reflect on the numbers we were facing here. There were only 1000 members of the Church over in Naples, just 800 in Rome, and only about 100 here in Sardinia. Of the roughly 1900 members within mission boundaries, only about 600 of them were active. We were facing daunting odds. I simply had to act more righteously so I could help bring more people into the Church. The weight was almost a physical presence on my shoulders.

We walked down a street of mostly two-story buildings. Quartu probably had 50,000 residents, but it seemed downright rural after Naples. I rang a doorbell at the next building on our list and opened my plastic flip chart to the "Happiness" list. A moment later, a woman about forty-five opened her door.

"Good evening, signora," I began. I held the list forward for her to see. "If you could have any two things on this list, which would they be?"

It was kind of an abrupt approach, but it got people involved right away, and the mission was really pushing this Happiness Approach right now. The list had several things that people usually wanted, such as "better family relationships," "better comprehension of death," "better relationships with friends," "more self-confidence," "better relationship with God," and "more peace in your life."

The woman looked at me and then at Elder Barker, and then she cautiously began reading the list. She finally said, "Better comprehension of death and more peace in my life."

"Well, signora," I replied, "we have a message that will explain how you can have *all* these things. Would it be okay if we talked to you and your family for a few minutes?"

The woman looked at us both again and then at the list one more moment, and then she nodded, moving aside to let us enter. The woman said her name was Signora Piras, and she motioned for us to sit. "My husband's at work right now and wouldn't be interested anyway, but I'd like to hear what you have to say." Normally, we weren't allowed to teach women without their husband being present, but I could tell by the look Elder Barker gave me that he was going ahead. There were no sister missionaries in our district, and Signora Piras was so much older than we were that it wouldn't look inappropriate.

The lesson went reasonably well and Signora Piras invited us to come back for another lesson. Though we were energized about that, the rest of the evening dragged by slowly. It was hard to keep feeling good about the one encounter when everyone else seemed so unhappy to see us.

The next morning passed without any further success. The following afternoon after lunch, we weren't in the mood for street contacting and got right to the tracting. There weren't many tall buildings in Quartu, but this afternoon we tracted out an area with several three- and four-story buildings. As we approached the main entrance of a three-story building, a thin man about fifty with graying hair rushed past us on the sidewalk and reached the door first. He turned and blocked our way.

"Don't you come in this building!" he said loudly. "I live here and I don't want you in my building!"

Elder Barker shrugged. "You don't own the whole building. There may be other people here who want to talk to us."

"I'm telling you! Don't try to come in this building!"

"What apartment number is yours?" asked Elder Barker. "That way we won't knock on your door."

"Don't knock on *any* doors! I'm warning you!" He unlocked the main door, went in, and pushed it closed with a loud click.

Elder Barker smiled at me and moved over to the intercom beside the door. He pushed a button. No one answered, but a moment later there was a buzz at the door as someone let us in. Elder Barker smiled again and pushed open the door.

We walked up to the top floor and began working our way downstairs. No one answered at the first door, and no one was interested at the second and third door, so we went down to the next landing and started over. I rang at the first door. A moment later, a woman answered. She was about forty, a little plump.

"Si'?" she asked.

"We're representatives of the Church of Jesus Christ," I began, "and we have a message about families we'd like—"

There was a loud screech behind us, and my companion and I turned to look. The man from the main entrance was at his apartment door on the far side of the landing. "I told you not to come in here!" he yelled. He reached into his apartment and pulled out a long pole with pruning shears on the end, a tree trimmer. I had yet to see a yard anywhere within city limits, so what he was doing with the tool I couldn't imagine. He pointed the shears at us. "Get out of here!"

I turned back to the woman. "So we were wondering if there was a time we could come talk to you and your husband."

The woman looked at us and at the man still shouting behind us. She shook her head and closed the door.

"We'd better leave," Elder Barker told me in English.

We started down the stairs while the man shouted, "And don't come back!"

I thought about just pretending to leave, opening and shutting the main door and then knocking on the doors on the ground floor, but then I thought it wouldn't be doing possible converts any favor making them members who had to live in the same building with the creep.

On the sidewalk, Elder Barker wiped his brow. "Mannaggia, that was scary!" he said. "What a psycho!"

I realized my heart wasn't even beating fast. The incident hadn't bothered me in the least. Being murdered on my mission might be the only way to avoid going to hell. I supposed it was good not to fear death, but I wondered if something might be wrong with a view of life that made death seem like a better option than living. I'd almost been happy when I saw the man threaten us with the shears.

I wondered if I should try coming back by myself one day to confront the man on my own. But martyrdom was only effective if it was forced on you, I realized glumly. I was stuck with living.

The next day was Preparation Day, our one day off for the week, though we'd have to work in the evening from 5:00 till 9:30. It was Elder Dorsey's turn to cook this week, so Elder Barker and I didn't have to head to the grocery, always one of the heaviest chores, even if the grocery was almost right across the street, also facing the square. My chore this week was cleaning the bathroom, and Elder Barker's was sweeping and mopping the apartment. Elder Shaw got to clean the kitchen.

We listened to a tape of Rondo Veneziano as we cleaned, moving to the happy, peppy, modern classical music. It made the other elders work briskly and happily, but while I found the music beautiful, I still felt almost too tired to move.

Since we still had to get up at 6:30 even on our day off, most of our chores were done by 9:00, even with breakfast and a shower thrown in. Then it was time to write letters home. But this morning, Elder Barker had a different plan.

"Hey, comp," he said, "let's go play a little broom hockey before it gets too hot."

He was smiling broadly, so I forced a smile, too, and nodded. I was already in my jeans, so we each grabbed a broom, and Elder Barker grabbed a small rubber ball as well before we headed up to the roof of our five-story building.

No one else was up here today, thank goodness. There was a little iron railing along the edge of the building, just above a six-inch lip of cement, and a couple of vents and pipes sticking up in various places, but mostly we had a wide, flat expanse to ourselves. I'd never understood James Taylor's song, "Up on the Roof," back in Biloxi, but it made perfect sense to me now in Italy, and I found the isolation up here somehow liberating. Sometimes, we dragged a couple of chairs to the roof on P-Day and wrote letters while sitting in the sun. But today I simply pretended to enjoy our game, smiling as Elder Barker laughed. Until I accidentally hit the ball over the side of the building.

The next few days passed uneventfully. Every time someone seemed remotely interested and talked to us for a few moments, I was happy, thinking maybe God could work through me after all. But then every time someone shut their door in our face or turned us away, I worried that my clear lack of the Holy Ghost meant I was going to hell.

Finally, it was time to do the radio show again, our one big project of the week. This time, our guest was Sister Padding. She and her husband had come to church this past Sunday as they'd said they would and had sat next to us, and when we heard Sister Padding sing, we were overwhelmed. Such an exquisite voice. After Sacrament meeting was over, I asked if she'd like to sing live on our radio show.

I'd never seen anyone look happier. "I play the guitar, too, so I can be my own accompaniment," she said. "How many songs should I prepare?"

"Is three too many?" I asked.

"That'll be perfect." She giggled. "I'm going to be famous."

We told her where to meet, and today when we walked up to the building, we saw Sister Padding out front with her guitar case. We went inside and up to the studio, where we explained to Sister Padding how the show would work.

Elder Barker and I took turns reading from Third Nephi about the physical effects Christ's death in Jerusalem had on the American continent. We read of his subsequent visit to the American Indians after his resurrection, breaking up the reading every six or seven minutes with a song from Sister Padding, "a local member of our church." She sang "The Streets of London" and "Annie's Song." Her voice cracked once during the first song, but she quickly loosened up and the second song went better. At the end of the show, we had her close with "Both Sides Now." Her eyes lit up as she started. But for some perverse reason, seeing her smile somehow made me sad.

Halfway through the song, Sister Padding faltered on one of the lyrics, and when I turned toward her, she had a panicked look on her face. She kept strumming for a moment, but she couldn't think of anything to sing. Then her eyes widened, and she burst forth with the last verse, singing it beautifully and hauntingly. But as soon as she finished, she grabbed her guitar case and ran out of the studio.

We headed immediately to Sister Padding's apartment after we left the station, but she wouldn't answer our knocks.

"Let's get her a card and slip it under her door," I suggested.

"Oh, Elder. She's a big girl. We have work to do."

But I insisted and twenty minutes later we slid the card over the threshold. I'd written, "Even the angels have a bad day once in a while." I didn't know what that was supposed to mean, of course. Elder Barker looked at his watch and motioned impatiently for us to go.

We did some street contacting in the afternoon without success. And we knocked on doors all evening, but no one was interested. Elder Barker and I ended up arriving back at the apartment around 9:15, fifteen minutes earlier than we were supposed to. I felt guilty again, but my attention was diverted for the moment by the gauntlet of teenage boys we had to pass another time to reach the door of our building. They glared and muttered as usual, but I thought we were going to get through without incident when suddenly one of the teens lunged at me, his spittle hitting me in the chest.

I ignored it and we closed the main door behind us. As we reached our apartment a few moments later, we could hear the phone ringing. Elder Barker hurried with his key and ran to the district leader's room to answer. It was dangerous to pick up before 9:30. If it were the zone leaders in Cagliari calling to check up on us, as they sometimes did, it wouldn't look good that we were in early, but it might be someone we'd given a card or pamphlet to calling to ask us for a teaching appointment.

But it was neither. "That was Sister Spissu," Elder Barker explained after he hung up, while I was wiping the spit off my shirt. Sister Spissu was a widow in her early forties, whose husband and daughter had been killed in a car accident shortly after they'd joined the Church. Her relatives told her it was God's way of telling her she was committing a grave sin by becoming Mormon, but she never stopped coming to church.

"What did she want?" I knew Elders Shaw and Dorsey stopped by to see her every couple of weeks. She probably just wanted to leave a message for them.

"She was upset," Elder Barker replied. "She didn't say exactly what was wrong, but she said she needed the priesthood over right away and we had to come immediately. I asked if she wanted Elder Shaw since he's the district leader, but she said she couldn't wait. It's an emergency. We better get over there fast."

"Is she hurt?" I asked as we locked our door behind us. "Is she sick?"

"She didn't say."

Sister Spissu lived eight blocks away, and as we hurried over, I prayed she hadn't cut herself with a knife and was waiting there bleeding rather than calling an ambulance. It wasn't good to rely on the Church for everything.

When we arrived at Sister Spissu's place, a relatively new three-story building, we rang the intercom, and she buzzed us right in. She lived on the top floor, and we hurried up the stairs. She was at the door waiting when we reached the landing on the third floor.

She didn't appear injured. "Hurry! Hurry!" she said, ushering us inside, looking about the hallway nervously.

We went in and she closed the door behind us. "What happened? What's wrong?" asked Elder Barker. I looked around the apartment, but everything seemed fine.

"This evening," Sister Spissu began, "one of my neighbors came over, a man in his twenties. I'd seen him in the stairway a couple of times before, but we've never talked much. He's new to the building. He has a roommate. I think they're students." She shook her head.

"Anyway," she went on, "it seems some of my mail was put in his box by mistake, so he came by an hour ago."

"Did he attack you?" I asked. What horrible thing had that man done to upset this woman so?

She shook her head again and then looked over her shoulder worriedly. She turned back to us and shivered. "He brought the mail over," Sister Spissu explained, "and we chatted a while. Everything seemed okay, and then he said he had to hurry back to fix dinner for his husband." She stopped and put her hand to her mouth.

"His *husband*," she repeated. "I was so horrified I made him leave right away, but it was too late. I prayed and prayed, but I've felt so uneasy ever since he was here." She grabbed Elder Barker's arm. "You have the priesthood. You've just got to cast out the evil spirit he brought."

My mouth fell open. Not once on my mission had I ever heard of an elder needing to cast out an evil spirit. In fact, not once in all my life had I heard of a priesthood holder casting out an evil spirit. We knew technically it was possible the situation could arise, but an evil spirit was a serious occasion, an incredible, remarkable event.

Elder Barker looked shaken, peering over his shoulder nervously, too. "Certainly, Sister Spissu," he said, his voice wavering a little. "Let's do it right away." He glanced about worriedly again.

Elder Barker raised his right arm to the square and in a trembling voice commanded any evil spirit in the apartment to leave immediately, in the name of Jesus Christ and by the power of the holy Melchizedek priesthood. We never rehearsed this kind of thing, so there was no telling if he was doing it right, but after he cast out the evil spirit, Elder Barker also offered a blessing on Sister Spissu and her home.

When my companion finished, Sister Spissu grabbed his hands and thanked him, tears in her eyes. He was smiling, but I had to fight to keep my face impassive. I hadn't felt any evil presence in the apartment before, and I didn't feel any different now after the blessing.

Was I so evil myself that I couldn't tell when there was an evil spirit around? While I felt wicked most of the time, I still didn't believe it was possible to be that out of touch. And if just being gay like her neighbor brought evil spirits around, why didn't Sister Spissu or anyone else notice anything around me? And why, for that matter, didn't she feel something was wrong about her neighbor while they were talking *before* he let her know he was gay? Something didn't quite seem right.

But Sister Spissu was a stalwart member of the congregation. And she'd paid her dues through intense suffering to be in tune with the Holy Ghost. She must know what she was talking about. Maybe I didn't bring evil everywhere I went only because I was still a virgin. Perhaps if I ever acted on my gay feelings, I would end up just as awful as Sister Spissu's neighbors, but while I was still a virgin, there was yet hope for me.

I wanted to see for myself if the neighbors were evil. I knew they must be, but it was agonizing to be so close to finding out for sure and not be able to. Sister Spissu gave us each a piece of cake, and then we went home in silence.

Back at the apartment, Elder Barker told the other elders about our experience while I went to our room and pulled out my Bible. I turned to the part in Luke that spoke of Christ casting out evil spirits from the man by the sea. I needed to understand more of what had happened tonight and what it meant for me. "Then went the devils out of the man," I read, "and entered into the swine: and the herd ran violently down a steep place into the lake, and were choked." Would even swine run to kill themselves in the sea rather than be near me?

The other elders sat in the kitchen talking and laughing, but I knelt by my bed and gave a halfhearted prayer before climbing under the covers.

Around 9:00 the next morning, the phone rang. It was Sister Spissu again, and she wanted to talk to Elder Barker. A moment later, he hung up and came back to our room. "Sister Spissu says she can't live in the same building with those queers. She can't really afford to move, but she asked us to keep an eye open for any vacant apartment."

I nodded, glad no one knew my secret. The missionaries would probably abandon every apartment I'd ever lived in.

"I have a better idea, though," said Elder Barker. "We'll get the faggots to move."

"How will you do that?"

"You'll see."

After a brief prayer, we left the apartment. The first thing Elder Barker did was head to a hardware store around the corner. He bought a can of black spray paint, and I started suspecting what he was up to. We walked over to Sister Spissu's apartment without a word and knocked on her door. Elder Barker didn't mention the paint but simply asked where the offensive neighbor lived, saying we wanted to talk to him and his roommate.

"Oh, you boys shouldn't talk to them," Sister Spissu warned us. "You should stay far away from that kind of abomination."

"We're just going to call them to repentance," Elder Barker assured her.

Sister Spissu said they lived on the floor below her, the first door to the left of the stairwell. We thanked her and headed down, but Elder Barker didn't knock on the door at all. Instead, he pulled the can of spray paint out of the bag.

"Anziano," I said, "you can't deface property."

"We'll make those freaks feel so unwelcome they'll be the ones to leave. It's not right that Sister Spissu has to move because of them."

"Let's talk to them," I said. "Ask them to stay away from Sister Spissu."

"Are you defending them?" Elder Barker demanded. "What kind of Latter-day Saint stands up for fruits? You give evil an inch and it takes a mile. The only way to deal with it is to root it out."

I said nothing.

"You know where the word 'faggot' comes from? It's the name of the sticks people used to put on the pile to burn queers at the stake. If we still did that, the world would be a happier place."

Elder Barker aimed his can at the door and sprayed the word "froci." I'd never heard it before. I'd have to look it up when I got back to the apartment. If it was some form of "gay," though, I wondered how Elder Barker had learned the word in the first place, or why he knew the origin of the word "faggot."

I was afraid someone would see us and report us to the police, so I was glad when Elder Barker put the can back in his bag and we left the building. "We'll keep coming by every few days," said my companion. "If they paint over the door, there's enough paint left in this can that we can keep spraying their door every few days until they get the hint and move out. We'll make them too miserable to stay."

I felt too miserable to stay, too. Try as I might to live righteously, it was too draining to always know that if people learned the truth, they'd despise me as much as I despised myself. It was exhausting to hide and pretend constantly.

Still, I managed to perform well enough today, talking to strangers about the Church as if everything were okay. I smiled and joked and laughed like usual.

This evening, when we went back to visit Signora Piras, we brought a filmstrip called "Man's Search for Happiness." It was a little outdated, adapted from a film shown at the 1964 World's Fair, but it was still powerful, addressing the questions, "Where did I come from? Why am I here? Where will I go when this life is over?" Carrying the projector around was a pain in the butt, yet sometimes we felt a prerecorded message carried the Spirit better than we did.

When we arrived, Signora Piras offered us each a glass of a bitter red soda, and as we all sat down, she said, "I heard your radio show yesterday. I thought it was very good." I was surprised that someone had heard us. We really did have an audience.

"Thank you," said Elder Barker.

"I also liked the music you played. Very soothing."

"Oh, that was Sister Padding. She's from England but lives here now."

"You mean the music was live? But it was so good."

I smiled. "Sister Padding will be glad to hear you think so. Maybe you could tell her yourself this Sunday at church."

She nodded and then we chatted a few more minutes. Finally, we started the filmstrip. Signora Piras seemed to like it, and I usually enjoyed seeing it again, but it always made me wonder at the end as we watched the righteous dead reunited with their loved ones in heaven what fate awaited me. I knew apostates were cast into Outer Darkness.

I thought of a passage in Second Nephi I had read several times this morning. "O wretched man than I am! Yea, my heart sorroweth because of my flesh; my soul grieveth because of mine iniquities. I am encompassed about, because of the temptations and the sins which do so easily beset me. And when I desire to rejoice, my heart groaneth because of my sins."

It was impossible to be happy even when things were going well because at the back of my mind I was always aware I couldn't ever truly share in the blessings of the gospel. I was always going to be outside the circle. Even serving a mission didn't bring me inside.

Elder Barker asked me to say a prayer, and then we shook hands with Signora Piras, gathered up our belongings, and headed home.

I wrote in my journal and then decided to read a little more of the Book of Mormon before bed. We read the scriptures in the morning, we read the scriptures during our lunch break, and we read the scriptures in the evening, but I never felt very enlightened. The stark contrast between what I was and what I was supposed to be was simply too painful to endure day after day.

At the radio station, we'd once played a Beach Boys song, and the words seemed written just for me. "I want to go home. Why don't they let me go home, home, home? Oh, oh, look out for Sloop John B. I want to go home."

But I didn't miss my home in America, I realized. I missed… I missed… I didn't know what I missed. I sat on my bed and looked at our picture of the Salt Lake temple on the wall and sighed.

My only hope was to somehow undergo a miraculous transformation. Paul had changed after his vision on the road to Damascus. Alma the Younger and the four sons of Mosiah had changed after their vision. Maybe I also needed a vision to find the strength to change. Sure, I was too evil to be worthy of a vision, but the sons of Mosiah had been evil, too, so maybe it could happen to me as well. If I couldn't change on my own, perhaps I needed to humble myself and let God do the changing for me.

But we were always in the city. How could you have a vision on a city street? Maybe an angel could appear in my bedroom. I suppose it wasn't likely, but it seemed to be the only chance I had of finding any peace.

I sat on my cot and listened to the other elders laughing in the kitchen.

Sometimes, it almost seemed we tried to stay so busy we didn't have time to think about our lives, about whether we really were happy out here doing this work. The other elders seemed downright oblivious to the question. But busy as I might be, I always found a few minutes each day to wonder. How was I ever going to get through two years, much less a whole lifetime, when a weakness I couldn't control threatened every day to destroy my life and my eternal happiness? It didn't seem fair that a sin I hadn't chosen had been thrust upon me and there was no way to overcome it. I felt like Sisyphus pushing a boulder up the hill every day, only to have it roll back down during the night. No matter how successful I was at fighting my gayness today, tomorrow the battle started from scratch all over again.

All I could do was hope for a vision, hope for a revelation, hope for some kind of miraculous change, and hope it came in time to save my soul. If I could just get one more baptism, one more person to testify on my behalf on Judgment Day, maybe I'd be okay.

I lay down without kneeling beside my bed first. I was going to hell anyway. What did it matter if I didn't pray tonight?

I turned on my side and stared at the dirt-stained wall for a moment. I worried my jumbled thoughts would keep me up late into the night, but I was asleep by the time my companion came into the room. I dreamed all night long, of falling rubber balls and cans of spray paint and arms raised to the square.

Yet when the morning light began streaming into the room, I felt as tired when I opened my eyes as I'd felt eight hours earlier. I forced a smile on my face, though, and strode out to the kitchen for breakfast, singing softly as I met the other elders, about bacon, and eggs, and French toast, too.

They smiled, and then I pretended to laugh.

The Ditch

It was nearing 3:00, almost time to head for the train station so we could go back to Ciampino. It was Preparation Day, our "day off," so Elder Wright and I had spent the morning doing shopping and then had come to Castel Gandolfo southeast of Rome to tour the observatory by the Pope's "summer home." After that, we'd walked from the crest of the volcanic crater down to the lake below, sat under an awning, and watched people boating on the blue, calm water of Lake Albano, while we wrote our weekly letters home to America as we snacked.

We had to wear our suits while we were out of the apartment, so we hadn't been able to relax as much as we wanted, but that was the reason for the rule. The Church didn't want us to forget we were missionaries and do anything inappropriate, like listening to the jukebox or flirting with girls. Of course, Elder Wright was flirting a little with two teenage girls anyway, and since the girls were putting coins into the jukebox, we couldn't help but hear the worldly music of Claudio Baglioni singing "E tu…"

I listened as Claudio sang. "And now there's no one else but you, only you and always you, and you're exploding inside of my heart…" In Italian, the words were beautiful, and when I saw one of the teenage girls wink at Elder Wright, who grinned back, I suddenly felt very alone.

Was I never going to stop feeling gay and learn how to want to share my life with a woman? I'd tried to cure myself for so long and hoped serving a two-year mission would encourage the Lord to heal me, but it hadn't happened. I hadn't specifically *asked* a priesthood bearer to anoint me with consecrated oil and give me a blessing. We all carried little vials of consecrated olive oil on our key chains, so I could have asked almost anyone, but I'd never told a living soul I was gay. I simply couldn't bear to let anyone know. Maybe God needed me to humble myself and ask to be healed through appropriate priesthood channels before He could do it.

But if it didn't work, if I didn't have enough faith to be healed, everyone would know I was gay, and I'd still be gay. What good would that do?

I took a last bite of my hard Italian bread covered with Nutella, a chocolate and hazelnut spread. Then I finished the last of my mineral water and looked back out over the lake. It truly was beautiful here, trees growing up all the sides of the crater. It was hard to believe that something which had once been filled with molten rock and poisonous gases could be so peaceful now. Birds twittered nearby and a butterfly lit on a purple flower at the water's edge. I wished…

"I guess we better head back, Elder Anderson," Elder Wright announced. "We've still got our cleaning chores to do." Our day off ended at 5:00, and we had to work from 5:00 until 9:30. We had no appointments set up, so we'd be tracting door to door all evening.

We stood, and I noticed a cute teenage boy was now chatting with the two girls. He had dark, wavy hair. "I'd like to get to know you" a new voice sang out on the jukebox.

Picking up our folders with our letters, we crossed the street and headed back up the sloping trail through the trees to the top of the crater. Before long, we were at the train station, and after only about ten minutes, an orange and yellow commuter train pulled up. There were lots of empty seats, so we took two by a window and looked out at the hills and farm houses as we left town.

The only other time I'd seen farms during my mission was out in Sardegna. One Church member who was terribly ill with some kind of blood disease had his wife call and ask us to come out. He wanted a blessing.

I'd anointed with the oil, and my companion had sealed the blessing, promising him a speedy recovery. He was still moaning as we left. The next day, he was dead.

It was easy enough to think it was my companion who didn't have enough faith, as he was the responsible one who gave the actual blessing, or that the man himself didn't have enough faith. I hoped it wasn't because I was gay and the Lord couldn't work through me that the man had died. Somehow, I didn't really feel responsible for that man's failure to be healed. I still mostly felt responsible only for my own failure.

I'd read that if one received healing, it also meant one was forgiven of his sins. The few times back home when I'd been sick, with strep throat or a 24-hour virus, and I'd called my home teachers from church, I hadn't been healed any sooner than the natural course of the illness. Of course, the one who was sealing the anointing always said, "according to your faith." It had irritated me to no end. I didn't have any faith. I was asking for a blessing so that *their* priesthood and *their* faith could make me feel better. If I could do it all by myself, what would I need them for? So once they said "according to your faith," I still hoped but wasn't surprised when I didn't feel better. Why couldn't they ever say, "You will be healed!" and make me believe it by their surety?

They probably didn't want to look like an idiot the way we did out in Sardegna. Still, it seemed to be asking an awful lot of a sick person that he also must accept the guilt for his own sickness. "You're only still sick because you're so weak and faithless." That sure was never the medicine I needed to help me feel better. And it seemed my whole mission was just more of that same nasty medicinal taste.

Why couldn't Church leaders announce that all gay members could be healed by a blessing from the apostles? If they said it firmly, I'd believe them. I'd have enough faith for that. If they were so close to God, why couldn't *their* faith heal me?

If being gay caused me to sin by not being able to marry, I wondered if diabetics were sinning because they didn't have enough faith to be healed, either, and remaining unhealed meant they couldn't obey the commandment to fast at least once a month. If their "sin" of omission was excused because of something "beyond their control," why wouldn't my sin of omission be excused as well? It always seemed like Church teachings made me the guilty one and no one else.

I looked over at Elder Wright. I didn't much like him. He obeyed most of the rules and was "good" enough, I supposed, but he simply wasn't very pleasant. He always kept trying to tell me how to do things. "That's not a good door approach. Try this." "That's the way you stop people on the street? No wonder you're not a zone leader yet." Naturally, his approaches were no more successful, but he did have the right attitude to rise in the mission hierarchy. Too bad there wasn't a cure for power trips.

The wheels of the train screeched, and we came to a stop rather abruptly. I didn't think much of it until the conductor ran past us a moment later. Elder Wright's eyes lit up. "Come on! Let's go see what happened!"

We hurried after the conductor, who stood near the door at the end of our car. I looked out and saw nothing but an embankment. Then I looked down and saw an old woman lying in a ditch, face down. She was wearing a dark grey skirt or dress and a black sweater, and she had a bandana or handkerchief over her hair. She raised one arm a few inches into the air. It trembled and lay back beside her head. Then she didn't move anymore.

"We hit that old woman!" said Elder Wright, looking at the conductor in astonishment. The conductor ran back toward the front of the train. We stayed by the door, and a few other passengers crowded behind us.

I saw a bag of groceries in the ditch, not far from the woman's legs covered with long black socks, only one foot still wearing a shoe. We were several feet past a street, but the road was just past a hill and a sharp bend in the tracks. The woman had probably been right in the middle of the two sets of tracks before she even knew the train was coming. The street was blocked by a lowered wooden arm, but she must have walked around it, not expecting it meant the train was really that close. I looked again at the woman. She still hadn't moved again. I knew she was dead.

Then an idea came into my head. What if we went out there and gave her a blessing? A shiver ran through me. Was this inspiration? Maybe this meant God did find me worthy. This might be God's way of blessing me.

What if everyone saw us heal her? They'd say she'd only been unconscious, but it would still make an impression. Perhaps this was the Lord's way of helping us make a start in this community. There were so few Mormons in Italy, and none in this town or back in Castel Gandolfo or in any of the towns along this train route, except for a handful in Ciampino.

We held the Melchizedek Priesthood. We held the power to act in God's name. We were elders who'd been through the temple. We had consecrated oil in our pockets.

My heart hurt, beating hard as adrenalin flowed through my body. What if I suggested the blessing to Elder Wright and he didn't want to do it? It took two people for a proper blessing, though one would do in an emergency. What if he thought I was stupid for suggesting it? What if we did it and nothing happened? Would people think we'd been giving the last rites, or would they know we'd failed? We could say the blessing in English so no one would understand, but then that seemed like proof we didn't have faith, and without faith, nothing could happen anyway.

Maybe this wasn't inspiration at all but just my own idea. What if being gay meant I *couldn't* have faith? No, faith was a commandment and commandments had to be obeyed. We needed to get out there before a doctor came along and declared her dead. We needed to do something now before her brain rotted from lack of oxygen, though God could probably heal that, too. Still, there was no point in demanding more of a miracle than we needed.

There were at least twenty people in our car looking on and ten gathered on the road. That could be thirty conversions if they were touched by the Spirit as they witnessed God's power. And if their families joined, that could be thirty or forty more. Then they might talk to a few friends who would join, and with so many people joining so quickly, a few more would get curious. Why, we could baptize a hundred people in just a month, form a new branch of the Church here.

It seemed incredible, but missionaries in South America were baptizing that many all the time. We were told in the Missionary Training Center that we could do it, too, even in Rome where the average number of baptisms in a month for all 120 missionaries was only twelve or thirteen. All we needed was faith like Ammon had in the Book of Mormon. And this might be exactly what the Lord needed us to do to get things rolling in Italy. We didn't even have one stake in the entire country. We should go out there and heal that woman.

I stared at the body in the ditch a few more minutes, a pear near the bag at her feet. I looked back at Elder Wright and then at the woman again. I should tell him, I kept saying to myself. I should tell him. My heart still hurt, and I prayed for the strength and courage to do what was right.

We could baptize a hundred people. This might even make the news. People all over Italy might get interested enough to let us into their homes. A thousand might eventually join. Maybe even a couple of thousand. And this might be the one final test of my faith that God needed me to pass before he could heal me of my homosexuality. This might be my one chance to do something truly meaningful with my life, my one hope to become straight and at least have a chance at getting into heaven. I had to say something to Elder Wright.

My heart beat harder. It *hurt*. I tried to breathe deeply. I had to have faith. I had to have faith.

More people were gathering on the road outside. My delay was going to be okay if I didn't wait any longer. There were even more witnesses now to be touched by the Spirit. It was time to go out there.

I saw an old man coming down the street, walking slowly down the hill, a mildly interested expression on his face, to see what everyone was gawking at. I almost smiled. He was sure in for a surprise. Even old people could change religion when they were converted by the power of the Holy Ghost.

Tell Elder Wright, I said to myself. Nudge him. Tell him.

I suddenly heard a tremendous wail, and everyone outside turned to look. It was the old man. He'd broken past the other spectators and was now kneeling in the ditch next to the bag of groceries. He screamed and cried and pounded the ground, pulling up grass and throwing it on himself. He beat himself in the face. I closed my eyes, but his agonized screams came into the train right into my soul. He sounded like he was being burned alive, screaming and screaming and…

"Come on, everyone, we'll transfer you to a bus and get you on your way," the conductor said, joining us again in the car. He opened the door on the opposite side of the car from the dead woman and her husband. We walked several yards around a bend to a couple of waiting buses, but even inside, I could still hear the man screaming.

"Darn!" said Elder Wright. "I already finished all my letters home." He looked out the window back toward the train as we pulled off. "Oh, well, I guess it gives me something to write about next week."

Long after we drove off, I could still hear the man's screams, even after I knew it was impossible. I closed my eyes and saw him in the ditch next to his wife. He must have loved her deeply even after all those years of marriage.

Why couldn't we be healed of cowardice and insensitivity as well as physical illness? But there was no cure, only "spiritual exercise," and no help from above to do the exercise. Maybe homosexuality wasn't physical, so God *couldn't* heal me. I'd been "exercising" for years and was still as "paralyzed" as ever. But character flaws were things you *did*, and I'd never done anything gay. This was what I *was*. It was physical. It was too hard to figure out.

Earth life was a pool of muddy water, and I'd dived in, thinking it was deep, and broken my neck. Now I was lying at the bottom of a shallow, dirty puddle, unable to move, and trying not to drown while people shouted, "Move! Swim! It's up to you!" Was drowning giving in to sin? If people couldn't exercise enough faith to be cured of the physical ailment of paralysis or stomach cramps or charley horses and drowned, were they morally responsible for bringing about their own early deaths?

I didn't know if I could hold my breath much longer. This filthy puddle covering my eyes was all I could see, was the whole world, and it seemed too ugly to be worth the effort.

No. I could still see more. I could see that man pulling up the grass and beating his chest. He loved that woman.

I felt my eyes water, but I quickly blinked them dry. I could not let Elder Wright see me cry. I glanced over at him. He was trying to catch the eye of a pretty teenage girl near the front of the bus. He hadn't noticed me blinking. Good. I gritted my teeth and stared out the window. My eyes were caught by the ditch along the side of the road, and they followed it like a track as we drove on.

Soon it would be 5:00 and time to get back to work, the start of a new work week. Faithful missionaries once again.

How did one get cured of faithlessness, if it took faith to be cured?

I kept staring out the window at the ditch, looking for an answer, but all I could see were weeds.

The 9:20 Express Train to Hell

"I'm so depressed, Elder Anderson. Why didn't God let me die in that earthquake? It's been months since then, and I still haven't accomplished one good thing. Why couldn't God just let me die? I'm never going to be a good person. I've done so many terrible things in the past. I can't learn the missionary discussions. I can't speak Italian. I'm useless and hopeless. Why can't I just die?"

Elder Quinn and I were standing at the tiny train station at Capannelle, waiting for a local to take us back to Ciampino. We rode the train almost every day in this district but there were no buses, since once we arrived at a town, it was small enough to walk wherever we wanted to go. Elder Quinn was not my official companion, but we were on a "work visit" because Quinn's companion said he was tired of Quinn's whining. "You don't mind working with him one night, do you?" his companion had asked me hopefully.

"No," I said. "I understand him."

So Quinn and I had spent the evening tracting door to door in Statuario, a town between Ciampino and Rome. He didn't enjoy it much, but he did it, and we were able to talk a good bit, which made the evening pass quickly. My companion often never talked at all.

Elder Quinn looked down into the pit at the train tracks. I remembered seeing a newspaper article about a woman who'd jumped in front of a subway in Rome to kill herself. Earlier in my mission I'd thought of jumping in front of a bus.

"Your companion doesn't help much, does he?" I asked.

Elder Quinn shook his head. "He just tells me to snap out of it, to be cheerful, to look on the bright side. You know none of that helps."

I did know. There was a certain level of depression where nothing else mattered. *Nothing* anyone could say made any difference, and I could tell who understood that by what they tried to say. If they tried to cheer me up, it proved they didn't understand, and their lack of understanding only made me feel more alienated and depressed. The very act of trying to cheer up a truly depressed person often made things worse. I felt better now than I had in the past, but I still remembered.

"Life does suck," I said.

Elder Quinn smiled. "Yes," he said. "It does. I've thought about going home to Canada, but my whole ward is depending on me. They're paying my way. I'm wasting their money, but I can't bear to disappoint them by going home."

I nodded. "It's not much better when it's your father paying for it. It's the same feeling."

"But there's so many more people I'm letting down."

I nodded, though I, too, felt the weight of pleasing my home congregation back in Biloxi who mistakenly thought so highly of me.

"Besides, I'm letting my parents down as well. I'm letting the mission down, and the Italians. I'm a failure to *everybody*." He sighed and stared down at the tracks again.

"How often do you think of killing yourself?" I asked.

He turned to me and slowly smiled. "All the time." He shook his head. "If I hadn't been so *stupid*, I wouldn't have run out of our apartment in Castellammare when the earthquake hit. I could have been killed when the roof collapsed right in the middle of the baptism. But I was still so new in the mission." We were both new then, having come out at the same time, almost a year ago now.

"Remember when we were leaving Salt Lake," I asked, "and our plane had engine trouble, so we had to land and change planes?"

Quinn nodded.

"Even then, I thought it would be best to die in a crash, but I didn't want anyone else to die, so I prayed for us to land safely."

"So you've thought about it, too?" Quinn's eyes looked at me hungrily.

"I can't tell you not to do it," I said. "I almost killed myself on my way here from Sardegna." I still wasn't sure it wouldn't have been the best decision.

"You were going to jump overboard?" He smiled at the idea.

I nodded. "It was stormy, so everyone else was below deck, and I was transferring alone, so I didn't have to be with my companion. It was the first time I'd been alone in ages."

"Felt good, didn't it? I mean, I feel like I'm alone all the time, but it's different to be alone *with* someone than without."

I nodded. "So I stood by the railing and looked in the ocean and thought, 'I could jump into the sea and everyone would think I'd slipped because of the storm.' I figured my family might be sad, but not as sad as if they knew I'd killed myself, and not as sad as if…" I thought again about the constant battle with my gay feelings.

"As if you lived," Elder Quinn completed. "I know."

We stood looking at each other a moment, and for the first time perhaps ever, I felt I'd connected with another human being. So often, I had to keep all my doubts to myself, afraid of the condemnation I'd receive if I voiced any of my deep concerns, but Elder Quinn understood. He was a total nothing in the mission, looked down on because even after a year, he'd only learned three of the eight missionary lessons the rest of us learned in two months. But he understood what I felt, and I loved him for it.

An orange and yellow local train pulled into the station, and the doors hissed open. Elder Quinn put his hand on my arm. "Let's take the next one," he said.

Soon the train was gone, and we were alone again on the cement platform. It was about 9:15, so at least we wouldn't be getting in before 9:30 to be criticized for not working long enough. I didn't like "faking" my work hours, but I did want to talk a bit longer, anyway. We could never talk like this in front of the other elders.

"My mother hasn't written me once since I came out here," said Quinn. "My father's only written twice. I tried to call my mom on her birthday, which we're really not supposed to do, but she'd moved without telling me, so I wrote my bishop asking him to find her new address." He shrugged. "I've been writing every week. I don't know how many of my letters she got before she moved."

It was unspeakable. The Church asked parents to write once a week to support the missionaries. Even though Quinn's parents were divorced, they were both members and knew the rule.

Elder Quinn looked off toward Rome for the next train. I studied his profile and the back of his turned head. He was fat, almost round, and some of the other elders made fun of him. He'd played football in high school, but not exercising after graduation had changed his body. I remembered once when he told me about his football buddies. "We were bad," he'd said, shaking his head, "really bad. I didn't think the Church would let me come out on a mission after I confessed." I'd asked what he meant by "bad," but he'd only shaken his head again and said, "really bad." I'd wondered since then if he was gay, but I knew he could have meant drugs or sex parties with girls, or almost anything. Still, homosexuality seemed the only terrible sin that was too terrible to name, so I still wondered. He had a girlfriend who'd stopped writing months ago, but then so did I.

I wanted to put my hand on Quinn's shoulder but was afraid to. If I reminded him of his homosexuality, that might push him over the edge.

Elder Quinn turned to me. "Did I ever tell you what happened last week?"

"When you woke up screaming?" We'd all been scared half to death, and Quinn's companion had yelled at him all the next day for it.

"I dreamed that when I finished my mission, they told me it didn't count because I wasn't good enough, and they made me come back."

"That *is* pretty scary," I said, laughing.

"And when I got back to Italy, my passport had expired and they wouldn't let me in. Then the Red Brigades shot up everyone at the ticket counter while I was trying to get back on the plane, and when I went to the veil to get in heaven, the voice on the other side said, 'Your passport expired. You can't come in.' So they sent me back to my body to lie in the hospital for eternity." He was silent a moment. "There's more, but I just can't tell it."

I tried to keep a blank face, but I felt annoyed. It was impossible to know how to help him if he could never quite confide in me, and yet I knew I couldn't confide in him either. What if his deepest secrets were completely different from mine? He'd never understand me. He must be feeling the same thing. And he might be right. What if he'd molested little children? I couldn't understand that. What if he'd raped teenage girls with his buddies? I couldn't understand that, either. Still, I'd have managed not to say anything awful to him, but I didn't know if the reverse would be true if I spoke up, and most people in the Church thought homosexuality was worse than any sin but murder.

"Do you think you'll go to the Celestial Kingdom?" asked Elder Quinn, talking of the highest degree of heaven, where God the Father and Jesus Christ lived.

"I want to," I said, "and sometimes I think if I want to bad enough, Heavenly Father will have mercy on me, but at other times, I think I'll be lucky if I make it to the Terrestrial." That was the middle kingdom, where reasonably decent people went, but there was no marriage allowed and no sex. Sex was reserved for the Celestial Kingdom and eternal marriages performed in temples. Not being with God and Jesus were supposed to be the reasons we didn't want to make it only to the Terrestrial Kingdom, but I knew most missionaries were thinking about the sex they'd miss if they ended up there.

"I'm hoping for the Telestial," Quinn said, mentioning the lowest level, where even creepy people but not out and out apostates went. One general authority had said even Hitler would make it to this kingdom. But the lowest was still part of heaven. Joseph Smith had once said if we knew how nice the Telestial Kingdom was, we'd all kill ourselves immediately to get there. But it certainly wasn't the place we were supposed to be aiming for.

"I really don't know if I'll go there or to Outer Darkness," Elder Quinn went on, talking of the place Satan and his followers lived. "Sometimes, I feel I'm so damned anyway that it doesn't matter what else I do in this life."

I turned sharply to look at him. Now I knew he was going to kill himself. Those were the exact thoughts I'd had aboard the ship during the storm. I'd felt damned to hell for being gay, so even if suicide was a terrible sin, it could hardly damn me any more than I was already damned. There may have been three heavens, but there was only one Outer Darkness. Once I qualified, it hardly mattered if I overqualified. People were ignorant when they said suicide was selfish. It was true that I wanted to avoid the misery I felt, but I knew perfectly well I was going on to where I'd still be miserable forever. I only wanted to die to spare the people I loved the pain of knowing me as I really was. I didn't think I could keep up a front forever. If I acted on my gay feelings after having had a testimony of the Church, I would be an apostate, the lowest of the low, as bad as Judas Iscariot. I would be worse than a murderer. So I'd stood at the ship's railing after leaving Sardegna and stared down at the churning waves, barely able to see them in the dark, but listening to their soothing roar.

"Do you think..." Quinn began, "do you think God would understand if I gave up?"

"I don't know," I said. "But I understand. And I can't believe I'm able to understand something God can't."

Quinn turned to look me in the face. Then he turned back to look toward Rome.

Was I going to be held responsible for what I'd just said? Was I encouraging him to kill himself? Maybe that would count as a murder against me. But if I was going to hell anyway, did that really matter? I almost *wanted* him to jump. I wasn't brave enough myself, but I so wanted Quinn to escape the misery I felt. Yes, he'd be miserable in hell, but that misery was going to come for us anyway. He'd at least escape *this* misery. So perhaps suicide was selfish after all, but it was unbearable to know every day with every fiber of your being that you so completely failed to be the person the Church expected you to be. It was like asking a person who was on fire to resist jumping into a pool of water. Was it selfish to want to put out the flames?

Maybe I'd jump with Quinn. Of course, if the Church knew he was gay from his earlier confessions, it would look like a lover's suicide pact. I couldn't tarnish my dying reputation when I'd managed to conceal my feelings for so long. But if he did kill himself, it might give me the courage to "trip" in front of a bus when we went to Rome for church some Sunday two or three weeks from now.

On the ship, the only thing that had kept me from jumping was hope. Despite everything, I had still managed to cling to a particle of it. Maybe, just *maybe*, things could somehow work out in my new area. If they didn't, I could always kill myself the next week. It was the way I'd made it through several months of depression now, long preceding the boat trip. I couldn't promise not to kill myself next week, but perhaps I could make it through a few more days first.

"Disse il ruscello un di', voglio a te confidar…" I began singing softly.

Quinn turned to me. "What are you doing?"

"When I was on the ship, I started singing hymns. I sang every verse of every hymn or Church song I could remember, in English and Italian. 'I'm the one that writes my own story,'" I began another song. "I sang for three hours on that deck during the storm. It pulled me through."

"And did things get any better? Are you happy now?"

I looked down onto the tracks. "No," I said.

Quinn nodded. "I used to wonder why God was torturing me so much. But then I realized it was all my own doing. I'm suffering because I'm scum. I really am just a bad person. It's my inner nature, and it's not going to change."

So *did* he mean his gay feelings? Or that he simply never enjoyed doing any kind of Church work at all? I remembered when we'd checked out referrals one rainy day near the hill town of Frascati, and we'd had to climb down several sets of stairs to get to lower levels in the town. "Let us go down," I would say formally, at first unconsciously using some of the dialogue in the temple film from the endowment ceremony we were never supposed to talk about.

"We will go down," Elder Quinn would reply, and we'd laugh as he said the temple film's response. After repeating the dialogue a while, though, Elder Quinn had put a stop to it. "We're really being irreverent," he'd said. "We shouldn't do this." He'd looked up as if expecting to be struck down. I supposed after going through the earthquake, that seemed a real possibility. It seemed to me now that someone who could stop the slightest form of irreverence couldn't be a spirit so bad he must be damned forever to hell.

"Maybe we expect too much from ourselves," I suggested.

"Elder Anderson," Quinn said quietly, "I can't speak Italian after a year. I only memorized three discussions after everyone else has been passing off all eight for months. I'm not expecting miracles. I just want basic competency, and it's beyond me."

"But there are ways to compensate…"

"Don't give me that crap," he said in a whine, squinching his face. "I have no 'special spirit' to get through to people. That's even weaker than my Italian." Elder Quinn did whine a lot, and I knew the other elders always rolled their eyes when he did. The tone was grating, but while everyone else thought Quinn was weak for whining, I knew he was at least being honest. I whined, too, but only in my journal or in my prayers. The other elders always thought I was doing fine. I put on a remarkable show of normalcy every day. I sometimes felt I could win an Oscar for my performance. That made the others happy, but wasn't that just plain old deceit? If everybody thought I was a great guy, but I was every bit as pitiful as Quinn, didn't that make me a hypocrite? And wasn't that about the worst sin Christ ever talked about? Quinn may have been weak, but he was honest enough to say what he felt, and he was honest enough to do what he had to about it. I envied him.

Elder Quinn turned away again to look for the next train. He stiffened as he saw a light approaching from the distance.

He inched just a little closer to the tracks, and I didn't know what to do. If I tackled him at the last minute to save him, was I really doing him a favor by forcing him to live a life he hated? He might put off suicide a little longer and eventually feel better and never do it, or he might simply end up hating me and still killing himself next week. I was Quinn's friend, but I didn't know what a true friend should do, or if I'd be brave enough to do it anyway.

I looked at his round body and remembered the way he'd ravenously eaten lunch earlier, the only pleasure he got out of each day. Did that mean he really wanted to live? Or was that too a form of self-destruction?

I decided I would let him go through with it. I'd make up something to tell everyone about tonight's work to make it look like he'd just started to do well, and that apparently this was all God needed before bringing him "home."

As the train approached, we could see it was a "real" train, not one of the locals. It was an express that wouldn't even be stopping here but barreling through at top speed. Quinn turned to me and smiled as if to say, "It's a sign. God does understand." He nodded once to say goodbye and then looked toward the train again. This was it. I held my breath.

But a hundred yards before the train reached the station, it started to slow down. It finally stopped completely before it even came to the station, something the express trains never did. Then it slowly started and plodded past us at five miles an hour, finally picking up speed after it left the station. No one had gotten on or off. The doors hadn't even opened. The train had simply stopped for no apparent reason. Perhaps it was ahead of schedule or something. It wasn't as if Quinn looked like he was about to pounce. There seemed no reason for the action.

But Elder Quinn turned to me with his mouth hanging open. "God *knew*," he said. "He didn't want me to do it yet." He shook his head in amazement. "He still wants me to do something else first." He looked up into the sky and then towards Rome again. "I guess I'll try, but He'd better help or I'm going to kill myself whether He's ready or not."

He stood staring at the tracks, and I came up beside him, placing my hand on his shoulder. "I'm glad you didn't go yet," I said. "I know it's selfish of me, but I like having you here. Even if *you* don't like you, and God doesn't like you, I like you, even with your secrets." For the briefest second, I wondered if there was something wrong with a gospel that created such despair, but I knew that was my own weakness trying to rationalize, and I felt guilty for yet one more sin. I stopped thinking and softly began singing the words to a hymn I knew. "We are all enlisted till the conflict is o'er. Happy are we! Happy are we!" We had to convince ourselves that things were okay if we were going to get through this. It had helped me before, and we both needed the help now.

Elder Quinn didn't say anything but kept looking at the tracks. "Soldiers in the army, there's a bright crown in store. We shall win and wear it by and by." I stopped singing then, unable to go on, and we just stood there on the platform, not looking at one another, each lost in our own thoughts. We stood in silence several more minutes until a local pulled into the station. Then we boarded silently, took our seats, and headed back home.

Let There Be Light

"Ever hear the one about the four Dagos who tried to change a light bulb?" asked Elder Farnsworth.

I was trying to study, since Elder Farnsworth had been chiding me earlier for struggling over a couple of scripture references when he'd given me a pop quiz on the train back to Ciampino from our tracting area. "Ethnic jokes aren't funny," I said, not looking up.

"Well, how about the one where the Pope, a rabbi—"

I looked up this time. "Elder, how can you make fun of other people's religion when people do that to us as Mormons all the time?"

"Sheesh, Elder Anderson, do you always have to be so grim? Lighten up a little."

"I don't have time to lighten up," I replied, feeling stupid. Before my mission, I'd joked around a lot, finally "blossoming" my last two years in high school, coming in second for "most popular", and even performing a two-minute comedy bit at the school's talent show. Then at church we'd been warned against "loud laughter," which had scared me because I liked to laugh. I felt sure that the cast and writers of *I Love Lucy* received extra points in heaven for making so many people feel good, even if only for half an hour at a time.

Since coming to Italy, though, laughter seemed part of another world. There was always so much pressure to perform that I felt I was in a race that everyone else had started before me, and hard as I might run, everyone was still up ahead. Trying to come from behind in a race where losing meant I was going to hell was not the situation that allowed me to joke with spectators or other runners along the way.

"It's not your time to begin with," Elder Farnsworth pointed out. "When we accepted our mission call, we dedicated these two years to the Lord."

"Well, the Lord apparently hasn't seen fit to include jokes into the program. Nothing in the White Bible about it." I tapped my shirt pocket where I carried my mission rule book everywhere I went. It was one of those mission rules that we have the book with us always, and that we read it once a week. I knew I sounded like a jerk, but I couldn't seem to help myself.

Elder Farnsworth shrugged. "I just don't think the Lord expects us to refuse to develop certain aspects of our character while we're out here. If He's perfect, He must have a perfect sense of humor."

"Shortsheeting my bed last night was not humor at its best."

Elder Farnsworth grinned. "I'll never be perfect in humor, though, unless I work on it, will I?"

I sighed and turned back to my scriptures. I didn't know how he thought I'd be in the mood to laugh anyway after he'd just told the other two elders in our apartment that I was apostatizing because I didn't know all the standard scripture references. He said it as a joke, of course, but how humorous was that? Why did people think criticism was funny?

One companion in Quartu had even criticized the way I walked. We were tracting an old part of town where the sidewalk was only about a foot wide. I'd walked in front of him once as we went down the street. "Don't walk ahead of me," he'd said. "I'm the senior companion." So then I walked behind him. "Don't follow me like a puppy dog," he said next. So I decided to walk beside him, which meant I was now on the cobblestones. "Don't walk in the street. You'll get hit by a car." People criticized constantly out here, all the time, every day.

Sometimes, my companions were deadly serious as they criticized, and other times they laughed, but it felt awful either way. Every time I put on my tie and the knot didn't come out right on the first try, I felt I was going to hell for wasting time or for putting the Church in a bad light by my poor image and example. Even when I did do things right, I felt I was going to hell anyway because I couldn't stop those gay feelings inside, even when I was so depressed I wouldn't have thought anyone could still be interested in sex. Every day, I felt the weight of damnation on my back. What was there to laugh about? Every "joke" about my incompetency seemed like another mile marker on the route to hell.

We were supposed to be an example for the world, a "light set upon a hill," our lives giving enough energy to the people of the world to motivate them to do good. But some days I hardly had the energy to force a smile on my face. The gospel seemed instead to drain energy from me. Perhaps it was my sins that did it, but wasn't light supposed to be stronger than darkness? Why didn't the light of the gospel overpower the darkness of my life, light me and make me a candle for the world to see? Maybe I was poor quality wax. I couldn't get my wick to light.

"Speaking of matches," I thought to myself with a comedian's intonation, there'd once been an incident down in Napoli involving a match. Two of the sisters had arrived home early for lunch and turned on the stove. But they'd forgotten there was no pilot light until several minutes had passed, and when one of the sisters went to light the stove, there was a huge explosion. The burners were blown across the room and the kitchen chairs toppled over. Even the kitchen door was knocked off its hinges. The sisters weren't hurt, but they were so frightened they ran out of the apartment to a neighbor's place. When the other two sisters came home and found the front door open and the kitchen in complete disarray, they thought someone had come in and kidnapped the missing sisters, so they called the police. In the end, the mystery was solved and everyone went out for a Margherita pizza.

The elders repeated the story to show how stupid the sisters were. But what purpose did that serve? I liked sister missionaries. They weren't required to be here like we were. They came because they were genuinely good. Seeing them always brightened my day.

But there were no sisters in our district now. All I had for light was Elder Farnsworth. This morning, after I groggily climbed out of bed and sat at my desk studying the scriptures before breakfast, still half asleep, Elder Farnsworth had come into the bedroom from the kitchen humming merrily. Seeing me slouched over my desk, he pulled up the serranda over the window and began to sing to the tune of an old Neil Sedaka song. "They say that waking up is hard to do. Now I know, I know that it's true. Some say that this is the end. Instead of waking up I wish that we were sleeping in again. I beg of you! Don't turn on that light! Can't we give sleeping another try? Come on, Elder, let's not be blue, 'cause waking up is hard to do."

On one level, I was impressed he could carry the impromptu song that far. On another, I just wanted to hit him for being so cheerful.

"I'm your senior companion," Elder Farnsworth reminded me from his desk, interrupting my thoughts. "So if I say the Lord wants you to lighten up, then—"

The light bulb in the ceiling went out with a little pop, and the room, with the serranda lowered down in front of the window, was cast into darkness.

"Caspita!" said Elder Farnsworth.

"Think the Lord is commenting on your Dago jokes?" I asked. How could God want me to laugh as if nothing were amiss, when almost everything important about me was wrong?

"I think He's telling us to take a break, to stop studying and get to bed early."

"I think I saw a light bulb in the hall closet."

"Oh, all right." He fumbled his way to the door. Once open, it let light in from the hallway. I tried to look at my scripture passages, but I couldn't concentrate any longer.

"I can't find the light bulb," Elder Farnsworth announced from the hall a moment later. "Elder Clark, could you help me look for it?"

"Elder Anderson can't help you? It's your room."

"He's too busy studying in the dark."

"I guess he's not very good at finding things, anyway. Unless he's with Elder Jacobs."

"Hey," said Jacobs.

They were talking about the time a couple of weeks back when we'd all caught the same train at two different stops and so ended up at the apartment at the same exact time for lunch. We'd all squeezed onto the tiny elevator, and Elder Jacobs and I, being the two junior companions, were closest to the doors since we'd followed behind the seniors onto the elevator.

When the doors opened, Elder Jacobs and I walked out, and the other two elders disappeared as the doors closed behind us. I hadn't really thought much about it, figuring they were going back to check on the mail, or that they were going up or down one floor to then race us to the apartment, making a game of it. I didn't think they'd sent *us* to the wrong floor until my key wouldn't fit in the lock, and a woman answered what I thought was our door with a raised letter opener in her hand. Elders Farnsworth and Clark had laughed all through lunch, calling us bad sports because we didn't find it quite as funny.

Sitting in the dim light at my desk, I wondered if it were true, if I really had lost all sense of humor, if humor had been burned right out of me. Missions were supposed to improve people, not turn them into bitter old men.

I smiled. At least I still had a sense of tragedy, if not a sense of humor.

Then I realized I had smiled. A rather cynical smile, of course, but it was something.

Elder Farnsworth came back into the room then holding a light bulb. He looked up at the ceiling. "Can you reach it?" I asked. He stood on the rug in the middle of the floor and stretched upwards. Elder Farnsworth was only five and a half feet tall, and our ceiling must have been ten feet high. I snickered. Morally, that was as bad as an ethnic joke, but he was so earnest I couldn't resist.

"You do it, smarty pants."

"You said I needed to see the humor in things."

"Very funny."

He handed me the light bulb, and I dragged my chair under the fixture. Even standing on that, however, I couldn't reach it. The ceiling must have been even higher than I thought.

"Close only counts in horseshoes," said Elder Farnsworth. "If you can't reach the light, let's get someone else."

"Maybe if I put some books on the chair," I said.

"You can't stand on the scriptures. You'll fall." When I gave him an odd look he added, "You're too symbolic, Elder. I don't think you live quite enough."

That was almost the same thing he told me a few days earlier, when a family from our congregation had invited all four of us to dinner one evening. We were sitting around the table talking, waiting for the food to finish cooking, and the family had the T.V. set on in the room. I'd have had to turn my head sharply to the right to look, though I could do it when I turned toward Elder Farnsworth. The T.V. was directly behind him, so he had no chance of looking, but we could both see the other two elders stealing glimpses whenever they could.

It was a rule that we not watch television for the two years we were here, but we were all drawn to it, as any American teenager would be. My last companion insisted we "fellowship" a family, supposedly to help them become stronger in the gospel, but all we really did was go over once a week and watch Japanese cartoons like *Speed Racer* with them in the evening. I always felt condemned in our work for not being more obedient, so when there was a rule I could follow but wasn't allowed to, I felt doubly frustrated.

With the T.V. off to my right during the dinner, I sneaked only a few glances at the screen. Since Elder Farnsworth wasn't looking at it, I knew he'd criticize me later if I did, and it wasn't worth it. Besides, I needed all the blessings I could get from obedience.

Finally, Elder Jacobs had turned to Elder Farnsworth and said, "You sure are being bravo. You aren't even trying to look."

"Of course not," he replied. "I can see the reflection perfectly clearly in that glass cabinet over there." He nodded toward the opposite wall. I looked over, and sure enough, there was a clear reflection. My mouth dropped open.

"That's obeying the Spirit of the Law!" Elder Clark laughed. "You flipper!"

"Elder," I said, amazed.

"Oh, Elder Anderson," said Farnsworth. "Live a little." I refused to look at the reflection, but I noticed the other two elders following Farnsworth's example, glancing frequently at the flickering light from the glass cabinet throughout the evening. It seemed hypocritical, yet they looked happier than I felt, and over the last few days, I hadn't been any more successful in the work than they'd been. Yet their smiles somehow made me think of all the conference issues of the *Ensign*, with pictures of grinning Latter-day Saints inserted in the middle of all the General Conference texts by the leaders of the Church. The effect was supposed to be, "What a happy people the Mormons are," but what I always wondered was, "How can they be so happy when there is so much suffering in the world?" It seemed almost sinful to be happy, knowing others were starving or sick or being tortured on such a grand scale worldwide. It felt like mockery to see them smile while I felt depressed, and I knew there were certainly people hurting a lot more than I was. Was creating a "show" of happiness supposed to be inspiring to others? Pagliacci did it, but he'd still been driven to murder in his underlying despair.

"Hey, Elder Jacobs!" Elder Farnsworth called out now. "Could you come here a minute?"

Elder Jacobs came in from his room down the hall. "Yeah?" said the six-foot, five-inch-tall missionary.

"Think you could help us change the light bulb?"

"I don't know." He stood up on the chair and could just barely reach the light. "Will I get shocked? You know the current is stronger over here in Italy."

"No, you won't get shocked. Would you please unscrew the bulb?"

Elder Jacobs looked at Farnsworth suspiciously in the light that filtered in from the hall. "If I won't get shocked, why won't you change it?"

"I can't reach it."

"Well, I'm afraid. Let Elder Clark do it." He stepped down from the chair.

"It's not an electric chair, you know," Elder Farnsworth muttered.

Elder Clark climbed up next, but being an inch shorter than I was, he couldn't reach the light, either.

"Pick!" Elder Farnsworth said, clapping me on the back. "I guess we can't study any more tonight, after all." Elder Clark stepped down, and Elder Farnsworth reached under the pillow on his cot and pulled out his pajamas. "Well, goodnight all!"

"So we're never going to study again at night, ever?" I asked. "We'll need to change the bulb sometime. I don't suppose we'll be any taller in the daylight." I looked at Elder

Jacobs. "We may be growing boys, but we're not growing plants."

Elder Farnsworth turned to me with a smile. "He made a funny. Elder Anderson made a funny." The other two elders looked at each other blankly, but Elder Farnsworth looked at me almost seriously and nodded.

I was hardly being funny, though. And yet, maybe there was only a fine line between mild humor and sarcasm. Perhaps I wasn't too far gone to go back across that line.

"Wait a minute," said Elder Clark. "I have an idea. Come help me, Elder Farnsworth." They walked over to Farnsworth's desk and began dragging it across the floor. We heard a dim shout from the apartment below, and Farnsworth and Clark giggled. The two missionaries lifted the desk and placed it down on the rug under the light. We were the only two elders I knew of in the mission with a rug, and I enjoyed seeing the orange, green, and black designs. Most floors were either marble or terrazzo, so anything we dropped broke on impact.

One neighbor above us in my last apartment in Quartu must have figured out our sleep schedule, because he would release a bag of marbles across the floor almost every night twenty minutes after we were in bed. We'd hear them rolling for five more minutes. "We'll laugh about this one day," my companion had said. But I wondered how something that wasn't funny could become funny just by the passage of time. Then again, before I saw *Arsenic and Old Lace*, I'd wondered how a movie about murder could possibly be funny, but I'd watched, and it was in fact hilarious. Humor must be one of those mysteries of God. I'd heard that some people with cancer had even healed themselves by watching comedies. Maybe the reason I couldn't cure myself of homosexuality was because I was too serious all the time. I thought I had to be serious with such a serious problem, but maybe what I really needed was to laugh more.

Elder Clark climbed up on the desk and reached for the light bulb. "Aha!" He twisted it out and handed it to Jacobs, who took it reluctantly, holding it gingerly as if he thought it might explode. Then Farnsworth handed the new light bulb to Clark, who reached up again and screwed it in. "Let there be light!" The room was flooded with the bright rays.

"Thanks a lot, Elder Clark," my companion said, picking his pajamas up from his bed and shoving them back under his pillow. "I appreciate your help."

"No problem." He and his companion headed back for their room.

"Help me move my desk back, would you, Elder Anderson?" I grabbed one end as he lifted the other, and we started carrying it back to its corner. I didn't lean over to make up for the difference in our height, so a couple of his books and a report he was making out started sliding across the surface. I stooped quickly to compensate just as Elder Farnsworth lifted up his side of the desk. His jar of pens jumped off and crashed onto the floor, sending glass everywhere. We heard another muffled shout from the apartment below.

"What happened?" exclaimed Elder Clark, rushing into the room as my companion and I set the desk down in the corner.

"The jar fell off," I said, sighing. I squatted down and began picking up some of the larger pieces. "Could you help us? This really made a mess."

"Sure thing." The three of us crawled along the floor, carefully picking up shards of glass from the rug, occasionally reaching under my companion's desk and bed for stray fragments. Within a couple of minutes, we had gathered up most of the glass, but I could still see tiny reflections of light coming from the rug, and I knew we'd never be able to pick out all the remaining minute pieces.

Elder Farnsworth and I thanked Elder Clark again for his help, and then Clark went back to his room. "What do you think, comp?" I asked. "Looks like we're going to have some painful prayers."

"People in some religions kneel on glass purposely," he said, rolling his eyes.

"Uh huh." Mormons just believed in a different kind of self-torture.

"Let's take it out to the kitchen balcony and beat it," Farnsworth suggested, grabbing one corner of the rug. "Needs cleaning, anyway."

We carried the rug through the kitchen and out onto the small balcony. Fighting with the empty clotheslines, we made it to the railing and hung the rug over. This was the same balcony from which we watched the old man across the street. He was usually there on his balcony each afternoon, talking to his cane. Once, a little over a week ago, we met him down in the street and talked with him a few minutes. After chatting briefly, we asked how old he was.

"I'm eighty-three." He'd paused and then corrected himself. "I mean, I'm ninety-three. No, wait. I'm eighty-nine."

Elder Farnsworth smothered a giggle, but I gave him a stern stare. "Well, what year were you born?" I asked.

He lifted his cane a bit and answered proudly, "January 30th."

Elder Farnsworth giggled openly, and I nudged him. "No, what *year* were you born in?" I insisted.

"Oh!" said the man, finally understanding the question. "1809."

Even I couldn't control myself after that. I felt bad for laughing, but Elder Farnsworth whispered that the man didn't know why we were. In fact, the man started laughing, too. Then he hugged us both before we left. He was probably just glad anyone would pay attention to him. I knew that thought should make me sad, but I'd felt better that day after running into him, and I felt better now remembering him. I felt good, too, remembering how Elder Farnsworth had insisted we bring some peaches to him yesterday that a member had given us. We'd stayed and talked with the old man for fifteen or twenty minutes. It hadn't seemed terribly "productive," and all I could think was that if I'd suggested it, I'd have been criticized for wasting time. I tried to let go of that feeling now and just remember the man's smile.

I looked at Elder Farnsworth standing along the railing trying to make sure the rug didn't slip out of his hands. I didn't understand him. Yesterday, he'd been so nice to that man when he couldn't get anything out of it, and the man probably wouldn't remember us a week after we left the area. And yet tonight, while we were tracting, he'd seemed to try deliberately offending another man.

We'd knocked on a door, and a man opened up, puffing away at a pipe and looking very superior. "I'm really not interested," he said and started to close the door.

"Please," said Elder Farnsworth, though I was already turning away. "We promise not to talk about how we disapprove of tobacco." I turned back in surprise. "You won't even know we think your smoking is a sin. No, sir, you won't feel any judgmental attitude coming from us. We just want to come in and teach you for a few minutes about the right way to live."

I stood with my mouth open, and the man looked from me to Elder Farnsworth and then began laughing. "I'm still not interested," he said, "but why don't you leave me a pamphlet or something?"

Elder Farnsworth handed him one, and after we left, he said, "Still disapproving? You'll make a great zone leader one day."

That threw me for a second, and I stammered, "It's just—it's just that—"

Elder Farnsworth stopped me on the stairwell landing between floors and put his hands on my upper arms to hold me. "It's not a sin to enjoy our work. Somewhere along the way, you've had your life drained out of you. The work is serious, and the mission has some hard rules, but when we agreed to give up two years to serve, it was two years of time, not two years of life. Elder, you must find a way to come alive."

Everyone beat me down out here, even Elder Farnsworth at times, and now I was blamed for being beaten. It wasn't a rejuvenating thought.

But on our way home, I'd noticed grass growing out of a crack in the sidewalk, and a flower growing out of a crack in a wall. Sterile places, I realized, but life found a way. Plants could make food with only water, carbon dioxide, and light.

All life on Earth depended on plants getting light, getting energy from light. The greatest creatures on the planet, the dinosaurs, had died because plants stopped getting enough light.

There was no comet dust which was clouding my vision, though. People right next to me seemed to be getting plenty of light, so why wasn't I? Was I in someone's shadow, my light blocked off? Maybe I'd closed my leaves like those tiny Mimosa plants I'd played with as a child, the leaves closing when I touched them, pestered into denying themselves light. Or maybe I'd experienced shock like plants that lost their leaves when transplanted. They had to pull on their reserves to make new leaves or die. Perhaps I was like a patch of grass someone had placed a board over. How could a blade of grass move a board out of the way to find light?

I smiled. Surely, my bizarre analogies were at least giving God a chuckle. I was good for something, anyway.

I looked at Elder Farnsworth again as he tried to wave the rug to dislodge the glass particles. I liked Elder Farnsworth. I didn't want to be so difficult for him. He was one of the few leaders who'd been nice to me at least part of the time. I ought to lighten my mood for his sake, if nothing else. But I wasn't sure I could change even for myself.

I tried to wave the rug, too, but even together, we didn't knock off many glass fragments. We could still see them shimmering in the rays from the streetlight. We shook harder, and with a whiplash effect, we made some dust fall out, and maybe a little glass as well.

"Just a second," said Farnsworth, leaving me with the rug while he went back inside. He returned a moment later with a broom.

Elder Farnsworth and I both held onto the rug while he tried to beat it with one hand. He couldn't get much leverage with the broom, but he did manage to hit the rug several times. Of course, he also hit the railing behind the rug, too. The sound of clanging metal echoed out into the night as the dust and glass particles fell freely from our rug and drifted downward. The shouts from the apartment below us weren't muffled anymore.

"Flip!" Elder Farnsworth was so startled at the cursing that he dropped the broom, which banged against the balcony railing below us before crashing to the street. We managed to hold onto the rug, though, and pulled it back over the railing, carrying it into our bedroom, almost tiptoeing. We spread the rug out on the floor, and then stood up and looked at it. The colors seemed brighter.

It reminded me of a tree we'd seen while getting referrals in the park one day. The sunlight had hit the tree at just the right angle and I took a deep breath as I watched the tree being transformed into a spectacularly beautiful image when the light was reflected from its leaves. I stared for a couple of minutes, and then the angle of light changed again, and the tree became ordinary once more, blending in with the other trees nearby.

I just needed to see myself under a different light. I'd seen actors under different lighting look very different, or clothes look a different color. One of my friends back home at church, a guy who always wore colored dress shirts with his suits and not white shirts like everyone else, had a brown car. It seemed so out of character that I finally asked about it. "I bought it at night," he explained. "And under the fluorescent lights at the dealership, it looked purple. It wasn't till the next day after I got it home that I realized what color it really was."

Was I seeing myself under fluorescent light or natural light? What was my true color?

"Looks nice," I said, nodding at the rug. "Cleaner than it's been in a while."

"Yes, it is. Thanks for helping me." Farnsworth stood looking at the rug while I went back to my desk and sat down, trying to find my place in the scriptures. I would learn just one more verse tonight, polish up just one small area rather than try to get all sparkling at once.

"Elder?" asked Farnsworth, not moving toward his desk and the report he'd been working on before.

"Yeah?"

"Do you have to study any more tonight?"

All that work to fix the light just to turn it off? I had to get those verses memorized sometime. Even if Farnsworth had only been teasing me earlier on the train, another companion later would be serious, and I'd already been out here for ages. I could be a little lighter on myself, but I didn't have forever to become a good missionary.

I looked at Elder Farnsworth, who looked now like a little puppy dog. "Can't we take a break once in a while?" he asked. "Hasn't my joking taught you anything about relaxing? Even the Lord took a break. What do you think the Sabbath is for?"

"Are you saying the Sabbath is a joke?"

His mouth fell open, and I smiled. It did feel good to play a little.

He slowly smiled, too, but shook his head. "Your humor still needs some work."

"Okay," I said, laughing, "we can go to bed."

"Spoken like a true senior companion." Elder Farnsworth nodded. "It won't be long now." He reached under his pillow and pulled out his rumpled pajamas.

"But how about some cookies and milk on our picnic blanket before we go to sleep?" I motioned to the floor. Elder Farnsworth grinned and went to the kitchen to grab what we'd need, and as I watched him struggling back with his hands full, I wished we didn't have separate cots. The realization made me feel depressed again.

But I smiled as Elder Farnsworth set the plastic cups on the rug next to our tiny milk cartons. Maybe I didn't have direct sunlight on me yet, but if I could somehow make artificial light long enough, perhaps I could survive. I sat on the floor next to Farnsworth, pouring milk for us both, and opening my pack of cookies, offering him first pick. "Elder?" I asked.

"Yeah?" He took a cookie, dipped it in his cup, and thrust it in his mouth whole, chomping as he waited for me to go on.

I tried to evoke my most casual air as I dipped a cookie in some milk and looked up at him innocently. "Ever hear the one about the four elders who tried to change a light bulb?"

Being Bravo

"Buona sera," I began but went no farther in my prayer, stopping as my companion started laughing at my mistake.

"We're not tracting him out," Elder Farnsworth said. "You can address him directly."

I smiled and began again, "Nostro Padre Celeste…"

We prayed in Italian and were always supposed to speak in Italian, but usually the Americans here in the Italy Rome Mission spoke English except when out of our apartments, and sometimes even then. I preferred Italian, wanting to use what I'd struggled so hard to learn, but it was impossible to speak Italian when everyone around me was speaking English. I knew a couple of the other missionaries back in Napoli who'd done so. I'd listen to half a conversation in English and the other half in Italian, as neither elder would give in. Obeying the rule to speak Italian could be done, but the other elders always rolled their eyes at the ones "trying to be bravo."

I prayed now in Italian, asking Heavenly Father to bless us that we might be able to reach those here in Ciampino who would be open to hearing our message, to help us be "Loyal to the Royal in Italy Rome," as our mission song declared. I also asked God to help us as we visited the two Mormon families later in Velletri. So far from either the

Tuscolano or Trionfale branches of the Church in Rome, they needed the strength we could bring them.

"…nel nome di Gesu' Cristo. Amen."

I lifted my head and opened my eyes, automatically reaching out to shake Elder Farnsworth's hand, but he was gone.

I heard a giggle and turned around. While I was praying, my companion had walked softly to the far corner of the room behind me.

"You flipper," I said.

"The good news is you were paying attention to God and not to me."

"And you were paying attention to…?"

He just grinned. "Don't dent your halo worrying about it."

I smiled. Elder Farnsworth frequently joked about my "halo" because I always insisted on doing things like dedicating our new tracting zone, or blessing a pear if we stopped to eat at a fruit stand during the day, or buying one meal a week for a man we'd met more than a month ago who was clearly struggling to make ends meet. Whenever one of the other elders in our apartment asked Elder Farnsworth why he kept talking about my halo, my companion would simply reply, "Oh, Elder Anderson's just trying to be bravo again."

It was 3:30, our two-hour lunch period was over, and we wouldn't be back until 9:30 tonight. Ciampino, just outside of Rome, wasn't much of a town, but we walked down to the main street and spent an hour walking back and forth, trying to work up the nerve to stop someone and attempt to interest them in the Church. In an hour's time, we only stopped two people, and neither was interested. I'd soon had enough of this "twenty-four hour" work, and we walked to the train station and bought tickets to Velletri, a little town several kilometers away.

We passed vineyards and a couple of other small towns along the way. I remembered once we'd stopped at a station and I'd asked my companion where we were. He'd looked out, read a sign, and then told me, "We're in Gabinetti." He laughed when I pointed out he'd read the sign for "bathrooms." Another time, my companion read the sign for the town of Albano but pronounced it "Al bagno," meaning "at the bathroom."

The train soon stopped in Velletri. It was still too early to visit either of our two member families here, so we decided to do a little "spirit tracting." That meant we were tracting outside our specified tracting zone, which was back in Ciampino, picking houses now as the Holy Ghost supposedly directed us. I never seemed to be especially inspired, but I gave it a shot now.

As usual, though, no one acted particularly interested today. I knew that I didn't often have the Spirit with me. My secret shame of being homosexual was still holding me back. We tracted for an hour without success and then called it quits. After stopping in a restaurant so Elder Farnsworth could use the bathroom, we headed over to see the Mangiapia family on the far side of town. I loved their name, and thinking of it put me in a better mood. "Mangia" meant "eat" and "pia" could mean either "slowly" or "softly," so their name meant basically, "Eat slowly." We had in the past taught people named Ciambella, which meant "doughnut," Salsiccia, which meant "sausage," and Mozzarella, which was of course a type of cheese. We'd even once knocked on the door of a family named Mormone. I'd felt sure *they'd* be interested, but I was wrong.

"Buona sera, Anziani," Sister Mangiapia said when she opened her door. "How are you this evening?" She ushered us inside, where her two children, Mario and Elena, about ten and twelve years old, were sitting. Her husband was still at work at their tiny pizzeria. They'd been members almost three years but rarely came to church because of the distance. Still, they were happy to see the missionaries when we came by maybe once a month.

The kids told us about school, Mario also sharing enthusiastic stories about his soccer team. Elena said she was talking to her friends about the Church and would let us know when we could go visit their families. The kids seemed comfortable chatting with us, never a given, and I had something I wanted to tell them, too. "Mario," I said, pulling out an envelope. "You said last time you liked to collect stamps."

"Yes," he said hopefully, looking at the envelope.

"I asked all the elders in the district to tear off the stamps on our letters from America. Would you like them?"

"Oh, wow, thanks!"

I hadn't wanted to favor one of the children over the other, but I couldn't think of anything special to bring Elena and so in the end had just bought a handful of chocolate Baci and handed them to her now.

"Thank you, Anziani," she said, blushing.

"Always trying to be bravo," Elder Farnsworth muttered to me under his breath.

We then turned our attention back to Sister Mangiapia. She worked part time in the pizzeria but tried to be home when the children returned from school. We told her about a man we were teaching in Ciampino, and she suggested maybe she and her husband could meet him sometime if things started getting serious. They couldn't get out to church much but wanted to help the kingdom grow if they could. She still read the Book of Mormon every day and prayed every night.

"Have you eaten yet?" she asked after the conversation began to drag.

"No," I said. We usually didn't eat dinner at all unless we had a dinner appointment with a family.

"Why don't you stop by the pizzeria? Alfonso will be glad to see you, and you can each have a couple of slices of pizza on us."

"Okay," said Elder Farnsworth. "Thanks."

We walked two blocks to the tiny pizzeria. Brother Mangiapia was behind the counter, but there was no one else in the store just then, so he wasn't busy. "Hello, Elders," he said, smiling broadly. I had only met him once before. I thought him a handsome man, with beautiful olive skin and a bushy moustache, and it was hard not to look at him too long. My eyes caught his, and I couldn't look away. Then he nodded at me as if he knew. I was terrified but kept looking.

"Elder Farnsworth, pick a couple of slices of pizza," he said.

Elder Farnsworth picked a slice of tuna fish pizza with tomato chunks and a slice of potato pizza. Brother Mangiapia handed him the slices.

"Elder Anderson, I need to talk to you in back for a minute."

My knees felt weak, but I followed Brother Mangiapia in back to the storeroom. Was he going to denounce me? I'd be sent home in disgrace if people found out I was gay. I'd tried so hard all this time to fight it, but I always felt completely transparent. It amazed me that no one had found out yet. And now it looked like somebody had.

"Elder Anderson," he said, looking me in the eyes and putting his hand on my shoulder, "I know."

"Kn-know what?" Maybe I could still bluff my way out.

He pulled me close and kissed me on the lips. I felt a thrill as his moustache rubbed against my face. But I pushed him away. "What are you doing?" My heart was beating fast and hard. I didn't know what to do.

Brother Mangiapia unzipped his pants and pulled his erect penis out. I couldn't help but look at it. It was…so pretty. I wanted to touch it. But I felt like I was being hit by a bus. How could we be having an innocent conversation one minute and he being trying to have sex the next? It was so abrupt. I couldn't quite fathom what was happening. "Want to suck me?" he said. "You can 'eat it slowly' if you like," he said, laughing. "I'll suck you if you'd rather. I only get a chance like this a couple of times a month."

"Brother Mangiapia," I said calmly, though I was trembling, "this is wrong. You can't do this."

"Don't you want to? I can see you do. Come on. We can't take too long." He started stroking his penis and licked his lips suggestively.

I was shocked by his crudeness. "Brother Mangiapia, what would your wife say?"

"My wife doesn't need to know. I satisfy her needs. If I have further needs of my own, that's my business, not hers."

I shook my head firmly. I'd never before had sex, and I certainly didn't want my first time to be in a back room, a "quickie" with someone I hardly knew. Of course, I planned to wait until I married a woman, but even if I did fall into sin with a man, it wouldn't be like this. It would be—

"Well, let's just keep this to ourselves then," said Brother Mangiapia. He zipped his pants back up and now cupped my crotch with his hand. He could feel that I was erect, too, so there was no denying I'd liked what I'd seen. He smiled and gave me a wink. "If you change your mind, just stop by again. We always like visits from the elders."

He looked in my eyes a moment and then leaned forward slowly and kissed me again. I didn't pull away and actually hoped he might try to stick his tongue in my mouth.

I'd heard that was called French kissing, but I wasn't sure. I finally broke away and wiped my lips. Brother Mangiapia laughed and winked again.

Then we both stepped back into the front of the store, and Brother Mangiapia urged me to take a slice of pizza. I felt I would be consenting to keep his secret if I did, but I didn't know that I wanted to report him, either. He was obviously committing a grave sin, yet I somehow felt stupidly protective of him, too. Was I being an accessory to sin if I kept quiet?

I took a slice of pizza bianca, the cheapest pizza available, only crust with olive oil and a few spices like rosemary on top. Elder Farnsworth had already eaten one of his slices, and we both left now with a slice apiece. "Thanks, Brother Mangiapia." Elder Farnsworth waved as we left.

"Have a good evening, Elders."

We walked to the corner and stopped to finish our pizza. "What did he want to see you about?"

I still felt myself trembling but tried to sound unconcerned. "Oh, he drank a cup of coffee and felt guilty," I said, "but I told him if he repented it would be okay." Lying was an offense that put you down in the Telestial Kingdom, but this was Brother Mangiapia's sin to confess, not mine. Besides, what if I told on him and he in turn told on me?

I had often dreamed of the time when I would be approached by another man. In college, I'd look hopefully at other guys passing my cubicle in the library. And in the bathroom, I'd hope to be groped from behind or pulled into a stall. I even picked up hitchhikers a few times, thinking maybe I'd be forcibly taken advantage of. I was too scared and too shy and too stupid to know how to approach a man myself, but I knew I'd be only too willing to go along with another man if the opportunity ever presented itself. Now it had, though, and I'd turned it down. So was I stupid? Or miraculously righteous?

Most likely, I was too shocked at the suddenness of the offer, and I'd probably start regretting the missed opportunity by nightfall.

This was a turning point in my life. I could feel it. If I could resist real temptation, maybe God would finally cure me.

But what had happened to Brother Mangiapia? Why wasn't *he* cured? He'd had sex with a woman regularly for over thirteen years, and he was still gay. He'd received forgiveness for past sins at his baptism and also been given the gift of the Holy Ghost when he was confirmed. Was he just not trying hard enough?

Well, *I* was trying. And I would be straight. "If thou canst believe, all things are possible to him that believeth." I believed.

Now I had to use the bathroom, so my companion and I stopped at the restaurant again where we'd gone earlier. As I stood there peeing, I looked at the toilet in the grimy room and knew that if there were indeed "many houses" in heaven, mine would be a grungy bathroom. Whether God pissing on my soul or was I pissing on it myself, I wasn't sure, but I definitely smelled piss!

I thought back on the communal bathrooms at the Missionary Training Center. I remembered how if I had to defecate, I was mortified to have anyone know, so I tried to get back to the dorm first after gym class, before anyone else was in the bathroom. But one time, I'd gotten in and saw another man's feet under one of the stall doors.

Normally, I'd have chosen the stall furthest from him and hoped not to be noticed. But that day, I didn't really have to defecate that badly, yet I still went in and sat down. I felt strangely intimate with the other man, sensing what I knew was a repulsive desire to thrust my penis into that hole I knew the man next to me was using. What a sick, sick person I had to be. What kind of horrendous creature was I to want to get into someone's asshole?

Of course, I was even more interested in having another man's penis, either in my hand, or in my mouth, even in my own asshole. I'd heard a guy at college one day joking, "If God had meant for a man to be fucked, he'd have given him an asshole." I thought such talk was base. And yet after the guy in the stall next to me left, I did go ahead and defecate, fantasizing that the pulling apart of my sphincter was being caused by another man getting inside of me.

I didn't see any possible way for redemption when my very nature was so appalling. Appalling wasn't even an adequate word to describe how low I was. Straight men didn't go in a bathroom and think about sex. Straight women didn't. People were right to loathe gays. I loathed myself, too.

After leaving the restaurant, my companion and I walked a few minutes over to the Stefanuccis' house.

Brother and Sister Stefanucci and their teenage daughter Gabriella were in, and they welcomed us inside. They'd been members five years, two years of that as the only Mormons in town, and even now they made up half the members here. It was a long time to be so alone.

Despite knowing there was another member of the Church who was gay, I felt more alone than ever. Before, I'd had just my own secret to worry about. Now I had two secrets. I wondered if I'd feel better if I talked to Brother Mangiapia, unburdened myself. I'd never talked to anyone about it before, not any family member, not any friend, not the bishop.

But what if the temptation to do more than talk was too great? Could I take the chance? I wasn't sure I could trust myself. Brother Mangiapia was proof that gays had no self-control. There was no reason to think I'd be any better. I needed to forget about it for now, though, and I tried to clear my head. I needed to focus on this other family who also needed our support. We were here to offer strength. The very idea almost made me sick, but I smiled and made a joke about the weather.

Brother Stefanucci told us how things were going for him at work. He didn't talk to his friends about the Church because he was afraid they'd abandon him. A couple of his friends didn't even know he was Mormon. It was too risky to let them know he was so different from 99% of the rest of the population. One of our mission programs was to give an address book to each member and have them write down the names and addresses of their friends we could visit. This was called "cultivating" the members. But it was clear Brother Stefanucci wasn't interested, so I didn't suggest it.

Sister Stefanucci told us she was worried her daughter Gabriella was going out with a boy who couldn't be trusted. Gabriella grew indignant at this and walked out of the room. "I think," said Sister Stefanucci haltingly, then turned her voice into a whisper, "I think they may be having sex."

For God's sake, tell her to use a condom, I wanted to say, but what I said instead was, "All you can do is let her know what's right, and that you love her no matter what. It's up to her to make the right decision."

Straight people could be forgiven easily enough for sex, anyway. It was a serious transgression for them as well, but even my own parents told me they'd had sex with each other before getting married. I wondered how you could repent of premarital sex if you'd ended up marrying the person involved and now couldn't face temptation for that sin anymore. How could you prove you'd really repented? That you wouldn't do it again under the same circumstances? Their forgiveness somehow didn't seem fair, but there certainly seemed to be no repercussions for my parents or others like them now, however serious sexual sin was supposed to be.

"Couldn't you talk to her?" begged Sister Stefanucci. "You're closer to her age. She'll listen to you. She won't listen to us."

I was irritated at being put in the position of moral leader. Of course, it was too far for the family to go to church on Sunday, so they never had a chance to talk to the branch president there, and he never came way out here. He'd be the appropriate person to deal with this. But we were here, and we were all they had. Yet why were they asking *me*? I wasn't even the senior companion.

"Okay."

"Go ahead. Knock on her door."

I motioned for Elder Farnsworth to follow, and I walked over to Gabriella's door and knocked, probably a little too timidly. "Chi e'?" she said from inside.

"It's Elder Anderson. Can I come in for a minute?" Wouldn't she see me for the hypocrite I was? Surely, everyone could tell.

There was a pause and then a begrudging "Si'." I opened the door and saw Gabriella sitting on her bed. I hesitated and then sat beside her, motioning for my companion to sit next to me.

"Parents can be hard to deal with sometimes," I said.

"Tell me about it."

"It's just that they remember the temptations they felt at your age."

"Please."

"And the temptations they probably still feel. Even if you get a little older and a little heavier, you still feel temptation. It never goes away." I hoped that wasn't true.

I looked at the floor and shook my head. Did all people talking about these things feel like idiots?

"You feel temptation here with me?" She tried to act flirtatious, and I saw Elder Farnsworth smile.

"Yes," I lied. "We can't even go on dates while we're out here," I said. Then I decided the best way to get through to her was to be completely direct. "We can't even masturbate for two years."

I heard Elder Farnsworth gasp, and Gabriella looked startled, too. "We're not saying you can't ever have sex," I went on. "We're just asking you to wait a couple of years, like we do. It's not the end of the world."

"Have you ever had sex?" she asked.

"I haven't, but Elder Farnsworth has."

"Elder!"

"She has to know it's okay to stop once you've started," I said. "It's harder to wait once you've had sex." I paused. "Apparently, it's rather nice. But it's worth waiting for."

Gabriella didn't say anything.

"Anyway, just think about it."

"Okay."

We left Gabriella and rejoined her parents, assuring them we'd had a good talk with their daughter. "Don't worry too much," I said. "She's pretty brava." It was ridiculous really to think that I could persuade the girl to be virtuous. Even though Elder Farnsworth had confessed to having sex before his mission, he'd repented and was now innocent. I, on the other hand, while still a virgin, was far more sinful, because what I wanted was an abomination. Maybe by talking to Gabriella, I had convinced myself to try a little harder to do the right thing. The whole incident left me feeling more stupid and sinful than ever. My "halo" felt like the ring of scum around the inside of a toilet bowl.

The Stefanuccis offered us some orange soda and asked us when there would be a temple in Rome. "We don't even have a stake yet," I said, Rome being several congregations short of that.

We chit chatted some more, not saying anything important, but the Stefanuccis didn't seem to want us to go. Finally, though, I glanced at my watch and realized we only had fifteen minutes before the train left. Elder Farnsworth offered a prayer, and then we departed.

As soon as we were out the door, we started running. It had begun lightly raining, so the cobblestones were slick, but we ran up the hill from their apartment, and then around a corner, and down another hill, hoping to make it to the station in time. We ran past paneficios and pasticcerias and alimentari shops. We ran past cheese shops and tobacco shops and butchers. We ran past a shoe store where a man was urinating on the metal grating that was pulled down over the door. Even running by, I found myself straining to get a peek. I slipped on a cobblestone and almost fell, but Elder Farnsworth caught me and we kept running.

This ridiculous race happened every single time we came to Velletri. We always stayed too long and had to fight to catch the last train. We called it "the Velletri Run." Why in the world did we always put ourselves in this position? We knew the right thing to do, but we always succumbed to temptation and stayed until it was almost too late. We deliberately put ourselves in a dangerous position for no real reason. We'd get in trouble if we didn't get back to our apartment and in bed before our 10:30 "lights out."

We ran past the Banco dello Spirito Santo and a gelateria and turned another corner. Finally, still running, we made it to the top of the last hill, and from here, we could see the train down at the platform. But had it just arrived? Or was it just about to pull out?

Oh, my god, I thought, suddenly realizing the implications. If we had to spend the night in Velletri, would we be forced to stay with the Mangiapias? The Stefanuccis wouldn't want two young men in their apartment overnight with a teenage girl, no matter how much they trusted us. Brother Mangiapia certainly wouldn't try anything with his wife present, but it would still be awkward. And what if somehow the sleeping arrangements ended up with Sister Mangiapia sharing a bed with her daughter, Elder Farnsworth sharing a bed with the boy, and me sharing a bed with Brother Mangiapia? Oh, my god. We simply had to catch that train.

We paused by a short, brick wall to catch our breath, our sides aching, and then we ran down the hill to the station, rushing past some teens listening to a jukebox and an old man walking along slowly with a cane. We ran through the train doors and collapsed into a seat.

Five more minutes passed before the train left.

"You like living on the edge, Anziano," said Elder Farnsworth, laughing.

"Not really," I said. "It's just that the edge always seems to get closer."

Thank God we were going to get home tonight. I could only be good one day at a time. Tomorrow's temptations would have to be dealt with tomorrow. I relaxed and put my books down, sitting back to enjoy the ride. Technically, while this counted as Travel Time in the statistics we turned in every week, Elder Farnsworth and I were still on duty and should be looking for people on the train to talk to. But I didn't feel like approaching anyone else this evening and so just looked out the window, wanting to forget what had happened earlier. I watched as the lights flashed by us outside and then dark shadows flew past, and I simply tried to enjoy the sensation of riding.

Riding trains made me feel sophisticated, made me feel I was really out in the world serving God. Once, I'd forgotten my flip chart of pictures on the train going into Rome. We got off at Capannelle and when we realized what had happened, we called the station in Rome to see if they could look for the binder and hold it for us. What they did instead was tell us the train was due to make a return trip to Ciampino and when they stopped at Capannelle, the conductor would step out with the binder and hand it to us personally, which was exactly what he did. It made me realize that people outside of the Church could have the Spirit sometimes, too. That was both encouraging and confusing. If we had a monopoly on truth but not on goodness, how did that make Mormonism any better than anyone else's religion?

Another time, Elder Farnsworth and I were in Rome and needed to return to Ciampino for lunch with the other elders. The local train was just about to pull out, so we made a mad dash for Binario 17. Just as Farnsworth started up the steps, the doors closed, catching him in between. The conductor looked horrified and helped Farnsworth squeeze in, but he shook his head at me, and I had to wait for the next train. It was a rare opportunity to be alone for a few minutes, and I briefly fantasized about escaping into the countryside and letting everyone think I'd been kidnapped, easy enough since we routinely received kidnap threats. But escaping would only be worthwhile if I had a man to escape with, and I didn't. I knew I had to be strong even when there was a good chance to sin, so I'd deliberately avoided looking at attractive men I might normally have hoped would approach me, and I caught the next train as soon as it pulled into the station. Bravo for one more day.

Elder Farnsworth and I rode the train into Rome at least twice a week, on Sundays for church, and also on Mondays to give our weekly stats to the zone leaders. We spent hours in Stazione Termini every week, and we saw a lot of the regulars there. There of course were the cab drivers trying to persuade people to hire them. There was a prostitute who wanted to welcome lonely men as they arrived in the city. Another regular was an old man who hung out with several other grungy people. I wasn't sure if they were homeless, but they were certainly poor and spent most of every day at the station. One day, the old man dropped his pants and flashed a woman in his group. She just cackled, and the incident was soon over, no one else paying any attention. I had gotten just a glimpse of the old man's genitals, and I felt ashamed of myself for experiencing such a thrill at seeing a dirty old man behaving in a dirty old way. Yeah, I was sure sophisticated, I thought disgustedly.

Another regular at the station was a middle-aged French woman, impeccably dressed. She ran around in apparent distress, telling people she'd lost her ticket back to Paris and was trapped in Rome unless someone would loan her fifty thousand lire, which she would pay back as soon as she got home. She must have taken in a huge amount of money every day, a good living. I was impressed that she didn't beg for one or two thousand lire but went for the big bucks with a big lie. Sometimes, it seemed that a bigger lie was easier to pull off. It must be true. It would be too audacious otherwise.

For some reason, this beautiful woman and her bold deception troubled me the most.

I couldn't help but think of Brother Mangiapia. If he hadn't surprised me so much, if I hadn't been worried about my companion being just ten feet away, I wondered if I'd have been strong enough to say no. I frowned. Perhaps it didn't matter why a person said no as long as they did.

Well, of course it mattered, I realized a second later. Otherwise, there would come a time when the situation was ripe for sin. And one had to be able to resist it then, too. I kept hoping my mission would make me stronger, but I felt as weak as I ever had. Why wasn't I slowly getting better? I seemed to be slipping further into the muck every day. Would God change me overnight on the last day of my mission if I hung in there and kept fighting? The Church said you could become heterosexual if you tried hard enough. It had to be true if they said it.

I thought back to the scene in the pizzeria storeroom, and I felt myself growing hard. Would it have been so bad, I wondered, to spend just five minutes alone with Brother Mangiapia?

I wanted to hit myself. How was I ever going to survive if I kept having thoughts like this? Did I want to lead a pitiful, shameful life like Brother Mangiapia, propositioning strangers in a dusty, dark room?

My companion and I were soon back in Ciampino around 9:15, fifteen minutes earlier than we were supposed to be. If you cut off fifteen minutes here and fifteen minutes there, it was hard to get your full sixty hours of work each week, the minimum for our Standard of Excellence. I told Elder Farnsworth I had to pee again and went in the station bathroom to delay us another minute. No one was in there at this hour, and I stood there looking around. Not everyone had the chance to physically see their own soul.

Since we lived only a block away, we still got back to the apartment early. I decided we could at least get some Dual Study time if I recited lesson H. I wanted to be able to report my monthly completion of the "Master's Art." If we didn't recite all eight of our memorized lessons at least once a month, as rarely as we taught them, we'd forget them.

I felt slightly better by the time we finished, and by that point, the other two elders in our district had come home, and Elder Farnsworth wanted to go talk to them. I was ready for bed, though it was still not yet 10:30. But our mandatory wake up time of 6:30 was fast approaching, and I felt especially tired tonight.

"Let's have our companion prayer now," I said before Elder Farnsworth left the room. "Why don't you say it?"

Elder Farnsworth began the prayer in English, and I stopped him and asked him to say it in Italian. "Trying to be bravo?" he asked.

"Yes," I said. "I am."

He began again, in Italian this time, and I quietly moved so I was just behind him. When he finished a moment later, I said, "Amen," and he jumped.

"You flipper."

"The Spirit moved me."

"Good night, Elder." He left the room smiling.

"Good night."

I turned out the light and crawled into my cot. I tried to sleep, but I kept seeing Brother Mangiapia in the storeroom, and I grew erect again. And though I hadn't masturbated in months, I couldn't seem to help myself tonight. I kept thinking of Brother Mangiapia, seeing that bushy moustache, and the dark fur around his penis, and soon I was sighing in relief.

And now I had just sinned. Would the one sin make it easier to sin again? To commit an even larger sin?

At least I still had a long while here in Italy to purge my soul. I could repent and move on. And maybe I could go back to Velletri and talk to Brother Mangiapia, after all, show him the error of his ways. Maybe that's why I'd been called to serve in this area, because the Lord knew that I understood what Brother Mangiapia was going through, and I'd be able to reach him when no one else could. I'd be like Alma the Younger and the sons of Ammon, whose sinful past made it easier for them to be beacons of light to others after they repented.

I shivered. Seeing Brother Mangiapia again would only make things worse.

And I wasn't going to let myself get worse.

"If ye have faith, nothing shall be impossible unto you." Jesus had said it himself, and Jesus wouldn't lie. I had faith, and I was going to become straight. That's all there was to it. Just because it hadn't happened yet didn't mean it wasn't going to. I was going to be bravo.

Pulling up the covers, I began humming to myself, thinking of the words to one of my favorite hymns.

I could hear one of the other elders entering the bathroom right next to my bedroom, and after a moment, I heard the sound of tinkling water.

My chest tightened, and I suddenly felt overwhelmingly sad.

I tried to clear my mind and not think of anything. If I couldn't think, I couldn't sin. I stared up into the blackness for a moment and sighed. But when I closed my eyes, the blackness formed itself into a clump of pubic hair. I heard the other elders laughing in the kitchen. I hugged my pillow and hoped and hoped, as I listened to the sound of a late-night train rumbling down the tracks.

Killing Babies

I was standing at attention in front of five other elders and four sisters at district meeting, while Elder Lucas, our senior zone leader as well as our district leader, pointed out my failures. "Elder Anderson, you're eight referrals short this week and six lessons short. You did get a full eight hours of dual study with your companion, but since he was sick and you both had to stay in half a day, I would think you'd have gone beyond the bare minimum requirements."

I nodded silently.

"What we need to see here is more sacrifice," Lucas continued. "What are you willing to sacrifice? Your companion is still new in the mission. You've got to make him work hard, too. As senior companion, you're responsible for the both of you."

I was about to reply when suddenly Elder Tate, another senior companion in the district, stood up and pointed at Elder Deiana, my companion. Tate glared at me and said angrily, "Don't kill the babies!"

Then I woke up and realized I was in bed. But I could still hear Elder Tate's bizarre words echoing in my brain. Only they weren't an echo. Someone was shouting.

"Don't kill the babies! Don't kill the babies!" It was Elder Tate. What was going on? I heard loud bumps and scrambling coming from the next room.

I crawled out of bed and made my way to the bedroom door. Elder Deiana had also been awakened by the commotion and followed me confusedly. Not understanding English perfectly, he probably understood even less than I did of what was happening.

"What's going on, Elder Anderson?" Elder Lucas demanded, turning on the hall light and coming toward us.

"That's what I was going to ask you," I replied. We could still hear banging coming from nearby. We could also hear moans and whimpering. Had someone broken in and attacked the other elders? We'd had several threats here in Rome, but could it really be? We always tried to be on guard, but maybe someone had gotten in anyway.

Elder Deiana and I glanced at each other, frowning, as Elder Lucas opened the door to the other elders' room and switched on the light. "What are you guys doing?" he shouted.

Elders Sterling, Deiana, and I crowded into the doorway behind him, trying to see whatever it was that was happening inside the bedroom. I could see Elder Sommers on his bed shaking, and I realized now that what I had thought was whimpering was actually laughter. "Look!" he gasped, pointing, and then was convulsed again with giggling.

The four of us moved further into the room and looked in the direction Elder Sommers had pointed. Under his desk, hitting the wall with his brush, was Elder Tate. He moaned again and then became quiet. "What's he doing?" demanded Elder Lucas.

Elder Sommers managed to stop laughing. Wiping his eyes, he said, "He's sleepwalking! It's great, isn't it?"

"Elder Tate!" said Elder Lucas loudly. "Hey!"

"Wait a minute," I said. "I heard it's dangerous to wake up someone who's sleepwalking."

"It's dangerous to let him go on," Elder Lucas countered. "If he keeps making so much noise in the middle of the night, he'll get us kicked out of our apartment."

"What's best for us may not be what's best for him," I returned. "Can't we think of a gentle way of calming him down?"

Elder Lucas looked disgusted and reached down under the desk, ripping the brush out of Elder Tate's hand. Tate continued to make stabbing motions in the air.

"Last night," Elder Sommers told us, "he started tossing and turning in bed, and he said, 'But I don't *want* to get married!' I almost died! I wish I could have heard the rest of that dream! He probably got some sister missionary pregnant. Probably Sorella Potter! No wonder it was a nightmare." He laughed again.

I tried to look under the desk at Elder Tate. He had a dream about not getting married? I wondered if he was gay, too, or just wanted to be single a while longer. I'd seen the returned missionaries back home in America, and every Sunday, two or three or four people would ask them when they were going to get married. It was the single most important commandment in this life, and after our mission was out of the way, there was no more reason to wait.

Since my mission hadn't cured me of my gayness, I dreaded going home. The pressure was bad enough now to be straight, and every month that went by after I returned, it would get worse. What if I was still gay two years from now? Three years? Four years? If just two people every week asked me when I was getting married, that would be over four hundred queries in just a few years. Bishops would be asking me, stake presidents, councilors, mothers of young women, everyone. I'd seen it already. I didn't need the nightmare Tate had had last night. I'd be living it soon enough.

"Hey, Elder Tate," said Lucas, more loudly. "Wake up." He shook Tate, who was now kneeling quietly under his desk. "It's probably those cookies you gave him before he went to bed, Elder Anderson. I told you not to eat right before bed." He nudged Elder Tate with his foot.

"Huh? Wha?" Elder Tate began, looking about foggily.

"Get out from under there. You woke everybody up."

Elder Tate sheepishly crawled out and stood, brushing off his hands and knees. "I'm sorry," he said, blushing. He was wearing only his garments. Our Mormon underwear what most of the elders slept in. Deiana had pajamas, though, and I wore blue jeans and a red plaid shirt. Elder Lucas said it showed I lacked the proper spirit, that I was too worldly, thinking of being a "civilian." I told him I just didn't think walking around in my underwear was modest, and he'd told me to grow up, that I'd never be a good missionary unless I developed a little more maturity. I said I didn't think underwear created maturity, and he told me I was too argumentative and needed to learn more respect.

It was as if in every possible aspect of life, I was never good enough. Nothing I could do was ever *quite* enough. I had to do more, do better, work harder, work smarter, be stronger, be *perfect*. It made me so tired that the one rule I could almost always obey was the one to get to bed by 10:30.

"What did I do?" asked Elder Tate, rubbing his head in a bit of a daze. "Did I say anything?" We told him what had happened and he looked even more embarrassed. "This doesn't happen too often really," he explained. "Usually, it's when I'm under more stress or I'm excited, like because of transfers or something."

Transfers had been about a week ago, so it seemed like a rather late reaction, and a strange one, too, since none of the new elders in this district, myself included, usually went around killing babies. Then again, the other day I had said something about women perhaps needing the right to control whether or not they wanted to reproduce, and that heretical, quasi pro-choice comment had gotten me a cold shoulder from a few of the others. I wondered now what Elder Tate had been doing with that brush. In his dream, was it a knife? Was he stabbing people he thought were murderers? I didn't really approve of abortion, but I sometimes wished my mother had had one with me.

"I hope you've got the stress out of your system now," Elder Lucas muttered. "Come on, everyone, let's get back to sleep."

We all reluctantly returned to our rooms. I wanted to quiz Elder Tate on just what he'd been dreaming, but he probably wouldn't tell me even if he remembered. While he may have gotten the stress out of his system, now it had been injected into mine. I'd never sleepwalked before from stress, though, and I hoped I wouldn't start now.

I stood still and suddenly felt weak. What if I *did* walk in my sleep some time? I was certainly under enough stress to cause it. Where would I go? I looked quickly at Deiana, who was climbing back into bed. What if I had a sexual dream about him and tried to get in bed with him? What if all I did was say, "Oh, Deiana!" or something sexual, and he heard me? One thing which had already happened three times during my mission was that I'd awakened in the middle of the night and found myself masturbating.

If my companion were awake and saw or heard me, he could report me to the President. I probably wouldn't be sent home for it, but it would certainly be embarrassing. And if it was in fact coupled with an "Oh, Deiana," I might get punched in the face. I hadn't dreamed of him yet, but I knew I wanted to, because I wouldn't allow myself to consciously fantasize about him. But how did you tell your subconscious to be careful? "Be good," I told myself now. "Be careful. Be strong. Be righteous. Don't let me down."

I could only do so much about my subconscious, but I could at least keep a brush-wielding avenger out for the night. I casually walked across the room and placed my chair in front of our closed door.

"What's that for?" Elder Deiana laughed. His accent wasn't bad but he slurred some of his words sometimes, making me feel I didn't know Italian nearly as well as I thought I did.

"I don't know." I laughed back. "If Elder Tate tries to come in our room, at least we'll hear him. You never know."

Deiana threw his pillow at me. "What if I sleepwalk and can't get out?"

I looked at the serranda to make sure it was down over our glass doors. I didn't want Deiana falling off the balcony three stories to the street. It was a bit too much to hope he'd mistake me for his girlfriend in a dream, and too sinful to hope, too. On the other hand, if he sensed somehow that I was gay, he might come beat me up in my sleep. It was no more ridiculous than a man beating a wall with a hairbrush.

I'd heard many of the elders talk about gays over the past year. "They should all be arrested." "They should be given electric shock therapy." "They should be castrated." "They should be executed." Every minute of every day, I had to be careful not to let some sign of my gayness slip out. "Watch yourself. Be careful. Watch yourself." But I couldn't guard myself when I was asleep. Oh, God, what if I said something now? What if?

"Do you ever sleepwalk?" I asked Deiana. Hopefully, he slept too soundly to hear anything I might say.

"No. Not yet, anyway." He laughed again. "I'm getting a lot of experience, though. If we learn by example, I'll be starting before long."

"What do you mean?"

"Back in my last district, we had a zone conference once, and some other elders had to travel all the way from Pescara, so they stayed with us overnight. One elder slept in our room with my companion and me. We all went to sleep, and then suddenly in the middle of the night, he jumped up and yelled, 'Stop!' and pointed at the door. Scared me half to death. Then he kept pointing but acted as if whatever he was looking at was moving. I thought a spirit had come into the room. Didn't sleep another wink all night. He told me the next morning he only did it when he felt stress, and said he had to confess something to the President during the conference interview. He'd dreamed some avenging angel had come into the room."

I threw Deiana's pillow back at him. "Go to sleep," I said, smiling. I climbed back into my bed and pulled the covers up to my chin, the way I used to do after I'd had a nightmare when I was a boy, as if the covers would protect me. I hoped they would tonight.

When I was a kid, I'd been a bedwetter. Both inconvenient and embarrassing. I had a plastic sheet on my bed at home, but when we went to visit my grandparents, I had to wear a diaper. There I was five years old having to put on a diaper, and everyone knew. It was humiliating.

Then there was the time my parents went on a weekend getaway, and I had to stay with neighbors for one night. I didn't pee every night, maybe only once every two or three weeks, but would this be one of those nights? I couldn't dare wear a diaper and have my friend find out, so I vowed not to fall asleep all night. We went to bed around 9:00, and I managed to stay awake until after 1:00, but I finally did fall asleep. Then toward morning, I dreamed I had to pee. I told myself I wouldn't do it, that I was strong.

But a few seconds later, my friend was yelling at me to wake up. He'd felt something wet in bed and realized it was me. He turned the light on and looked at me in horror. I'd begun crying, saying, "I thought I was stopping it in my dream." He'd told all the kids in school, and it wasn't until I finally outgrew bedwetting around age eight that I was able to face sleep again with ease.

I remembered my first success at avoiding wetting the bed. I was eight and woke up around 4:00 in the morning with a strong urge to urinate. But I'd woken up, I realized, in time to save myself. The only problem was that the bathroom was all the way down a dark hall, and the light switch was at the far end. I was still afraid of the dark, and I couldn't face that long hallway by myself.

So I urinated on the carpet in the corner of my room, and when my mother noticed the wet spot the next day, I blamed it on the dog. My mother looked at our tiny chihuahua, looked at the wet spot, and then looked at me, and I knew that she knew. I was mortified, and I realized what a freak I must be to have done something so abominable. But after that night, I never wet the bed again, and I found the courage to face that long, dark hallway in the middle of the night. Yet even now, twelve years later, I still worried about losing control in my sleep.

But I'd learned to have at least a little of that control when I slept. Before my mission, for example, I could tell myself right before going to bed what time to wake up in the morning, and I'd wake up in time to turn off the alarm before it rang. Out here, I was usually too tired to get up until I had to. I could tell myself, "6:25, 6:25, 6:30, 6:20, 6:25, 6:25," and still not even start waking up until that alarm rang. When I was too tired, my subconscious didn't listen. "Please be good. Please be good," I told myself again.

I remembered another time as a young teenager at a Boy Scout campout. I'd heard from some kids at school that boy scouts liked to fool around on camping trips, "jerking off" together. I was instantly intrigued by the story but also terrified when it came time to actually go camping. What if some of the guys wanted to fool around, just to "experiment," but they could see I really liked it, that it was more than just play for me?

And what if I got my usual early morning erection when we first got up from our sleeping bags? Did all boys get that? Or was that a particular sign of gayness? I didn't know. Perhaps I'd get an erection and my tent mate would think I wanted him and would tell everyone. I'd be laughed at. I didn't know what to expect. All I knew was that I was afraid to sleep because in my sleep, my penis seemed to have a mind of its own. As it turned out, though, being a Church-sponsored troop, nothing sexual at all happened the whole weekend. I was both relieved and disappointed.

I was almost afraid to sleep now, but it had already been such a long day, and soon enough, I couldn't concentrate on anything anymore. Various scenes of Tate with his brush, Deiana undressing, the man who'd turned us away this evening closing his door, and the Id from *Forbidden Planet* rampaging across the countryside all jumbled together in my brain. There was one final scene of Elder Lucas tiptoeing around me as I slept, trying to quietly enclose me in a shark cage, whispering to the others that I was too dangerous to be walking around free. Then I was alone in the room, still in the cage, and my Id was outside, trying to break into the cage to get me. Finally, the images faded away, and then there was only darkness and rest.

The next thing I remembered was seeing metal bars strewn about the bedroom, and in the middle of the room was a shredded pillow. Someone was pointing to the pillow and screaming that it was dead. It was dead! I woke up to the sound of shouting coming from the next room. "Elder Tate's dead! Elder Tate's dead!" It was Elder Sommers, shouting hysterically.

I jumped out of bed quickly, getting my foot tangled in my blanket and tripping onto the marble floor with a loud whump. "Elder Tate's dead!" I shouted as loudly as I could, still half asleep, scrambling to my feet. "Elder Tate's dead!" I ran to the door, forgetting about the chair and running right into it in the dark. I howled with pain, jumping up and down on one foot.

Elder Deiana quickly switched on the light and pushed the chair aside, opening the door. Elders Lucas and Sterling were running down the hall toward us. "Who's dead?" yelled Elder Lucas. "What happened?"

I was still moaning loudly and holding my bruised shin. Elder Deiana looked totally confused, especially since we were all speaking English. "What's going on?" Elder Lucas demanded again. Frustrated by our lack of cooperation, he shoved open the door to the other elders' room. He went inside, followed by Sterling and Deiana. Even I managed to limp after them. "Who'd dead? What's going on?"

Elder Sommers was standing on his bed, leaning against the wall with his hand on his heart. "Oh, Elders!" he breathed.

"Where's Elder Tate?" asked Lucas. We looked under his desk but couldn't see any sign of him. I glanced toward the balcony doors. They were closed and the serranda down.

"He's under my *bed*," Elder Sommers said. "That's what I was shouting. He startled me when he crawled under my bed."

"Then who said he was dead?" Elder Lucas looked about coolly. "I'm sure I heard someone say he was dead."

Still standing on one foot, I mumbled, "I guess I said it. That's what I thought he shouted. You see, I was having this dream, and—"

Elder Lucas groaned. "Not you, too? Come on, let's get back to bed. Remember, you guys, we still have to get up at 6:30. If we're still sleepy, we know who to get mad at."

Everyone nodded, looking at me, knowing that Lucas was a stickler on wake up time. A few days ago, we'd all been out late and took a wrong bus, getting stranded halfway across Rome, having to wait another hour and a half for a bus in the right direction. We didn't get to bed until after 2:00, but Lucas still insisted we all get up at 6:30 the next morning. "It's the rule," he said. "We have to obey all the rules."

Then Deiana had been sick two nights ago, and I'd been up half the night with him, helping him to the bathroom, but Lucas had come in the next morning at 6:30 and told me to get out of bed. Deiana could sleep in because he was sick, but I was healthy, and the Lord still expected me to obey the rules. I could see a couple of the others looking at me now the way I'd wanted to look at him then.

"What about Elder Tate?" asked Elder Sommers. "He's still under my bed."

"Leave him there," said Lucas. "The bed'll muffle any more noise he makes. I'm going to sleep. If anybody makes another sound, I'm going to throw him out of the apartment and bolt the door." With a last, tired glare in my direction, he stalked out of the room toward his own.

He wouldn't threaten to throw Tate out, but he could threaten *me*. Not that he'd do it, of course. He'd only make me wish he had. But the way he said it made me remember Karl Malden in *Fear Strikes Out*, constantly demanding more and more and more of his son until his son finally had a nervous breakdown. I'd seen the movie shortly before my mission and when I saw Anthony Perkins yelling at his father, "You're killing me!" I thought, "Oh, my goodness! That's me!" But Jimmy Piersall's father had been selfish in his demands. The Church was only trying to help me. God himself had commanded us to be perfect. I *had* to be better. I *had* to be.

I rubbed my shin again. "Sorry, guys." I realized that my subconscious self, my *real* self, had caused everyone trouble.

Elder Deiana helped me back to our room, and as he gently helped me onto my bed, I felt an immense wave of depression. I *liked* the feel of his hands on my body. "Sorry to keep you up," I said. "I know you're still not feeling good after the other night."

"No problem, Elder," he said with a smile. "A little give and take is fair enough. I hope your leg feels better in the morning." He tousled my hair and then went to turn out the light and get into his own bed.

"Golden dreams," I said, using an Italian phrase to wish him a good sleep.

"Take your own advice," he replied. "I know you can do better than that last one." I heard shuffling in the dark and suddenly felt lips brush against my forehead. Then Deiana climbed back into his bed again. "Be at peace tonight," he said softly.

"Thank you." I tried to close my eyes but couldn't. Even though the room was almost completely black, I stared upward into the darkness. He kissed me, I kept thinking. He was Italian, so it didn't mean anything, but he kissed me. I shook my head slowly against the pillow and sighed wearily. Please be good, I told myself, listening to Elder Deiana turn over in his bed. I closed my eyes tightly then and still saw the same darkness. Please be good, I told myself. Be better. Be stronger.

I'd heard that some people could direct their dreams by telling themselves ahead of time what to dream about. I tried to focus on rebuilding that shark cage, making it hardier and more fortified. I would put in extra bars. I would weld them to the frame. I'd make my cage strong. I remembered how the Id had gotten through a dozen steel doors in *Forbidden Planet*, but I'd make my cage better than a steel door. I'd make my cage out of titanium. That was better, wasn't it? It had to be.

I closed my eyes even more tightly. I wouldn't let my true self out, I thought firmly. It was going to be okay. I'd be safe. And then, continuing to talk myself into safety and security, I tried not to think about dead babies.

Pissing in Peace

I had finished breakfast and scripture, and all the other elders except Deiana had finished their showers, so I headed for the bathroom. I was able to use the toilet before Deiana came in, which was nice and made me feel I'd already accomplished something for the day. Guys were guys, and though most of the elders I'd lived with on my mission had no inhibitions, I still preferred my privacy at times. But when six guys had to share one bathroom, privacy became a rare commodity.

Once I'd been brushing my teeth after lunch when another elder had come in and sat on the toilet. He was certainly the one in the more compromising position, but I'd still felt a flash of irritation. Another time I'd gone into the bathroom and had just unzipped my pants when an elder came in and began talking to me about a problem he was having with his companion. I appreciated his willingness to confide in me, but with a "shy kidney," I could hardly concentrate, feeling stupid for not being able to urinate, and thus hardly able to offer any good advice. Of course, he didn't really want advice; he wanted someone to listen. Still, I generally listened better with my pants zipped up.

I was at the sink now starting to shave when Elder Deiana came into the bathroom. "Buon giorno," he said, starting to strip.

I watched him take off his brown pajama top but then looked back in the mirror, wanting to keep looking but afraid he'd notice. I could probably get all the privacy I needed if I'd just go ahead and make everyone uncomfortable, yet alienation and privacy weren't quite the same thing. So instead, Deiana and I had a system where he'd take a shower while I shaved and washed my hair. That way we could clean up without getting in each other's way. I usually showered last out of all six elders so no one would have any reason to come in the bathroom and I'd get a few more minutes alone, but I also got very little hot water, okay in warm weather but less pleasant in the winter.

When it was cold, I'd wash up at the sink and pretend I took a shower so the others wouldn't think I was weird. "Did you hear about Anziano Johnson?" I'd heard a missionary gossip once. "He never takes a shower! Can you imagine being his companion?" I had met the guy once and found him to be quite normal. It turned out he came from a rural desert community and automatically took sponge baths to conserve water, and he didn't want to begin any wasteful habits here in Italy that would be a problem after he went home. But the rumors preceded him, and there was always someone joking about his body odor. I felt I had to be careful not to invoke the wrath of the missionary grapevine. Adjusting to new companions every couple of months was tough enough without having them already decide not to like me in advance.

Elder Deiana began singing "La famiglia dei gobbon" as he started showering, and I finished shaving. When I was younger, I'd longed to be able to shave to prove I was a "man." Now that I had to do it every day, I wished I could be like some of the other elders who only had to shave once a week. I was considering growing a beard for at least a little while when I went home to America, when I no longer needed an "innocent" face to present to people. I had tried to grow a beard before my mission, but my bishop and so many other members had made comments about my setting a poor example that I had shaved it off. And after my mission, I'd have new examples to set, "for the youth." I wasn't sure I was up to hearing continually how I had to avoid the appearance of evil. Being "man enough to grow a beard" now had a new meaning, I realized.

Damn, did every decision have to be such a moral issue? It was just a beard, for goodness' sake.

Elder Deiana finished singing around the time I started washing my hair, which I liked to do at the sink so I wouldn't be in the shower so long, thus decreasing my chances of having the bathroom invaded while I was naked. Deiana tried to begin a conversation, but I couldn't hear him very well. Even some of the Italian elders, used to showering maybe twice a week before their mission, quickly learned that while they were still in Italy, they had nevertheless moved into a different culture since the majority of missionaries here were American, and it wasn't long before the Elder Johnson stories brought them to conform their behavior to the standard. Elder Comesano was the only one I knew who'd refused to shower daily, but he'd been used to showering or bathing three or four times a week anyway, and he refused to let other people run his personal life. When he needed to bathe, he would. There were still a few comments made about him, though most people left him alone. But I knew I didn't have his charisma.

Elder Sterling walked in the bathroom then as I was rinsing my hair, and he squeezed past me to get to the toilet. As he stood there, Elder Lucas came in, too, with a laundry bag full of clothes. "Hi," he said.

With my head still in the sink, I replied, "You can put your clothes in the machine, but please don't start washing them until I've finished my shower."

"Oh. Okay." He frowned and stood there a moment considering something. Lucas and I weren't on the best of terms anyway. Being our senior zone leader, he seemed to feel he needed to check up on me continually as a senior companion in my companionship. It wasn't enough that I had to tell him my daily goals each morning during our fifteen- minute devotional, and that I had to tell him my weekly goals each week during our district meeting, but he'd demand, not ask, every evening to know if I'd accomplished those goals, and demand to hear the results of my weekly goals in district meeting. "You only taught two lessons this week, Elder Anderson?" he'd say in front of everybody, checking a list of my goals from last week. "You said you'd teach five. What happened?" To me, a goal was something to aim for, not a contract written in blood, but rather than teach me ways to be more effective, he'd just say things like, "Don't you take this work seriously? These are promises you're making to God, not to me."

It was a mission rule that we had to send a copy of our work hours and how we'd spent them—teaching, tracting, visiting members, getting referrals, traveling, or whatever— to both our zone leaders and to the mission president. We also had to include a letter to each sharing our feelings. If anything seemed amiss in our hours, if they were too low, or too high, or too perfectly used, a "work visit" was often arranged, where one of the leaders would come for a day or two to work with the elder in question to see if he was working properly. The only time Elder Lucas seemed to want to do a work visit with me or my companion was after I'd stated my goals for the day during devotional, and I'd planned a particularly interesting day, like getting referrals in the Villa Borghese in the morning and tracting near the Coliseum in the evening, or if I'd managed to get a teaching appointment or something like that. Then he'd often go with my companion to fill my day's plans and make me figure out something else to do with his own companion.

But even if he wasn't so intentionally obnoxious, the mission rules handed down through the zone leaders were often hard to live by anyway. We couldn't decide if we needed to wear our suit coats or not based on the temperature. No, we had to have an edict from the president. "It is now May 1. You don't have to wear your jackets anymore." Were we too stupid to tell if it was cold? The sister missionaries weren't advised about *their* jackets. Why were we?

Music had always been controlled, of course. We used to be allowed to listen to the Mormon Tabernacle Choir, music from Latter-day Saint musicals such as *Saturday's Warrior* and *My Turn on Earth*, and classical music. One sister was reported for listening to John Denver on her earphones, and a few zone leaders didn't think the classical music some of the elders were listening to was appropriate and reported this to the president, who became so disgusted that he outlawed all music. So now the most we could hope for was to have a neighbor with a loud radio. Back home, Lionel Ritchie wasn't one of my favorite artists, but now it felt good to hear his voice coming through our open window.

We also needed ten hours of individual study each week, each hour of personal study being reported weekly to our leaders as well. We could study the scriptures, Church books, and the *Ensign*, which was the official Church magazine, along with grammar and our missionary discussions. One elder had bought a newspaper once and been reported to the president, even though it was the day after the Pope was shot and was certainly something worth following. I'd bought a book by Italo Calvino to read when I returned to America and had been reported for that just because someone thought I was reading it now. Elder Lucas would sometimes pop into my room and say, "Just wanted to make sure you were studying." I'd learned how fast to turn the pages of a book so it would look like I was reading, while I sat at my desk and thought about whatever subject I needed to. And my journal contained not only my account of each day's activities, but also whatever other topic or issue I'd been meditating on.

My latest was a "stop and smell the flowers" theme, which I'd started two weeks ago when I felt I was always hurrying about trying to fill someone else's goals. I stopped one day in front of a bush of blue hydrangea and just stared at their beauty. Deiana had been a little impatient at first and would only let me look for twenty seconds, but he was getting now to where he knew once or twice a day I'd stop to admire some flowers. I hoped he didn't feel it was too feminine a thing to do. It took maybe two or three minutes out of the entire day, and yet I still had to constantly battle the feeling I was sinning. I'd decided to keep up the practice until I could admire the beauty of the flowers while not worrying about doing so.

Elder Sterling, finished now with the toilet, pulled a cord to flush it, and clapped me on the back as he passed by to leave the bathroom. Just yesterday, he'd come in the bathroom while I was urinating and stood beside me as he casually unzipped and urinated as well. I was okay if I'd already gotten started, but I still wished mission rules didn't insist on no locked doors inside the apartment.

Lucas, after accidentally bumping against me, pushing me slightly against the sink, now opened the circular glass door of the washer, bumping my leg, and began shoving his clothes inside the machine. Would it kill him to wait until I was finished? Then again, was it killing me to let him go ahead now and load the machine? Perhaps not, but I still gritted my teeth until he left the room.

When Deiana turned off the shower, I dried and combed my hair as he toweled off. Since our hair could only be a certain length, I'd recently had a haircut, and I had one pesky little strand that didn't want to stay down. I was glad someone hadn't come in and brushed his teeth while I tried to comb my hair. It annoyed me enough that the others came in while I was in the bathroom, but when they would interrupt me and not let me finish what I'd started, it was all I could do not to push them out of the way. I probably *should* have pushed them out of the way, but even if they were rude, I didn't want to be. And yet, if the alternative was to always be shoved aside myself, I wondered if maybe I should think more about it.

Elder Deiana was still drying off, but I had nothing left to do, so I began slowly undressing. I was afraid to be naked in front of the other elders. I'd survived the communal showers at the Missionary Training Center for two months by staring the entire time I was showering at the shower spigot above me, but I was always afraid I'd get an erection out here and then everybody would *know*. It was hard enough dealing with my gay feelings without having everyone suspect every move I made. I was always quite open for the most part in my yearly interviews with my bishops back home and in my interviews every couple of months with my mission president here, confiding all of my feelings, good and bad, but this was one part of my character that I never let anyone invade.

I smiled as I took off my shirt. Didn't they manage to invade it, anyway? I'd read every pamphlet or book chapter the Church had ever published on the subject. How could it help but emphasize all my self-doubts about my inferior, weak, obviously self-indulgent nature? Wasn't my letting those ideas into my head allowing these people to invade this private part of my character? Was the fact that I still couldn't tell if I was legitimately bad or if the Church was wrong on this one, single point a sign of that invasion, or merely a sign that I wasn't in tune with the Spirit enough to truly repent?

My bishop back home would chat nicely about something for a few minutes as each interview began, to put me at ease, but it was hard to relax knowing he was preparing his list of questions. I never wanted to be startled by a question I hadn't considered, so I went in with a very prepared and rehearsed supply of answers, which just convinced me more that I was in deep need of spiritual help.

The answers were usually true, as I had very little in the way of actions to hide really, but I still went in with my guard up, not wanting to *have* to answer even when I was innocent. It still seemed like none of his business.

"Do you smoke?" he'd ask.

"No."

"Have you ever tried it?"

"No."

"Do you think about trying it?" He wanted to cover every possibility, and I knew it.

"No."

"Have you used any drugs?"

"No."

"Do you want to?"

"No."

"When you go out with girls, do you kiss them?"

"No."

"Really? Not even a peck?"

"I don't date much."

"Do you pet, touch her body or her clothes in private places?"

How come she was allowed private places, and I wasn't, is what I wondered, but what I said was, "No."

And the questions would go on. Usually, I'd have to confess only one sin, masturbation, tell him how frequently I committed it, and how long it had been since the last time I did it. Usually five or six weeks, since I scheduled the interview in advance. And because I'd never actually done anything gay, I convinced myself that I didn't have to tell him I wished I had. Just talking about masturbation was always embarrassing enough, but to lie to a bishop was a major sin, and besides, in his position, he was surely spiritual enough to see through me, which would be even more humiliating. However, I'd learned the trick of looking down at the floor as I confessed but then looking him straight in the eyes when I shook his hand firmly when the interview ended, to show how I had cast off the sin and guilt through repentance, the final step of which was confessing to the bishop.

The Church called masturbation "self-abuse," but even though I tried to believe everything the Church said, that always felt ridiculous. I could accept it was a sin, but it seemed that so personal a sin should be between me and God since no one else was involved or hurt in any way, and I resented having to share such information about myself. Bishops were supposed to keep all the information they heard private, but I knew that leaders gossiped, too, and I didn't feel it fair I had to worry about others finding out. Of course, if I didn't sin in the first place, I wouldn't have a problem.

But the probing by Church leaders at times was also done in public. It was a commandment to partake of the sacrament every Sunday, but it was also a commandment *not* to partake if we had an unresolved sin in our lives. So if I didn't take the bread and water, everyone would know I'd done *something*, even if they didn't know exactly what.

The temple, though, was the worst. The only time we had to be naked, during the initiatory when we were anointed with water, we did get to wear a sheet with a hole for our heads, and the man anointing us would just reach under the sheet. That wasn't too bad. Of course, once through the initiatory, the temple worker had to help us put on our first pair of Mormon underwear. Then we had to wear a pair of those garments at all times. They were one-piece underwear, knee-length, with a T-shirt attached, and a slit in the back and a slit in front, since there were no pants to pull down. We had to buy our clothes for the rest of our lives based on their capacity to conceal those garments. There was still personal choice involved in selecting our underwear, of course. While we had to buy Church-sewn garments, we could pick the cotton, or the nylon, or the Bemberg…

The hardest part of selecting my first garment was figuring out how to guess the right size. I selected a pair and went into a dressing room. But as I looked at the thing, I couldn't figure out how to get into it. Surely not through the arm or leg holes. I tried to get in through the slit in the seat but got stuck. I managed to pull it off, and after I put my suit back on, I stuck my head out the door and sheepishly asked a female temple worker there in the garment room, "How do you put these on?"

She smiled pleasantly. "Through the neck, dear."

The neck? How odd. But I tried and it worked. So after I chose my size, the first of my garments was sent on ahead to the initiatory booth to await my naked body.

But the endowment ceremony itself was even more difficult. We had to make the most serious commitments of our lives, agreeing we'd rather be killed than reveal them, and we had to make these commitments in front of fifty or a hundred people. Sure, we were given a chance at the beginning of the meeting, *before* we knew what was coming, to leave the room, but even then, we had at least fifty pairs of eyes on us, ready to judge in an instant.

And the same went for the vows. "I will only have intercourse with my spouse to whom I am legally and lawfully wed," was one of the first. But I didn't know if I could make a commitment like that which had to last the rest of my life. What if I did succumb to a man once? I couldn't say, "I'll try." I had to say I'd do it and accept the eternal consequences of breaking that promise made "in front of God and these witnesses."

Could I stop the program for a moment and talk to someone? No. Could I leave? Not without everyone knowing I was a sleaze and reporting it back home to everyone. So what was left? I lied and pretended to make a covenant I had no way of knowing I could keep, what should have been a personal commitment to God between two people becoming just a show.

I didn't know why I kept ruminating when I needed to focus on getting in and out of that shower. I just wished the Church would leave some part of my life for *me*. That private part didn't have to be only for sin; it could be simply for thinking a little or to relax. Was relaxing or thinking a sin?

Perhaps. I remembered that Deiana had mentioned once he'd never been circumcised, and I was curious every time I was in the bathroom with him to see what a foreskin looked like. But I could never get up enough nerve to do more than glance at him, which didn't tell me much. I felt I'd be betraying him to look at his body when he didn't know I was gay, so I didn't look. And again today, I could see he was standing in full view if I'd wanted to peek, but I kept my eyes elsewhere. So couldn't the Church trust me with a little privacy?

I finished undressing and stepped into the shower. Within a minute or two, Elder Deiana was dressed and left the bathroom. Finally, I was all alone. I knew that as missionaries we had to be with our companion twenty-four hours a day, but I hadn't realized it meant *twenty-four hours a day*. If someone felt he needed to kneel by his bed to pray, he just got used to someone sitting across the room flipping pages of a book as he talked with God. In a few apartments, we had a hall closet we used as a "prayer closet," but even that was hardly private, as several times, other elders popped in without warning, "just to check" on whoever was in there. I'd had no idea what the checking was for until one elder was caught masturbating with a porno magazine he'd smuggled into the apartment and was threatened with being sent home. If he was sent home, it would be a major disgrace, as everyone in his home congregation would speculate on the reason for his early return. He'd never live down the shame. After accepting the restriction on prayer closet access, the elder was allowed to remain.

If an elder wanted to rest after working several hours, he needed a companion he could talk into taking a break rather than one who would report his loafing. And if he felt like working hard, he had to hope for a companion who would let him do so and not drag him down. Compromising was great exercise, but it was nice now to have a few minutes just for me. Even when the Law of Consecration which we'd accepted in the temple was to be enforced on some future day, when we'd have to give all our income to the Church, we were supposed to be allowed *some* private property. Surely, I deserved a little of that now as well. I closed my eyes and let the lukewarm water flow over me.

The shower was over too quickly, the water turning cold before I was even half through. After drying myself off, I began dressing. As I pulled my shirt on over my garments, Elder Lucas stuck his head in the door. "Okay if I wash my clothes now?"

God, only a couple of minutes of peace a day, and it was over already. It always went by too fast. "Sure," I said, shrugging.

Lucas started into the room.

"No, wait," I said. "Could you go out for a minute? I'm not finished yet."

As he left, Lucas mumbled something about my needing to make up my mind, and certainly it was dumb to think one more minute could really make any difference. Soon that would be gone, too, but still, I took my time as I buttoned my shirt, and then I put on my socks and shoes, being completely dressed now except for my tie, which I usually only put on right before I left the apartment, putting off that last bit of confinement as long as possible. After I was finished, I stood in front of the mirror for a few seconds, taking a couple of deep breaths. Then I closed my eyes as I let the last one out. I simply had to believe I deserved something more for myself than the opportunity to write in my journal, "I had a good day. I pissed in peace."

"Okay," I called. "You can come in now."

Lucas came in immediately and pushed a button on the washing machine. Then Elder Sommers walked through the open door and headed for the sink to brush his teeth. Lucas passed by me on his way out, grumbling again, and I left, too, going to my room and sitting down at my desk to start the day's next task.

I picked up my lesson book and flipped to the D discussion, about eternal progression, and I began studying it. Progress. Personal and eternal progress. It was a beautiful principle, probably the one Church ideal I believed in more than any other, that I could be a better person one day than I was today, and that later still I could become even better than that, on through eternity as long as it took for me to become perfect.

I used to think that the goal of perfection meant we all had to become the same, but here in Italy, I'd seen new flowers, tasted different foods, spoken a different language, and I realized that the best, most perfect rose could never inspire the exact same feelings as a perfect hedge of five-pointed star jasmine. I didn't need to conform always to Lucas's or even the Church's standards. I could try to develop in ways that I alone wanted to. Or needed to. There had to be room just for me somewhere.

The trick now was to really believe that and to act accordingly without feeling guilty.

I opened my journal and wrote, "When I get home, I will wait two weeks, and then I will grow my beard, and I will keep it no matter what anyone says." I looked at the vow and smiled, but then I thought that something which sounded so formal needed a witness and looked over to see if Deiana might be willing.

But I shook my head, still smiling, and closed my notebook. I prayed briefly, committing myself to my goals for the day, and then I turned back to my studies. Too bad I couldn't read that Agatha Christie novel in Italian I'd bought when my companion wasn't looking. But perhaps a language lesson today instead of the missionary discussions.

I picked up my dictionary and flipped through several pages. *Automiglioramento* might be a useful word to know.

As a Man Thinketh

When I turned eighteen, I stopped masturbating. I'd just heard the stake president at church say that "being gay isn't something you are, it's something you do."

I'd been dumbfounded. I'd never done anything gay, yet I still knew I was gay. Then it hit me. I *did* do something gay. I fantasized about sex with men. I masturbated. So that was why I could never seem to change. I would have to stop *all* gay activity, even mental activity, before I could be cured.

I figured starting at eighteen would give me one full year before I left for my mission, and that would be enough time to heal myself. For the next year then, every time a stray sexual thought would come into my head, I'd start singing a hymn if I was alone, and if I was in public, I'd would simply recite the lyrics in my head.

I successfully avoided all gay thoughts and masturbation for an entire year, but I was mystified when I turned nineteen and realized I was still gay. Maybe it took just a little more time.

Now I'd been out on my mission for ages, and I was painfully aware I hadn't become straight yet. Of course, my record of no fantasies and no masturbation had been broken a couple of times out here in Italy, and all I could hope was that it didn't put me back at start, that I wouldn't need two or three more years yet of 100% abstinence before being cured. Maybe it took seven years altogether to be healed. That was always a religious number. Or maybe twelve. That was a lifetime, though. I'd be 32 before I could get married. What if it took forty years? Would it even be worth the trouble then? All I knew was I had to keep trying till it was done. I thought my companion, Elder Deiana, was attractive, but I'd never fantasized about him even once. Surely, that had to count for something.

All I wanted from him was friendship. We got along well enough, I supposed, but somehow our relationship was still polite, not genuine. Of course, since I'd had no real friends before, I realized I might not recognize true friendship if I had it. But I really wanted to think of Deiana as my friend. I wanted him to actually *be* my friend. I looked at him now as he came back into our bedroom from the balcony.

"Sei pronto, Anziano?" he asked.

"Yes, I'm ready." I offered a prayer and we left the apartment. The other elders had gone out fifteen minutes earlier with the *mostra* and headed down to Via Nazionale. We caught the next bus and soon joined them on the sidewalk where they had already set up the display to attract attention. Elder Lucas was talking to a man and pointing to something on the streetboard as he talked. Elders Landrith and Sommers were talking to each other, and Elder Sterling was standing by himself looking bored till one of the sister missionaries from our district went over to talk to him.

Elder Deiana and I positioned ourselves amongst the other missionaries and got ready to approach anyone who looked even slightly interested in our display. I wished I could get five referrals in one day, do something that would impress Deiana so he'd think well of me. But as soon as I thought that, I felt guilty for having the wrong incentive for missionary work. Most people walked right by the streetboard without even a glance, but I wanted Deiana to have a successful mission, so I had to find some new contacts.

I bit my lip. I was still working for the wrong reason. I had to do this for the people themselves. I needed to focus. After about twenty minutes, I saw a man looking at a picture of Joseph Smith praying, so I approached him.

"Sir," I said, "in the Old Testament, the Jews were always guided by the prophets. Wouldn't it be nice to know that God had called a prophet to guide us today in these troubled times as well?"

The man turned and walked off without even looking at me. I hated street contacting, but we had four more hours of it before we could go home for lunch, so I just moved back to my position and waited for the next passerby who looked approachable.

I always felt desperately alone when doing street contacting, even when there were eight of us here together. I looked over at Elder Landrith. He'd studied one year toward his music degree before coming on his mission. The man seemed gentle and nice, and I wondered if he might be gay, too, but it didn't seem right to assume that every refined person was gay. Mozart wrote beautiful music, and he certainly hadn't been gay.

Several months ago at a zone conference, Elder Peterson, who I knew only slightly, had run into a sister missionary he hadn't seen in a long while. He'd gushed, "Oh, I just *love* your hair!" and a couple of the other elders had looked at him oddly, with a mixture of fear and disgust. Was that a gay thing to say? Too bad I was too chicken ever to try to raise the subject with him. I'd heard once that up to 1 in 10 people might be gay. Did that go for Mormons, too? We had 120 missionaries in this mission alone. Why, that could mean possibly twelve of us were gay, but they were as invisible to me as if they didn't exist at all. Would pretending we didn't exist make us go away? If only the subject weren't so taboo, if only we could talk about it, maybe we could help each other out, give each other a hand.

Those statistics reminded me of my freshman Biology course in college with Dr. Pinter. She was so smart and fun and enthusiastic. She made learning hard things like the Krebs cycle and ATP production fun. She told us about a species of frog that were true hermaphrodites, and about a species of eel in which every single member was a functional female for several years until they all eventually grew to be functional males.

Dr. Pinter also told us about a species of fish in which there was one male for every 24 females, but if the male was killed, one of the females changed into a male almost overnight. There were enough of these species, she told us, that they were divided into two groups, one for those which were born females and then turned into males, and one for those which were males first and then became females.

It certainly made me wonder. But human beings were different. God wouldn't play around with our gender.

And yet Dr. Pinter had also told us that in addition to the usual XY chromosomes in men and the XX in women, there were some people born with XXY, some with just a single X, some with XXX, some with XYY, others with XXYY, and even some with XXXXY. Maybe there were even some other variations. I couldn't remember it all.

But I did remember that she told us the rate of these occurrences ranged from about 1 in 1000 to 1 in 5000, and I did the math. With a global population of over four billion, that meant over 800,000 people were born with just the X, two million were born with XXY, another two million with XYY, and still four million more with XXX, and this wasn't even counting all the other abnormalities. That added up to well more than all the Mormons worldwide, more than all the Jews slaughtered during World War II. Millions and millions of people who appeared perfectly normal but who were in reality sexual freaks like me.

Was it possible that being gay was simply a genetic mistake or natural variation as well, that it wasn't just a mental aberration? And if it were, was there really anything I could do about it?

Well, this wasn't truly about science, was it? It was about morality, and morality didn't change. Then again, I remembered, polygamy in the Church was seen as moral at one time, even a commandment, and now you were excommunicated for it. That seemed like a significant change. And Joseph Smith himself had once said something to the effect that, "What is wrong at one time can be, and often is, right at another."

But being gay could never be right. I was just allowing Satan to influence my mind if I let myself think otherwise. I wanted to be a respectable man, someone like Dr. Kildare. Or the father on *The Brady Bunch*. Someone anyone could see at a glance was sound.

Another man stopped to look at the streetboard, and I approached him, smiling pleasantly. Then I approached a couple more men who hesitated as they passed the streetboard. I didn't get a single referral, naturally, but Elder Deiana got one late in the morning.

I could never tell him I was gay. Yet it would be nice to talk about some of my other problems once in a while. I wished I could fully trust *anyone* at all. I suddenly felt alone again. The hours passed excruciatingly slowly, but finally it was time to head back to the apartment for lunch.

Elders Lucas and Sterling, Landrith and Sommers, and Deiana and I all climbed in the back door of the bus headed for Monte Sacro, lugging the heavy *mostra* with us, and since we had our monthly passes, we didn't try to move forward to the ticket box but stayed in back where it was roomy. After a full morning of 24-hour work, it was a relief to be heading back to the apartment for a break. Technically, we were still on duty, even on the bus, but I relaxed and didn't worry about contacting anyone else. I casually looked out the glass doors to the street below, and a young woman's face caught my eye.

The girl must have been about twenty, our age, slim, with short, black hair. She seemed fixated on us, like she'd just seen a long-lost friend. The bus took off, and the woman started running down the street alongside the bus. When we got caught in traffic, she kept running on ahead. Then when we pulled up at the next bus stop, she was there, panting, and climbed on board immediately.

"You're Americans, aren't you?" she said in English with only a slight accent. "I love Americans." She was addressing Elder Lucas.

"Yes, we're Americans," he said, clearly amused.

"Are you here for a visit?"

"No, we live here."

"Oh, that's terrific!" The girl brushed some hair away from her eyes. "I'm Marta."

"Anziano Lucas." He took her offered hand, still looking amused.

"Anziano?" she asked with an upraised eyebrow.

"We're Mormon missionaries."

"Oh, how awful!"

"We don't mind."

At this point, Elder Deiana nudged me and said in Italian, "She seems awfully fresh."

Marta looked at him and smiled but then turned her attention back to Lucas. "But do you ever get to go out and have fun?"

"We have one day off a week," he said. "We usually play soccer or go sightseeing. And that's the day we do our grocery shopping and write letters home."

Marta looked horrified. "That's it? You don't date? You don't see your girlfriends? What about sex?"

"We don't have sex."

Marta's mouth fell open. "But it's a biological need," she said. "Like eating." She looked around at the rest of us. "You've been brainwashed. You're wasting your lives away."

"Just two years," Elder Lucas said, still smiling.

Elder Deiana nudged me again and said plainly in Italian, "Is she talking about sex? What a hussy."

Marta looked at him again and laughed, and I told Deiana in Italian, "She's Italian, you know. She understands everything you say."

"No, she isn't," he replied. "She's American."

Marta laughed again.

"Cheerful, isn't she?" said Deiana, still in Italian.

Marta laughed even louder.

"Very cheerful."

Marta slipped a piece of paper into Elder Lucas's jacket pocket. "If you ever get horny, give me a call," she said. "You may look like missionaries, but you're still men underneath."

The bus pulled up to another stop, and she made her way to the door. She gave Deiana a quick peck on the lips and said sweetly in Italian, "You really need a girlfriend," with a perfect Italian accent. Then she hopped off the bus.

Deiana still refused to believe Marta was Italian, and we all talked about the encounter the rest of the way home. Elder Lucas looked pleased with himself for being the center of attention, and I wondered why she'd picked him. He was by no means the best looking in our group. Deiana was, but even if Marta preferred Americans, both Landrith and Sommers were better looking than Lucas. Maybe Lucas simply had an air of authority, and she liked that. Who could ever tell what was in another person's mind?

I looked at Deiana. I couldn't forget what he'd said right after Marta got off the bus. "I don't need a girlfriend. I have you."

While Elder Sterling prepared lunch, Deiana took a nap, which was against the rules, but I tried to get in a little studying. Normally, I read from the Book of Mormon, these days in Italian, but lately I'd felt a need to understand the Old Testament better, and right now I was in Proverbs. When I got to chapter 23, verse 7, the words jumped out at me. "For as he thinketh in his heart, so is he."

I realized glumly that my comparing the attractiveness of the other elders proved I was still gay inside. I remembered former President Jimmy Carter a few years ago admitting he'd committed adultery in his heart. People had attacked him severely for saying it, but I bet it was true of almost everyone else, too. It was certainly true for me, and I had to stop. If I read enough scriptures, if I prayed enough, if I was a good enough missionary, I could do it.

We'd been told recently at zone conference we were being too negative. "If you think positive thoughts," our mission president had told us, "you'll get positive results. The power of God is released when we think faithful thoughts. Just keep saying to yourself, 'If God be for me, who can be against me?'"

It sounded good, but how could I believe God really was for me in the first place? Either he'd made me gay, which seemed to suggest he didn't like me very much, or I'd somehow become gay through my own sinful nature, which certainly meant God would not like me now. Why should he help me when he probably just wanted to send me straight to hell?

How could I think positive thoughts when the Church told me my very existence disgusted God and every righteous person on the face of the Earth?

If "in my heart" I considered myself disgusting, though, didn't that act by itself make it a reality? I needed to think of myself as good before I could become good in actuality, but how could I ever consider myself good when the Church kept telling me every day that I was evil?

I remembered reading Gerald Pearson's book, *There is a Way Back,* when I was a teenager. I hoped I wasn't too far gone that I couldn't get back to a more righteous state. Why couldn't I be more like Gerald Pearson?

After lunch, I read a little more and prayed again before getting ready to leave the apartment. I smiled as we went from building to building. "We're going to get in," I told myself. "This family wants to hear us." "This man is ready for the gospel right now." Still, as usual, we had no success.

Then this evening around 7:00, Elder Deiana and I stopped by to see the Bocellis. They were a young couple around thirty who we'd baptized last week. I'd baptized one person back in Napoli, five in Sardegna, and then these two with Deiana. I was officially one of the highest baptizers in the mission, and everyone thought I was holy. Except perhaps for Elder Lucas, who somehow seemed a little miffed that I'd baptized more people than he had. But I knew it was all an illusion, that it was pure luck I'd found receptive people, that deep inside I was still a horrible person damned to hell if I couldn't change. Yet it felt good nevertheless to be part of the process that brought others to the Church, even if I personally wasn't going to be blessed for what was, after all, their own private decision to accept the gospel.

We rang the Bocellis on the citofono outside their building and when they buzzed us in, we took the elevator up to the third floor.

"Anziani!" said Sister Bocelli, opening the door. "Good evening!" She ushered us inside, where Brother Bocelli shook our hands warmly. He was slim but muscular, with a hard-looking face that struck me as very masculine.

Elder Deiana and I sat on the sofa, and Brother and Sister Bocelli sat in two chairs nearby. They had a huge painting of Roman ruins on the wall, and a Persian rug covering part of the marble floor. The marble didn't mean they were rich, though. We had one in our apartment, too.

"Find any other good investigators?" Sister Bocelli asked. "We don't want to always be considered the newest members around here." She laughed.

"No, I'm afraid not," I said. "But we're trying. You have any questions about anything that happened in church Sunday, or anything you've been reading in the Book of Mormon?"

"Not yet," said Sister Bocelli.

"Oh, I do," said Brother Bocelli.

"Yes?"

"Is fasting really that important? It's not much fun, and I don't see the point."

"My father never fasts on Fast Sundays," I said. "He has it in his mind that all the Church is after are fast offerings, so he feels if he gives money equivalent to two skipped meals, he doesn't have to fast. But if you approach fasting with the proper attitude, it can be a truly uplifting experience."

"Fasting helps us focus on the spirit rather than our body," Deiana said.

"Well, it makes *me* think *non-stop* about my body."

"Our mission president told us our attitude is the key." Deiana smiled, so pretty. "We can achieve anything our mind can conceive. When we've fasted once a month for a while, we learn to think instead of just feel."

"It's because of the way I feel that I joined the Church."

"We make our bodies obey our spirits," I added. "We don't let our spirits be subject to what our bodies want."

"But my body doesn't want anything bad."

I shrugged. "Then maybe you don't need to fast. But most of us do."

There was an awkward silence for a moment.

"Oh, I have another question," Sister Bocelli said.

I nodded at her, happy to change the subject.

We chatted for maybe twenty or thirty more minutes, and I was just about to signal Deiana it was time to leave when Brother Bocelli spoke again. "Something's been bothering me," he said thoughtfully. "Sunday afternoon after services, Tea and I went to the Catholic church for the baptism of her sister's baby girl."

"Well, that's okay," I said. "We certainly don't want to cut you off from your family."

"The thing is, we haven't told them yet we're Mormon. Tea's parents and grandparents were there. And we didn't want to upset them on a special day. So we dipped our fingers in the holy water and made the sign of the cross and took communion and pretty much acted in every way as if we were still Catholic. Tea said it wouldn't matter, that we were still Mormon on the inside, but I just wondered what you thought."

Deiana and I looked at each other, and I could tell he was going to leave this one to me. Though it really wasn't the same thing, for some reason I thought of the Marranos in Spain, after the Inquisition began in 1492 and all Jews were forced either to convert to Catholicism or be tortured and killed. Many pretended outwardly to be Christian but secretly continued practicing Judaism in private, for the rest of their lives. I was sure God still considered them Jews, as they did themselves.

I wasn't quite sure what to say now, but I just started speaking, hoping for the best. "Religion so often divides us," I began slowly, "and people use it all the time to hurt others. I don't think it should be used to cause pain. So I think not making a point of no longer being Catholic was probably the right thing to do. God knows what's in your hearts."

I wasn't sure I was correct, but everyone seemed to relax. I tried to lighten the mood then by bringing up a couple of innocuous subjects. We talked of our favorite oldies songs, from the days when songs seemed more innocent, when Johnny Mathis crooned so soothingly. And we talked of our favorite movies from the 1950's and '60's. As Elder Deiana and I stood up to go, I thought of James Dean and Sal Mineo and sighed. They had something I didn't. You could almost taste their testosterone. I bit my tongue hard for the nasty thought which came to mind. Why couldn't I be good and wholesome like Tab Hunter? Or tough and hard like Montgomery Clift?

We tracted for another hour after leaving the Bocellis, and on one apartment door we saw a sign, "Thieves took everything already. Don't bother robbing us again." In another building, a woman screamed when she opened her door and saw us just before we were about to knock, and a few minutes later, her husband came out with a gun to escort us out of the building. Crime was certainly high in Italy, but good grief. Did we really look like robbers?

We got home a little after 9:30, and the other four elders were already home. Elder Landrith told us of the lesson he and his companion taught tonight to a family of four, and then Elder Sommers added, "But they were just pretending to be interested. When we finished, they brought out their green Bible and started trying to convert *us*. They were Jehovah's Witnesses."

"But at least we got a lesson in," said Elder Landrith. "It'll look good on our stats."

We joked for a few minutes about "Jay Dubs," as we called them, and I had a glass of milk and a couple of Bucaneve cookies. Deiana had run out of his, so I gave him a couple of mine, watching him stick his tongue through the hole in the middle. Then Elder Sterling joined us in the kitchen. "Come listen," he said, smiling and motioning for us to follow.

We went to the living room, which Elders Lucas and Sterling used as a bedroom, and found Elder Lucas on the phone. Elder Sterling looked at us and put a finger to his lips. "I could see you at church," Elder Lucas was saying in English, "but we couldn't visit you at your apartment. We could send two sister missionaries over, though. Then if you had any questions they couldn't answer, you could talk to me at church about it."

We looked at each other and shrugged. He was talking to an English-speaking contact, a woman apparently. We got lots of English speakers from other European countries and from Africa. Two of the sisters had recently baptized a woman from Ghana. It didn't seem like a big deal at this stage. Deiana, of course, couldn't follow the conversation at all. I hated that we always spoke English in the apartment and left him out. I translated for him whenever I could.

"Okay, Marta," Lucas said, "if you change your mind, you have our number now, too. Goodbye."

So that was it. Lucas had called the number Marta had slipped into his pocket. He was pretending he was doing missionary work when in reality he was simply flirting. I suppose it wasn't important, but I still found it slightly annoying. I went back to the kitchen and finished my cookie.

The next morning at Devotional, Elder Lucas suggested we do the *mostra* at Piazza Barberini. We usually only did the *mostra* once a week, as a kind of treat, since it was marginally less painful than regular street contacting, but he was the senior zone leader, and if he said we needed to do it twice in a row, then he must be receiving inspiration.

We took turns carrying the heavy display, and it was Deiana's and my turn to carry it downtown today. Two other elders would carry it back. We left first because it would take us longer to walk with it after getting off the bus, and we had the streetboard set up near the subway entrance by the time the other elders joined us. No sisters came along today.

I got two referrals, and Elder Deiana got one, making me feel pretty good about Lucas's decision. We were supposed to stay till about 1:00, but I had to pee pretty badly, so Elder Deiana and I decided to leave around 12:45. We caught the subway to Termini and while in the train station, I overheard two American women, one of them asking the other, "I wonder which bus we take to get to the Vatican."

I stopped for just a moment. "You catch the 64 right out front, and it'll take you straight there."

"Oh, thank you! Thank you!" the woman said. "That's such a help! And by the way, you speak English so well!"

"Thank you." I briefly considered asking her about religion, but it seemed too mean to try converting a Catholic pilgrim on her way to the Vatican. Yet I was supposed to feel I was doing her a favor. No matter what I did, it never quite felt like the right thing. Could that *really* just be because I was gay?

Deiana and I caught a bus for Nomentana then, but we somehow caught it going the wrong way. I thought I'd die before getting home to the bathroom, but soon it finished its route in and started its journey back out again. By 1:30 we were back at our building and took the elevator up to our floor.

But as we neared our door, we could hear movement inside the apartment. Someone was in there. Two other missionary apartments had been robbed in the past couple of months, and now it looked like ours was suffering the same fate. I wasn't sure what to do, but I wanted Deiana to see me as strong. I wanted to be like Rock Hudson, or maybe Farley Granger, a real role model of a man if ever there was one. I'd go through the neighbor's apartment and climb across their balcony to ours. I'd scare the thieves out, and Deiana would be waiting to jump on them in the hallway when they tried to leave. Deiana agreed, and I knocked on the neighbor's door. "Remember," I said to Deiana, "jump on anyone who comes out our door." He clenched his fists with determination.

A woman answered and I explained the situation briefly. She allowed me in but ran behind me, shouting "Ladri! Ladri!" so loudly I thought the thieves would surely hear.

I went out her kitchen door to a tiny balcony and swung my left leg over the railing, looking down at the ground far below. I reached over and stepped onto the balcony of our apartment and then grabbed the railing and pulled myself over. It probably looked brave but was mostly stupid. Wouldn't it have been better to have asked the neighbor to call the police? Why hadn't that been the first idea to come into my mind? I thought about going back to do just that, but I didn't want Deiana to think I was chicken, so I took a deep breath and forced open the kitchen doors.

Elders Lucas and Sterling looked at me. "What in the world are you doing out there?" demanded Lucas.

"What are *you* doing here?" I countered. "We left before you!"

"Well, Elder Sterling has to cook this week, so we left just a couple of minutes after you. I guess we know the fastest bus to take."

"Oh."

"You didn't answer my question. What are you doing there on the balcony?"

I didn't want to answer but knew it would get out eventually, so I decided to just tell him. "I thought you were thieves, and I was going to surprise you."

"What a dolt," said Lucas. "Where's your companion? You're not supposed to leave him alone."

"He's out in the hall," I said, feeling my face flush. "I'll go get him."

I started through the apartment, wondering if Deiana was going to think I was an idiot, too. I didn't really care if Lucas thought poorly of me, yet I didn't want Deiana to. I guess how he reacted to me now would tell me a lot about the way he truly felt. Could someone *else* thinking positively about me, I wondered suddenly, actually make me a better person? The idea had never occurred to me before.

I'd thought acting like a man would make me feel stronger, more heterosexual, more natural. But my self-doubts never seemed to leave. The constant awareness of my completely alien nature was like an oppressive weight, suffocating me. I just wanted to be a regular guy and hang out with my companion as friends. But now I had to face him as the doofus I was. Would he call me a *cretino*? Or just laugh innocently and punch me in the arm? As disgusted as

I always was with myself, deep down I still believed I was truly worthy of friendship, so maybe that was enough for God to work with.

Still trying to figure out what to say, and looking back over my shoulder toward the kitchen, I opened the front door and stepped out into the hall.

Then, with a loud yell, Deiana ran forward and pounced on me, pinning me to the ground.

And even though I got an erection almost immediately, I still pissed my pants.

"Elder Anderson, is that you?" asked Deiana, lying on top of me. His weight felt wonderful.

"There were no thieves," I struggled to say. "Sorry about that. It was just the zone leaders."

Deiana got up, laughing, and reached down with a hand to help me up. Then he saw the wet spot on my pants and grew concerned. "Hurry up, Anziano. Let's get to our bedroom before the others see. I'll walk beside you to block their view."

I was mortified and felt my face burning, but Elder Deiana helped me up and then handed me the flip chart he'd dropped on the floor earlier, so I could cover myself.

"These things happen," he said with a shrug, "but there's no sense letting Lucas know." He put his hand on my cheek and patted it gently. "Now let's get inside and out of those clothes."

Deiana gave me a wink, and we whooshed down the hallway and straight to our room without being stopped. I quickly changed and started a load of laundry before lunch. My pants were finished drying before time to leave, but I wore a different suit anyway.

"It's a brand new you," Elder Deiana said as we prepared to leave for the evening.

I must have still looked uncertain, though, because Deiana grinned sweetly and said, "We're friends, Anziano. Any secret you have is safe with me." Then he patted me on the cheek again. "I'll tell you one of mine tonight so you'll feel better."

I suddenly felt warm inside in a way I never had before. Deiana liked me. What else could possibly matter?

The answer started creeping back into my mind almost immediately, but I forced it right back out. Just for today, I was going to be positive. Just for today, I was going to be happy. I could always be miserable tomorrow. I could be despicable again then. But not today. For the rest of this day, I was going to have a friend, even if I knew deep down I could never really open up even to him. "Let's go spread the gospel," I said, picking up my scriptures and smiling.

We prayed and then headed back outside, humming the same hymn in unison as we strode briskly together down the street.

Deiana reached over and squeezed my hand. After the briefest pause, I squeezed back.

Bus Surfing

"Come on, it's 3:30," I said to Elder Deiana, picking up my notebook and Bible. "You ready, Anziano?"

"Si'," he replied before heading for the bathroom to brush his teeth. I smiled and opened my notebook, studying the crude map I had drawn a couple of weeks earlier. Elder Deiana and I had tracted out almost half the streets in our new tracting zone in northeastern Rome, no small feat considering that nearly every apartment building was seven or eight stories high. Several doormen, however, had "helped" us speed along in our zone by refusing to let us into their buildings. Some wouldn't even allow us to use the citofono, or intercom, outside.

Deiana was pretty good with portieri, though. We were able to sneak past a few each night, and if we got caught, he could usually laugh or talk his way out of a potentially sticky situation. "Oh, I'm sorry," he'd say. "We didn't see you sitting right there in your desk by the door." The portieri were never pleased, but my companion's obvious lie and the twinkle in his eyes would usually get us off the hook without being shouted at too loudly.

Elder Deiana glided into the room then, showing me his clean teeth in a wide grin. He picked up a Book of Mormon and a few pamphlets from his desk. "Ready?" he inquired innocently.

After Deiana offered a brief prayer, we headed out of the apartment and down the street toward the bus stop. It was annoying to have to run half a block right after lunch to catch a bus, so we walked quickly down Via Franco Sacchetti and hoped we'd be close to the bus stop if the bus suddenly turned the corner. Just yesterday, we'd had to race for the bus, but Deiana had had to pause to avoid being hit by a car. I didn't realize he wasn't right behind me until the bus took off and I saw him waving at me. I'd stepped off the bus at the next stop and walked back to my companion. We'd had to wait another fifteen minutes for the next bus.

Resting at the bus stop now, I glanced at Elder Deiana. He was a few inches shorter than I was, about 5' 6", with short, straight black hair and olive skin, wearing a stylish Italian suit compared to my American polyester monstrosity. He was looking at a pretty, dark-haired girl who was reading a book. Deiana was always pointing out girls reading books. "Antonella read that one, too," he'd say, or "Antonella told me that one was garbage." I'd heard enough praise of Antonella to expect her to be swept up in a chariot of fire. "I like a girl who takes care of her body," Deiana explained, "but she's also got to use her mind."

A girl's mind was about all I cared about when meeting her, and I liked that Deiana at least put that somewhere on his list of priorities. I wondered if he'd find me attractive if I was a girl, but I had no desire to be a girl, and I didn't want him to be one, either. I liked Deiana as he was.

I'd never told anyone about liking guys, and I'd hoped two years as a missionary would purge those sinful feelings out of me, make me worth liking as a person. The feelings were still there, though, and I didn't know what I was going to do about them, but I was sure that God had had a purpose in mind when he'd given me a companion I could really love. Maybe being with Deiana would satisfy that need I had to have at least one man love me during my life.

I looked over at Deiana again. He had a contented grin as he continued to look at the young woman reading her novel. He seemed to be sentimental about a lot of things. So was I. I think that's why I dreaded the next day so much. Transfers. Deiana and I had already been together for two months in the Rome Four district, and I had never stayed with a companion for longer than that. It was almost certain one of us would be leaving in two days.

It seemed as if those two months had flown by, but I could hardly remember a time without him. Friendships usually came and went with transfers, but Deiana and I shared something special. We weren't just compatible companions. We were friends and really cared about each other, especially when we could sense that the other was discouraged or feeling depressed about something. Like that time I had cooked eggs and potatoes for him one morning, the day after he'd received his "Dear John" from Antonella. Or the time he'd washed the dishes for me one afternoon when it was my turn. I'd been discouraged with our lack of success in the work, and I felt like a failure. But I decided that if Deiana thought enough of me to help me out, I must have something going for me. I hadn't made many friends back in America, and I certainly hadn't made many out here. It was refreshing to have someone sincerely care about me now. Especially another man.

I had felt reasonably close to a couple of other companions previously. Nothing too special, but I would've liked to keep in touch after we'd been transferred. It was against mission rules to write letters within mission boundaries, of course, so when transfers had come, that was that. Maybe we'd see each other again at a zone conference, and maybe not. Would I break that rule for Deiana, though, and keep in touch after transfers? Would he be willing to break it as well?

"Anziano Anderson," my companion interrupted my thoughts. "Arriva l'autobus." We crowded in behind the other passengers. Since we'd already bought a monthly pass for eight thousand lire, we squeezed by some of the other passengers and made our way to a reasonably vacant spot near the front of the bus, where we grasped a metal bar above our heads as the bus took off.

Sometimes, we talked to the other passengers, trying to get their addresses so we could teach them, but usually my companion and I just talked to each other. It had been during our on-bus conversations that I had learned a lot about Deiana's past. Almost every time we passed the army outpost on Via Nomentana, I heard another story of the year Deiana spent as an Italian paratrooper. Even though his service had been obligatory and difficult in many ways (hassles with leaders and rules, mostly—Deiana sometimes had a big mouth), he seemed to enjoy a lot of the things he'd had to do that year. He told me of the times he and his buddies had clogged the bathroom drains in the barracks and had slid naked on their stomachs in the three-inch deep water, and about how they would terrorize the new "allievi" in the middle of the night by making them leap off of upper bunks in the dark onto mattresses they couldn't see. He reminisced about using the big guns on the base and the war games they played. Once, due to a miscalculation, a huge shell from the opposing team had landed almost at his feet. Fortunately, the ground was wet from rain and the shell had sunk about ten feet before exploding.

Last week after relating one of these stories, he'd paused, fingered the dog tag he still liked to wear almost every day, and had then handed the tag to me nonchalantly. He'd quickly turned to talk to a nearby man about the Church before I could say anything. Now I wore the dogtag every day. Another time when I'd asked about parachuting, he'd told me, "I was scared to jump out of that first plane, but since I had to go, I decided I might as well take a picture of myself falling," and he'd given me a copy of the picture later.

It was also on the way to our tracting zone near Piazza Bologna where I learned about some of Deiana's hobbies. He liked mountain climbing in the Alps, north of his home in Milano, and he enjoyed camping. I was surprised to find myself interested to hear about his hobbies because I had little desire to participate in them, though I had to admit his example with weightlifting had gotten me to work out with him twice a week so far. And his soccer lessons each Preparation Day had made the game at least reasonably fun, though I'd never been much into sports before.

More than that, though, I think we discovered we were both simply nice, that because we never tried to take advantage of each other or insist on having our own way, that it was a pleasure to be together. Once, Elder Lucas, our zone leader, had ordered a "work visit" with Deiana, intending to take my place as companion for an evening. But while Lucas was brushing his teeth after lunch, Deiana had pointed silently to the door and led me outside so he could work with me instead. "You're my companion," he'd said, giving me a light kiss on the forehead. "I want to work with *you*."

"Our stop's next," Deiana said, pushing a square red button near a window. We edged over to the two doors near the center of the bus. When the bus stopped, we jumped down and crossed over to Viale XXI Aprile. We usually had to wait for the light, but our timing was just right this time. We passed a blue and white police van, always parked in the same place, and about seven young policemen.

We'd been right by that police van when Deiana told me about the time he was in Milano on his way to school one morning and saw a carabiniere get shot to death by the Red Brigades. The carabiniere had been just a young man serving his obligatory military term but had had the misfortune of standing next to a higher officer, who had been seriously wounded in the incident. I think it was also as we passed the van on our way home one night when Deiana reminisced about the fights he and his friends in the military used to get in with the local punks in Livorno, where they were stationed, and about the time he was beaten in Milano after refusing to give up his wallet to a couple of thugs. He lost his wallet, anyway, but he said he always loved a good fight.

A few minutes later, we were on Via Pisa, so I opened my notebook and checked to see which building we needed to tract out next. We had to walk about two thirds of the way down the street before we could start. We entered the elevator and pushed 7. At least we didn't have to pay ten lire each trip up, like down in Napoli. Most of the elevators in Rome were free.

"You're awfully quiet tonight, Elder," Deiana told me as we stepped out of the elevator on the top floor. "Anything wrong?"

"Just thinking a little," I replied, smiling. "Wears me out."

"I can understand that." He smiled back and pushed the doorbell of the first door.

A moment later, the door opened. A middle-aged woman answered. "Chi e'?"

"Good evening. We're representatives of The Church of Jesus Christ of Latter-day Saints, and we have a short message we'd like to share with you and your family." Elder Deiana paused. "Is your husband in?"

"No." She closed the door.

"Oh, well. Good evening," he replied.

"Not your type, Elder." I pushed the next doorbell. "What is your type, anyway?" I wondered if his type had changed any since Antonella.

"Can I give a long answer?" He laughed.

"Sure."

"Well, she'd have to be pretty, have auburn hair—"

"Auburn?"

"Uh huh. And be fun."

I pushed the doorbell again. I wasn't sure if I heard anything, so I knocked. "What do you mean by 'fun'?"

"Oh, you know. Crazy. We can joke and laugh and have fun."

"Oh." We started down the stairs.

"But," he added, "she has to be serious at the right times."

"Like when?" I pushed the first doorbell on the sixth floor.

"In the park or in the car."

The door opened. "Chi e'?" said a guy about our age.

"Hi! We're from the Church of Jesus Christ. Is your father home?" I asked.

Before I even finished my question, the father was at the door, but he wasn't interested in our message. At least he was nice about it. He closed the door and Deiana pushed the next doorbell. "So what kind of car did you have?" I asked.

"A Fiat 500," he said, looking indignant when I snickered. The "cinquecento" was probably the smallest car made by Fiat, so tiny it made a Volkswagen bug look big. "Better than a moped!" he added defensively.

"I'm sure! So, just how serious do you like to get in the park or in your 500?"

We heard some rustling in the apartment in front of us, so we knew someone was looking at us through the peep hole. Deiana decided to give his approach to the door, but he got no response. We went down to the next floor. I pushed the first doorbell.

"Well, if I know her well enough, we'd probably French kiss."

"Yeah?" I paused. "I hate to sound ignorant, but I've never kissed a girl before. Just exactly how do you go about French kissing?"

Deiana looked incredulous for a moment, though I was sure he didn't know *why* I'd never kissed a girl, and I would have preferred to die than ever tell him. "Well, when you kiss," he said, "you just put your tongue in her mouth and tickle the roof of her mouth. Girls love it."

"And what does she do?"

"Chi e'?" said an old, female voice from the back of the apartment.

"Good evening!" I said loudly. "We're—"

"Chi e'?" the old woman shouted, a little closer to the door. It was useless to answer yet. "Chi e'?" she shouted again. Now she was almost close enough. "Chi e'?" she repeated yet another time, right at the door. I explained who we were and our purpose, but she was sure we were thieves and told us to go away. I pushed the next doorbell.

"Oh, girls do the same thing," Deiana continued. "Guys love it, too."

"I'll have to try it one day."

"You don't know what you're missing."

In the next building, we discussed relatives. Deiana almost died when he heard the country names of my Southern relatives, my Uncle Buford and Aunt Betty Jo, and my cousins Mary Lou, Thelma Rose, and Bertha Sue. A woman opened her door as Deiana was laughing, but fortunately, she was good-natured and liked to see two boys who seemed pretty decent. Since her husband was home, she let us in and we taught them our first lesson, about Joseph Smith, the Book of Mormon, and the restoration of the Church of Jesus Christ. They weren't terribly interested, but we left a Book of Mormon and a couple of pamphlets along with our card, which had the address of the local congregation and the missionaries' phone number. Who knows? At least we planted a seed.

Of all the different things we did as missionaries, tracting was one of my favorites because my companion and I were able to contact a lot of people and still have time to get to know each other better. We could discuss the work and new ideas, experiment with different door approaches, and get to meet with people in their homes where they felt most comfortable. It had taken me a while before I learned to enjoy it, of course, but it had almost always been better than referral taking on the street.

Not that tracting was always fun. After all, there was the time that woman had chased us out of her building with a pair of scissors, and over near Piazza Sempione last month when that man had pulled a gun on us. And there were a couple of doors shut in our faces each night along with being kicked out by portieri. But even those experiences were okay when shared with a friend.

I'd always been afraid of having to be with a companion for twenty-four hours a day, every day. Surely there would be habits and characteristics that wouldn't blend well. That was true, I'd found out, but after a year and a half, I had learned to tolerate an awful lot of habits. I'd had a couple of rough companionships, but Deiana was not only okay, he was absolutely the best companion I'd had out of twelve so far. We had a lot of good times, but still there were days when having a good friend by my side was the only way I survived emotionally or spiritually.

We had always been told, "Love the country, love the people, love your companion. Then you'll be an effective missionary." I'd always tried to put that into effect, and I'd found that it was true. All of that came together in my present companion, which made me appreciate him more than my other companions. But no one had prepared me to be separated from the people I had learned to love.

Frankly, I'd never expected to love at all. When I was a child, my Sunday School teacher had once asked us all to go home and tell our fathers we loved them, insisting our fathers needed to hear it once in a while. That night right before bed, when my father was in the kitchen getting something to drink, I'd said, "I love you, Daddy." He hadn't even looked at me. I supposed he'd felt awkward, but at the time I thought it meant he didn't love me at all.

I grew leery of the word "love" just after the one incident, and when my aunt told me she loved me a few years later, all I was able to manage in reply was, "I sure appreciate you, too." And whenever I felt particularly close to any other friend or relative, which truthfully hadn't been all that often, the only thing I'd been able to say was, "I like you." The word "love" just wouldn't come out. I felt it for Deiana, but I wasn't sure I'd be able to risk saying it again. I had tried a couple of times during the past few weeks, but the words simply would not come, in English or Italian.

Now Deiana and I were probably going to be split up. I only had six more months before I went back to America. Why, I might not ever see Deiana again after two more days. Ever! I slipped my left arm around Deiana's right as we turned onto Via Livorno. It was common custom among Italian friends, even guys, to hold hands or walk arm in arm. I had quickly picked that up during my time with Deiana, although I knew I'd be clobbered if I ever tried that with an American companion.

The first time Deiana had held my hand in public was during a district meeting with the other elders and sisters all around us. I'd been so surprised I didn't know what to do. I could feel my face turning red, but I *liked* holding his hand, so I didn't pull away. Then one evening, I had casually been rubbing my neck to get a crick out of it, and Deiana had come over and given me a massage. To feel his strong hands against my skin was wonderful. *Wonderful.* I was so afraid I'd fall in love with him, and yet I never felt that any of the contact we had was sexual. It was the touching between two friends, and I thanked God he'd sent me to a country where I could actually touch another man, and it was *all right.*

It was time for a break, so Deiana and I walked over to a nearby bar and ordered two glasses of Ferrarelle orange soda, my favorite. We watched a teenaged kid playing a pinball machine, and we talked to the bartender for a moment. He said he'd had the missionary lessons a few years ago, but he didn't care to hear any more. "Keep on working, though. I believe what you're doing is good." He wouldn't let us pay for the sodas. After thanking the bartender, we left and headed back to Via Livorno.

Deiana suggested a pee break then, but there was no place nearby with a public bathroom other than the bar we'd just left. So he led me into the next apartment building and up to the top floor. Then he found a door which led up to the roof. It was dark up here, but light enough to see because of the streetlights and apartment buildings all around. Deiana walked to the edge of the roof and unzipped his pants. "Come on," he said, smiling.

I had a hard time peeing in the presence of another man, and even using a public restroom by myself was difficult because I was always afraid someone else was about to come in. But this was Deiana, and I felt more comfortable with him than I ever had with anyone else, so I walked up to the edge of the roof and unzipped, too.

"Let's go," he said, and started urinating, right over the edge of the roof. I couldn't believe it. But a thrill went through me as I contemplated being so naughty, and I soon followed his example. When we finished, he laughed, and we headed back for the door leading down to the stairwell again.

The rest of the evening went fairly well. We only got in one more door, and that for only fifteen minutes, but we did have some good talks with people in the hall. One man said he'd come to church on Sunday, but of the hundreds who had said that to me, I had yet to see someone actually come out. There was always the chance, though. We'd see.

Deiana and I also got to talk more in between doors and buildings. I thought I already knew almost everything about him, but I did learn a couple of new things. For example, he could say some English curse words quite well. That jerk on the scooter who spit at us didn't know what was going on, but I sure did. He had that pronunciation and accent just right. I wondered who'd taught him.

We left our zone and started back to the apartment at about 9:00. We only had to wait a few minutes on Nomentana before a 136 came along. There weren't many people on the bus, so Deiana grinned at me and said in English, "Bus Surfing, U.S.A."

"In bocc'al lupo, Anziano," I said. It was an expression used to wish one luck, which translated literally to "in the mouth of the wolf." Legend had it that Rome had been founded by Romulus and Remus, two orphans who'd been raised by a wolf, so the expression was a wish that the recipient would be as fortunate as Romulus and Remus had been. The phrase had sounded ominous to me the first time I heard it, but I'd seen that a lot of things which seemed negative at first could turn out to be positive in the end.

Elder Deiana and I started bus surfing. We balanced ourselves in the back of the bus and tried to stand without holding onto or leaning on anything. I cheated on a couple of curves and almost fell at one stop, but Deiana had been practicing longer and was really rather good. My balance had been getting a little better lately, though, since I'd been practicing more with Deiana. A few odd stares did come our way, especially from one old, large woman in black who scowled at us several times, but we were so used to being stared at as missionaries that it didn't bother us at all. We either ignored the staring passengers or smiled back at them.

Within twenty minutes, we were back on Franco Sacchetti, where we pushed the button and hopped off the bus. At least at night we could get off at the same stop. Last week, when we'd been coming home for lunch at 1:30, the bus had been so crowded that only Deiana could squeeze off at the right stop. Then I'd had to battle for a minute with a "pasta mamma" and some young teens and get off at the next stop a couple of blocks away.

As we slowly walked back to the apartment, Deiana looped his right arm around my left, and he rested his head on my shoulder. We looked up at our building and saw that the lights were on in our apartment. The other elders were already home. We rode the elevator up to the third floor and started to walk down the hall.

Deiana didn't slow down as he spoke. "Ti voglio bene. Sai?"

I didn't hesitate, either, in my reply. "I love you, too, Elder."

Washing Dishes

"Okay, are we all agreed then?" Elder Lucas asked. District meeting, the almost always painful two-hour meeting we held once a week to evaluate our behavior of the previous week, set goals for the coming week, and inspire each other on to missionary greatness, was almost over. Elder Lucas sat slumped in his chair, leaning backwards with one arm thrown over the back, feigning casualness. He didn't have his tie knotted up to his throat like the rest of the elders, again trying to create a false sense of openness, though I doubted anyone was fooled, especially after the announcement he'd just made.

The four sisters and six elders looked at each other, trying to judge each other's reactions. Before I could say anything, Elder Lucas continued. "Good," he said, nodding. "Then it's settled. We'll each get sixty-seven hours of work this week, twelve hours of individual study, and eight hours of study with our companions." He looked around in calculatedly sedate triumph. "Each companionship will get seventeen referrals, and thirty hours of our work will be tracting and teaching." We were already expected to work sixty hours a week, of course, and sometimes even that wasn't easy. We were also expected to have personal study ten hours a week. Just where Elder Lucas expected us to find those extra nine hours, I wasn't sure.

I felt I was already a hard worker most of the time, and I didn't see the need of adding those extra hours as an "offering unto the Lord." The worst part, though, was that I wasn't given a choice. I was told I was going to do it. So much for free agency. Maybe taking orders was fine for the military, but I wasn't in the Marines.

I had thought when I accepted my mission call to Italy upon turning nineteen that learning the language, the missionary lessons, and working every day would be hard, and it was, but that turned out to be the easiest part by far. Dealing with the "mission leader personality" was the only challenge out here that really amounted to anything. The problem was that instead of progressing to the possibility of solving it, I seemed to be steadily growing away from that.

I had found these problems in almost every district, but it seemed worse here in Rome 4, or maybe I was simply growing less obedient and more provocative. During my first week in the district with Elder Lucas, I'd overstepped my bounds by trying to correct him, my superior by three degrees. Elder Lucas had brought up sex at the dinner table, explaining that he hadn't realized masturbation was a sin until he was interviewed to come on his mission, and he wished he hadn't been circumcised because he believed the foreskin protected the head of the penis, ensuring even greater sensitivity during sex. Having struggled my whole mission to suppress my own sexual feelings, I didn't feel up to listening to him, particularly as he didn't express any guilt over committing a sin I'd struggled with for years, *knowing* it was a sin and having to face two bishops more than once as I had to confess. They were embarrassing meetings, and whatever repentance I'd been granted was painfully won, and there Elder Lucas was, acting like for him, it was okay to have masturbated.

"Do you really think that's an appropriate topic for dinner conversation?" I'd asked, too irritated to be more diplomatic.

"You have heard of a penis before, haven't you?" Elder Lucas had responded immediately.

We couldn't date for two years, couldn't masturbate ever, and talking of sex seemed counterproductive at best, but I wasn't good at replying under pressure, plus I then felt the weight of his position in the hierarchy, so I said nothing.

That wasn't the end of it, though. The next day, my companion, Elder Stuart, and I'd had little success in the work, and Elder Lucas said, "You sure you're following the Holy Ghost, Elder Anderson?" Other leaders had said the same thing, so it didn't prove any special malice, though he did seem to say it rather zealously. Then two days later, he zapped me again. "You didn't teach a lesson tonight? Weren't you even *trying* to find a family?" I noticed that the other two elders hadn't taught either but received no reprimand. And the next day, I heard, "For goodness' sake, Elder, show some enthusiasm! You're so dull. I can just imagine what your honeymoon will be like." That remark certainly had little to do with missionary work, and it didn't teach me how to do better. I wanted to say, "You want me to fondle myself at the door?" but said nothing. He apparently was never going to get over my one comment.

With my feelings just as gay as they'd ever been, I wondered if he could somehow see it in me. I'd been out on a "work visit" with a zone leader in Naples once who'd wanted to check up on my work habits, and as we were walking through a park, he'd suddenly gone crazy, trying to attack a man just a little older than us, in his early twenties. I'd restrained him, and the man had walked off. Then the zone leader had explained that the guy had winked at him. It made me nervous that Lucas seemed fixated on my sexuality, as if he had secret information even if I did succeed in the work, but it also made me try harder to suppress those feelings, just in case he wasn't sure.

Somehow, I still had to find a way to stop being gay. But goodness, what more could I do? I'd never done anything gay yet, though the desire to do something evil was always there, always strong. Was it even possible to change? Maybe being with Elder Lucas was God's idea of an incentive for me to suppress those desires, or it was a punishment for not having done so already. Perhaps I'd have to be with Lucas until I could look into his probing eyes without worrying.

Anyway, we'd finished the business of our district meeting, and it was now time to bear our testimonies before we concluded. This was the part I used to think was the most intimate, the part that would bring us all closer. Now I mostly saw people lying, trying to impress others, or intimidated into submission. Occasionally, someone seemed to believe what they said, but then I could never be sure if they were ignorant or truly faithful. What I saw depended on my mood. Today, I needed to believe that faith was possible, so I tried not to be too judgmental.

Sister Larson stood up first. "I'm so grateful for my companion," she began. "She helps me so much. We work hard together, and I know we'll see success." She went on, explaining how she knew the Latter-day Saint Church was true, that Jesus Christ was the Savior, and that the Book of Mormon was the word of God. After she finished, the other missionaries bore their testimonies one by one.

I wasn't in the greatest mood and didn't feel like saying much, but I knew everyone had to bear their testimony during the meeting. I'd tried not to bear one once before, and everyone had waited in silence for three or four minutes before I finally decided to say something. "I know The Church of Jesus Christ of Latter-day Saints is the true church, and I say this in the name of Jesus Christ. Amen." A couple of the others had given me odd glances for my short testimony, but no one had said anything. I just didn't like that I *had* to bear my testimony, whether I felt like it or not. No wonder people thought we were a cult that brainwashed people. I sometimes wondered myself.

My companion, who was new in the mission, began bearing his testimony in broken Italian, and Elder Lucas translated Elder Stuart's Italian into something the Italian elder in our district could understand. I smiled and tried to pay attention to what he said. "I know we can do what Elder Lucas has told us, and I know we'll be blessed. I feel the work will really start growing in this area." New missionaries were almost always fired up. At least their enthusiasm seemed genuine. I felt Elder Lucas did it just to become a leader in the mission, not because he felt he could help us by leading us, but because he simply enjoyed the power.

Soon the Monday meeting was over and we all chatted for a few minutes before the sisters headed to their apartment for lunch. Elder Lucas was the cook for the elders this week, so he went into the kitchen and started getting things ready for the meal. I went straight to my room and started studying. With so little time left us to stay in the house, I figured I'd better use my time wisely. I pulled out my lesson book and began studying F, which was "Truth versus Error." The concept I was working on was about forgiveness.

"What'd you think of the meeting?" Elder Stuart interrupted. He sat down at his desk and looked over at me.

"What can I say?" I shrugged. "They're our leaders, right? They're called of God, aren't they? They're supposed to be inspired, right?"

"Supposed to be?"

"Let's just say my testimony of Elder Lucas isn't as strong as my testimony of other things."

"That's what I thought. What are we going to do about getting sixty-seven hours? I said I'd do it, but on our best weeks, we've only gotten sixty-two, and then my studying suffered."

"Do we have a choice? If we don't do it, he'll criticize us all week and tear us apart next district meeting." Not that I should care what he thought about us, but I did. Besides, it was too uncomfortable to be berated and ridiculed in public.

"That's an incentive?" Elder Stuart asked wryly. "Aren't we supposed to be doing the work to help the people?"

"I think I heard those words again—'supposed to be.'"

We tried to get some studying in before time to eat, not wanting to fall behind on the first day. I was growing hungry since our meeting had gone overtime, but I was used to eating only two meals a day, so I concentrated on my lesson. "To be forgiven, we have to forgive others," said my book.

I stopped. I hadn't noticed that before. Well, I had to have noticed it since I recited that line all the time, but it had never sounded quite so direct until then. I knew I really disliked Elder Lucas. I also knew I had evil thoughts of my own. Did this lesson say I had to forgive Elder Lucas for all the times he'd hurt me before I could be forgiven? I didn't know if I could pay that price. Facing embarrassment with my bishops had been one thing, but this price was far too steep. Wasn't that what the Atonement was for in the first place, so that Jesus could pay the price that we couldn't?

I knew I was rationalizing, though, and this ideal of forgiveness was too important to me to toss aside. Besides, didn't I have to prove somehow that I was better than Lucas? I'd read the prophet President Kimball's pamphlet condemning gays as selfish and hedonistic. If Lucas was petty or vindictive, it was because he was a human being and just hadn't progressed as far as he could in these areas yet. If I acted the same way, *my* weakness was because I was gay. I shook my head, knowing how stupid that was, but still wondering if it somehow were true. I had to be better than others just to prove I was equal.

But prove to whom? The world? They didn't know I was gay anyway. To God? Maybe. But surely he could see into my heart. He'd know what weaknesses I had and why I had them, which ones I was responsible for and which ones, if any, I wasn't. Then who was I trying to impress? Perhaps I simply needed to prove something to me. I thought for a second. I wanted to be better than I was. And certainly something I wanted in my character was not feeling disgust or hatred for another human being.

But how could I forgive Elder Lucas for deliberately hurting me, when he didn't even ask for forgiveness but continued the hurts? Was that how God felt when I repented of masturbation and then did it again, when I told Him I'd try not to fantasize again about guys but would do it not three days later? I hurt God over and over again and still expected Him to forgive me. Or at least hoped He would. So surely that's what I had to do for Lucas. But didn't forgiveness mean not holding those past actions against him? If "forgive and forget" had to go together, was it possible to treat Lucas as innocent when I knew he was still plotting?

Just last week, I'd been searching for my scissors for days, asking everyone in the district two or three times if they'd seen them. No one had. Then two days ago, I'd gone to Elder Lucas's desk to get the phone number of a local congregant, and I'd found my scissors in his top drawer. Maybe I was judging, but I couldn't believe he hadn't known they were there all along, that he hadn't deliberately stolen them. Of course, it was hardly a crime that brought the world to an end, but still, it *irritated* me.

And there was a certain cumulative effect to his petty offenses. When my companion was cook for a week, Elder Lucas found something bad to say about every meal. "That's not balanced." "These apples aren't too good." "Took you long enough, didn't it?" I lived and worked with Elder Stuart twenty-four hours a day. Cutting him down hurt me, too, if not simply because I liked him then because the criticism brought Stuart's mood down, which both affected my mood and also hurt the work. What made the hassling worse, though, was that these comments were usually followed by, "You've been around Elder Anderson too long," or "I think your companion's corrupting you," or even "That's something I'd only expect Anderson to do." Once he even said, "Thank goodness it's Elder Anderson's turn to take out the trash. I don't want to look at this stuff any more than I have to." I'd been so tempted to take his plate right then and empty in into the trash, and I kicked myself all evening for not having done so. I wondered how the others could pass it off as a joke. Elder Lucas was laughing as he said it, but I knew it was meant to hurt.

Elder Stuart didn't get a lot of that, however. Most was more clearly directed at me. A couple of Sundays ago, I'd been asked, five minutes before Sacrament meeting began, if I'd give a ten-minute talk. I had two five-minute talks written in my notebook and made up a story to tie them together. But after the meeting, Elder Lucas said, in Italian so all the members could understand, "That wasn't very good. We're supposed to be setting an example here."

Honestly, I couldn't understand why Elder Lucas *hated* me. Could it *all* be from that one comment I'd made weeks earlier? Would we run into each other at a mission reunion ten years from now, and he'd ask, "Can you handle talking about a penis yet?" So I didn't feel up to talking of masturbation at dinner, and maybe it was because I felt so insecure about my sexuality, but was that really so catastrophic? Could we never get past that? Surely, we could at least tolerate each other, learn to live together civilly. But he went out of his way to provoke me. I knew that the best, most infuriating response on my part was to be totally unaffected, but I couldn't play that role convincingly. Knowing he meant to hurt made me mad, and while I could be silent, I couldn't erase the cold expression from my face.

Then a new idea struck me. Maybe he wasn't doing it all out of spite. Perhaps he wanted to provoke me as some kind of incentive. He wanted me to retaliate, feeling that standing up to him would make me better able to handle rejections when going door to door, better able to turn those rejections into acceptances. I frowned. If that was such a noble goal, why wasn't there a class back at the Missionary Training Center on How To Be An Obnoxious Missionary? Then again, maybe that's what went on in those special, private zone leader meetings with the mission president. Still, I was sure it wasn't the Church that wanted me to learn self-defense. It was Lucas who took it on himself to teach me to develop "gumption" because he in his superior state knew I was a worthless human being without it.

Yet I remembered reading an account of Joseph Smith publicly criticizing Brigham Young severely and unfairly, and when Brigham had responded humbly, Joseph had said, "You passed the test." The account had deeply disturbed me, as Joseph's actions had seemed rather crappy, but I tried to remember that he was a prophet, and God must have told him to do it, and surely God knew what was right. But Lucas was no Joseph Smith. With Lucas, it didn't even seem he was simply letting the power go to his head. Even if he were just a regular missionary, I felt he'd act much the same way.

I tried to remember other leaders who'd been nicer, but there weren't many. One zone leader back in Napoli, though, had been okay. When our phone was out of order one week, he'd had to go outside and make a few phone calls. His companion was busy writing out a report one day, so he asked me to go along with him. I agreed and we headed down the street in search of a phone booth or bar.

We'd found a booth not too far away and he went inside, dialed, and started talking to someone at mission headquarters. It was the middle of February and I walked back and forth a bit while the zone leader talked, rubbing my arms and trying to keep warm. He glanced out at me, put down the phone, and took off his coat. I couldn't figure out what in the world he was doing. Then he took off his sweater, tossed it to me, and put his coat back on before picking up the phone again.

"Let's eat!" Elder Lucas shouted down the hall. "Hurry it up! We've got work to do!"

We marched into the kitchen and squeezed around the small table. If we were really careful, all six of us could fit. Elder Stuart, who was assigned to wash the dishes that day, moaned when he walked into the kitchen. The room was a mess, with sauce spilled on the stove and floor, and a couple of pots and several utensils scattered throughout the kitchen, all covered with either white, green, or red goo.

We sat down and stared at the food on the table. "What is it?" asked my companion.

"Spinach pie, of course. It'll be good for us. We'll need our strength this week. We've got liver for tomorrow."

Someone halfheartedly asked a blessing on the food, and we began to eat. I had a yellow plastic bowl instead of a plate because Lucas had somehow managed to get half the dishes in the house dirty. Even the yogurt cup I was drinking from had something floating in the water. I glanced at Elder Stuart and sighed.

The next two days passed in much the same manner. One way my companion and I found to get more hours of work each day was not to go home for lunch. We ate a prosciuto crudo sandwich from an alimentari grocery shop or picked up some grapes and cheese from some other shops and studied together in the park. A couple of hours less a day with Elder Lucas didn't hurt any, either. If forgiveness meant forgetting the offense, then avoiding him seemed the best way to get him out of my mind. I knew that wasn't real forgiveness, but I put that thought out of my mind as well.

My turn to wash dishes came on Thursday afternoon, so we ate in the apartment. When I walked into the kitchen, I almost collapsed. *Every* dish was dirty. Every one. I said nothing but ate quickly and began washing while the others were still eating. One elder tried to make a joke about it. "It'll help you get ready for marriage." I wanted to laugh, but I said nothing, hating myself for being mad and unable to shrug it off. Elder Lucas was the one who'd committed a deliberate act to hurt, and yet because I allowed it to hurt me, I was now the bad guy. And I hated Elder Lucas for that.

We were supposed to leave at 3:30, but I was still in the kitchen cleaning the stove before I mopped the floor. Elder Lucas stuck his head in the door. "Get crackin'. You never get out of the house on time."

If he wasn't still here, too, he wouldn't know that, I thought. He should practice what he preached. Besides, I *was* usually out of the apartment on time, especially the last few days when I hadn't even come in for lunch. He was obviously just trying to get to me. I *hated* that it worked. I stopped cleaning and looked out the window, counting slowly to ten in Italian. A minute later, I felt a hand on my shoulder. "How's it coming, Elder Anderson?" asked Stuart. "Can I help?"

"I've just got the floor left, but thanks." I started pushing a rag around with a broken broomstick.

"I'm sorry. I should've come in earlier to help. Or at least read to you so we could get some Dual Study time."

"No. I needed to be alone to think."

"Why didn't you say something? You know he did it on purpose."

"I wanted to, but I was afraid."

"Of him?"

"Of what I would say. You know, he's nice to the others. They don't even notice what he does to me. Or to you."

"Well, he mostly leaves me alone. How do you keep from getting mad? I almost died when I saw this kitchen."

"I've been seething all week, and it hasn't done me a bit of good. It makes me feel rotten, and it doesn't hurt him a bit. If anything, it makes him happy."

"Well, you're cook next week. You can get him back."

"Yeah."

I still had to pray and rest for a few minutes, so we didn't get out of the house until 4:00. I didn't care, though. We'd still have a good evening. Elder Stuart suggested we make up for the lost time by having him read aloud to me on the bus as we went to our tracting zone, so we could double up on our hours, getting companion study and travel time out of the same period, but which would go in separate columns on our statistics sheet, a little sneaky, but something our consciences could live with under the circumstances. Elder Stuart then took over most of the door approaches as we tracted, easily doing two or three for every one that I did, until finally I loosened up and was able to do my share.

After a few hours, I became thirsty, and when a woman said, as had everyone else this evening, that she wasn't interested in our message, I asked if she would still mind giving us a glass of water. I'd gotten through a reluctant door before with that approach, though tonight I was really mostly interested in the water. The woman returned a moment later with two glassfuls, but just as she reached the door, she spit into each glass and held them out to us.

"No, thanks." I smiled pleasantly as we walked away.

"Shouldn't we dust our feet at her door or something?" Elder Stuart asked a moment later. "How could you be so calm? I wanted to throw the water in her face."

I shrugged. "It didn't bother me," I said, realizing it was true. My first thought, in fact, had been, "Won't that make an interesting letter home?" I *expected* non-members not to like us. I'd never felt peer pressure at school because my classmates there weren't my peers. The people at church were. And not even my classmates at church. They so often didn't know any more about the Church than non-members. It was my teachers and other LDS leaders who were my peers, who were the ones I wanted to please, who I wanted to emulate. Now on my mission, my peers were the other missionaries, but I didn't even like half of them. Still, for the first time in my life, I felt real pressure from my colleagues, and I hated it. I'd preferred back home standing alone. So why couldn't I stand alone out here and just be myself? Why did I have to conform my life to what others wanted?

"You're incredible," Elder Stuart said. "To be so accepting. That must be why the Lord put me with you as my first companion."

"He put you with me because you're not a trial like everyone else," I returned. "Having one person I can like keeps me sane. Just barely."

"What would you do if Elder Lucas were your companion?"

"Probably slit my wrists." I laughed, but Elder Stuart didn't.

"Why turn your anger on yourself? Wouldn't it be better to kill him?"

"But murder is a sin, Elder."

"And suicide isn't? I'm not saying you should kill him. I'm just wondering why you don't *do* something."

"Well, he's not my companion. You are. And we need to get back to work and find someone who wants to listen."

We came in that evening at 10:00 instead of the usual 9:30, and I tried to get a last bit of studying done before we had to be in bed at 10:30. Besides, if I went to the kitchen for a snack, I'd probably have to talk to Elder Lucas. I hadn't been studying five minutes, however, before he opened our bedroom door. "How'd it go tonight?" he asked, coming into the room. "Teach any lessons?"

As the zone leader responsible for every missionary in the area, it was in fact his business how we did, but I still felt he was butting in. His question didn't *feel* professional. It wasn't my position to make that judgment, but I didn't look up from my lesson book as I replied. "Yeah."

"Really? Did you get a return appointment?"

I didn't answer right away, hoping to show him I was trying to get in all my study hours as he'd ordered, and knowing my answer would make him feel victorious despite our success. "No," I said curtly.

He didn't press me anymore about it but started talking with my companion. He made some jokes, talked about his evening, and announced that he'd just finished reading a paperback Church book, *Jesus the Christ*. He'd studied it so thoroughly, he said, it was now falling apart. Walking over to our trash can, an old detergent box with a plastic grocery bag for a liner, he tore out the pages of the book and threw them in. This time I did look up.

"Uh, we just emptied that," I said. "Do you think you could put your trash in your own can?"

"Oh, sure. I'm sorry." He picked up the can and left the room. "I'll empty it for you."

"Leave the bag."

I shook my head and turned back to my lesson, but I was no longer in the mood to study. Some of what Lucas had been saying could have been friendly if I wasn't already absolutely sure I disliked him. I wondered if maybe I'd been too harsh. Maybe he was finally trying to be nicer, and I had to be able to let him.

"Elder?" said my companion. "I smell smoke."

Two seconds later, Elder Lucas marched back into our room, carrying our smoking trash can. "I got rid of the trash," he announced, laughing, little flames reaching into the air, "and I left the bag in."

I tried hard to keep my voice calm. "If you'll get that out of here, I'd like to get some sleep."

The next day was Preparation Day, our day off having been changed recently from Monday to Friday. Elder Stuart and I left the apartment as soon as we finished our chores and headed to the park. Elder Lucas had been upset about our wearing blue jeans out of the house, saying we were setting a bad example and he'd have to include this in his weekly report to the president, but I needed to get away, and I wasn't going to lie on the ground wearing a suit.

Elder Stuart and I walked around the park, lay on the grass and wrote letters, and even explored some one-hundred-year-old ruins that were supposedly sealed off. One stone staircase had a jagged hole, so we had to stretch carefully over the missing steps. I wondered if anyone else had been up there in recent years and found my answer in the form of discarded hypodermics on an upper floor. I'd heard someone say this had been Mussolini's house, and I wondered if it would ever be restored or if the people wanted everyone to see the rotting shell as a reminder.

As a native Mississippian, I realized how long people could hold grudges. The North still didn't allow much development in the South. But Southerners held their grudges, too. My great-great-grandfather had fought at Vicksburg, but when we went up to see the monuments, my mom would say, "Don't look at that one. It's a Union monument. *Here's* a Confederate one." And the war had been over almost a hundred years before I was born. I didn't know enough about Italian politics to understand all their grudges, but I did know the government here was divided into so many factions it collapsed about once a year, the factions unable to work together. I heard that Mussolini's granddaughter was thinking of going into politics. I wondered how she'd do. I wasn't sure I'd want her in power.

Elder Stuart and I made our way back down the crumbling stairs and out of the building. We played soccer with some kids for a while and then rested on the ground.

"I'm glad the weather's nice," Elder Stuart said, looking up into the sky.

"It's been a good day. I'm glad you suggested coming here."

"Too bad we have to go back." He laughed.

"Yeah."

We became silent, watching a young couple lying down nearby, and three kids chasing each other. How could so many people look this laid back and carefree? Why did I have to be constantly making so many major moral decisions? I was surely overreacting by making trivial things into Heaven or Hell issues. Perhaps I needed to be more like everyone else, just relax and do what I wanted. Couldn't I simply give Elder Lucas the Italian "up yours" arm gesture and be done with it?

I shook my head. I guessed, as stupid as it sounded, I honestly did believe in the Golden Rule, to do unto others as I wanted them to do to me. Although scared of being murdered, I'd twice picked up hitchhikers back home because I thought that one day I might be stranded and need a ride. I was always nice to the Jehovah's Witnesses who knocked on my door in America because I knew one day I'd be a missionary and would want people to be nice to me. I didn't like people to criticize me, so I rarely criticized them.

Okay, okay. I said *one* thing to Lucas, but did I have to suffer eternally for it? Hadn't he already "gotten me back"? Maybe if I apologized to him, things would get better, but that thought almost made me sick. He disgusted me. How could I apologize, especially since he'd paid me back, and especially since I wasn't even wrong in the first place? I watched a cloud drifting slowly overhead, and then I closed my eyes for a moment.

A Catholic priest walked by. How awful to be celibate forever, I thought. At least I had a carrot dangling before me. One priest had angrily slammed the door in my face, though perhaps his irritability derived from his sexual frustration. Another had talked with us for an hour, and one had even suggested we visit a woman he knew in the building, saying she might be interested in our message.

Then I remembered another priest I'd talked with, the one who had been to Africa. He'd told me of a boy who'd been stung by a scorpion and chased it around until he finally killed it. By that time, though, the poison was already streaming through his body and he died. The priest had said it was too bad the boy didn't forget the scorpion and focus on the more urgent problem of getting rid of the poison.

The rest of P-Day went well, and we taught a partial lesson later in the evening. Elder Lucas and his companion taught a full lesson, and the other two elders got a good "call back."

The next morning was Saturday, our one sure day of working the *mostra* since it had taken so much trouble standing in different lines for hours dealing with the IRA (the Italian Run-Around) until we received our permit. We'd spent a dozen mornings fixing up the display the way we wanted it, with a presentation of the family on one side, a historical line showing the ancient church, apostasy, and restoration on another side, and a depiction of genealogy, the welfare program, family gardens, and other Church programs on the final side. It was a nice diversion from our other morning activities.

Fortunately, Lucas didn't participate much while we were putting it all together. Surely, our animosity would have come out in the display itself, and people looking at it would have sensed vaguely that something wasn't right. I wondered if even now while I was working with Elder Stuart, maybe miles from Elder Lucas, if people could still sense that something was wrong somewhere inside, and it affected how they responded to me. All this time I'd been feeling people could sense my homosexuality and responded negatively to that, but maybe it was my impurities rather than my irregularities that people could sense inside me.

"You and Elder Stuart carry the mostra," Elder Lucas ordered as we got ready to leave the apartment. It was our turn to carry the heavy streetboard downtown to Piazza della Repubblica, so we started out of the apartment ahead of the others, hoping we'd all get to the bus stop at the same time.

After we set up the board at the piazza, we spread out and looked around for anyone who might glance at the pictures and messages. This was usually a good morning to get the addresses of people who wanted to hear a little more about the Church, and Elder Stuart and I had only gotten six referrals of the seventeen we needed for the week.

"Good morning, sir," I said to an elderly man looking in our direction.

"Good morning."

"Did you know there was a prophet of God and twelve apostles on the Earth today?" I asked, noticing which picture he was staring at.

The man said nothing and didn't even look at me before walking off. "Why did the Lord have to call him to this mission?" I heard Elder Lucas remarking to his companion several feet away. I didn't think he meant me to hear, though, because he shut up and walked away when I turned my head in his direction.

Elder Stuart and I ended up with two more referrals by the time we started back for home, making eight for the week, three more than we usually got. It was true that raising our goals had also raised our achievement, even though we still fell short of the new goal and would still be told we were shirking our duty. Succeeding at missionary work was surely something that pleased God, though, even if it made us miserable. So was Elder Lucas the demon I felt him to be? I looked around the piazza at the people uncomfortably averting their eyes so we wouldn't stop them. Being uncomfortable wasn't essential to being good, but making other people uncomfortable somehow didn't feel right, so I simply couldn't agree that Lucas's tactics were justified. But doctors had to make people uncomfortable before they could make them feel better. I sighed. It was just too complicated.

I didn't feel like talking to any more people, so Elder Stuart and I left a little earlier than the others since I had to cook. On the bus on the way home, Elder Stuart nudged me. "Kind of a long morning." He smiled. "What's for lunch? No pig liver casseroles like last week, I hope."

I'd only learned to cook six meals to fulfill my quota each time it was my turn to cook for a week, and while no one raved over my meals, they were at least edible. "Ciampino Chow-Down Chili," I said, "bread, corn, sofficini, and blood oranges."

"Sounds good. Sounds like you'll get a lot of dishes dirty, too." He laughed. "Today's Elder Lucas's day to wash dishes, you know."

"Yes, I know."

When we arrived at our apartment, I threw my mail on my desk without reading it and went straight to the kitchen. Opening a few cans of beans after putting some ground meat in a skillet, I marveled at my situation. I'd been on a mission for ages, over a year and a half, and it was *still* hard. Didn't it ever get easy? I remembered one of the quotes we'd had to memorize in the Missionary Training Center. "That which we persist in doing becomes easy to do. Not that the nature of the thing has changed, but our ability to do has increased." But this mission never seemed to get easier. And our leaders always compared the mission to our life, so was life always going to be like this, too?

I was so tired of it all. What more was it going to take to prove myself? I jerked back the lid on the can of corn. I still had five months left. If I'd made it this far, I supposed I could stick it out. Enduring to the end was a principle I believed in. Of course, we were told that endurance didn't simply mean surviving but overcoming. I had to know for myself that I wouldn't run away from a difficult problem. Maybe Elder Lucas or I would be transferred soon and I wouldn't have to be with him any longer, but if it wasn't him, there would surely be someone else I couldn't get along with. I had to learn to deal with him because there would always be at least one "Lucas" in my life.

Was I being a doormat? The scriptures said to turn the other check. But I only had two cheeks. Just how many offenses was I supposed to put up with? Maybe not retaliating was a sin itself in some situations. Maybe it was right sometimes to fight back. Was I just a big, gay sissy afraid of a good fight? Even the early Mormons, after being kicked out of New York, and Pennsylvania, and Ohio,

Missouri, and Illinois, finally stood up for themselves when they learned the U.S. Army was coming after them in Salt Lake. They put straw in their houses, ready to burn them rather than have their property confiscated again, and they aimed their guns, ready to fight. And the Lamanites in the Book of Mormon who let themselves be killed rather than spill blood by fighting back at some point finally began defending themselves. But then, those were all life and death situations. All I was really facing was a few mean words, some of which were even true.

But even if I'd been wrong to criticize Elder Lucas that day at the table, why couldn't *he* be the one to forgive me? Why did *I* always have to do all the work?

I wanted to teach him a lesson. I should get the kitchen as dirty as I could and see what *he* thought about it. The best defense was a good offense, wasn't it? I'd had my strategy wrong all along. But then I reluctantly remembered F. "To be forgiven, we have to forgive others."

"Oh, please," I said out loud. I just didn't know if I could do even a part of it. I closed my eyes for a second, my hand on my head, and then I looked at my watch. The others would be home in ten minutes. I quickly set the table and started washing the skillet after the meat was cooked. Then I washed the boiler after putting the steaming corn into a bowl on the table. I had just finished cleaning the skillet I'd cooked the sofficini in when the other elders walked through the door.

"Just in time," I said, putting the pot of chili on a cloth on the table. "Let's eat!"

A Wife of Whoredoms

"One man with two women," said the woman at the door, looking at us in disgust. "You certainly look like Mormons to me."

Sorella De Feo laughed. "Well, we're not married. We—"

"So you're just his whores?"

"We're missionaries," said Sister De Feo, smiling, "and we'd like to talk to you about families."

"If you think families are so important, why don't you settle down and get married instead of going door to door bothering people?"

"So what you're saying," I said slowly, butting in, "is that you'd rather we come back tomorrow at 7:00?" I smiled pleasantly at her.

The woman stared at me a moment. Then she laughed. "No," she said, "but I have a coworker who might be interested." She gave us the name and phone number of a woman, and Sister De Feo put it in her Book of Mormon.

Then we moved on to the next door.

"Nice referral," said Sister De Feo, looking at me with a twinkle in her eye.

"Well, the trick is to find the referred person as interested as the person giving the referral thinks they'll be. Sometimes, they give us the name of someone they just want to annoy." The sisters laughed.

We were doing a "zone bust" this evening, all the missionaries in our part of Rome getting together and switching companions for the evening, just to spice things up. It was one of the rare times that as an elder I was able to work with the sister missionaries. I was with Sisters De Feo and Eldredge tonight.

I'd known Sister De Feo for ages since she'd started her mission in Naples, shortly after I'd arrived there. Now, since she only had eighteen months to serve compared to my twenty-four, she was almost finished while I still had several months left. This would probably be her last area. I'd always liked her, enjoying talking to her at church or in district meetings and zone conferences when we happened to be in the same areas. She'd also been in Cagliari while I'd been in Quartu on the island of Sardinia, so we'd seen each other quite a lot over the past year or so.

"Do you think I ought to introduce you two as my wives the rest of the evening?" I rang the next doorbell.

"I *would* like to serve another mission one day with my husband when we retire," said Sister De Feo. "Maybe a temple mission or as a mission president."

A man answered the door, and I gave my approach. He wasn't interested, so we moved on down to the next floor in the building. We kind of had an unspoken agreement. If a man answered, I did the approach, and if a woman answered, Sorella De Feo and Sorella Eldredge took turns.

I rang the first doorbell on the next floor, and another man answered. "Good evening," I said. "We're with the Mormon Church. We'd like to talk to you a few minutes this evening about the Book of Mormon. What would you think if you learned the American Indians had written a book of scripture just like the Bible?"

"I don't even care about the Bible," he said, smiling wryly, "but thanks anyway."

"But reading the Book of Mormon gives you so many more religious stories to make fun of," I said earnestly.

"Now that *is* tempting," the man said, laughing. "Do you have a pamphlet? That'll give me something to start with. If I get some good material from that, maybe I'll give you a call."

I handed him a pamphlet about Joseph Smith's first vision, and we moved on.

"Your approaches are a little unorthodox, Anziano," said Sister De Feo.

"The Lord works in mysterious ways," Sister Eldredge pointed out.

"Exactly," I said. We laughed again. I actually spent most of my mission depressed, but I could put on a good show when I tried, and tonight with the sisters, I wanted to try.

We continued tracting for another hour, not getting in, but having fun chatting to each other as we worked. Sister Eldredge was from Tooele, Utah, and had graduated with a Marketing degree from Brigham Young University. She said she'd hoped that would make her particularly useful as a missionary, but she'd only baptized two people in the ten months she'd been out.

Sister De Feo, as I knew already, was from Bari down in southern Italy. She was an only child, and her uncle was a Catholic priest who had a chapel on the bottom floor of the building her family lived in. Her parents were still devout Catholics. Sister De Feo had become interested in the LDS Church at sixteen, but since her parents wouldn't approve of her joining, she had to wait till she was eighteen. Then she cut her hair short so it would dry quickly, and she was secretly baptized. But one day, Sister De Feo's mother discovered her Book of Mormon hidden under her mattress and had beaten her with a broom when she came home from work. Her father had had to pull her mother off of her.

She was grounded for a year, and since she couldn't afford to move out on her own, she had to put up with it. She could only sneak in maybe one church meeting every couple of months, but then one day when she turned twenty-one, she decided she wanted to go on a mission. It would get her out of the house, let her be with Church members, and let her serve God. She secretly sent off her papers to the proper authorities, and even after she received her mission call, delivered of course to a friend's address, she waited until the day before she left to tell her parents. The vast majority of missionaries, probably 99%, paid their own way, but the Church was particularly interested in having natives proselytize in their own countries, so they were willing to foot the bill, $250 a month for rent and food. Sorella De Feo's mother tried a different approach this time and told her that if she ever wanted to return to God, she'd be welcome. Her mother had only written three times since she'd been out, though Sister De Feo wrote home weekly. She'd baptized four people so far, all in one family in Cagliari.

Sister Eldredge got a Call Back at another door, but that was the last of our success this evening. We had to stop around 8:00 because the sister missionaries had to be back home by 8:30 whereas the elders had to stay out till 9:30. We worked our way back to Piazza Sempione, where we met up with the other missionaries who'd come for the zone bust. I found my companion, Elder Stuart, and after wishing Sisters De Feo and Eldredge a good night, Stuart and I tried to work another half hour before heading home ourselves.

"That Sister De Feo is really something," I told Elder Stuart after we were back in our room. "A real Latter-day Saint."

Elder Stuart laughed. "I think someone has a crush," he said, winking at me.

I could feel myself blushing, though the accusation was ridiculous. I was still as gay as I'd ever been, despite trying non-stop to convert to heterosexuality. But it had certainly crossed my mind over the past year that if I had to marry a woman, Sister De Feo wouldn't be a bad choice.

"Had to marry," I thought with a shudder. What an insult to any woman to phrase it like that. Being with Sister

De Feo might actually be pleasant. For me, anyway, if not for her.

She never had a mean thing to say about anyone, not even her companion back in Naples, Sister Witherspoon, who everyone knew was awful. In all the time I'd known Sister De Feo, I'd never even heard her use words like "mannaggia" or "caspita," extremely mild expletives on the order of "goodness gracious" and "my word." I remembered hearing that back in Cagliari, she'd spent a couple of hours each Preparation Day for several weeks cleaning the house of a member who had broken her leg. And in Naples, despite her limited wardrobe of eight outfits that had to last for eighteen months, she'd donated one to a woman who'd lost everything in the earthquake. And she was always nice to me, even when other people weren't.

"No," I said, "but I definitely would like to keep in touch with her after she goes home."

"Robert and Patrizia sitting in a tree," Elder Stuart sang in a childlike voice. "B-a-c-i-a-n-d. First comes love, then comes marriage. Then comes Roberto in a baby carriage." He laughed again, and I did, too.

But it made me think. If Sister De Feo wanted to marry in the Church, her options were limited. There weren't many eligible Italian Mormon men. She might be willing to consider me. I wasn't much of a catch, but perhaps a gay Mormon was better than no Mormon at all. Still, as missionaries, we weren't even supposed to be thinking of marriage or dating. Right now, I just wanted to be Sister De Feo's friend.

I had always planned to get married, of course. Not only was it a commandment, an absolute requirement if one wanted to reach the highest degree of the Celestial Kingdom, but I also wanted children. My father had always been a good provider financially, but he never made me feel loved or even liked. I was simply a moral obligation. I knew I could do better for my children. I would talk to them, play with them, make them feel important. That had to start at a young age. You couldn't be distant for twenty years and then suddenly turn on a switch and be close. I just hoped my kids didn't turn out to be jerks, or creeps, or mean-spirited. It would be easy to be good to good children, but I'd have to be good even if mine were just average kids. In the year before my mission, I'd already started going to garage sales and buying baby clothes and children's books at inexpensive prices. I didn't know if I'd be as good a provider as my father had been. Maybe it was impossible to be good in all areas.

I remembered as a teen thinking that going through the temple would make me "a man," but now that I'd been through it, I still felt as immature as I ever had, just as unprepared to be a father. I'd been given a new name in the temple, one I was forbidden ever to tell anyone or even write in my journal. I was never even to say it out loud. But though I'd only heard the name once, I knew I would always remember it. The name was Hosea. I was shocked to learn upon studying the Biblical Hosea later that he was commanded to choose a wife "of whoredoms." Would I have to choose a promiscuous woman to marry? And would that turn out to be a punishment or a blessing? Sister De Feo certainly didn't seem the type to qualify, though she had once told me, "There are things you don't know about me." But maybe as a gay man I needed someone really experienced. Or did the name simply mean that my very nature, even as a virgin, was so decadent that I was a whore myself? I wasn't quite sure what the Lord intended by giving me that name, but I reflected on it often.

I didn't often think about women, though. Once, my companion and I had been walking down the street, and a pretty teenage girl had come up to us and said hi in a very friendly manner. I thought she was flirting with the young Americans, so I said hi rather curtly and kept walking.

Fortunately, however, my companion recognized her as the daughter of a couple we'd taught a lesson to a couple of weeks previously. I paid so little attention to girls that I didn't remember ever having seen her before.

But I was thinking more about women these days, so the next morning, rather than do our usual street contacting, I took Elder Stuart to see Rosa, a member of our congregation. I had also briefly considered coming back to marry this woman if I didn't marry Sister De Feo, because I also liked her, but that was out of the question now after what she'd told us on our last visit. I'd been impressed with Rosa right from the start. She was about thirty-five, way too old for me, but she was so sweet that I didn't care about the fifteen-year age difference. Even with no money, she always found ways to do nice things for other people.

For a new member of the congregation with poor eyesight, Rosa had bought a notebook and written the words to some of the more popular hymns, all in large print. For another member who was feeling depressed, Rosa wrote a poem specifically about the woman, making her feel special.

She babysat one day a week for free, to give another member in the congregation a break on child care costs.

Rosa was from Trieste, where her mother had abandoned her at the hospital when she was born. She was raised in an orphanage by nuns who used to beat her, so when she was sixteen, she ran away and married the first man who paid any attention to her. He beat her, too, but he did give her a son, Sergio. But as soon as her husband learned she was pregnant, he left. So Rosa raised the boy on her own, working part-time in the day as a cashier and, she'd told us without shame, part-time at night as a prostitute. The instant she told us, I couldn't help but wonder if that meant I was supposed to marry her.

When Sergio was six, Rosa brought him into a gelateria for a treat, and as they were leaving, a car ran off the road and right into the shop. Rosa was hospitalized for seven months before she could learn to walk again. Sergio had been killed outright.

But Rosa went on. She gained a lot of weight because it was so hard to walk, but she soon ran into two sister missionaries and before long was baptized. She had just a part-time job now as a check-out girl at the grocery, and lived in a rented room in someone else's apartment, but she was happy, and she came to church every week. She often went with the sister missionaries on teaching appointments, and she taught the Primary children on Sunday. The children all seemed to like her, recognizing that she was genuinely interested in them, and she was able to maintain control even over some of the more unruly ones.

A month ago, though, Rosa learned she had terminal cancer, and she had only a few months to live. That's what she'd told us on our last visit. Now she was just trying to enjoy as much of life as she had left.

It was almost 9:30 in the morning when Elder Stuart and I rang her doorbell. A woman answered and nodded resignedly when she saw us. "Rosa's in her room," she said.

We knocked at her door, and Sister De Feo let us in. She was there with her companion, Sister Moyes. "Salve, Anziano Anderson," she said when she saw me. The sisters weren't allowed to say "ciao" to us. It was too intimate.

"Two visits in one day," said Rosa, sitting on the edge of her bed, wearing a black skirt and a bright red blouse. "How lovely."

"Visiting sweet young ladies like you is the closest we get to dating," I said. "It's good we have the other sisters here as chaperones. You know you can't trust guys." I smiled, but then I thought she might take that as a reference to her no-good husband, and I felt stupid. "Did we interrupt you?" I asked, hoping to change the subject. "We did kind of barge in unannounced."

"I was just telling her about my mother," said Sister De Feo.

"How is she?" I asked.

"You know she hasn't been too happy with me the past few years," Sister De Feo replied. "But she sent me a nice letter a couple of weeks ago, and it gave me the courage to send my Church books home in the mail. It gets so heavy carrying them when I get transferred. I'm glad she's making more of an effort to accept me."

"Your mother is lucky to have a daughter like you," Rosa said. "I wish I could read more Church books. I need all the positive influence I can get."

We chatted for another twenty minutes, trying to make the work sound more successful than it really was to cheer Rosa up, but she was so cheery she was cheering us up instead. Elder Stuart and I ended up leaving at the same time as Sister De Feo and Sister Moyes, so we walked them to the bus stop. Then they headed off to Viale Regina Margherita while we went on to Via Nazionale.

"So was that visit to see Rosa," Elder Stuart asked after we'd all separated, "or to see Sister De Feo?" He smiled.

"I had no idea Sister De Feo would be there," I said, blushing again. "She didn't mention it last night."

"Uh huh." He nodded knowingly, still smiling.

Elder Stuart and I walked up and down Via Nazionale, pretending to make an effort at taking referrals from men on the street. We passed a bookstore, and I looked in the window longingly. I'd saved about four or five thousand lire each month over the past several months, so I had a tidy sum. I'd bought two Church books in Italian earlier in my mission and read both of them, but now I wanted to buy some Italian literature to send home to read once I finished my mission. We weren't supposed to waste our time in bookstores, so I wanted to wait till I'd saved up a little more and then just make one trip, one big sin instead of several tiny ones, getting economy-sized guilt.

Although I'd read the entire Book of Mormon in Italian, it wasn't the same as reading literature. I wanted books that showed what it was really like to live here, so I could always "come back" by picking up a book. Through the store window, I saw a copy of *The Secret Garden* in Italian, and I wished I could read something like that, too, just for fun. I already had a copy in English back home saved to give to my children. Maybe if I married an Italian, I could raise my children to be bilingual and would need copies in both languages.

Back at the apartment for lunch, we didn't tell the other elders about our visit to Rosa. They would have thought we were wasting time. In the evening, though, Elder Stuart and I worked harder at tracting, feeling we needed to atone for the "unproductive" visit.

And we actually got in. A man and his wife and thirteen-year-old daughter all listened to our lesson about the restoration of the Church. They didn't even laugh when Elder Stuart said that Joseph Smith went to "pay" in the woods. They didn't want to make a return appointment, but they did buy a Book of Mormon for a thousand lire and promised to read it. That wasn't likely, but hopefully it wasn't a totally fruitless evening.

Knowing we probably wouldn't be coming back, we deviated from our normal script a little and told them about temple marriage and how their family could be "sealed" together for all eternity. That was a really big point among Mormons, but I wondered, as I watched the father correcting his daughter a little too harshly on an unimportant point, why we necessarily wanted to be with our families forever if we couldn't even handle twenty years with our kids as it was. My dad was never actually mean to me; he was just indifferent. But did I want to be with someone for eternity who was indifferent? I'd be closer to my children, I vowed, and they'd want to be with me.

If I ever managed to have children at all. Could I marry someone without first telling them I was gay, and if I told them, would they want to marry me?

We had no more success the rest of the week, so Sunday was a relief, a day to relax in the company of other Church members. We took the bus to the Nomentano branch just outside the city limits, where the Church rented a house to use as a chapel and classrooms. There was even a yard, with grass, and an olive tree. I'd never realized an olive was as hard as a rock while it was on the tree. Who'd ever thought to soak olives in brine so they'd be edible? It impressed me that someone had been so inventive and clever. I wondered if I could ever do anything beyond my own experience. At least go beyond my desires for a man and discover heterosexuality. Living in Italy, being a missionary, all this was God's way of helping me expand myself.

I decided to seek out Sister De Feo and try a little benign flirting. She wasn't socializing with the others, though, hanging back, standing off to the side and looking at the floor. Had she heard something new about Rosa?

If Rosa took a turn for the worse, I wondered if I could somehow propose to her now and ask if she'd be married to me in the temple after she died, by proxy. We routinely did temple marriages by proxy for married couples who'd died without the benefit of the temple. I wondered if the Church would allow a half proxy marriage in our situation. I'd never have to face Rosa as a husband until after I died, and by the time I was in the afterlife, surely I'd finally be cured of homosexuality. Maybe that was the only fair way for me to marry, when I wouldn't have a chance of ruining a woman's life here.

But it seemed too weird an idea. What would people think of me if I suggested such a thing?

"You okay, Sister De Feo?" I asked, pulling her aside. I suppose I really liked her better than Rosa, but she was my age, and healthy. It was a little too scary thinking about coming back to visit her after my mission was over. If I asked her to marry me, she might say yes.

"Oh, I'm okay," she said, unconvincingly.

"What happened?" I asked.

She looked at me a moment and then shrugged. "Well, I got a letter from my mother yesterday."

"And that's not good news?" I asked. "She didn't become a Jehovah's Witness, did she?" I smiled, though I immediately felt the joke was inappropriate.

"She said she got the package of Church books I sent." She paused. "She told me she was happy I was finally repenting and getting rid of all that trash. She said she burned the books on the back balcony."

"Oh, Sister De Feo," I said. "I'm so sorry." There was an awkward silence between us. It was an inane thing for me to say, I thought. How could I think of being anyone's husband when I couldn't even talk to a friend?

She shrugged again. "It's only books. They can be replaced. It's just that I feel tricked. My mother never had any intention of accepting me. You don't know what it's like to be considered evil by your own family."

I nodded, though in fact I knew what it was like to be considered evil by *everybody*. At least Sister De Feo had Church friends who thought she was terrific, other missionaries, members of the branches she'd served in. *Everyone* would think I was slime if they knew the truth about me. Even Sister De Feo, most probably. It was unbearable realizing the people you loved would be appalled even to talk to you if they knew your secret. But maybe Sister De Feo wouldn't hate me if she knew. Not completely.

"Which books did you lose?" I asked.

Sister De Feo mentioned several books. I was pleased to hear her include *La Grande Apostasia* and *Il Miracolo del Perdono*, the only two Church books in Italian I had. I could bring her my copies next Sunday. That left only six more to replace. After Sacrament meeting, I pulled aside the member in charge of selling Church books and arranged to meet at her home to buy a few more from the list. The Italian literature to send home to America would have to wait.

The Miracle of Forgiveness, by the prophet Spencer W. Kimball, had been an important book for me, as there had been an entire chapter on homosexuality. I remembered one passage in particular explaining that while homosexuality was "repugnant" and "detestable," it could definitely be overcome. The prophet criticized those who said otherwise, insisting, "To those who say that this practice or any other evil is incurable, I respond: 'How can you say the door cannot be opened until your knuckles are bloody, till your head is bruised, till your muscles are sore? It can be done.'" He said it so confidently that I knew he must be right, and I knew if I tried just a little harder, made my knuckles a little bloodier, I could finally put all this behind me.

Maybe a tiny act of generosity would induce God to offer me a little more help. Of course, it was wrong to expect something in return, but that just proved how imperfect I still was. I could never do a good deed purely for its goodness alone. Being gay made me a weak person all around.

I intended to wait till the following Sunday to give Sister De Feo the books, but I started worrying that she would continue to feel bad in the meantime, so Wednesday evening after I knew the sisters were back in their apartment, Elder Stuart and I stopped by with a bagful of five books, all I could afford from the list.

"Anziano Anderson, I don't know what to say," Sister De Feo said from the doorway of the sisters' apartment. "It's too generous. Really."

"You've made a lot of sacrifices to be here," I replied. "I can make a few."

"Well, I can't thank you enough. I—" She stopped.

"What is it?"

"I have an idea," she said. "I can bring these to Rosa tomorrow and let her borrow them for the next few months, until…well…" She shrugged. "I just arrived in Rome, so I probably won't be transferred for my last four months. It'll make her happy to have some Church books to read. I won't be reading them again right away, and if it helps her even just a little…" She shrugged again. "I probably should have given them to her as a gift right from the beginning, rather than trying to send them home for myself."

I suddenly thought again that maybe I really could marry Sister De Feo. I should have seen by myself that Rosa was in the more desperate situation, but Sister De Feo had been the one to realize it. Maybe if I couldn't marry Rosa before she died, and I couldn't marry her by proxy in the temple, I might be destined only to get married to her in the Millennium after she was resurrected. Since she was so nice, and fit so well with my temple name Hosea, I should have been thinking of her more than I was.

Both Sister De Feo and Rosa were nice. Would God let me have two eternal wives? Of course, I wouldn't likely be able to handle being with one woman, so I didn't know why I was thinking of being with two. I smiled but felt a little sad, wishing I could feel closer to either of them than I suspected was ever going to be possible. As much as I genuinely liked these women, what I felt for them still paled in comparison to what I'd felt for my favorite companion, Elder Deiana. If I needed marriage to qualify for the Celestial Kingdom, and yet marriage forced me to live with a woman who could never feel fully loved, how could that commandment ever be considered righteous for either of us? Was it possible for God to demand something sinful? If I truly felt any love at all for these women, would it mean I would specifically *refuse* to marry them?

I didn't love Elder Stuart, but I liked him, and I gave him a pat on the back now, though I didn't really know why.

He turned to me in the hall and looked at me curiously. Sister De Feo grinned.

I suddenly remembered my last visit to the temple in Provo before coming to Italy. Our group of seven elders went to the temple once a week, on Preparation Day. Instead of a regular companionship, I'd been in a threesome in the Missionary Training Center, and I'd liked both of my companions. Near the end of the endowment ceremony, which we did in proxy for various deceased people, a select group of eight or ten people formed a prayer circle in front of the rest of the participants. It usually alternated between male and female in the circle, a man holding a woman's hand, and she holding the hand of a man next to her. It had been that way every time I'd gone through the temple, so I thought it was a rule. But on our last visit, there had been too many men, and I was put in the circle between my two companions, getting to hold the hands of two men instead of two women. It seemed like a sign to me then, though I wasn't sure just what it meant. And I wasn't sure why it reminded me of Sister De Feo and Rosa now. And Elder Deiana. I didn't know if even two women could compensate for never being with one man.

The other two sisters who lived with Sorella De Feo and Sorella Moyes had just finished baking some cookies, and they gave a handful to Elder Stuart and me. We ate them standing in the hall outside the sisters' apartment, since we weren't allowed inside. They also brought us each a glass of milk, and after we finished, we shook hands and left.

It was too late to do much more tracting, and a little too early yet to go home, so we just walked for a while. "That was really very good of you, Elder Anderson," said Stuart. "I won't tease you about her anymore."

I smiled. "If there were only a few more nice people out here, this mission wouldn't be such a bad place." Most of the time, it was miserably hard, but once in a great while, it was wonderful. I didn't really fit in, though, which always made me a little wistful, and I doubted I ever would.

Did the ministering angels in the lower degrees of the Celestial Kingdom feel bad because they didn't make it to the top to be gods? Did they always feel out of place, too? It was still the Celestial Kingdom, wasn't it, and they'd still earned the right to be there, hadn't they?

I didn't want to come in second. I'd always thought Olympic athletes who seemed peeved about winning a silver medal were bad sports, but now maybe I understood them a little better. I wanted first place, too.

"Well, I don't think the mission's so bad," said Elder Stuart. "I like it here." He punched me in the arm. "But maybe that's because I'm with you."

I smiled and clapped him on the back again. If I could replay the few good moments of my life throughout eternity over and over like a tape and experience anew what I'd felt at the time, that might not be so bad. As long as I didn't have to relive all the bad moments instead. I forced myself now to talk to a middle-aged man walking by, hoping to create another nice memory, but he gave me a disgusted look and moved on. Then Elder Stuart and I walked around the dark streets of Rome aimlessly for another twenty minutes, not knowing what else to do, before finally heading on home.

Bloodletting

The alarm rang at 6:30. I jerked awake, jumped out of bed, and crossed the room to silence the beeping. I had to put the clock on the other side of the room or either Elder Stuart or I would just reach over and turn it off without quite remembering to get out of bed. But if we weren't up and in the kitchen or bathroom by 6:35, our zone leaders came in to call us to repentance.

"It's not daytime again, is it?" moaned Elder Stuart as I turned the light on. "It was just day yesterday." He sat up and slid his feet to the floor.

"Hey," I said, smiling, "we have a great day ahead. We get to walk the streets and get referrals." It was tedious work both of us disliked, stopping strangers on the street to try to interest them in the Church, and we'd be doing it from 9:30 till 1:30. It was like pulling teeth, or getting blood from a stone.

Elder Stuart stuck out his tongue. "How can you smile when you say that?"

"Months of practice polishing my hypocrisy."

"I see why the Lord assigned you as my trainer." He grinned and stood, stretching. He had the slightest erection but seemed unembarrassed by it. I felt awkward and looked away, pulling on my slacks and stepping into my dress shoes. I was afraid he'd be able to tell I was gay if I looked.

After Elder Stuart had his pants on, I pulled up the serranda over the balcony doors, letting the morning light in through the glass. Part of why it was hard to wake up was because it was pitch black with the serranda lowered all the way so that not even between the slats could any light get through. Sleeping in complete darkness made me feel like a vampire. I turned off the overhead light and sat back on my bed, looking out at the dim light from outside.

I'd been out on my mission over a year and a half and only had eight baptisms. It was a lot really for this mission, but a friend of mine in South America had already baptized 62. I always felt I wasn't doing enough. And yet every month, I cashed a check for $250 from my father to get through another month. We were supposed to pay our own way, but my mother hadn't wanted me to get a job as a teenager. She'd wanted me to get good grades at school.

I'd worked a few days for men in my ward when they needed temporary help, but all my work altogether hardly paid for more than the first month out here. I knew that numbers weren't the most important thing, but it had been a while since my last baptism, and I couldn't help but feel like a parasite taking money every month with nothing to show for it. It wasn't as if my character were improving, as if there were any benefit of any kind.

I yawned and stood up. No sense in getting depressed before the rejections started at 9:30. Plenty enough time for that later.

Elder Stuart read the scriptures while I went to the kitchen. One of the other elders was taking a shower. I was usually first in the kitchen, and today I wanted to pretend I was eating, rattle my cereal box and wash a bowl in the sink. I was continuing a special fast I'd begun yesterday after our one communal meal at lunchtime. As missionaries, we weren't supposed to fast more than the first Sunday of each month. Extra fasting, apparently, would weaken us. But it wasn't as if there was any chance I'd become less effective in the work, as I wasn't effective at all.

I was fasting for help in finding someone who'd be interested in the Church, for help being more spiritual, and for help in somehow finally not feeling gay anymore. It was too much to ask from one fast, yet all of it seemed too important to leave out. But pretending I was eating this morning wasn't only so no one would know I was breaking a rule; it was also because fasting was only effective if you did it without making a show. I hoped by doing it "right" to at least counterbalance my motives a little.

I went back to my room to read from the Book of Mormon and pray. Then at 8:30, the six of us in the apartment gathered in the zone leaders' room for devotional. After a hymn and a prayer, Elder Lucas began, asking Elder Fois and his companion their plans for the day, and then asking me what my companion and I had planned.

Elder Lucas sat with his arms folded, frowning. "Knowing you guys," he said, "those plans won't be very effective anyway. So it's just as well I called the hospital yesterday and volunteered us to go in today to give blood."

We sat in silence for a moment. Then Elder Fois said, "It's against mission rules to donate blood."

"That's when there's no specific purpose for it. If it's just to be good, we're good enough already as missionaries. If it's to help the world, we're already helping by spreading the gospel."

"It's because it weakens us physically and we have to be on our feet all day."

"You should be sitting in someone's home teaching most of the time. If you're not, you need to work harder."

"How can I work harder when I'm weaker?"

"Christ fasted for forty days and you can't give a few milliliters of blood? If it weakens you that much, it's your spirituality that's weak, not your body." Elder Lucas laughed pleasantly, and Elder Fois looked at the floor.

"So why *are* we giving blood?" Elder Stuart asked.

"You too?" asked Lucas, turning his eyes upward. "If any of you were sensitive enough, you'd remember that Brother Cafiso's father is in the hospital with cancer. Brother Cafiso has fasted five days in the past two weeks, and his father needs a transfusion today."

"You're not supposed to fast more than once a month," Elder Fois pointed out. "God hears us then. If we don't like His answer, we're not supposed to try forcing *Him* to do *our* will."

Elder Lucas just stared at Fois without a word, and Fois looked down again. Finally, Lucas said, "The letter of the law is supposed to make us better, not be used as an excuse to get out of difficult things." He looked around the room at each of us. "And you, Elder Anderson?" he asked. "What do you think of giving blood?"

"You know I always support you when you make decisions as our priesthood leader." I tried to sound sincere, but the words themselves seemed laden with sarcasm. Or with hypocrisy. Of course, I always did in fact do everything Elder Lucas asked, so I did "support" him, even if I disliked him. And since I did what I said, it wasn't exactly hypocrisy. After all, God didn't ask us to enjoy obeying his commandments. He just asked us to do it. But somehow, doing something I didn't like did feel like hypocrisy. I wondered why Elder Lucas couldn't have explained the situation to us and asked us to help rather than volunteering our blood for us. Agreeing to go felt like agreeing that his methods were right.

"Good," said Lucas. "I hope everyone had a hearty breakfast because it's time to head on to the hospital."

"Now?" asked Elder Fois. "We usually don't leave the apartment until 9:30."

Elder Lucas sighed. "Can you find it in your heart to give up some of your own time instead of work time? We still have converts to find."

Elder Stuart and I went back to our room to put on our ties. Elder Lucas didn't like us attending devotional without them, and he usually made fun of me, but Fois had distracted his wrath today.

"You were pretty quiet back there," Elder Stuart said. "But I know that quiet."

"It's not right to force people to give a gift." I shrugged. "If it's not freely given, it does the giver no good anyway."

"Well, I guess Elder Lucas's point would be we aren't doing it for us but for Brother Cafiso's father."

I nodded and felt stupid, thankful I'd kept my mouth shut in front of Lucas. At least when Elder Stuart said it, he didn't mean to insult me, but Lucas would have said it not only because it was true but also to be hurtful. It irritated me that I was still so selfish that any time I even attempted to do something good, I worried about Celestial points. I knew I couldn't get any "points" until I stopped wanting them and instead wanted simply to do the good things, but then even my desire to want to do good for its own sake was still being shaped by the desire to forget that what I was really after was the points. That must be why I could never seem to reach the level of goodness I wanted, because the goodness was merely a steppingstone and my conscience knew it.

Because the hospital was on the other side of Rome, it took us three buses and well over an hour to get there. I thought the whole time about passing out at the hospital and having Lucas laugh at me. I'd never liked needles much, but when I was a boy, after I'd already developed a fear of needles, I had a TB test. I'd been dreading it and was so relieved to see how painless it was that ten minutes later in a drugstore with my mother, I passed out. She'd rushed me back to the doctor, who was concerned enough that he decided to do a blood test to see what had caused me to faint.

Even at that young age, I knew why I'd passed out, and as the doctor drew blood, I fought not to get woozy again.

Years had passed before another incident, this one when I was eighteen, right before my mission, when I had a flu shot. I was sitting on the doctor's table, he gave me a shot in my arm, and then he turned around. I saw green blotches and thought, "Gee, this is the same color green I saw right before I…" and the next thing I knew the doctor was reviving me.

"I know why I passed out! I know why I passed out!" I'd said while he tried to keep me from falling off the table.

The doctor laughed and said it happened to lots of people and not to be embarrassed. But I was. And if I was embarrassed if front of understanding people, it was going to be just that much worse in front of Lucas.

I didn't know why I should care what someone I didn't like thought about me. Because I was afraid he was right not to like me? I *was* a wimp. It wasn't so much that I felt my fear of needles made me seem gay. I wasn't effeminate, and I knew that lots of what most people considered masculine was macho nonsense. And though my gayness had seemed like the most gigantic obstacle when I first started my mission, the longer I was out here and the more I learned about myself, the less important that seemed to become. I hadn't done anything gay yet that might keep me out of heaven, but I sure did a lot of other things that could. So while my gayness still worried me, other areas did, too.

When other guys easily lifted heavy objects I couldn't, no amount of consoling myself on my GPA at school could make up for the self-disgust I felt at never using my body.

Losing thirty pounds on my mission so that I now weighed 150 did help me feel a little better, but my contentment could never last long before some other bit of reality intruded. One stupid little needle that I knew didn't hurt was going to prove yet again how weak I was.

We walked through the gates to the hospital, and Brother Cafiso met us at the door. He led us to the blood donor station, and we stood in line to have our blood tested before we could donate. "Now, you didn't eat this morning, did you?" asked the nurse.

"Yes," said Elder Fois. "Weren't we supposed to?" The corners of his mouth almost turned upward, but he fought it.

"Oh, no, not for this. You'll have to come back tomorrow, but we can still test you this morning."

I could still give, I thought, and get it over with, but I'd have to admit I was fasting, so I decided to just spend another day worrying instead. I followed the line and soon enough was sitting with my finger in the nurse's hand. A huge rush of an invisible force welled up inside me in the one second the sharp metal prick came down. The force felt like the cloth swab I used to pull through my clarinet back home to clean out the spit after I was through playing. The feeling just pulled right up through my body, and then— prick!—it was done.

Now it was simply a battle to have the nurse finish squeezing my finger before I fell on the floor. Squeeze. Drip. *Squeeze*. Drip. "Okay. You can go."

I still felt in control enough to make it to another chair, and I sat with my head lowered to my chest to try to prevent the green splotches. I couldn't put my head between my knees without being obvious. But I could feel the sweat forming on my forehead and stomach, that cold feeling I knew. So I lowered my head further and breathed deeply.

Damn! I thought. I didn't *want* to give blood. I didn't *want* to help Brother Cafiso's father. I wanted to be left alone. Surely, there were enough people without phobias to give the necessary blood. If I was going to be bad by giving with such a grudging heart, and bad to be so hypocritical as to be pushed to do what I hated, if I wasn't going to get *anything* out of this, why did I make myself go along with it, suffering physically and still hating myself? If I was going to hate myself anyway, at the very least I ought to have the comfort of not getting stuck and fainting.

"I hate giving blood," said Elder Fois, sitting beside me. "I always feel sick for two days."

"You make too big a deal out of it." Elder Lucas walked up beside us. "We used to do this as a family all the time back home. My dad even does pheresis once a month."

"Pheresis?" asked Elder Fois.

"They take blood out of one arm, spin it in a tube to separate the plasma or platelets or whatever they need, and put the rest back in your other arm. It takes a couple of hours. Giving blood only takes five minutes. When my dad was out of work for three months, he did pheresis every week."

"I'm so impressed," I said. I regretted it instantly, but I just couldn't resist.

"Are you really?"

"Somehow, the story reminds me of the widow's mite. It's easier for some people to give than others. If this is hard for Elder Fois, you're not helping anyone by being a jerk about it."

Elder Lucas raised an eyebrow. "All I did was tell an encouraging story. If you take such offense to it, it must be hitting pretty close to home."

My wooziness evaporated. "And I suppose *that* wasn't a jerky remark?"

"Methinks the lady doth protest too much. You're too sensitive for your own good. I get so tired of it."

"No one's forcing you to sit here and talk to me."

"You better watch that attitude, Elder. You know I have to report all of this to the President."

I said nothing but returned his gaze without flinching, trying to make my face a complete blank. He finally smiled and walked away.

I hated that man. I hated him. How in the world had the Lord called Lucas as a leader? "Mysterious ways" almost seemed like a cheap justification for the mistakes some leaders made in choosing the others. Giving blood was going to be ordeal enough. Why, *why* did everything have to be compounded by leaders like Lucas? Didn't I *just* go through this with him?

"Thanks, Elder Anderson," said Fois. "But I guess he's right. We really ought to be big enough to do this. We're already giving up two years of our lives. What's a day or two more?"

I nodded but stood up and walked to a window. It was thick with dust, and there was a chicken bone on the sill. I didn't need Fois to thank me, but I didn't need him to go against me, either. I remembered in fourth grade, a friend was being teased and pestered on the playground during recess, and though I was scared of the bullies myself, I felt I had to go help. All I did was say, "Hey, leave him alone," and they did, but then my friend turned to me in a rage. "I don't need you to fight my battles!" I'd felt so stunned that I'd walked away embarrassed, and we never did play together after that. I'd always welcomed any help that came my way. It seemed strange other people didn't feel the same way.

I remembered another time in junior high, kids were teasing another boy, calling him a "homo." I'd already realized by then I was gay, but I didn't really believe anyone else in my school or town might be. In any event, it was a mean thing to say, so I again told the torturers to leave the boy alone. They did but switched their attack to me. "Standing up for a fag. You must be one, too." The other boy ran away, leaving me wondering if only gays cared about injustice. Wouldn't a nice straight person help out, too?

But any time over the next several years I heard gays criticized on T.V. or in school, no one ever stood up for them or even said to live and let live. There always seemed to be a kind of feeding frenzy like when sharks smelled blood. Even the ones who didn't say specific mean things still laughed at what the others said. I sometimes remained silent, unless the talk was of someone I liked. Then I could use a niceness defense for the person. The others would look at me funny, but they'd be quiet. It was usually so easy to get them to stop, I wondered why more people didn't do it. I wondered why I didn't do it more, either.

Even today, Lucas had made my intervention uncomfortable, but he *did* shut up.

"Here come the results," said Elder Stuart, who'd walked up to stand beside me. "It's like waiting to hear if your lottery ticket will be called."

He smiled, and I did, too. "Not that you'd ever actually buy a lottery ticket," I said. I'd done so once, hoping to win and run off to another city where I could pretend to be Italian.

"Oh, of course not. It's against Church policy." He smiled again, and I laughed.

The nurse waited until we all looked at her. "Two of you have low iron and won't be able to give blood." She struggled over the strange names on her list. "Elder Lucas and Elder Stuart."

Elder Fois slumped his shoulders a bit, but Elder Stuart took a step toward the nurse. "Couldn't I take an iron pill or something?"

"No, no. Just you other four come back tomorrow. And don't eat breakfast first."

Elder Lucas seemed totally unconcerned. I suspected that because his family had frequently given blood, he'd often tested low for iron and knew he couldn't donate. It seemed odd that he so specifically asked us to eat when the nurse was so adamant we not. I wondered if he'd said to eat because he knew if we all skipped breakfast and came down today, he wouldn't have to give blood, but he would have had to miss a meal. This way, he lost nothing and even got to fill up half his morning with "important" work.

"New rule," said Lucas. "Whoever is cook, we need to start eating liver once a week."

No, "we" didn't need to, I thought, *he* did. And he could buy it on his own, rather than use our combined district money, but I said nothing.

"Can't we just take a pill?" Elder Stuart asked.

"Liver is good for you," said Lucas. "It cleans the blood. Come on, now. It's time we got back to work."

Elder Stuart and I retraced our bus route to our section of Rome and then started walking the streets, looking for likely people to stop. "I feel like a vampire sometimes," I said, remembering again how I'd felt that morning. "I know we're bringing something good to people, but I still feel like I'm stalking victims and pouncing."

Elder Stuart laughed. "I know what you mean. But we've got to look at it differently. We're not vampires, we're bloodhounds, sniffing out the people who are ready for the gospel." He crinkled his nose and sniffed.

"But bloodhounds are still seeking prey, aren't they?"

Elder Stuart shrugged. "No analogy is perfect."

We stopped half a dozen men, several minutes passing between each contact, and finally it was after 1:00, time to go home for lunch even though we hadn't taken any addresses. As we walked to the bus stop, Elder Stuart pointed across the street to a *farmacia*. "Let's stop in there a second," he said, and we went in. I was always amazed to find that people here could buy hypodermics in the drugstore and give themselves injections.

Elder Stuart picked up a bottle of iron pills and headed for the counter. "You don't like liver?" I asked.

"I want to give blood tomorrow. I don't really mind. I'll take your place if you want, and we won't tell Elder Lucas."

I smiled. That was so sweet of him, but I knew I couldn't use the word "sweet." "Thanks, Elder," I said. "I'll live to regret turning down your offer, but I guess I'd better go ahead and give, too."

"See? You're a good guy," he said, plopping down a few thousand lire on the counter.

"No," I said, "I'm not." I paused as a new idea began forming in my mind. "In fact, I've got a devilishly fun idea."

"What?"

We left the store and continued toward the bus stop.

"Elder Fois is cook this week, but if you could distract him for a few minutes, I could crush some of these pills and mix them in the spaghetti he's cooking for lunch. Then tomorrow morning, we can say we've prayed very hard that we can *all* help Brother Cafiso, and we feel confident that the Lord has recognized our faith and answered our prayers. We'll challenge Lucas to come back to the hospital and be tested again. If he won't, we'll say he doesn't have enough faith and prove it when you can give, and if he does come, he'll have to give, too."

Elder Stuart laughed. Then he looked at me, burst out even harder, and had to turn away. "It's always the quiet ones," he finally managed to say. "You know, he may not mind giving blood."

"It doesn't matter. I'll have the satisfaction of forcing him into it, just like he always forces us into things." I suddenly felt much better and stopped a man just before reaching the bus stop. My smile must have been convincing because we finally took our first referral of the day.

While the sauce was simmering and pasta boiling, Elder Stuart asked Fois to discuss something personal in our room, and I quickly dumped ten crushed iron pills in the sauce, just over one and a half pills per person if we ate all the sauce, which we usually did. Then I poured in a little extra sugar to cover up the taste of the metallic "spice." I was calmly standing on the kitchen balcony when Fois returned.

"That sauce smells good," I said when we all sat down to eat, not to throw anyone off the track but to spur Elder Lucas into taking an extra large portion so I couldn't have as much. I suppressed a smile when I saw I was right.

The meal went pleasantly enough, and it did feel nice to eat again after twenty-four hours. I savored the feeling and hoped the fast helped. Maybe sacrificing imperfectly would still make it easier someday to do right.

As usual, I said very little during the meal and tried to eat fairly quickly so I could go back to my room, but Elder Lucas apparently felt satisfied with the morning's activities and didn't feel the need to talk to us much during lunch. He couldn't let the entire meal pass without at least one dig, however, so as Elder Fois passed out the blood oranges for dessert, Elder Lucas turned to me and casually asked, "Made out your will?"

"Excuse me?"

"For tomorrow when you have your heart attack."

"I'm sure I'll be just fine, but thanks for your concern. It's touching."

"You were looking pretty pale this morning."

"I suppose it's the low iron affecting your eyesight."

Elder Lucas smiled. "I expect it's your lack of character affecting your circulation. I've been praying about this all morning, and since none of you can eat breakfast in the morning anyway, I think you and Fois need to skip any snacks later this evening, too, and make a fast to help increase your will to serve others and overcome your selfishness."

"But…" Elder Fois began.

Elder Lucas held up his hand. "Of course, it's up to you. No one can force you to do the right thing. That's something that has to come from within. I just offer you the challenge."

I wanted to say something right then about my own challenge, but I knew it had to wait until morning so Lucas wouldn't have time to think about it. "Sure," I said. "I'm up to a fast. I see more and more each day why you're a zone leader and I'm just a senior companion. We're blessed to live with you, rather than be off in one of the other districts without the benefit of your daily guidance."

Elder Lucas seemed to ignore my comments, holding out his orange well in front of him as he concentrated on peeling it. I tried to sound sincere and felt I was getting pretty good at it, though I wasn't sure that was truly an accomplishment. I actually did look forward to another fast because I still clearly had so much imperfection to purge from my system. The tiny refinements would take more than a lifetime, and I was still working on major issues, but at least I wouldn't have to feel guilty over this fast.

Suddenly, a spray of water hit my face. "Sorry." Elder Lucas withdrew his orange back toward his plate. "Elder Fois, you're right to offer us a healthy dessert, but try to find one a little less messy." I looked down at the red spots on my white shirt.

"Why does life have to be so difficult?" I asked Elder Stuart later while we were tracting out a lower income area, one of the few in our section of Rome. I swatted at a mosquito as we stood before a citofono, trying to get someone to buzz us into the building.

"There must needs be opposition in all things," Elder Stuart quoted.

"That wasn't my question. I asked *why*."

"Well, so we'll appreciate heaven. We wouldn't realize how wonderful it was if we hadn't come here first."

We buzzed another name and waited for a response. "Then you're telling me we should beat our children for a while so that later when we treat them nicely, they'll realize how great they have it?"

Elder Stuart laughed. "Earth life is just a short class to prepare us for the rest of eternity. God has to put obstacles in our way or we'd never learn anything. Mosquitoes teach us patience." He waved one away.

"Caribou sometimes run headlong off of cliffs trying to escape mosquitoes," I said. "Sometimes, there are just too many."

"Or that's a God-given example of impatience, to show us the evils of it."

"What do we need to learn patience for if heaven is so fantastic?"

"To put up with the people on the planets we create."

"I guess so," I said, thinking that was what lightning bolts were supposed to be for. I pushed another button, wondering if the intercom even worked. "I talked to a veterinarian once," I went on. "He said someone had brought in a kitten that seemed sluggish. The poor thing was covered in fleas, and it had lost so much blood it died. When we see so many people who are spiritually dead, I wonder how much of it is their fault, and how much is because of all the bloodsucking that goes on in this world. Sometimes…"

"We aren't kittens, and we aren't caribou," Elder Stuart said. "We're human beings, and God never gives us more than we're able to bear. You remember I Corinthians 10:13."

I nodded and motioned for him to follow me to the next building. "Yes," I said. "The gospel is a great big flea collar. I'll have to use that in a talk sometime." Elder Stuart laughed, and I did, too, but I wondered if my collar's effectiveness had expired or if I'd bought the wrong brand altogether.

We didn't teach any lessons during the evening, and there were no cookies and milk as consolation before bed. I kept us out an extra half hour so we didn't get home until 10:00, though I knew that was hard on my companion. I just didn't feel up to the temptation of food, and I didn't want to listen to Elder Lucas. Still, I felt bad over not giving Elder Stuart enough time to unwind before bedtime at 10:30. Just more of my selfishness.

"Sorry I'm not giving you much time to snack before bed," I said as we rode up in the elevator.

"Oh, I'm fasting, too. You're my companion." That was all he said, and I wished I could squeeze his hand in appreciation. After some of the companions I'd had, I really did realize how lucky I was to have Stuart. Maybe there was some truth to this "opposition" stuff.

"Out pretty late, aren't you?" Elder Lucas asked when we walked in the apartment. He was eating some bread and cheese. "Teaching a lesson?"

"No."

"I didn't think so. Dinner appointment?"

"Oh, for goodness' sake, stop needling him all the time," said Elder Stuart. "You really do have a bloodlust, don't you? He's doing everything you want. Can't you leave it alone?" He stalked off to the bedroom, but I deliberately stayed in the kitchen to talk to Elder Fois while Lucas continued to smack his lips as he ate.

"Okay, off to bed, you two," Elder Lucas ordered when he finished eating. "I can't guard the kitchen all night."

Elder Stuart was already in bed. I undressed in the dark and then climbed into my cot, anxious for a change for morning to come. Making Lucas go to the hospital might be sneaky, but Christ did say to be cunning, and maybe God needed me to do this to "chastise" Lucas. If God used leaders to shape us, He probably needed us to shape leaders, too. And maybe God was simply standing up for me against a bully by giving me the iron pills. I'd be refusing His help to ignore the plan.

If I wasn't being deceived and led astray instead. Trying to decide which possibility felt strongest, I finally fell asleep.

Soon, the alarm was ringing, and I turned it off. "Oh, it's not daytime *again*, is it?" asked Elder Stuart. "I'm *sure* it was day just yesterday."

We crawled out of bed and dressed for the morning. But as the reality approached of challenging Lucas's faith and making him go to the hospital, I began to worry. There was no chance of getting caught, so that wasn't a problem. And it wasn't even that the hospital would be far less oppressive without Lucas there. Elder Fois's companion was sure to tell him if I fainted or anything, so the ridicule would be coming in any event.

"Maybe we ought to go on without him," I suggested to Elder Stuart.

"Oh, he's coming," he said. "And I'm going to tell him before he eats breakfast." He started for the door.

"He could have bought some iron pills on his own. He heard you mention it twice at the hospital. If he's chosen not to help when he could, maybe we'll be helping him do something good and he'll actually be blessed for it."

"And shouldn't we want that for him?" Elder Stuart reached for the door handle. "God knows what's in his heart."

I put my hand on his that was resting on the handle. "That's the whole point. Damn, I *want* to do this, too, and I guess I'll be judged for that. But I just can't bear to think I'm sinking completely to his level. I have so little self-esteem out here. I simply can't afford to shatter any of it. We've just *got* to be better than he is."

"But if you want to do it, you'll be held accountable for it, anyway. You may as well get the satisfaction if you're going to get the punishment. And if you're holding back for an ego boost to feel superior to him, that's just something extra to be punished for on top. Then it'll just be your ego keeping the hospital from having more blood, and that can't be good."

I put both hands to my temple and closed my eyes. "I know, I know, I know, I know." I breathed deeply and then looked at Stuart. "There is no way to redeem this situation. I'll have to accept that. And I'm responsible for your desire to go through with it, too, since I thought of the plan."

"I'm responsible for what I feel," Stuart said.

I nodded and then sighed, shrugging. "There's an awful lot I don't know," I said, "and I hate not knowing. But one thing I do know is that it's wrong to force Elder Lucas to go up to the hospital with us. I could easily rationalize another answer, but I just *know*.”

We were both silent a moment, and finally Elder Stuart took his hand off the doorknob. “You’re a good man,” he said. “I’m glad you’re my companion.”

“No, I’m not.” That was one of the other few things I knew. “But I’m better for knowing you.” He was, after all, about the only one in our group who sincerely wanted to help Brother Cafiso’s father.

“You’re such a sucker.” He grinned, and I grinned, too.

“Tell you what,” I said. “If we can get out of the hospital early enough, we’ll take a bus up to Prima Porta and do some street contacting. I’ll treat us to lunch so we don’t have to come back here, and we can tract out the area until it’s time to come home.”

“Let’s go give some blood,” said Stuart. “And if you pass out, I’ll treat us to dessert after lunch.”

We waited until Elder Lucas was in the shower, and then we quietly left the apartment. He’d end up having to go to the hospital after all, since he couldn’t trade my companion for his who still had to go, but hopefully we’d be gone before they arrived. We caught a bus the instant we walked onto the street, and I sent a silent prayer of thanks upwards.

The air seemed different so early in the morning, fresher. I looked out the window at the buildings we passed every day, and I found myself smiling. I looked at Elder Stuart, and he was smiling, too. This was surely the only good day we were going to have all week, but maybe that was enough.

I heard Elder Stuart humming, and I wondered how Brother Cafiso and his father were feeling.

Maybe giving blood could be a healthy thing, not only for the receiver. Doctors in the past had used leeches on patients, and I'd heard the idea was being practiced again by some respected physicians. Maybe it was like fasting and could have some kind of purging benefit.

Oh, stop trying to make it good, I told myself. I just needed to go with the flow, accept things without questioning so much. Like fasting, maybe giving blood or suffering or obeying or even simply enduring could only have a spiritual benefit if one didn't make a show of it. I was going to give blood, I was going to get sick, I was going to get better five minutes later, and that was all there was to it. Maybe God made us come on missions so he could do pheresis on our spirits and isolate the parts he wanted to take out. I had to stop fighting centrifugal forces.

I focused on the scene outside the window. We passed an open market selling fruits, vegetables, and some bread. There was generally lots of fresh seafood around, too. I remembered I'd seen eels and squid and things. Maybe when Lucas insisted on liver, I could buy some unidentifiable seafood and tell him he was eating leeches instead.

I shook my head. So all the imperfections weren't purged out of me yet. Maybe that was okay. It was *supposed* to be a slow process.

But if I didn't get purged at least of my gayness, I might be excommunicated when I got home. That might be God's way of letting "bad blood" out of the Church, but I didn't want to be drained from that body by leeches like Elder Lucas back home. Maybe I was a white blood cell and *he* was an infection, and …

Oh, for goodness' sake, stop thinking, I told myself.

I sat back and relaxed, listening to the sounds of the city coming alive. Elder Stuart began humming. I reached over and patted his leg. He turned to me and smiled.

Almond Milk

I opened the letter from Elder Deiana, smiling in anticipation. We were discouraged from writing to anyone within the mission so we'd neither waste time nor spread gossip, but I was glad Elder Deiana had broken the rule. He was doing well, thank goodness, but life just wasn't the same in Pescara, he said, as it had been in Rome Four with me. There was even a P.S. from his companion. "I don't look forward to meeting you," wrote the companion. "I'm so sick of hearing about you I'd probably punch you in the face."

How sweet. Deiana missed me. I opened my journal and looked at a picture of him. I sent all my photos and negatives home to Mississippi since I had to carry everything I owned here in Italy in just two suitcases, but I did keep a photo of Deiana. I'd taken several, one of him in jeans studying outside on the balcony, another of him knocking on a door while we were tracting, and yet another of him on a bus. But the only one where his face was clear was the photo of him in his pajamas in bed, his knees bent, his legs halfway up in the air from having just plopped down on the mattress. He was looking directly into the camera, directly at *me*, and smiling. In bed. His legs in the air.

Oh, no. I felt a tightening in my crotch and immediately began rehearsing the words to a favorite hymn. "The Spirit of God like a fire is burning! The latter-day glory begins to come forth!"

Damn. Almost an entire month without any sexual fantasies. At least I'd stopped this one before it went too far. I'd been sure that serving two years as a Mormon missionary would change me, but the time was quickly drawing to an end, and I was still wishing…still wishing…

"We thank thee, O God, for a prophet, to guide us in these latter days!"

I read the scriptures for the next several minutes before my companion, Elder Stuart, called everyone into the kitchen for lunch. Elder Stuart was a good comp, nice and a decent worker, but no one could replace Deiana, and I didn't expect Stuart to try. Deiana had been very nurturing, even though I was the senior companion and had been out far too long to still need to be milk fed. But he had in fact fed part of me that had remained unnourished, and while I was no better at the work now, and no better at putting up with jerky missionaries, I still felt stronger somehow.

I'd managed not to talk about Deiana endlessly since he left, despite wishing we were still together. In some missions, companions stayed together six months or more, but here it was only a month or two. Of course, if I'd stayed with Deiana six months, it would have killed me to leave him.

Arriving in the kitchen, I sat next to Elder Stuart, who sat nearest the stove. "What do you have planned for this evening?" asked Elder Lucas, our senior zone leader, as he began to eat. He asked us our goals each morning during devotional and checked up on us each evening when we came in, but sometimes he liked to pressure us in the middle of the day as well.

"We're converting a family," said Elder Stuart, smiling. It was a private joke between us, to always tell Elder Lucas more than we really expected, because Lucas always said we weren't ambitious enough. We really did have plans to teach a young family, but Stuart had pushed it up one notch. Deliberately lying was the only way we could please some of our leaders. Stuart and I pretended we were "joking" rather than lying, so we could believe it was Lucas who was wrong in demanding our lies. But I knew we were both wrong, that something just wasn't right in a system that demanded lies over truth for the sake of a good appearance.

"You have an appointment?" asked Elder Lucas.

"Of course," said Elder Stuart.

"We told you that this morning," I reminded him.

"Oh, that's right." He continued eating, but I knew more was coming since he hardly ever spoke to me without insulting me in some way.

"Well, what are we going to do about the work visit?" asked Elder Ballantine, the junior zone leader.

"I guess you can take Elder Stuart out to teach the family," said Lucas. He turned to me. "He's a greenie," he explained, as if I didn't know my companion was new to the mission. I made up games all the time to make learning the language and missionary lessons more fun, wanting to make his missionary childhood nicer than mine had been, hoping to mother him just a bit. "He needs the teaching experience," said Lucas. "So you and I can go check out some referrals."

"That sounds good," I said, trying hard to make my smile look real. "That means we'll be teaching, too. Still something good to write in my journal." Elder Stuart touched my leg under the table to let me know he understood I was still playing the game, turning the referral into a teaching appointment, to show my positive attitude.

"You spend too much time in that journal. You should study more."

"It's a commandment to write in our journals," I said.

"We're here to be good missionaries. You use your journal as an excuse not to work hard."

And you use the work as an excuse never to think, I wanted to say but couldn't. If Elder Deiana were still here, I was sure I could have gone on to say it. I needed to be that strong by myself, though, and felt angry that I wasn't.

Elder Stuart and I both knew that Lucas wanted the work visit to keep me away from teaching. His secondary purpose, I suspected, if the teaching went well, would be to persuade Stuart that the following lessons should be entrusted to the zone leaders because of their experience. They'd thus be able to tally up the baptism as their own, but, more importantly, they'd actually have the experience of working with the people and watching the Holy Ghost work on them. I wasn't sure which was more important to the zone leaders. They apparently did have the Spirit with them, however, since they were in fact generally good baptizers. Maybe it was best after all that I wouldn't be teaching the family tonight. It was certainly more important for the Church to grow stronger here in Rome than it was for me to have a spiritual experience.

Just before he had to leave, Elder Stuart came up to me in the bathroom as I was urinating. "I won't let them take our family," he whispered. "If the lesson goes well, I'll tell the family I'll be coming back with you, and I'll take out my appointment book and not let Elder Ballantine schedule anything.

"Just have a good time tonight," I said. "If—"

Elder Lucas came into the bathroom, heading for the sink to brush his hair, which was so short it didn't need brushing. "I'm sure Elder Anderson can pee by himself," he said casually, looking into the mirror as if he were barely aware of us.

Elder Stuart moved over toward the sink as I zipped up. "Need any help with your hair?" he asked. Elder Lucas gave him a cold stare, so Elder Stuart shrugged innocently and left the bathroom. Elder Lucas then looked at me, his eyes resting just a second too long on my now covered crotch, as if he were looking for evidence that my companion had touched me.

I hated being inspected by other men, even with my clothes on. I'd seen so few other men naked that I was never sure there wasn't something distinctive about a gay body. When I was twelve, I'd peeked through a crack in the bathroom door at my grandparents' house, trying to catch a glimpse of my grandfather, but a glimpse was all I got, and it wasn't enough. Elder Lucas already made critical comments about my lack of muscles, complaining I didn't lift our homemade cement weights along with some of the other elders. I was slim enough, about 145 pounds, but I wasn't built. I knew Lucas didn't like my body, and I didn't like him looking at it.

I was sure Elder Lucas was one of those people who could spot someone gay in an instant. I felt constantly intimidated, afraid he'd one day blurt his suspicions out loud. It had been a general worry for years, which was wearying enough, but he amplified the fear, and spending time with him was downright exhausting.

I remembered when I'd discovered masturbation at thirteen how excited I was. Though I hadn't read any Church literature on it yet, I was still sure it was wrong. Then I made a second discovery, much more terrible—this white stuff left a stain. I realized it when my mother came to my room one day and sat beside me. My red chenille bedspread was in a clump at the foot of the bed, and my mother absentmindedly pushed it aside so she could sit. Then she stared a second, lifted it toward her face, and said, "This smells like…people." She looked at me, and I knew that she *knew*.

After that I only masturbated in the shower, but, even so, there was evidence, because sometimes in the middle of the night I'd dream about a man and wake up to find wet, sticky underwear. I was mortified, but Mom always did the laundry, so I knew she knew what was happening, and all I could hope was that it wasn't just gay boys who had dreams. When my folks were gone, I checked my dad's underwear drawer, and every last pair was spotless. Was that because he was grown or because he wasn't gay? Several times out here in Italy, I'd had those dreams, but at least I got to do my own laundry now, and, fortunately, my Bemberg garments didn't stain like cotton did. Still, it was amazing how much energy I spent guarding my laundry bag and checking my garments before changing clothes in front of my companion. It just couldn't be right to live in such constant fear of nature, but I did, and I felt that fear again now.

"Do I pass inspection?" I asked. Six hours with Lucas this evening, from 3:30 to 9:30. It was days like this which made two years seem an eternity. Elder Lucas didn't reply and continued brushing his hair, so I squeezed past him and headed for the door.

"Wash your hands, Elder. You'll be out representing the Church. Don't be disgusting."

He refused to move away from the sink, however, so I finally leaned over and washed my hands in the tub.

I stopped feeling fear then and felt anger instead. Even if Elder Lucas were perceptive about sex, he surely could never suspect me of being gay. Whenever he looked at me, he must see instead my utter hatred of men, since that was virtually all I felt when I was in a room with him.

We had to take two buses to get to the first address, given by someone the zone leaders had talked to in a park outside their tracting area. I knew Elder Lucas was grading me on my referral-taking performance this evening, and, though this was my least favorite missionary activity, I wondered if I should do it for the evening just to avoid his criticism. But as I saw a man at the second bus stop, I simply didn't feel like talking to him. Elder Lucas was the leader.

Let him lead, let him be the first to approach someone. Maybe I wouldn't do any street approaches even if he did do a few. Show him I wasn't going to be bullied.

The man was about thirty, with dark hair and a moustache. He was dressed neatly but casually, and he kept glancing at me, trying to read my nametag. He didn't smile, but he didn't look mean, either. He looked a little bit like Deiana, which was probably why I finally moved over a few feet and spoke to him.

"We're missionaries with the Church of Jesus Christ."

He nodded. "I figured. You the guys who don't believe in blood transfusions?"

"That's Jehovah's Witnesses," I explained. "We believe in science and medicine."

"Really? Science like evolution?"

"Well, that's a little complicated. We're kind of in the middle on that one."

The man laughed. "How can you be in the middle? We either evolve or we don't."

"We don't believe in evolution," said Elder Lucas, joining us.

The man nodded. "That's what I figured."

"That's not quite true, Elder," I said. Then I turned back to the man. "Would it be okay if we came over sometime to explain it all more fully?"

The man thought for a moment. "Will you two come? I'm not sure which one of you to believe, but I want to hear both sides."

"Sure," I said, though I almost considered passing up the opportunity rather than meet that demand.

The man told us his name was Sandro and gave us his address, asking us to meet him around 9:00 that evening. I smiled, grateful not to have to work a second evening with Lucas. "See you then," I said as he stepped onto his bus, which had graciously arrived just in time. It was awkward to conclude a conversation and then still be stuck at the same bus stop for five more minutes.

"Elder Anderson," Lucas said after the bus pulled off, "don't ever contradict me in public again."

We soon caught our bus and checked out our first referral. No one was home. We took another bus and checked out a second referral. The wife was home but the husband was out. Could we come back the following evening? Elder Lucas said yes, and we walked to the next address, or tried to. It was a stationery shop. No one inside had heard of the man who'd given us the address.

We taught a partial lesson at the next address and were told that was enough. I expected Elder Lucas to comment about my lack of spirit at the meeting, though he himself had done the actual teaching, but he said nothing, and we went on to check out the remaining two referrals. Nothing.

"Time to start tracting," said Elder Lucas around 6:30. "We can still teach a lesson before checking out your referral."

"We can teach two," I said. "There's time."

He looked at me coldly. "We're nowhere near our tracting area," he went on. "Are we near yours?"

I shook my head.

"Guess we'll have to do some Spirit Tracting. Where does the Spirit tell you we can find a family?"

"Peru?" I suggested, knowing of the phenomenal baptism rate in many South American countries.

"Funny. Lead the way."

We tracted out two nearby buildings without receiving so much as a Call Back, but I was relieved Elder Lucas's door approaches were no better than mine. I used a couple of his so he wouldn't try to teach me his way, but neither his nor mine brought us any luck.

"The Spirit told you to come over here?" Lucas asked as we entered our third building. "What Spirit are you listening to?"

"Did you ask for guidance?" I returned. "Feel free."

"Don't try that crap on me," he said, "trying to make this my fault. I'm the zone leader, and it's my responsibility to train you to be a better missionary. And that means *not* doing all the work myself but making *you* do it. Parents don't do their children any favors by refusing to teach their kids how to work and be responsible. So get us in a door."

"Yes, Daddy." I didn't get us in a door, though, and neither did he. We'd already taught a partial lesson, which meant we'd already had as much success as anyone usually did in one evening. Finally, around 8:30, we headed over to check out the referral we'd taken at the bus stop.

Sandro opened the door when we arrived around 8:50 and ushered us in. A friend of his, Alberto, was also there. "I told him about you, and he wanted to come," Sandro explained. "I hope that was all right."

It would be nice to baptize one of these guys, so Lucas would leave me alone for a while. I asked Alberto to offer a prayer before we started, but as he prayed, I realized I'd just hoped to use these men as ammunition, treating them simply as objects. Obviously, they'd be happier in the Church, so I was thinking of them, too, but I knew that wasn't what had inspired the thought. I opened my eyes during the prayer and stared at the plastic-covered flip charts in my lap.

I used to be a nice guy before my mission. I was almost sure of it. But maybe I'd only been nice because I'd never truly been under any real pressure. It was how one acted under pressure that showed one's true character.

And just one evening with Lucas made me see these men as statistics. It made me not want to teach them well, so they wouldn't want us back, but that too was selfish, to avoid giving them the gospel to protect my ego. Yet while I knew it was my fault for letting Lucas's pressure make me more selfish, it seemed there had to be something wrong with the kind of leadership I'd experienced my whole mission which made that kind of selfishness almost inevitable.

In fact, the whole idea of the mission was to use other people, to baptize others to prove to God we were worthy of the Celestial Kingdom. We came to score Celestial points and said so openly, as if this were something to be proud of. I'd felt selfish that my private goal had been to cure myself of homosexuality, but I only wanted that so I'd be eligible for heaven, so wasn't it all the same thing? We came to "help" others, thinking really only of ourselves.

I wished Deiana were here. He'd made me feel human. He'd broken his share of the rules while we were together, drinking tea, keeping us out after 10:30, talking to girls, and other things which irritated me, but at the same time I'd finally stopped feeling I had to obey every single rule perfectly. But I knew I'd have to break the mission rule next Preparation Day and write him a letter back for the one I'd received today.

Alberto finished praying, and I started the lesson, talking of Joseph Smith's first vision. The two men looked at each other doubtfully. Then Elder Lucas talked about the restoration of the priesthood and the translation of the Book of Mormon from the golden plates buried in the ground.

It was my turn to go on from there, but Sandro stopped me. "That's all very interesting," he said, "but we really have more scientific questions."

"Like evolution?" I asked.

"Yes, but other questions, too. Do you believe in a soul? How was the world created? Is there life on other planets? Do you think sex is natural? Do you think homosexuals are born that way? Do you believe in birth control? Is it natural for a man to have sex with more than one person? You do believe in polygamy, don't you?"

"You seem to be pretty preoccupied with sex," Elder Lucas said. "It's probably natural to have sex with as many women as you can, but the scriptures tell us we must overcome the natural man and live by a spiritual law."

"And homosexuals?" asked Sandro.

"That's not natural," Elder Lucas replied. "It's against both natural and spiritual laws."

"Well," I said, looking at Sandro and avoiding Elder Lucas, "it probably is natural to homosexuals to be homosexual, but…"

"But you guys can have six wives and it's okay," said Alberto.

"We don't practice polygamy," said Elder Lucas.

"But we used to," I said.

Elder Lucas turned to me and said in English, "Let me handle this, Elder."

Alberto looked miffed that we'd said something in another language and went to the kitchen. Elder Lucas explained to Sandro about polygamy, then about temple marriage, and finally about eternal sex available through a successful temple marriage to those worthy couples who obeyed all the commandments while on Earth.

All the commandments. That was never going to happen. It was odd, but the idea of eternal sex was one of the main goals I had in keeping the commandments. As much as I knew I wanted it now as a virgin, I couldn't imagine facing an eternity without it. And yet eternal sex seemed like a rather bizarre goal for the top of the list, reserved only for the most righteous of the righteous. Sex as an incentive for good deeds, as our main incentive even for missionary work. Part of the rest was certainly godhood and creating planets, but peopling those planets by providing spirits entailed billions of sex acts, and I knew from talking with other elders that this was something they looked forward to, whether it was with one wife in heaven or twenty, and most believed in polygamy in the Celestial Kingdom, even if they never admitted that to their girlfriends back home.

I remembered my Sunday School teacher telling our class of fourteen-year-olds that if for no other reason, we should stay in the Church and be good so we could have eternal sex. It was a way of keeping us in line sexually, to threaten to take sex away from us. It was a relief that sex was seen at least somewhat positively in the Church, since so many religions saw it almost always in a negative light, but our view still didn't seem fully positive. And though I *did* want that sex for eternity, it still seemed that something must be wrong with a philosophy that offered sex as its ultimate reward.

"Only those who've been married in Mormon temples have sex for eternity?" asked Sandro. "What about Catholics? Or people who live together for twenty years?"

Elder Lucas began answering, but even to me the answers sounded weak. If people didn't have a chance to be married in the temple but still lived a good life, they'd have the chance to have a temple marriage performed vicariously for them. So, yes, Catholics could have a good, eternal marriage, but fornicators, even if they really loved each other, wouldn't have any rights eternally. As I listened, I realized I wasn't sure any longer I even wanted to be with a wife eternally. I might be happier in a lower kingdom, where I could just be friends with people like Deiana. I was sure being with him had been more satisfying than sex with a woman. Maybe things did all work out for the best.

Alberto motioned for Sandro to join him in the kitchen, and I wondered as I heard him stirring a spoon in a glass if he were poisoning some drinks. He came out a minute later, but Sandro stayed in the kitchen this time. "He's preparing some Latte di Mandorle for you," Alberto explained. "I tried, but I can never get it right."

"Almond milk" was a thick, white syrup mixed in a glass of water and tasted like the icing on wedding cakes. I rarely had the chance to drink it, but I was suspicious, since cyanide was supposed to taste like almonds. Once someone had spiked a drink for us with alcohol, and though I'd never tasted alcohol before, I knew something wasn't right and stopped drinking. But for goodness' sake, these men couldn't have known ahead of time they wouldn't like our answers. Most likely, they were trying to show they were nicer than we were, serving people who stood ready to bar so many others from heaven. If I had a choice, I'd certainly prefer their company eternally to Lucas's.

Sandro came out a few moments later with four glasses, two of wine and two of almond milk. I took a sip, and it didn't seem quite normal, but it was okay, probably only my imagination, and I figured that to die as a martyr was better than living a mediocre life; in fact, it was what I'd prayed for most of my mission, so I went ahead and drank it all.

Elder Lucas was slower but drank his, too, as he explained how sex wasn't dirty but sacred.

"But why can't two people who deeply love each other share that sacredness even if they aren't married?" Alberto asked.

"Because if they truly love each other, they *will* get married and make a formal commitment," Lucas replied. "And if they're engaged, they'll show they have the strength to withstand adultery by withstanding fornication."

Alberto rolled his eyes, though this was one of Lucas's answers which did make sense to me. "What about homosexuals?" he demanded. He and Sandro looked at each other, and it finally dawned on me they were both gay. How had I missed that? I'd just thought they were liberals. I looked to see if Elder Lucas had noticed.

"You need to repent and find a good woman," he said. He'd probably noticed right away.

"And avoid all sexual fulfillment," said Alberto. "No, thanks. If God gave us sex organs, I think He expected us to use them to the best of our ability."

"Sexual fulfillment now or sexual fulfillment for eternity," said Lucas. "It's your choice."

"God cares about the fall of a sparrow," asked Sandro, "but can't care about me if I'm not part of a heterosexual couple?"

"Homosexuality is a manifestation of a deeper spiritual rot," Elder Lucas said calmly. "If you don't cut out the dead tissue soon, the gangrene will spread throughout your system, and there is no recovery from total spiritual death. Most homosexuals are already spiritually dead. I can't judge them, but I expect most will be cast into Outer Darkness with Satan because there's nothing left to salvage."

The two men looked stunned for a moment, and then Alberto laughed. I knew what Elder Lucas said was right, but I still felt as though I'd been stabbed or scalped or had my fingernails ripped off. But none of that really described the feeling I had when I heard Church leaders talk about me. Once when I was a boy, I'd put a broken plastic toy in a campfire and then poked it with a stick. The toy melted onto the stick and kept burning, and I marched around triumphantly with my torch, until a tiny drop of plastic dripped onto my head. The burning, searing pain was intense, but after I ran inside and stuck my head under the faucet, all my mother could find was a tiny blister the size of a pea. That was the closest pain I could associate with hearing what God thought of me. Burning plastic was dripping inside my chest. And yet I knew that when Church members said these things, they truly had no clue of the pain they inflicted, seeming surprised if anyone ever acted hurt. If people felt pain, it was their own fault for doing something wrong. It was simply the realization of their sin and its consequences that caused their pain.

"God seems to be a bit of a pervert," Alberto said. "He seems awfully fixated on my penis."

"God cares about all sin," Elder Lucas said stiffly.

"And yet the only children I'm allowed to teach are my own," said Sandro. "I can't just be a good uncle, or a good elementary school teacher, or help society in some other way. I absolutely *must* bring children into this world."

"God made the commandments, not me," Lucas replied. "I'm just here to tell you about them. It's up to you to follow them."

It felt awful hearing the men ask the same things I'd asked myself over and over. Lucas was so cool and collected, so sure he was right. He *sounded* right. And yet I knew there were plenty of families where the parents didn't have family prayer, or always teach the kids the right principles. Those families weren't heavily praised, but they were still respectable, just by the mere fact of being a family. It was almost as if God was saying, "He used his penis in her vagina, as I intended. The rest we can work out." It did seem hard to accept at times.

And these two men looked so good together.

Oh, but that was Satan tempting me. I looked at Elder Lucas. I needed his strength. I hated needing him of all people, but I couldn't let my pride keep me from the truth.

"What if I told you that when I prayed and asked God if He approved of my being gay, He gave me a wonderfully warm and confirming answer?" Sandro said it sincerely, as if such a thing could have really happened.

"Then I'd say you were praying to the wrong source."

Alberto laughed again. "These guys have their minds made up," he said to Sandro. "If they don't like the evidence, they just claim it doesn't exist."

"No," said Lucas, "you're the ones doing that. The evidence is all around you."

"You know," Sandro said, shaking his head, "you act like sex is the most important part of a relationship, or the only part. It's good, but really, we know lots of couples who have been together for years, and the most important thing—"

"Don't try to justify it to them," Alberto interrupted. "It's demeaning."

Sandro sighed and patted Alberto's knee. Then he turned back to us. "What it boils down to," he said, "is that you believe in a God who would let us experience the joy and beauty of sex and a loving, committed relationship, and then would deny it to us for eternity, while we know there are others up there in heaven who are having sex all the time. This God would *want* us to have a perfect memory of our lives as our punishment, would want us to remember what love and sex had been and what it had meant for us. And just because we didn't understand the rules, or because we were weak, or because we made a few mistakes, your God would punish us for millions and billions and trillions of years for those few mistakes made over thirty years." He nodded. "I don't think I want to know any more about your Church. You can leave now."

"I can tell you in the name of Jesus Christ that—"

"I said you could leave now," Sandro repeated. "I'm hardly going to stop loving this man because some kid told me his cruel god said to."

"You guys are lovers?" I asked. I hadn't figured that out yet. I thought they were just friends.

"Shut up," said Elder Lucas in English. He stood up, and I did, too. God, how I wished I could talk to them. I wondered if I could bring Elder Stuart here another day, if Stuart would tell anyone we'd come. I wished I could come alone. Even Deiana I couldn't tell everything to. I wondered if there would ever be anyone in my life I could really talk to. These men apparently had talking, friendship, *and* sex. That was certainly too much to hope for, but I thought I could settle for no sex if I could just really talk to someone. Deiana had been the closest I'd ever come, and that was damned satisfying.

I realized then that Deiana was exactly what I'd been hoping for when I came on a mission. Yes, I'd wanted to serve God, but I also wanted to have a deep friendship with other men. It was why I could so look forward to a mission that other nineteen-year-olds in the Church dreaded. The most miserable aspect of my mission hadn't been the lack of success in the work but the lack of decent men to become friends with.

I truly loved the Church, though, and so did Deiana. I could have become a Catholic priest or joined the Navy if all I wanted was male company. Neither experience would be much more miserable than this one. It was sharing the company of someone who loved the same things I loved that made the miserable things like Lucas bearable. Yet despite the love I felt for the Church, I was glad Deiana had broken a rule to write me, and I knew I wouldn't feel the least bit guilty by doing the same thing. Loving the Church and loving the rules wasn't always the same thing. Of course, it was apostasy to think that way. Our eternal exaltation rested even on the smallest of rules, we were constantly reminded. And yet it felt very "right" to be "wrong" at times. Something just wasn't fitting into place.

Sandro opened the door to the apartment, and Elder Lucas and I stepped out into the stairwell. Then Alberto came to the door. "So you really don't want to stay and have sex with us?" he asked mockingly.

"Alberto," said Sandro.

"Well, you know we have to tell them."

"You are so disgusting," Elder Lucas said.

"Is oral sex a sin?" asked Alberto.

"Yes," said Elder Lucas.

"Not for married couples," I amended, shrugging. It was another positive aspect of Mormonism that virtually all sex acts inside of a loving temple marriage were acceptable. It was so good to see that our Church leaders weren't small-minded about these things. It was another proof that the Church really was true, even if I didn't understand everything about its rules.

"So you don't even want to watch?" asked Sandro, and Alberto looked at him oddly. Sandro shook his head at Alberto and then suddenly pulled me back into the apartment and shut the door. Elder Lucas banged on it and shouted. I was too surprised to do anything. Were they going to rape me? I knew I should feel upset, but instead I felt my penis becoming erect, and I hoped they wouldn't notice. I wouldn't be able to tell anyone about it, but maybe it was an answer to my prayers. Maybe it would be so unpleasant that it would destroy all homosexual desire. Finally, finally, God was coming through for me just at my weakest moment.

"I can't go through with this," said Sandro.

Oh, no, please, you have to, I wanted to say. But I knew I was still just being wicked. I suddenly knew I was always going to want this. The wave of depression made me go flaccid instantly.

"You wimp," returned Alberto.

"I'll tell this once," said Sandro. He put his hand on my shoulder. "We shouldn't have done it," he went on, and I wondered again if they had poisoned us. "It's just that we get so sick of religious people. You have to understand, we go through so much."

So I *was* going to be killed on my mission, after all, and by a gay person, of all things. It was just too appropriate. God, knowing that because of my gayness my only chance for exaltation was martyrdom, chose my own failure as my ticket to heaven. After coming this far, however, it was still a bit irritating. If God was going to let me be killed, He could have done it months ago before most of the crap I went through. Of course, maybe He had to wait until I realized for sure that it was impossible for me to change. That was something now that I finally understood. Being gay was a permanent condition. It had never occurred to me before.

"It's okay," I said.

Alberto laughed. "What's okay? You don't even know what we've done."

"It doesn't matter."

Alberto covered a smile and then hid his head against Sandro's shoulder. Sandro looked at me and then down at the floor. "We masturbated into your drinks. You drank me and your friend drank Alberto." Alberto tried to smother his laughter by burying his face in Sandro's back.

"He's not my friend," I said.

"I do think we should tell that guy," Alberto managed.

"I'm really sorry," Sandro said. "It was juvenile of us."

"Fuck 'em both."

I remembered as a teenager the first time I tasted my ejaculation. It had made me gag. But I'd heard that gays had oral sex, and I simply had to know what it was like. The next several times I tried to taste it, I gagged again. Apparently, it was an acquired taste. But I kept trying, fantasizing about another man, pretending I was taking him in my mouth, wishing someone would seduce me.

There was one very cute weatherman on the Weather Channel, and, if no one was home, I knew his shift, so I'd turn on the T.V., masturbate while looking at him, and then sometimes quickly put my ejaculate in my mouth, pretending it was his. I always felt like the degenerate sleaze I was afterward, knowing no one else could possibly be as perverted and disgusting as I was, and yet somehow the idea of physically becoming one with another man was more satisfying than repulsive, and I kept fantasizing, wanting to pray for the experience to become real one day, but never daring to. Living with missionaries hadn't filled that emotional need. I'd been very good about not masturbating and about controlling my thoughts out here, but now with Lucas, of all people, I'd had the experience I'd wanted for ages. I felt closer to Lucas for a moment but then instantly more distant from him than ever.

He was still banging on the door. "I'm going to call the police," he shouted.

"Oh, shut up, Elder," I said loudly. Then I turned back to Sandro, wondering if I didn't tell Lucas, if I could bring Elder Stuart here one day and ask Sandro if I could have the same kind of drink I had last time.

No, that would be a sin. But could I enjoy what happened today without it being a sin? I should feel mad and tricked and violated, while instead I felt glad I had Sandro rather than Alberto inside of me. I felt…I felt *good.* And I knew suddenly that I wanted to have this feeling again.

This must mean, though, that being gay wasn't entirely sexual. Sandro and I hadn't done anything more than shake hands, and yet we'd had a sexual experience that was deeply emotional. If the emotion was the most valid part of that union, how could the Church say it was simply lust? Something just wasn't right.

But maybe I wasn't able to think clearly, not right after my drink had been raped.

I laughed out loud, and Sandro and Alberto took a step back. "Sorry," I said. Then I shook hands with each of them. "Life is too complicated for me to know if I should be mad or not." Sandro looked at me intensely, and I suppressed an urge to kiss him. "I guess I'd better go. Thanks for an interesting evening. You won't feel slighted if I don't write about this in my letter home?"

"You have our address." Alberto winked. "You can write to us."

Of course, I could never write down my full feelings anywhere and have the danger of someone ever finding it. My one comfort was knowing that if I ever committed suicide, no one would ever know why.

Alberto leaned over and shrugged. "Maybe you should cum in your friend's coffee." He laughed, but Sandro shook his head. Alberto kept chuckling.

It wasn't funny, though. It was people like Alberto who made me think the Church must be right, that homosexuality was indeed low and vulgar. But people could also make heterosexual sex low and vulgar, so that didn't prove anything. I didn't know what to think.

"Why couldn't you have just poisoned us?" I asked.

Sandro smiled. "Good luck, kid," he said, patting me on the shoulder again. "I hope you really do believe in evolution. It's the only thing that'll keep you from becoming extinct." He opened the door, and I joined Elder Lucas in the hall. We started downstairs immediately, passing a couple of people peering out their doors at us on the next landing.

"What happened in there?" Elder Lucas demanded.

"They said they'd had sex with a Mormon missionary once, and they wondered what became of him."

"Who was it?"

"They didn't say."

"Well, that's not very helpful. How can I report that to the president? We can't let gays go around representing the Church, can we? Are you sure they didn't tell you his name?"

"I'm sure," I said, "but you can always go back and ask them yourself."

"Funny."

We left the building and walked briskly along the street to a bus stop. "Do you have to report everything to the president?" I asked.

In an almost emotionless voice, Elder Lucas answered, "I'll have to report that you don't think so."

Then, remembering what he'd said this afternoon, I added, "Will you write about it in your journal?"

"Something that filthy? I don't want my kids reading that one day. You want your kids to read about talking to faggots?"

"Knowing the truth is surely better than lying. Isn't that why we're out here, because leaving people in ignorance isn't the Lord's plan? How can our kids make real decisions without knowing what life is like?"

"I'm *not* telling my kids about this. You're disgusting."

"Well, you tell the president and I'll tell my journal. Fair enough?" I would also tell Deiana, at least about some of it, just to see what his reaction might be. I wouldn't *know* I couldn't talk to him about everything unless I tried. Simply broaching the subject would be liberating. Unless Deiana reacted like Lucas. It didn't seem fair that I had to risk so much for the chance of receiving some tiny bit of decency. But taking a risk was the only way to receive any decency at all, so what choice was there?

The first bus that passed wasn't ours, so we waited silently for the next. I thought about the brief two months Deiana and I had spent together, and how I knew even at the time that that experience made the rest of my mission worthwhile. We'd probably never see each other again. But would finding a more permanent friendship after my mission like the one I'd had with him make my whole life worthwhile? It was too much to think about.

I had to clear my mind again, so I began humming the tune to a hymn. "Ye Elders of Israel, come join now with me."

Elder Lucas looked at me disgustedly, and I smiled in return, humming along until I came to the refrain. "O Babylon, O Babylon, we bid thee farewell," I sang out softly. "We're going to the mountains of Ephraim to dwell." Elder Lucas stared off down the street, looking for our bus, and I hummed the tune again as I rehearsed the second verse in my mind. But I stopped then, not going on to the third verse, my other thoughts refusing to be kept out.

My mission was supposed to make me a better person, I thought, seeing Deiana in bed in his pajamas. It wasn't a sexual image this time, however, but a comforting one. Why did feeling close to another human being make me feel so alone? Why would anyone *want* me to feel bad about being close to another person? Something just wasn't right.

I joined Elder Lucas, glad our time as companions was almost over, and looked down the street, wishing I were with Deiana, and looking forward to being with Stuart again soon. I stood next to Lucas, alone, waiting in the dark for the bus.

"Every time I have to work with you just wears down my soul," Elder Lucas muttered.

Listening to him almost made me sick. I felt my stomach churn, but remembering what was inside my stomach in some bizarre way calmed me. "Well, don't force yourself to work with me," I said. "The Lord doesn't expect a seasoned missionary like you to put up with the strain. That's why he gave me a greenie."

"You think you're so smart."

"No," I said, "actually, I think I'm pretty slow. But I'm catching up." Elder Lucas looked too disgusted to say anything, so I went on, hating myself for being this petty but unable to resist. "Why don't you show me how spiritual you are by taking a referral before we get home?"

"I already told you," he said through clenched teeth. "I'm supposed to make sure *you* know what you're doing. That one referral you took tonight was evil. Why don't you try to redeem yourself before we get home? Think you can take a referral at 9:30 at night?"

I thought about playing my exaggeration game again by replying, "I can get two," but the time for games seemed to be over. "I don't know if I could or not," I finally said. "I know you can't, though, or you'd do it to show me up. Frankly, I just don't care to try anymore."

"I'll have to report that, Elder."

I smiled. "I feel like a late bloomer sometimes, but I do wonder how old you'll be before you grow up."

"That'll be quite enough, Elder. I can have you transferred to the boondocks if I want. To Sassari or Pescara. You better show some respect."

I believed Lucas was a jerk, but I believed the Church was true. I believed that homosexuality was wrong, but I wanted nothing more than to be gay and be Mormon. I liked the Church for the most part except for this one thing. Of course, questioning the one issue made me wonder about a few more, made me wonder if I might be experiencing Stockholm syndrome without realizing it. Would it really be such a sin for a woman to have a career? Did we all need to have children? Some people weren't cut out to be parents. I pitied Lucas's kids. But if I hadn't been forced into questioning in the first place, I could have probably gone a lifetime in ignorant bliss. Despite everything, though, I still wanted to be Mormon. And for the first time, I also wanted to be gay. That combination could never be, and yet I couldn't give up either one.

People could be addicted to harmful substances.

"I'm the one that writes my own story," I recited the Church song in my head. "I decide the person I'll be. What goes in the plot, and what does not, is pretty much up to me."

The bus came, and soon we were back on Franco Sacchetti. "Just a minute, Elder," I said, directing Lucas to the bar on the corner that was about to close. We often bought milk and cookies here for a bedtime snack. Elder Lucas rolled his eyes but followed.

I bought a bottle of Latte di Mandorle, and though Lucas couldn't possibly know why, he still glared at me. I shrugged. "My companion has a lot left to experience out here," I said. "I wouldn't be a good trainer if I neglected almond milk. You can have some too if you want." Elder Lucas turned away in disgust and, carrying my bottle, I followed him back home.

"You need a souvenir to remember tonight?" Lucas asked in the elevator on our way up, scowling at the bottle in my hand.

I looked at him and couldn't help but laugh. "Imagine, Elder, how much you could contribute to the world if you used all that energy you spend in hating me for something positive instead."

"Imagine if *you*—"

"Oh, Elder, get a life already. And don't do it by sucking out mine. Get your own life. I want to keep mine for myself."

"I'm going to report your insolence, Elder."

I laughed again. "Do it then and leave me alone. You're nothing but a daddy's boy, a president's boy. So go run and cry to him."

The doors opened onto our floor and Elder Lucas pushed past me to leave first. "I'm through talking to you."

"Thank God." I knew I shouldn't provoke him but I couldn't seem to help it. I felt every bit as petulant and arrogant as Alberto had been tonight. I felt injected with a new energy that wouldn't let me go back to what I was, though I didn't think the new me was going to be much of an improvement. Following Lucas to our apartment, though, I knew I'd better try to calm down. I had five more months left, and as miserable as it had already been, they could make it worse. Maybe I'd tell the president that Sandro told me he'd spiked my drink, and I was belligerent due to the alcohol. My whole mission was a lie, anyway; what did it matter if I lied a little more?

Elder Stuart greeted me at the door with a smile and a tap on his pocket planner to show me he'd gotten a return appointment. I smiled back and handed him the almond milk, explaining how to make it and then heading straight to our room, asking him to tell me about his evening in the morning. I kicked off my shoes, pulled off my suit, and plopped right in bed, though it wasn't even 10:00. I was going to need a full night's rest to face the next day.

But lying in bed with the lights off, instead of falling asleep I saw Sandro's face. And then I saw even more of him. This time I didn't try to kick out the images but let them come inside of me. It felt good, and not only sexually. I liked feeling close to another man. When I didn't try to fight it, it felt good.

Eventually I tried to clear my mind, and just before 10:30, Elder Stuart came back into the room. He quietly undressed and slid into his bed. For the first time, I let myself fantasize about him, too. Then I felt guilty. Even if I could ever accept my gayness and accept the idea of finding a real and complete friend, I could hardly justify promiscuity, and yet I had just fantasized about two different men, one of whom was already "married." Maybe it was true, then, that gays were all degenerates, and just letting myself go for a few minutes had already pushed me further down that road.

I didn't know what was going to happen. I was excited, and scared, and most of all tired. Five more months. And instead of going faster, the last few seemed to absolutely drag by. I felt very tired. All this time, and I still didn't know if I was going to make it.

I let my fingers caress my nipples lightly, feeling the symbols woven into my undershirt over each nipple, one to remind me to stay on the right course, the other to remind me that the Lord expected us to live strictly following His rules. "God, what in the world do you want from me?" I asked silently. I put my arms down beside me and tried to focus on the blackness I saw when I closed my eyes, and I cleared my mind the way I often had to at night in order to sleep, chanting silently to myself. "Nothing. Nothing. Blackness. Nothing. Nothing. Blackness. Nothing. Emptiness. Emptiness." After a while I finally fell asleep.

P-Day Man

"Traitor!"

My companion spewed the word at me. We'd been together almost a month in the Rome Four district here in northeastern Rome. I was senior, having been out on my mission twenty months, while Elder Andrews was still green, this being his first area. In fact, I was his trainer, even a higher calling than that of district leader in some respects. As Andrews's first companion, I was considered his most important, his shaper, his molder. Andrews was the second greenie I had trained.

"Elder Percy," Andrews said, stalking out of the bedroom, "let's do another work visit. I'm not working with this…son of perdition."

"God created Adam and Eve," said Elder Percy, looking at me with disgust, "not Adam and Steve."

Elders Percy and Andrews were soon out of the apartment. I wanted very much to see Elder Collins, Percy's companion over in the next room, but we'd been forbidden from speaking to each other after what had happened last night. Our zone leaders, Lucas and Ballantine, who were over not only this district but two other districts as well, lived at the far end of the hall in the living room. They had phoned the president this morning and were to escort Collins and me to the mission home at 11:00 for an interview.

My whole future would be decided in this interview. If I was sent home in disgrace, everyone would know I'd committed some horrible sin, and gossip would follow me the rest of my life. If I was allowed to finish my twenty-four months, I could continue to lead an upstanding life in the Church. But now I wondered if I wanted to.

I stood at my bedroom door and looked over at Collins's door, which was closed. I could probably slip a note under it quickly without the Z.L.'s noticing. Maybe if I—

"Go study the scriptures, Elder Anderson," Lucas ordered from down the hall. "I think you need it."

Elder Lucas had never liked me, and just two days ago when he'd criticized me for only teaching a partial lesson when Andrews and I had an appointment to teach a full one, I'd said to him, "They weren't ready for the gospel. Would you rather I stayed just to get good stats for the week, or would you rather I spend the time looking for someone who is truly interested?"

"If you had faith," he'd countered, "you could have won them over with the Spirit. Their not progressing to baptism will be on your head."

"I haven't seen you baptizing anyone lately."

He'd been so mad he'd stormed out of the room. I knew what he was hoping the president would say to me today.

I went in my room and closed the door, looking out the window at the apartment buildings surrounding me. This was a new part of Rome with sparkling, new buildings featuring balconies by every window. Most people had plants or chairs on their balconies, but we had clotheslines on ours. I knew I could climb from my balcony over to Collins's, but why bother? It was Collins who had reported what happened to the Z.L.'s, Collins who had freaked, Collins who had initiated the kiss in the first place.

Collins had been feeling ill yesterday afternoon and had wanted to stay in. Andrews and I had a teaching appointment over by Piazza Sempione, one I'd been trying to set up for a week, with a family of five who really seemed they'd make it all the way to the baptismal font. But I knew Percy would just sit and complain all evening if he stayed in, making Collins feel worse, so I pulled a work visit and switched companions for the evening.

Collins and I had done it before. We'd started out in Napoli together, where we'd gone through an earthquake and Communist demonstrations. Later, we'd ended up in Sardegna at the same time and by then knew the language well enough to risk working with each other a few times. We had taught and baptized a teenage boy and a family of four together just by contacting them together first on work visits.

Our companions had been jealous, since the average baptism rate was three converts in two years, and Collins and I had practically done these five in our spare time.

Collins was a little pushy, in my view, but I never asked more than once. If someone wasn't interested, I moved on. One week, I'd somehow gotten eighteen referrals, addresses of people I had stopped in the street. The weekly goal was fifteen, and most companionships got around ten, while I usually only got five or six. But I had also taught nine discussions on my best week, while the goal set by the mission president was eight, and the average per week was probably only two or three. Early in my mission, I'd had an entire month when I'd only taught one.

Collins generally did better than I did and was considered a likely candidate for district leader come next transfers for his remaining few months. I knew I'd never be a leader, though. I hated filling out my hours sheet into the various categories: street contacting, member visits, teaching, tracting, individual study, companionship study, and travel time, and though I'd been meticulous about it for a long while, now I usually just divided 70 hours randomly to fill the slots. I insisted on wearing blue jeans instead of a suit when I left the apartment on Preparation Day. I even slept every night in my jeans just so I could feel like a real person. Collins had nicknamed me "P-Day Man" back in Sardegna, and the title had stuck with me ever since.

I also disobeyed the coat rule, which said we had to wear our suit jackets every time we left the apartment until the day in May when the president said we no longer needed to. I saw that the sister missionaries had no coat rule and so simply decided for myself if I was hot or cold. The Z.L.'s never let me go without an argument each time I tried to leave the apartment. I usually ended the argument by waving good-bye and walking out the door.

But the president had still liked me. He'd told me once, "I never have to worry about you. You just go out and do the work." I guessed he was worrying now.

It had all seemed innocent enough last night. Collins was achey from feeling bad and had asked me to give him a massage. I knew I liked Collins and that I was attracted to him, but I wasn't terribly concerned because I had no idea Collins might be gay. I'd thought I was the only gay missionary in existence. Two of my notebooks were filled with journal entries as I debated back and forth over what to do about my homosexuality.

I had known for years I was gay, though I'd never had sex with anyone. I knew I loved my early morning seminary classes five days a week as a teenager, and that I loved my Boy Scout meetings, and speaking in church, and blessing the sacrament after I was ordained a priest at sixteen. I knew I loved reading the scriptures, organizing church dances, singing in the church choir, and mowing the lawns of elderly members. My family had never been close, but in the Church, I felt like part of a huge, real family. I didn't understand why I was gay, but I knew that if it kept me from these people, then it was wrong, and I decided never to let anything happen.

Going on a mission had been my goal since I was thirteen. I knew I could purge myself through serving God full-time for two years. The Lord would see I was trying and would help me the rest of the way.

It had taken me half a year to learn how to make a decent street approach. And going door to door had been quite tedious the first couple of months, but I finally learned how to turn tracting into a game, and zone leaders twice had sent me for a day to other districts to show the missionaries there how to have fun and still work. Most district leaders and zone leaders thought I was being irreverent, though, and ordered me to "get serious about the work of the Lord." I would do so when they watched but then went back to my own style later. After working with twelve companions, I'd seen that everyone had his own style, and that that was okay.

I had baptized eight people in twenty months. When my Z.L.'s told me I wasn't working properly, I wondered what they meant. I finally decided they meant I was doing things differently than they did.

That's when I started wondering about being gay again. Was it really wrong, or was it just different? I thought back to what Elder Percy had said earlier about God not creating Adam and Steve. I'd heard the claim several times over the years, and it always struck me as odd. I knew, of course, that being gay was wrong, but using Adam and Eve as an example seemed a poor way to prove it.

We had to be like Adam and Eve because they were heterosexual, but there was no other way we had to be similar to them. What was their race, for instance? They couldn't have been white, and Asian, and black, and Hispanic, and aborigine, and Arabic all together, could they? We didn't have to be farmers and hunters like they were. They weren't Mormons, or Christians, or even Jews yet, so we didn't have to practice religion the same way they did. We didn't have to live in the same place they did.

We didn't need to have our children marry each other, did we? And were sterile people automatically sinful for not having any kids at all? What of the tens of thousands of celibate people in the world? Did people run up and shout into Mother Teresa's face, "God created Adam and Eve, not just Eve!" Even Catholic priests who hated gays used Adam and Eve as an example, despite not following their example themselves.

So just how much like Adam and Eve did we have to be? Only in this *one* aspect of heterosexuality? Nothing else in the world mattered in our comparison to them except our sexual orientation? I knew I was guilty of worldly reasoning when I thought like this, and normally I tried to repent and think the way I was supposed to. But now, I decided that when I got home, I'd finally have to start reading up on the issue, reading things from the gay point of view, not just the Church's. I loved the Church, but was it possible it was wrong? I wasn't prepared to accept that yet, but I was definitely going to look into the matter when I got home.

I'd already fallen in love with one of my companions, but I hadn't let on to anyone. I could control both my actions and my thoughts. It was too fun to be in Italy, too nice being a missionary despite the constant rejection and cursing and hassles with other missionaries. While walking back home the other day, I had looked up at the apartment and thought, "Despite everything, you will always look back at this mission as a special time in your life." I knew it even now.

I didn't want anything to keep me from finishing my two years. I felt alive out here in a way I never had before, notwithstanding the difficulties, and I wanted to keep that feeling as long as possible. One elder had been sent home for sneaking off to see an X-rated movie. Another had been sent home and excommunicated for having sex with a young woman. Two more had been threatened after kissing a girl. I didn't know what to expect for Collins and myself.

I hadn't even been thinking anything sexual last night while I was rubbing his back. Collins had taken off his T-shirt so I could massage his bare skin, and while I enjoyed the feel of him against my fingers, I was thinking about the lesson Percy and Andrews were teaching, hoping they weren't lousing things up, and wondering what I might try if they did.

I'd been massaging for close to an hour before Collins turned over and looked up at me. Then he sat up, his face only inches from mine. I thought, "Gee, isn't he cute? I'm glad we're friends." And before I could think anything else, Collins had leaned forward and kissed me on the mouth.

It was a long kiss, maybe thirty seconds, but we never opened our lips. I had never French kissed and wasn't sure I'd know how even if I tried. I didn't pull away, though, and that was why I was in trouble now.

I opened the two glass doors and stepped onto my balcony. The sky was deep blue, and there was a light breeze. The woman across the way was watering flowers on her balcony. She looked up and smiled, and I waved.

I heard the doors to Collins's balcony squeak open and turned to look. Collins came out hesitantly and stood silently at the railing for a moment, only a couple of feet away. He glanced over his shoulder toward the kitchen balcony and then whispered, "I've been praying all morning. I'm going to tell the president I'm sorry and I'll never do it again, that he can interview me every week or put me in a threesome instead of a companionship, but that I want to stay and work. I feel peaceful about it. Have you been praying? How do you feel?"

I shrugged. "I'm not going to apologize."

"What!" Collins leaned over the railing toward me. "Anderson, you've got to!"

"I only apologize when I'm sorry."

Collins straightened up and took his hands from the rails. "I'm going to tell him to keep us out of the same areas. I think it's best." He waited a moment and then added, "I can't ever speak to you again."

He stood there a moment longer and I nodded. Then Collins went back to the door, pausing a moment to turn to me again. "Good luck, Elder," he whispered before going inside.

I nodded again and then turned to look back over the city. A man was walking his dog on the street below, and I could hear teenagers playing soccer somewhere around the corner. An old woman was dragging a two-wheeled cart behind her, loaded with a huge bag of groceries. I watched as a soccer ball came careening down the sidewalk, bumped into the cart, and then bounced back up the street.

The woman stood looking forlornly at her spilled groceries. The man with the dog walked on. No one stopped to help her. I looked down at myself, still in my jeans, and this not even P-Day.

I started down the hall, but when I got to the door, Elder Lucas came out of his room, staring with wide eyes. "Just where do you think you're going?" he asked.

I opened my mouth to answer but then just turned and opened the door instead, walking out without a word.

Transfer Cookies

I picked up a triangle-shaped carton of milk and a roll of Bucaneve cookies and brought them to the bar. "You need anything else, Elder Wharton?" I asked.

"A ticket home," he mumbled.

"Don't you want any transfer cookies?"

"What?"

"Those black and yellow cookies. You drop them in a glass of milk. If it turns black side up, you stay. Yellow side up, you get transferred."

"Well, how come you got those other cookies? Don't you want to know if you're getting transferred?"

"I've already been everywhere," I replied. I'd started my mission in Naples, then gone to Sardinia and Ciampino, and I'd been here in Rome for several months. "I can adjust to wherever they send me." There was still Ostia and Pescara and Caserta, or even another part of Naples. I'd spent so much of my mission hating my life, but lately, I felt a thrill being here, a thrill just in being alive. Rome was a pretty nice place, whatever my other problems might be.

"I'm not going to have to adjust again if I go somewhere else, am I?" Elder Wharton curled his lip and sighed.

"You've been in Italy one month," I said. "You still have about six more months of adjusting to do. It took me a year, but most people aren't as slow as I am."

"A year? That's forever!" He looked down at his still new shoes and kicked the floor gently.

"Do you want any cookies?"

"I guess so." Elder Wharton picked up a roll of cookies and placed it next to mine on the counter. He started to fish in his pocket for some change, but I shook my head.

"I'll get it."

"Thanks, Anziano Anderson."

We left the bar and walked a block to our apartment on Franco Sacchetti. We pushed open the tiny elevator doors and squeezed into the cubicle, riding up three floors. The zone leaders, head over our apartment and the missionaries in three other apartments, were already home, one talking on the phone and his companion in the kitchen. The other two elders hadn't returned yet for the evening. It was only 9:25. We weren't supposed to be in until 9:30. We should have loitered at the bar a few more minutes.

I remembered when Elder Lucas, our senior zone leader, had spoken to us after the last transfers. The first thing he did the following morning after the new elders arrived was hold a special meeting in our apartment. "I've been going over last month's stats," he said, very businesslike, pacing in front of us, "and I've decided we must work harder." He pointed to the elders from the room next to ours. "You're averaging four referrals a week," he said. "The minimum goal, the *minimum* goal, is fifteen. I know that if you exercise your faith and do the work we've been commanded to do, you'll reach your goals. Remember I Nephi 3:7." The two elders dropped their heads and mumbled their renewed commitment.

"And Elder Anderson," he said, turning to me, "you have a new greenie. You've only been averaging five referrals a week. You *must* do better this month. The Lord is giving you a chance to make up for your past. He's given you a greenie straight from the Missionary Training Center who doesn't know about your past problems so you can have a fresh start, too."

I saw Elder Wharton turn to look at me questioningly, and I couldn't help but laugh. "Well, I guess he knows now, doesn't he?"

"Elder," said Elder Lucas sternly, "we'll be watching your performance very carefully. You had better work harder." He smiled and began pacing again. "Next," he started to go on, "I'd like to talk about—"

I motioned to Elder Wharton, and we headed past Elder Lucas toward the door. "What are you doing?" he asked, his mouth hanging open as he finished speaking.

"I can be more productive out on the street than sitting here watching you congratulate yourself on your leadership abilities." We walked out, and neither of us spoke until we'd been at the bus stop a few minutes.

"What was that all about?" Elder Wharton finally asked.

I shrugged. "I am so sick of mission leaders who think they're Brigham Young. I'll bet Elder Lucas himself doesn't get even more than six referrals a week." A man passed us on the sidewalk, but I didn't even try to talk to him. "Of course," I added with another shrug, "that doesn't mean we shouldn't be getting more, too."

I could see that Elder Wharton was still debating over his next question, but I wasn't going to answer it unless he asked. "And the rest?" he finally said.

"They found out I'm gay," I replied, looking right at him. He blinked and then looked down. "Not that I've ever had sex, of course. I don't have any idea what I'm going to do about being gay when I get home. I think I still believe the Church is true, but I also think it's okay to be gay. Anyway, I'm not going to deal with it any more than I need to until I'm off my mission. I do like being here. And whether or not the Church is true, if there are people here who are dissatisfied with what they have, I don't see why I shouldn't at least offer them something different. Family Home Evening is a good program. A lay ministry has several advantages. The emphasis on volunteering is good. Fasting once a month is good. There are a lot of things I like. But for all its usefulness, hierarchy isn't one of them."

Elder Wharton was now looking off down the street for a bus, which was still nowhere in sight.

"So do you have a problem with my being gay?"

Elder Wharton glanced at me for a moment, looked away, and then turned to me again. "I...I don't mind," he said.

I relaxed and decided to try a little harder to help him get adjusted to his new life, but over the following weeks, I could see that Elder Lucas's comments kept him from ever feeling very comfortable. "You two sleep with your bedroom door open," Elder Lucas had said that first night. "You be sure and tell us if he tries anything, Elder Wharton."

"You sure you don't want to watch?" I countered.

"I'm going to have to report that to the president, Elder."

Did the president get a kick out of these things, too? I wondered but didn't say anything. Elder Wharton looked at me briefly and glanced away.

A few days later, one of our appointments cancelled at 8:30, and we were far from our new tracting zone, so we came home. "9:00?" asked Elder Lucas. "Elder Wharton, I know you're just a junior companion, and he's supposed to be training you, but as your zone leader, I'm authorizing you to tell him he has to stay out later. If you have to set the example, do it. It's a pretty low day when an elder out for only a week has to train his trainer."

Elder Wharton looked at me, and then he looked at Elder Lucas, and then he looked at me again, not knowing who to side with. I told him later to play along with Elder Lucas in public or he'd regret it, but he told me, "You're my companion. The Lord put me with you. That means I'm supposed to be loyal to *you*."

Sometimes, fortunately, Elder Wharton wasn't directly involved in the conflict, like with the shower incident. Elder Lucas had forbidden me to go in the bathroom while the other elders were taking showers. I was last out of six, getting to use cold water, and generally no one came in the bathroom while I was there, something I'd longed for my whole mission. I should have kissed another elder sooner.

But a couple of weeks back, while I was finishing my shower, Elder Lucas came in to throw his laundry in the washer. He seemed to be taking his time, but I didn't want to come out of the shower before he left. Finally, though, I'd taken all the cold water I could, and I turned off the shower and stepped out to dry myself off.

Elder Lucas looked me up and down, a disgusted expression on his face.

"Doesn't meet up to your expectations?" I asked. "Well, the water *was* cold." Since I'd started doing push ups and sit ups every morning a couple of months earlier, I felt more comfortable with my body than I ever had in the past.

"I'm going to have to tell the president you said that." He brushed past me to leave.

"Maybe I'll tell him myself."

Sometimes, a day or two would go by with no major conflict, but even though Elder Lucas had just criticized me again today at lunch, I still always expected further criticism, and arriving home at 9:25 provided more than enough ammunition.

"A little early, aren't you?" Elder Lucas asked as I walked into the kitchen to put away my milk. I didn't answer. "What if there was a golden contact out there walking the streets on or the bus, or in that next building you should have started tracting out? What if he was only in the mood tonight to be receptive to the gospel?"

"If he was in the mood tonight and never will be again, he's probably too flaky to stay in the Church, anyway."

"It's not our place to judge, Elder. You don't win the race by stopping a foot from the finish line."

There may have been some logic to what Elder Lucas said, but I wasn't in the mood to hear it. Perhaps because I knew he might be right. It was only five minutes, of course, but there were three degrees in heaven, and if I wanted to go to the highest one, didn't I have to do better than just a good job? I no longer believed that being a dedicated missionary was going to change my orientation, but I still wondered if I had to do something extraordinarily good to make up for being gay, even if I never did anything with another man. Would I need converts as character witnesses on Judgment Day? Even if I didn't, had I let someone down by not giving 100% tonight? I hated guilt trips, but I *did* feel guilty an awful lot. The only problem was that I wasn't sure guilt ever made me a better person. It seemed like a useless emotion. Maybe it was time I outgrew it.

"We'll stay out late tomorrow night," I said.

"You can never make up lost opportunities," returned Elder Lucas.

"Should I just kill myself now?"

He put his glass in the sink and looked at me coolly. "Don't miss any more." He left for the bathroom and a second later, Elder Wharton walked into the kitchen.

"What was that about?"

"Elder Lucas wants us to work harder. He says we're slacking."

"Jeez! You work me like a dog now." He picked out two cups and placed them on the table next to our cookies.

I took out a triangle of milk I'd bought the day before and cut off the corner, pouring some milk for both of us. I worked as hard as any missionary companion I'd had in the past year and a half, but I also knew there were times with all of them that had been full of loafing. Travel time was the easiest way out, waiting at bus stops or riding the bus or metro to our tracting area, and not talking to people about the Church along the way, though we might be traveling half an hour or forty-five minutes.

"Transfers tomorrow morning," said Elder Wharton. "I'd like to go where the people are more receptive."

I smiled. "They rarely transfer you to another country in the middle of your mission, but once every five or six months, someone gets shipped to the New York Italian-speaking mission. I wouldn't hold my breath, though. Their baptism rate isn't any higher."

"They're baptizing a lot up in Milano and down in Catania. Sixty a month. We're only getting fifteen here in Rome."

"Sixty a month for 120 missionaries. That's one per companionship, but some of those are families all baptized by one companionship, so not everyone is baptizing."

"Still, it's better than fifteen, isn't it?"

"Yes."

"What's wrong with us? Are we bad?"

"I'm not sure that's a relevant question, but Elder Lucas thinks so. I'm sure he's going to tell us to raise our goals."

Elder Wharton rested his chin on his hands. "I guess we'd better then. If I have to be miserable, I may as well get something out of it." He looked blankly in front of him for a moment and then looked at me. "So show me the cookies."

I opened his roll and poured out a few cookies. "It's the first one," I said. "Drop it in and see."

Elder Wharton held the cookie over the cup, closed his eyes and whispered, and dropped the cookie. It landed black side up. "And what does that mean again?"

"It means you don't have to write home tomorrow. Now it's my turn." I dropped a cookie into my milk. It landed yellow side up.

"Aw, no fair. You're getting transferred with my cookie."

"I've been in Rome Four six months," I said. "Besides, it's just a game." Sometimes, my whole mission seemed like a game, though not often a very fair one. All this work, and sometimes I still felt like just buying a ticket and going home, this close to the end. All the effort I'd invested into fighting my gayness, and I still felt like going off with the first cute Italian I saw, just for sex, without even having a relationship first. All this work for so long, and I was still right on the edge, closer to the edge than ever.

How could I survive for fifty or sixty more years? I was playing a game with the cards stacked against me. I was playing Solitaire, and God had taken an ace out of the deck before handing it to me.

This must have been very much how Adam felt when forced to choose between disobeying one of two commandments. If he didn't eat the fruit, he couldn't procreate since Eve was being cast out. And if he chose to leave so he could procreate, he'd have to eat the fruit and break that commandment. But God hadn't yet given him the knowledge of right and wrong, so it was impossible for him to sin no matter which choice he made. But for me, there was no way to *avoid* sin. Were we just assuming God was nice? Maybe He really wasn't. What verification did we actually have? Maybe He was just a very powerful Zone Leader who enjoyed his position of power.

"Well, maybe it would be good to be transferred," Elder Wharton said. "We only had one good contact, and he flaked out on us last week." He slowly twirled a cookie on the table. "And I'm so down about not getting a letter from home this week. Things'll have to get better soon one way or another."

I did understand his depression and knew it might take him a while to come out of it fully, but I wanted to try to help him what little I could. "You know," I said, "there are hymns we can sing when we feel low." I smiled when Elder Wharton gave me a sour look. "Do you know 'Tragedy'?"

Elder Wharton gave me a puzzled frown, and I began singing to the tune of a Bee Gee's song. "Tragedy! When your contacts fail and you get no mail, it's tragedy!"

Elder Wharton smiled then, and I sang a few more lines, ending with, "With no one to baptize, you're going nowhere!" He shook his head, and I put my hand on his shoulder. "Your mission will turn out okay," I said. I scooped out my cookie to eat it. "And we'll find out about transfers tomorrow for sure."

That night as I lay in bed, I wondered where I might be sent, or if there was anywhere in the mission I still wanted to go. I'd started out in Napoli and then gone to Quartu. It had been bad enough at the time, but now that I was used to big cities, I didn't think I could handle a small town again. Cagliari might be okay, though. Ciampino had been nice, but it was a Roman suburb rather than a small town, and Rome Four was great. Naples was too poor and dirty. More baptisms there, but such a depressing place. Maybe Rome One or Rome Three or E.U.R. would be okay, somewhere here in the city. Terni or Sassari would be too far from everyone except mission leaders.

Elder Deiana was in Pescara, but if I were sent there, he'd undoubtedly be sent somewhere else. He'd written me once after the rumors about me spread across the mission, saying he didn't see what the big deal was, that he'd kissed me goodnight several times. Of course, he knew the difference between an Italian kiss and a gay one, but it still made me feel good to hear him say it. It would be awkward to see him again, but I'd gladly face him if I were transferred to his district.

Of course, wherever the Lord wanted me is where I'd go. That's what I'd written on my mission application form, expecting to be sent to North Dakota or Kansas. I could hardly believe it when I'd opened my letter two months later and read, "You are hereby called to serve as a full-time missionary in the Italy Rome Mission." Rome. Well, that wasn't too bad, I thought.

I went to the kitchen that day and waved my letter in the air. My mother stopped cold and looked at me. "Where?" she asked, her face expressionless.

"It's someplace that has food you like," I replied.

"Mexico," she said glumly. "You're going to Mexico."

"Nope. It's another place that has food you like."

"Italy!" She started jumping up and down. "You're going to Italy!" It was where the Lord wanted me, but it didn't hurt that my mom liked the idea, too. It was a shame my father liked small town Mississippi life so much he'd turned down my suggestion that he and Mom come to visit Rome for a week when my mission was over. It might be the only chance my mom ever got to come, and I'd have been proud to show them around.

Being sent to an important city had at first made me feel important, particularly when we were told we were the Lord's elite, serving right at the center of the Catholic Church, right on "Satan's doorstep." Then being overwhelmed by the cultural and historical importance of Rome as well as its size had made me feel insignificant. I'd met too many nice Catholics to feel any longer that I was really in the midst of evil, but I still believed the Lord had a plan for me and that He would send me where He wanted me, to fill whatever assignment I had to fill there, so I was anxious to see where God would ask me to go next. People here generally just looked at us a little mystified and said, "What are you doing here? Go to Africa." As if that wasn't just as culturally insensitive.

Elder Wharton and I ate a few more cookies in silence, and then we went to bed. I would save the special "snowflake" cookies I'd bought today to celebrate tomorrow night if one of us was being transferred away.

The next morning, Elder Wharton and I had to leave at 8:30 instead of the usual 9:30 because we'd be losing time when we came back at 10:30 for the transfer meeting, so we skipped our usual Companion Study and got right to work. There was a man about thirty also waiting at the bus stop, and I thought, "What the hell?"

"Excuse me, sir," I said, watching Elder Wharton jump from the corner of my eyes.

"Yes?"

"We're representatives of the Church of Jesus Christ of Latter-day Saints, and I was wondering if you knew any of our church members here."

"No. I see you boys around the city sometimes, but that's about it."

"Have you ever read about the Mormons or seen anything on T.V. about us? I'm just curious as to your perception of Mormons."

We chatted for five more minutes until the bus came, and the man was nice enough, but he wasn't really interested. We stayed in the back of the bus while the man went forward, and when he seemed out of earshot, Elder Wharton asked, "So we're supposed to do that all the time?"

"Theoretically."

"Flip. And I have twenty-one months left."

As we hung onto the metal bar above our heads and looked out the windows, I realized I didn't feel as good about my street approach as I'd expected. It was an accomplishment in a sense, but it was already over. I should already be approaching someone else on the bus. No victory, of any degree, lasted longer than the incident itself. All I felt all day long was pressure to do more. It never let up. I felt caught between accepting the pressure as a realization of what God expected, and rejecting it as an unrealistic goal forced on me by others. Somehow, I always seemed to experience both feelings at the same time.

"This our stop?" asked Elder Wharton, hand poised over the red button. I nodded, he pressed, and soon we were back on the street.

We walked along the sidewalk, and I felt too tired to talk to anyone. Besides, it was Elder Wharton's turn, though I knew of course he wasn't strong enough yet to do it without prodding. So we walked down another street, and down yet another. Finally, I thought I'd try again.

"Good morning. My name is—"

"Oh, go fuck yourself."

The man walked off, and Elder Wharton leaned over. "What did he say?"

"He said he's not interested."

We walked on a ways further, and then Elder Wharton pointed across the street. "There's a bar. Can we sit for a minute?"

I would have preferred the mechanical activity of walking, but I shrugged and we crossed the street. Two boys were playing pinball inside, and a man in a business suit drank coffee at the bar. Elder Wharton and I sat down at a little table near the ice cream freezer.

"I wish bars at home were this nice," Elder Wharton said.

"You been to many?" I smiled.

"Oh, no, of course not. But you see them on T.V."

"There'll be pandoros and panettones in here next fall. Christmas cakes. You'll like your first Christmas here. You know, no matter how bad things get, you can still stay, 'Well, at least I'm in Italy.'"

"Is that important to you?"

"I've studied a lot of Italian history since I got here. I'd like to come back after I finish college. Maybe live here."

"Really?"

"I don't know if I could live just anywhere in Italy, but Rome I like. Of course, it's hard for Americans to get work here, but I could try. Maybe get a job at the embassy. I think Rome's a great city." I laughed. "This is the only thing Elder

Lucas and I have in common. His mother's parents were Italian. He told me he might come back, too."

Elder Wharton shook his head. "I can't imagine you two actually having a pleasant conversation together."

"Miracles happen out here in the mission field, Elder."

We were silent for a moment, and then Elder Wharton asked, "Do you really think I'll make it?"

"You'll make it."

"Sometimes, I feel my life is crumbling all around me."

"You just have to believe you're good even when everyone else is telling you you're bad."

"Is that how you make it?"

I shrugged. "Self-esteem is a talent. What little I've got I've developed out here, but I don't get much chance to practice, and developing talent takes practice. It's not like riding a bicycle. This is easy to forget."

"But…how can you practice self-esteem when you're always doing something wrong?"

"Ultimately, I think we have to stop caring so much what other people think, and just do what feels right to us."

"And how in the world do we do that?"

"I'm only a senior companion," I said, laughing. "I don't know *all* the answers."

We walked up and down a couple more streets, and I managed to talk to one more man, and he did give us his address, though I didn't expect it would amount to much. Elder Lucas would say that was just my own negativity creating a self-fulfilling prophecy. I didn't want to have an aura of negative energy, though, so I smiled brightly and started to walk at a brisker pace.

Elder Wharton seemed too preoccupied with transfers to concentrate, and it made me think back on past transfers. We only had a day to pack after hearing them, the president afraid we'd stop working once we knew we were going to another city, something I'd never even been tempted to do, but the quickness of the transfers always made them a bit shocking to the system. There was no time to psych ourselves up for the change.

Once, early in my mission, I was in a district with an elder who was finishing up his twenty-four months. On transfer day, when it would be announced formally he was heading back to California, everyone in the district wore black death buttons that men pinned on their shirts or coats to show they were in mourning. Someone in the district made a death poster like those plastered all over Napoli, with the elder's name on it. We had a good time teasing him about going home.

I remembered at another transfer meeting, this one about a year ago, the district leader had gathered everyone together in a park and read out the most baffling transfers. One elder was to go to a district he'd already served in, with an elder he despised. He sat through the rest of the meeting in a daze. Another elder, out for only two months, was to become a new district leader, and a sister with only one month left was to be demoted to junior companion.

Finally, the district leader could take it no longer and, looking at the suffering missionaries, burst out laughing. "April Fool!"

Afterward, I'd commented to another elder, "Thank goodness Sister Blanke wasn't sent down. Could you imagine finishing your mission as a junior companion?"

A sister who had only two months left, and who had never been anything but a junior companion because she couldn't master the language, had overheard. "I don't think that's so terrible," she said.

I felt like an idiot.

At most transfer meetings, though, all that happened would be that someone would learn their new companion's name, and immediately all the others would begin telling stories about him or her. "He never takes a bath." "She flirts with all the men on the bus." "She punched a man on the street once." "She punched *me* once." "He never brushes his teeth." "He never speaks English, and he jumps all over you if you do." And on and on.

The gossip had surprised me at first, since I'd always been taught it was a sin. But "sparlare" was one of the first Italian words I'd learned. I'd never wanted the responsibility of being a district leader, but I remembered the shock I'd felt when I overheard two zone leaders once discussing a report they were making to the mission president. "Elder Cowley only gave us soup and sandwiches for lunch one day last week. That was pretty pitiful, even if the food budget was low. That's not someone I want to suggest for D.L. to the president. Cowley needs to learn to sacrifice." I didn't think

I was D.L. material, but I liked Elder Cowley. He'd ended his mission two months ago still just a senior companion.

Another elder had been caught writing letters home telling everyone he was assistant to the president, the highest a missionary could go, higher even than zone leader, while he was actually only a senior companion who could barely speak the language. He must not have realized the president sent a letter to each missionary's home bishop to be read at his homecoming, listing every position he'd held during his mission, but the elder did know he'd never make it in mission politics. I thought it pathetic he even cared. But I suppose that was how some people saw me, trying to please leaders I didn't like.

"You don't think I'll get a jerk next time, do you?" Elder Wharton asked, nudging me.

"There's no telling," I said.

"A mission is like playing 'Mother May I?'" he said, shaking his head. "Did you see the way Elder Lucas looked at us when we left this morning, as if we were walking into a trap, like we were doing something wrong by leaving early? I feel I'm being tricked even when I think I'm doing something right. I feel someone's always trying to catch me at something."

We were silent a moment, and I remembered the time I'd come into our bedroom one evening after Elder Wharton had gone to bed. He evidently didn't expect me back from the kitchen so soon because I saw his blanket move near his crotch a couple of times before he made a startled "Oh!" when he saw me. Then he pretended to be asleep, when it was too obvious he wasn't. I'd gone over to his bed, leaned down, and whispered, "You can't possibly think I would care, Elder Wharton." He'd opened his eyes and looked at me guiltily. I patted him on the head and whispered, "I'm still a little thirsty. I think I'll go back in the kitchen for a few minutes. Good night." I was sure being caught masturbating wasn't what Elder Wharton was referring to now, and I wished that wasn't the first thing that had come to mind.

"No," I said, "a mission is more like a contact lens."

"Huh?"

"It's helped me see more clearly."

"Oh."

"Don't you ever hear people talk about how great their contact lenses are? 'They're just so wonderful. I wouldn't want to go back to glasses for anything. I'm so happy with—oh, wait a second. It's gone behind my eyeball.'" Elder Wharton laughed as I rolled my eyes back and acted like I was trying to get something out of my eye. "But they all insist they're happy with those contacts," I went on. "Even with cleaning them every day and everything."

"And a mission is like that?"

I laughed. "It is for me. It's been painful and uncomfortable and tedious, but I wouldn't trade my experiences for anything."

"Why?" Elder Wharton looked unconvinced.

"I don't really know. I just know I feel alive out here. I'm forced to deal with myself. Elder Lucas is the contact lens behind my eyeball, like many other missionaries before him. At home, I might avoid them. Out here, I have to face up to them, which means I have to face up to myself, too."

"I'd rather have perfect eyesight to begin with."

"Me, too."

We stood on the sidewalk while I tried to work up the energy to stop someone but couldn't. "Let's go tract out just one building," I finally said.

"In the morning?"

"Someone may have called in sick to work to take the day off, and we'll catch him at home."

"Do we really want to bring a liar into the Church?"

"One more can't hurt." We looked at each other and laughed.

"Time for the *parolacce*," I said when we reached the top floor of a building and Elder Wharton rang the first bell.

"Oh, pick, not again," he said.

"*Serratura*," I enunciated carefully.

"What the flip does that mean?" he asked, just as the door opened.

"Lock," I said, smiling at the woman who opened the door.

So Elder Wharton somehow had to find a way to work the word "lock" into his conversation with the woman at the door. Giving each other a bizarre word just before the door opened was a technique I'd learned from another companion as a way of staying alert and keeping the tracting from becoming too monotonous. Elder Wharton always bitched about the game, but I could see him perk up whenever I started it, and he usually ended up in a better mood for the rest of the evening, so I'd throw out words for twenty minutes or so every few days. It helped him with his vocabulary, at the very least.

Since we were only doing the one building this morning, I switched to the "flip chart" game halfway through, waiting until after Elder Wharton knocked on a door before opening my binder of plastic-covered pictures at random, to a scene of a baptism in a forest, or to a family praying, or to a picture of the Earth, or whatever. Elder Wharton then had to focus his approach around that. When he'd made a comment about it one time in the apartment, Elder Lucas told him, "You really think Elder Anderson is teaching you the proper respect for this work?"

In turn, I recounted the story of an apostle who'd gone to talk to another apostle in the Church Office Building in Salt Lake, and upon opening the office door had found the man on the floor, slapping his leg with his head bowed. The first apostle stepped back outside and returned later, unable to keep from asking what the man had been doing. "Oh," said the second apostle, "I was telling the Lord a joke, but he'd heard it before."

Elder Lucas had just stared at me, but Elder Wharton had laughed. I saw him smiling now as he finished an approach about Church welfare farms, using his limited vocabulary, to match a picture I was showing. The woman smiled, too, but wasn't interested. We were soon finished with the building and back out on the sidewalk.

We looked at a couple of children playing on a balcony nearby, and at a woman pinning laundry onto a line on another balcony. Another woman came out of a bread shop with a fresh loaf of warm, round bread. Then she walked into a cheese shop next door. A man came out of a pizzeria just beyond that, taking a bite out of the single slice he'd bought.

I looked about, trying to decide in which direction to walk. I pointed, and we started off. I talked to one last man before we headed back to the apartment for 10:30. We arrived at 10:25, and soon all six elders and four sister missionaries from a nearby apartment were there.

Elder Lucas called everyone to order, and first he started running down the transfers from the other districts in our zone. Then he began with our district, starting with the sisters. One was going to Pozzuoli, and the three others were staying, with a sister coming down from Terni. Then he began with the elders. Both zone leaders were staying, one of the other elders was going to Napoli One, and his replacement was coming from Napoli Three.

"And now for the last companionship," said Elder Lucas. "Elder Wharton, you're staying here."

"The transfer cookie was right," Elder Wharton whispered to me.

"And Elder Anderson gets transferred to…New York."

There was a collective gasp from everyone in the room. I sat there stunned and missed most of the rest that was said in the meeting. After the sisters and the other two elders left, Elder Lucas told my companion to leave us alone for a few minutes. Elder Lucas's companion left for the kitchen, taking Elder Wharton with him. Then Elder Lucas closed his bedroom door.

"I'm sorry it's come to this," said Elder Lucas. "If you had only listened to me."

"What do you mean?"

"I've told you over and over to shape up, but you are the worst missionary I've ever seen. When the president asked all the zone leaders if we knew who might be good for New York, I told him you'd be right for it."

"You think I'll work harder in New York?"

"Oh, I don't care. I just want you out of Italy. You're too weak. I love this country, and I want missionaries here who'll work for it."

I stood up and walked to my room. "Come on, Elder Wharton," I said as I passed the kitchen. "Let's get back on the street."

I was quiet as we left and as we rode to Villa Borghese, and I was quiet as we walked through the grounds and finally ended up by a fountain. Elder Wharton didn't say anything, but he kept looking at me expectantly, and I didn't know what to say.

After we stood in front of the fountain probably five minutes, I said, "New York."

Elder Wharton breathed heavily. "Are you glad? Or mad?"

"I can't go to New York." It was the first time I'd realized it. "I can't stay, either," I said. How could I tell people I still believed the Church was true?

"Why?" he asked. "You're not going home, are you? You only have three months left. You can make it, can't you? New York won't be that bad. You'll see."

I suddenly felt ill and barely made it to a trash can before throwing up. I leaned on the can for a couple more minutes and then made my way to a bench and sat down.

"You okay, Elder Anderson?"

I nodded. "Just tossed my transfer cookies. Maybe we should try again."

"Oh, Anziano."

"I suppose Elder Lucas is right. He says I'm too weak." Not that I felt I really needed to work any harder. But perhaps I did need to develop a stronger personality. If I didn't, maybe the Church would try to force me out of my membership as Elder Lucas was forcing me out of Italy.

It might well be that the Church was true, but even if it were, it was clearly led by men who did what *they* wanted, not what God asked. The scriptures did say that God couldn't force anyone to be good, so that must go for Church leaders, too. 90% of those I'd seen rise in the mission hierarchy had been creeps. Yet they were the kind of men the Church always seemed to put in leadership positions. They were the ones who would rise in their congregations back home. They were…they were the ones who were leading the Church right now. Surely, they weren't all unpleasant. I'd had a few good leaders in my life, certainly, but the good guys were definitely in the minority.

Yet even if only *some* of the leaders were jerks, what good did it do that the Church was true? Sometimes, I felt I was in the mouth of a ravenous wolf. How could anyone tell when something was part of the Church or when something was the idea of some creep? Was being gay even wrong in the first place, or was that just the opinion of a few men at the top? The jerks lower in the hierarchy might not be totally responsible for what they did because they were simply following other jerks, but where did that leave me? It meant I could no longer trust the Church.

In a way, having my beliefs decided by someone else had been easy. It was going to be harder to make every decision on my own. But even when trying to believe the prescribed beliefs, I'd still thought a little too much, and I never fully fit in. Maybe it wouldn't be so different now. I'd just be free to do it without guilt. And there were certainly some things the Church said which I did believe. I wasn't going to chuck the whole thing just because part of it might be wrong.

Perhaps I shouldn't even care if I was forced out of the Church but leaving it should be my decision and no one else's. I'd still have three more months to work on that decision before going home. I almost laughed. Wouldn't it be funny, I thought, if during my homecoming talk in Biloxi I announced I was leaving the Church? We were sometimes told our missions could be considered a success if the only person we converted was ourselves and we came back a true believer. Although I had believed completely two years ago, I had still hoped to strengthen my faith even more. I still *wanted* to believe, but I wasn't sure I could any longer. If I wanted to maintain any kind of control over my membership, though, it meant I had to stop refusing to deal with my gayness. I had three more months to get this contact lens out from behind my eyeball.

Naturally, in a new mission, I'd be just a junior companion these last few months. But maybe that was okay, after all. I'd have less responsibility, more time to think. At the same time, I didn't feel up to following a senior companion's every order. I might try to develop a little stubbornness as my last mission goal. New York might be a good place for that. I ought to be able to learn something useful there. Maybe how to stop playing by the wrong rules.

"So you'll go to New York?" asked Elder Wharton.

"Yeah, I'll go," I said, smiling a little. "It's an important city. I guess even if things get kind of bad, I can always say, 'At least I'm in New York.'"

Besides, I'd heard a little about Greenwich Village being a gay neighborhood. That might be interesting to check out. Missionaries weren't allowed to visit Pompeii, but perhaps Greenwich Village wasn't too far from Little Italy. And many people always dreamed of going to New York. If I found I liked it, I might even think of moving there eventually. That might be more realistic than moving to

Rome. I definitely didn't think I could face small town Mississippi life anymore.

I smiled. I'd certainly miss Rome, and Deiana, and my life here, but it would have been over soon regardless, and maybe it was time for me to start changing my life anyway.

"That's right, Elder," said Wharton. "You write me and tell me how you're doing, and I'll write and tell you if I'm doing any better here."

"I'll have to get you to send me a Pandoro next Christmas."

"Sure, Elder."

"Come on," I said, standing up. "There's a museum in this park I've been meaning to see for months. Let's go."

"But it's a workday. What'll Elder Lucas say?"

"What's he going to do? Send me home?"

Elder Wharton smiled, and I put my arm around his shoulders. He nodded, and together we slowly started off through the park.

Acknowledgement of Previous Publication

"P-Day Man," published in the Summer 1991 issue (#66) of *RFD*

"Bus Surfing," published in the March 1992 issue (#174) of *Christopher Street*

"Pissing in Peace," published in the May 1993 issue (#201) of *Christopher Street*

"Washing Dishes," published in the May 1994 issue (#213) of *Christopher Street*

"The 9:20 Express Train to Hell," published in the Summer 1994 issue (Vol. 2, #4) of *Backspace*

"The Ditch," published in the December 1994 issue (#220) of *Christopher Street*

"Bloodletting," published in the May 1995 issue (#225) of *Christopher Street*

"Killing Babies," published in the Fall/Winter 1995/96 issue (Vol. 4, #1) of *Backspace*

"The Shepherd Boy," published in the December 1995 issue (#230) of *Christopher Street*

"Almond Milk," published in the anthology *In Our Lovely Deseret: Mormon Fictions*, Signature Books, Salt Lake City, 1998, ed. Robert Raleigh

"Transfer Cookies," published in issue 9:3-4 (2007) of *Harrington Gay Men's Literary Quarterly*

"The Rift," published in the Autumn 2009 issue (Vol. L, #3) of *The Massachusetts Review*

Books by Johnny Townsend

Thanks for reading! If you enjoyed this book, could you please take a few minutes to write a review online? Reviews are helpful both to me as an author and to other readers, so we'd all sincerely appreciate your writing one! And if you did enjoy the book, here are some others I've written you might want to look up:

Mormon Underwear

God's Gargoyles

The Circumcision of God

Sex among the Saints

Dinosaur Perversions

Zombies for Jesus

A Gay Mormon Missionary in Pompeii

The Gay Mormon Quilter's Club

The Golem of Rabbi Loew

Mormon Fairy Tales

Flying over Babel

Marginal Mormons

Mormon Bullies

The Mormon Victorian Society

Dragons of the Book of Mormon

Selling the City of Enoch

A Day at the Temple

Behind the Zion Curtain

Gayrabian Nights

Lying for the Lord

Despots of Deseret

Missionaries Make the Best Companions

Invasion of the Spirit Snatchers

The Tyranny of Silence

Sex on the Sabbath

The Washing of Brains

The Mormon Inquisition

Queer Quilting

Racism by Proxy

Orgy at the STD Clinic

An Eternity of Mirrors

Please Evacuate

Recommended Daily Humanity

The Camper Killings

Let the Faggots Burn: The UpStairs Lounge Fire

Latter-Gay Saints: An Anthology of Gay Mormon Fiction (co-editor)

Available from your favorite online or neighborhood bookstore.

Wondering what some of those other books are about? Read on!

Invasion of the Spirit Snatchers

During the Apocalypse, a group of Mormon survivors in Hurricane, Utah gather in the home of the Relief Society president, telling stories to pass the time as they ration their food storage and await the Second Coming. But this is no ordinary group of Mormons—or perhaps it is. They are the faithful, feminist, gay, apostate, and repentant, all working together to help each other through the darkest days any of them have yet seen.

Gayrabian Nights

Gayrabian Nights is a twist on the well-known classic, *1001 Arabian Nights*, in which Scheherazade, under the threat of death if she ceases to captivate King Shahryar's attention, enchants him through a series of mysterious, adventurous, and romantic tales.

In this variation, a male escort, invited to the hotel room of a closeted, homophobic Mormon senator, learns that the man is poised to vote on a piece of anti-gay legislation the following morning. To prevent him from sleeping, so that the exhausted senator will miss casting his vote on the Senate floor, the escort entertains him with stories of homophobia, celibacy, mixed orientation marriages, reparative therapy, coming out, first love, gay marriage, and long-term successful gay relationships. The escort crafts the stories to give the senator a crash course in gay culture and sensibilities, hoping to bring the man closer to accepting his own sexual orientation.

Let the Faggots Burn: The UpStairs Lounge Fire

On Gay Pride Day in 1973, someone set the entrance to a French Quarter gay bar on fire. In the terrible inferno that followed, thirty-two people lost their lives, including a third of the local congregation of the Metropolitan Community Church, their pastor burning to death halfway out a second-story window as he tried to claw his way to freedom. A mother who'd gone to the bar with her two gay sons died alongside them. A man who'd helped his friend escape first was found dead near the fire escape. Two children waited outside a movie theater across town for a father and step-father who would never pick them up. During this era of rampant homophobia, several families refused to claim the bodies, and many churches refused to bury the dead. Author Johnny Townsend pored through old records and tracked down survivors of the fire as well as relatives and friends of those killed to compile this fascinating account of a forgotten moment in gay history.

Missionaries Make the Best Companions

What lies behind the freshly scrubbed façades of the Mormon missionaries we see about town? In these stories, an ex-Mormon tries to seduce a faithful elder by showing him increasingly suggestive movies. A sister missionary fulfills her community service requirement by babysitting for a prostitute. Two elders break their mission rules by venturing into the forbidden French Quarter. A senior missionary couple try to reactivate lapsed members while their own family falls apart back home. A young man hopes that serving a second full-time mission will lead him up the Church hierarchy. Two bored missionaries decide to make a little extra money moonlighting in a male stripper club. Two frustrated elders find an acceptable way to masturbate—by donating to a Fertility Clinic. A lonely man searches for the favorite companion he hasn't seen in thirty years.

The Golem of Rabbi Loew

Jacob and Esau Cohen are the closest of brothers. In fact, they're lovers. A doctor tries to combine canine genes with those of Jews, to improve their chances of surviving a hostile world. A Talmudic scholar dates an escort. A scientist tries to develop the "God spot" in the brains of his patients in order to create a messiah. The Golem of Prague is really Rabbi Loew's secret lover. While some of the Jews in Townsend's book are Orthodox, this collection of Jewish stories most certainly is not.

The Last Days Linger

The scriptures tell us that in the Last Days, wickedness will increase upon the Earth. When leaders of the Mormon Church see a rise in the number of gay members, they believe the end is upon them. But while "wickedness never was happiness," it begins to appear that wickedness can sometimes be divine. At least, the stories here suggest that religious proscriptions condemning homosexuality have it all wrong. While gay Mormons may be no closer to perfection than anyone else, they're no further from it, either. And sometimes, being gay provides just the right ingredient to create saints—as flawed as God himself.

Mormon Madness

Mental illness can strike the faithful as easily as anyone else. But often religious doctrine and practice exacerbate rather than alleviate these problems. From schizophrenia to obsessive-compulsive disorder, from persecution complex to sexual dysfunction, autism to dissociative identity disorder, Mormons must cope with their mental as well as their spiritual health on a daily basis.

Am I My Planet's Keeper?

Global Warming. Climate Change. Climate Crisis. Climate Emergency. Whatever label we use, we are facing one of the greatest challenges to the survival of life as we know it.

But while addressing greenhouse gases is perhaps our most urgent need, it's not our only task. We must also address toxic waste, pollution, habitat destruction, and our other contributions to the world's sixth mass extinction event.

In order to do that, we must simultaneously address the unmet human needs that keep us distracted from deeper engagement in stabilizing our climate: moderating economic inequality, guaranteeing healthcare to all, and ensuring education for everyone.

And to accomplish *that*, we must unite to combat the monied forces that use fear, prejudice, and misinformation to manipulate us.

It's a daunting task. But success is our only option.

Wake Up and Smell the Missionaries

Two Mormon missionaries in Italy discover they share the same rare ability—both can emit pheromones on demand. At first, they playfully compete in the hills of Frascati to see who can tempt "investigators" most. But soon they're targeting each other non-stop.

Can two immature young men learn to control their "superpower" to live a normal life…and develop genuine love? Even as their relationship is threatened by the attentions of another man?

They seem just on the verge of success when a massive earthquake leaves them trapped under the rubble of their apartment in Castellammare.

With night falling and temperatures dropping, can they dig themselves out in time to save themselves? And will their injuries destroy the ability that brought them together in the first place?

Orgy at the STD Clinic

Todd Tillotson is struggling to move on after his husband is killed in a hit and run attack a year earlier during a Black Lives Matter protest in Seattle.

In this novel set entirely on public transportation, we watch as Todd, isolated throughout the pandemic, battles desperation in his attempt to safely reconnect with the world.

Will he find love again, even casual friendship, or will he simply end up another crazy old man on the bus?

Things don't look good until a man whose face he can't even see sits down beside him despite the raging variants.

And asks him a question that will change his life.

Please Evacuate

A gay, partygoing New Yorker unconcerned about the future or the unsustainability of capitalism is hit by a truck and thrust into a straight man's body half a continent away. As Hunter tries to figure out what's happening, he's caught up in another disaster, a wildfire sweeping through a Colorado community, the flames overtaking him and several schoolchildren as they flee.

When he awakens, Hunter finds himself in the body of yet another man, this time in northern Italy, a former missionary about to marry a young Mormon woman. Still piecing together this new reality, and beginning to embrace his latest identity, Hunter fights for his life in a devastating flash flood along with his wife *and* his new husband.

He's an aging worker in drought-stricken Texas, a nurse at an assisted living facility in the direct path of a hurricane, an advocate for the unhoused during a freak Seattle blizzard.

We watch as Hunter is plunged into life after life, finally recognizing the futility of only looking out for #1 and understanding the part he must play in addressing the global climate crisis…if he ever gets another chance.

Recommended Daily Humanity

A checklist of human rights must include basic housing, universal healthcare, equitable funding for public schools, and tuition-free college and vocational training.

In addition to the basics, though, we need much more to fully thrive. Subsidized childcare, universal pre-K, a universal basic income, subsidized high-speed internet, net neutrality, fare-free public transit (plus *more* public transit), and medically assisted death for the terminally ill who want it.

None of this will matter, though, if we neglect to address the rapidly worsening climate crisis.

Sound expensive? It is.

But not as expensive as refusing to implement these changes. The cost of climate disasters each year has grown to staggering figures. And the cost of social and political upheaval from not meeting the needs of suffering workers, families, and individuals may surpass even that.

It's best we understand that the vast sums required to enact meaningful change are an investment which will pay off not only in some indeterminate future but in fact almost immediately. And without these adjustments to our lifestyles and values, there may very well not be a future capable of sustaining freedom and democracy…or even civilization itself.

The Camper Killings

When a homeless man is found murdered a few blocks from Morgan Beylerian's house in south Seattle, everyone seems to consider the body just so much additional trash to be cleared from the neighborhood. But Morgan liked the guy. They used to chat when Morgan brought Nick groceries once a week.

And the brutal way the man was killed reminds Morgan of their shared Mormon heritage, back when the faithful agreed to have their throats slit if they ever revealed temple secrets.

Did Nick's former wife take action when her ex-husband refused to grant a temple divorce? Did his murder have something to do with the public accusations that brought an end to his promising career?

Morgan does his best to investigate when no one else seems to care, but it isn't easy as a man living paycheck to paycheck himself, only able to pursue his investigation via public transit.

As he continues his search for the killer, Morgan's friends withdraw and his husband threatens to leave. When another homeless man is killed and Morgan is accused of the crime, things look even bleaker.

But his troubles aren't over yet.

Will Morgan find the killer before the killer finds him?

What Readers Have Said

Townsend's stories are "a gay *Portnoy's Complaint* of Mormonism. Salacious, sweet, sad, insightful, insulting, religiously ethnic, quirky-faithful, and funny."

D. Michael Quinn, author of *The Mormon Hierarchy: Origins of Power*

Selling the City of Enoch is "sharply intelligent…pleasingly complex…The stories are full of…doubters, but there's no vindictiveness in these pages; the characters continuously poke holes in Mormonism's more extravagant absurdities, but they take very little pleasure in doing so….Many of Townsend's stories…have a provocative edge to them, but this [book] displays a great deal of insight as well…a playful, biting and surprisingly warm collection."

Kirkus Reviews

"The thirteen stories in *Mormon Underwear* capture this struggle [between Mormonism and homosexuality] with humor, sadness, insight, and sometimes shocking details….*Mormon Underwear* provides compelling stories, literally from the inside-out."

Niki D'Andrea, *Phoenix New Times*

"Townsend's lively writing style and engaging characters [in *Zombies for Jesus*] make for stories which force us to wake up, smell the (prohibited) coffee, and review our attitudes with regard to reading dogma so doggedly. These are tales which revel in the individual tics and quirks which make us human, Mormon or not, gay or not..."

A.J. Kirby, *The Short Review*

"The Rift," from *A Gay Mormon Missionary in Pompeii*, is a "fascinating tale of an untenable situation...a *tour de force*."

David Lenson, editor, *The Massachusetts Review*

"Pronouncing the Apostrophe," from *The Golem of Rabbi Loew*, is "quiet and revealing, an intriguing tale..."

Sima Rabinowitz, Literary Magazine Review, *NewPages.com*

The Circumcision of God is "a collection of short stories that consider the imperfect, silenced majority of Mormons, who may in fact be [the Church's] best hope....[The book leaves] readers regretting the church's willingness to marginalize those who best exemplify its ideals: those who love fiercely despite all obstacles, who brave challenges at great personal risk and who always choose the hard, higher road."

Kirkus Reviews

In *Mormon Fairy Tales*, Johnny Townsend displays "both a wicked sense of irony and a deep well of compassion."

Kel Munger, *Sacramento News and Review*

Zombies for Jesus is "eerie, erotic, and magical."

Publishers Weekly

"While [Townsend's] many touching vignettes draw deeply from Mormon mythology, history, spirituality and culture, [*Mormon Fairy Tales*] is neither a gaudy act of proselytism nor angry protest literature from an ex-believer. Like all good fiction, his stories are simply about the joys, the hopes and the sorrows of people."

Kirkus Reviews

"In *Let the Faggots Burn* author Johnny Townsend restores this tragic event [the UpStairs Lounge fire] to its proper place in LGBT history and reminds us that the victims of the blaze were not just 'statistics,' but real people with real lives, families, and friends."

Jesse Monteagudo, *The Bilerico Project*

In *Let the Faggots Burn*, "Townsend's heart-rending descriptions of the victims…seem to [make them] come alive once more."

Kit Van Cleave, *OutSmart Magazine*

Marginal Mormons is "an irreverent, honest look at life outside the mainstream Mormon Church….Throughout his musings on sin and forgiveness, Townsend beautifully demonstrates his characters' internal, perhaps irreconcilable struggles….Rather than anger and disdain, he offers an honest portrayal of people searching for meaning and community in their lives, regardless of their life choices or secrets." Named to Kirkus Reviews' Best of 2012.

Kirkus Reviews

The stories in *The Mormon Victorian Society* "register the new openness and confidence of gay life in the age of same-sex marriage….What hasn't changed is Townsend's wry, conversational prose, his subtle evocations of character and social dynamics, and his deadpan humor. His warm empathy still glows in this intimate yet clear-eyed engagement with Mormon theology and folkways. Funny, shrewd and finely wrought dissections of the awkward contradictions—and surprising harmonies—between conscience and desire." Named to Kirkus Reviews' Best of 2013.

Kirkus Reviews

"This collection of short stories [*The Mormon Victorian Society*] featuring gay Mormon characters slammed [me] in the face from the first page, wrestled my heart and mind to the floor, and left me panting and wanting more by the end. Johnny Townsend has created so many memorable characters in such few pages. I went weeks thinking about this book. It truly touched me."

Tom Webb, *A Bear on Books*

Dragons of the Book of Mormon is an "entertaining collection....Townsend's prose is sharp, clear, and easy to read, and his characters are well rendered..."

Publishers Weekly

In *Gayrabian Nights*, "Townsend's prose is always limpid and evocative, and...he finds real drama and emotional depth in the most ordinary of lives."

Kirkus Reviews

Gayrabian Nights "was easily the most original book I've read all year. Funny, touching, topical, and thoroughly enjoyable."

Rainbow Awards

"The pre-eminent documenter of alternative Mormon lifestyles...Townsend has a deep understanding of his characters, and his limpid prose, dry humor and well-grounded (occasionally magical) realism make their spiritual conundrums both compelling and entertaining. [*Dragons of the Book of Mormon* is] [a]nother of Townsend's critical but affectionate and absorbing tours of Mormon discontent." Named to Kirkus Reviews' Best of 2014.

Kirkus Reviews

In *Invasion of the Spirit Snatchers*, "Townsend, a confident and practiced storyteller, skewers the hypocrisies and eccentricities of his characters with precision and affection. The outlandish framing narrative is the most consistent source of shock and humor, but the stories do much to ground the reader in the world—or former world—of the characters....A funny, charming tale about a group of Mormons facing the end of the world."

Kirkus Reviews

Lying for the Lord is "one of the most gripping books that I've picked up for quite a while. I love the author's writing style, alternately cynical, humorous, biting, scathing, poignant, and touching.... This is the third book of his that I've read, and all are equally engaging. These are stories that need to be told, and the author does it in just the right way."

Heidi Alsop, *Ex-Mormon Foundation Board Member*

In *Lying for the Lord*, Townsend "gets under the skin of his characters to reveal their complexity and conflicts....shrewd, evocative [and] wryly humorous."

Kirkus Reviews

"Townsend's collection [*The Washing of Brains*] once again displays his limpid, naturalistic prose, skillful narrative chops, and his subtle insights into psychology...Well-crafted dispatches on the clash between religion and self-fulfillment..."

Kirkus Reviews

In *Missionaries Make the Best Companions*, "the author treats the clash between religious dogma and liberal humanism with vivid realism, sly humor, and subtle feeling as his characters try to figure out their true missions in life. Another of Townsend's rich dissections of Mormon failures and uncertainties..." Named to Kirkus Reviews' Best of 2015.

Kirkus Reviews

"Written in a conversational style that often uses stories and personal anecdotes to reveal larger truths, this immensely approachable book [*Racism by Proxy*] skillfully serves its intended audience of White readers grappling with complex questions regarding race, history, and identity. The author's frequent references to the Church of Jesus Christ of Latter-day Saints may be too niche for readers unfamiliar with its idiosyncrasies, but Townsend generally strikes a perfect balance of humor, introspection, and reasoned arguments that will engage even skeptical readers."

Kirkus Reviews

"While the author is generally at his best when working as a satirist, there are some fine, understated touches in these tales [*The Last Days Linger*] that will likely affect readers in subtle ways….readers should come away impressed by the deep empathy he shows for all his characters—even the homophobic ones."

Kirkus Reviews

Orgy at the STD Clinic portrays "an all-too real scenario that Townsend skewers to wincingly accurate proportions…[with] instant classic moments courtesy of his punchy, sassy, sexy lead character…"

Jim Piechota, *Bay Area Reporter*

Orgy at the STD Clinic is "…a triumph of humane sensibility. A richly textured saga that brilliantly captures the fraying social fabric of contemporary life." Named to Kirkus Reviews' Best Indie Books of 2022.

Kirkus Reviews

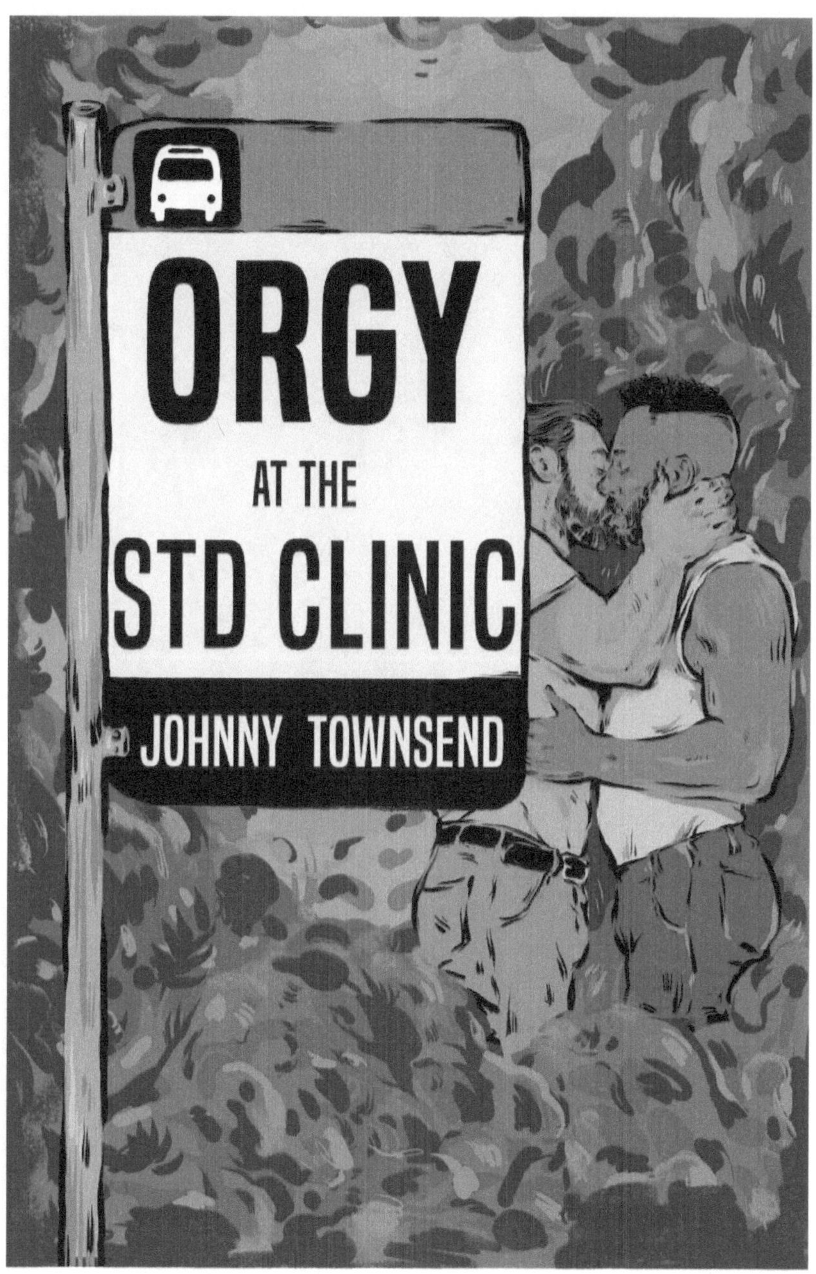
ORGY
AT THE
STD CLINIC
JOHNNY TOWNSEND

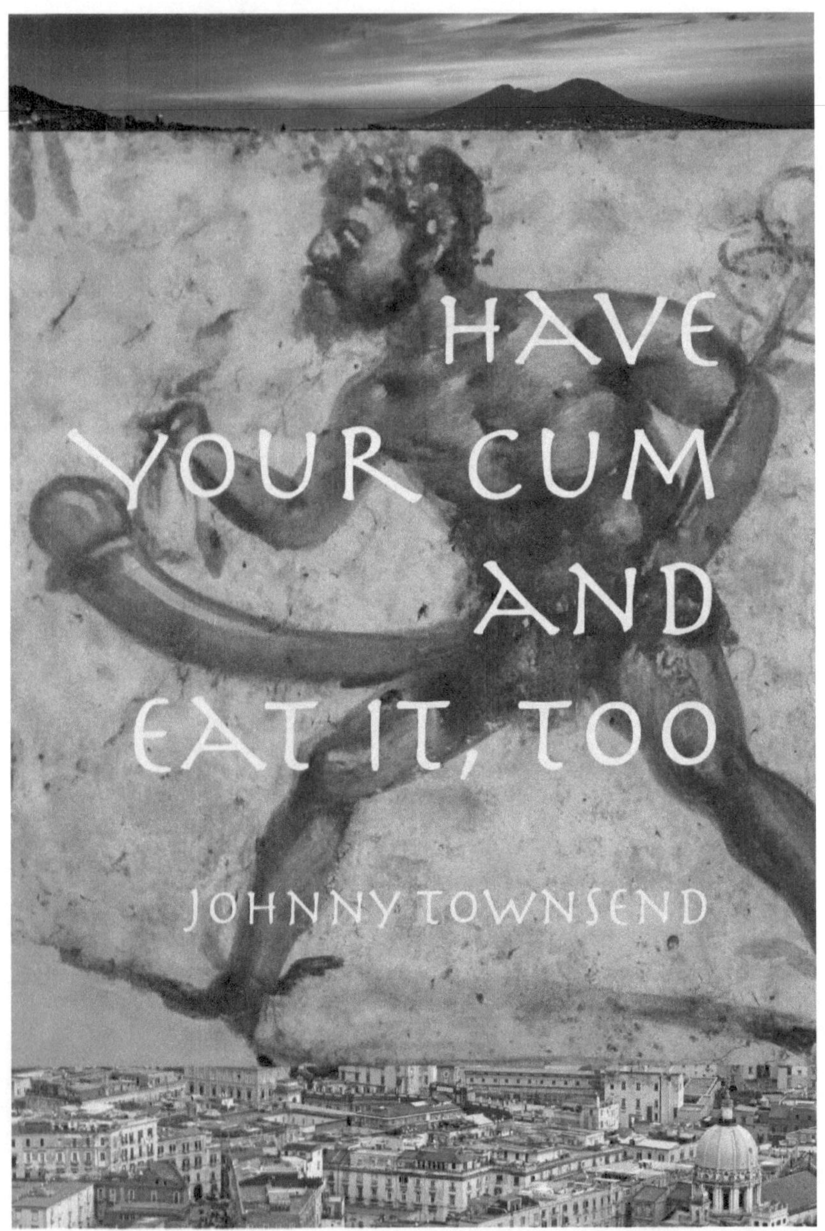
HAVE
YOUR CUM
AND
EAT IT, TOO

JOHNNY TOWNSEND

www.ingramcontent.com/pod-product-compliance
Lightning Source LLC
Chambersburg PA
CBHW031234310726
48971CB00004B/1015